PRAISE FOR
TRUE BELIEVER

"Brace yourself for this unforgettable bull ride. Carr's blistering novel will make you a TRUE BELIEVER."

—K. J. Howe, internationally bestselling author of *Skyjack*

"Gritty, intelligent, and a brilliant sequel to *The Terminal List*. Jack Carr once again delivers a bomb cyclone of a thriller."

—Dirk Cussler, coauthor of #1 *New York Times* bestselling author Clive Cussler's *Celtic Empire*

"In *True Believer*, Carr delivers another engaging, action-packed read with an impossible-to-fake authenticity other writers can only dream about. One of the best books of the year."

—Simon Gervais, former RCMP counterterrorism officer and internationally bestselling author of *Hunt Them Down*

"Don't start *True Believer* until you can read it through all the way to the end. What a ride!"

—Kurt Schlichter, Senior Columnist at *Townhall* and author of *Wildfire* and *Militant Normals*

"Jack Carr creates an incredibly vivid, emotional, action-packed tapestry of carnage and death."

—Justen Charters, Black Rifle Coffee Company, *Coffee or Die Magazine*

"Jack Carr is simply one of the top writers of political thrillers."

—Bookreporter.com, Best of 2019 pick

ALSO BY JACK CARR

The Devil's Hand
Savage Son
The Terminal List

TRUE BELIEVER

A THRILLER

JACK CARR

EMILY BESTLER BOOKS
—
ATRIA

NEW YORK   LONDON   TORONTO   SYDNEY   NEW DELHI

For those who continue to operate
at the tip of the spear

EMILY
BESTLER
BOOKS

ATRIA

An Imprint of Simon & Schuster, Inc.
1230 Avenue of the Americas
New York, NY 10020

First Emily Bestler Books/Atria Paperback edition September 2021

EMILY BESTLER BOOKS / ATRIA PAPERBACK and colophon are trademarks of Simon & Schuster, Inc.

For information about special discounts for bulk purchases, please contact Simon & Schuster Special Sales at 1-866-506-1949 or business@simonandschuster.com.

The Simon & Schuster Speakers Bureau can bring authors to your live event. For more information, or to book an event, contact the Simon & Schuster Speakers Bureau at 1-866-248-3049 or visit our website at www.simonspeakers.com.

Interior design by Dana Sloan

Manufactured in the United States of America

10 9 8 7 6 5 4 3

Library of Congress Cataloging-in-Publication Data is available.

ISBN 978-1-5011-8084-2
ISBN 978-1-9821-7144-5 (pbk)
ISBN 978-1-5011-8086-6 (ebook)

Somewhere a True Believer is training to kill you. He is training with minimum food or water, in austere conditions, day and night. The only thing clean on him is his weapon, and he made his web gear. He doesn't worry about what workout to do—his ruck weighs what it weighs, his runs end when the enemy stops chasing him. The True Believer doesn't care how hard it is; he only knows that he wins or he dies. He doesn't go home at 1700; he is home. He knows only the cause.

—ATTRIBUTED TO AN UNIDENTIFIED U.S. ARMY SPECIAL FORCES
   INSTRUCTOR, FORT BRAGG, NORTH CAROLINA, DATE UNKNOWN

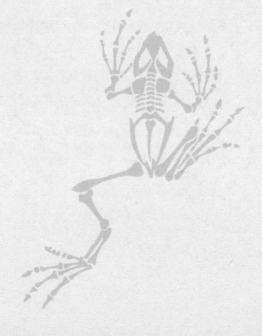

PREFACE

THIS IS A NOVEL of redemption.

True Believer explores the psyche of a man who has killed for his country and broken society's most sacred bond in a quest for vengeance. Can this man, who transformed into the very insurgent he'd been fighting, find peace and purpose, and learn to live again?

These are not unlike the questions facing veterans of the wars in Iraq and Afghanistan as they prepare to leave military service. Can they find purpose in their lives? Can they identify their next mission, and can it be productive, positive, and inspiring to those around them?

The issues surrounding transitioning veterans are numerous and complex: constant deployments since 9/11, vampire hours overseas—operating at night, grabbing a few precious hours of sleep during daylight—survivor's guilt born of dead friends and teammates, life-altering physical wounds, traumatic brain injury, and post-traumatic stress. These factors combine with sleep-aid dependency, excessive alcohol use, and marital problems to form a caustic cocktail from which it is difficult to recover. For those who have lived their lives in a constant state of hypervigilance, as our DNA dictates is necessary to survive and prevail at the tip of the spear, identifying a new mission in a postmilitary life can be a daunting task; the team is family, the team is purpose, the team is home. Returning to spouses, children, diapers, soccer practices, and leaky roofs can sometimes pale in comparison to the adrenaline and focus of planning and executing an operation to capture or kill a high-value individual downrange.

You've topped off magazines; replaced batteries in NODs, weapons mounted lights, and lasers; gassed up vehicles; studied the target's pattern of life, the target area, and the routes to and from the objective. You've gone over every contingency you can think of. Air assets will be overhead as elements of the Combined Joint Special Operations Task Force observe via a video downlink from a Predator UAV or AC-130 gunship. A Quick Reaction Force is standing by to provide reinforcements if necessary. Your mind is focused. Your team is ready, just waiting for the trigger to execute. You are part of the most experienced, effective, and efficient special operations man-hunting machine ever assembled.

Replicating that life in the private sector is an exercise in futility. The operator's search for the sensations of the battlefield on the home front can manifest in unproductive and unhealthy endeavors. A new mission with a constructive purpose is necessary, one that fulfills the quest to be a part of something greater than oneself. The old life will always be a part of us, but we need to move forward.

Although it certainly informs my writing, I am not a frogman anymore. Instead, I explore the feelings associated with my time in combat on the pages of my political thrillers. It is my hope that those real-world experiences add depth, perspective, and authenticity to the story. Serving my country as a Navy SEAL was something I did. Past tense. I've turned in my M4 and sniper rifle for a laptop and a library as I fulfill my lifelong dream of writing novels.

In the pages of *True Believer*, I examine a similar transition for my protagonist, James Reece. Feeling responsible for the deaths of his family and teammates, betrayed by the country to which he pledged his allegiance and sacred honor, what could possibly give him purpose? What mission could make him want to live again? These issues are the same ones confronting those who have fought in the mountains of the Hindu Kush and along the banks of the Tigris and Euphrates in the cradle of civilization, and, though explored through the medium of a fictional narrative, are no less valid. We are the accumulation of our past experiences. How we channel those experiences and knowledge into wisdom as we move forward is critical.

What's past is prologue. Written by William Shakespeare in *The Tempest*, it is also inscribed on a monument outside of the National Archives in Washington, D.C.

How true that is.

Jack Carr
Park City, Utah
December 18, 2018

- Though this is a work of fiction, my past profession and its associated security clearances require that *True Believer* go through a government approval process with the Department of Defense Office of Prepublication and Security Review. Their redactions are included as amended and remain blacked out in the novel.

- A Glossary of Terms is included for reference.

PROLOGUE

AHMED TURNED UP HIS collar and cursed the snow. He'd never liked the cold, despite his hometown of Aleppo being a far less temperate destination than most Westerners envisioned. He'd found Italy's Mediterranean coast in the summertime to be a paradise and would have gladly made it his home. His current bosses, however, wanted him in London. Frigid, dreary, snowy London. It was temporary, he was told; six months' work with his head down and his mouth shut and he could live wherever he wanted. His plan was to travel back south, find an honest job, and then send for his family.

Tonight, his job was to drive the van. His destination was the medieval market village of Kingston upon Thames, in southwest London. Ahmed didn't know the nature of his cargo and didn't much care so long as it was unloaded quickly. Whatever he was carrying was heavy. He felt the brakes struggle to handle the load whenever he stopped at the many traffic signals along his route. He turned the white Ford Transit delivery van's heat to its maximum setting and lit a cigarette. Traffic was terrible, even for a Friday evening.

Ahmed pulled the cell phone from his pocket: 7:46 p.m. He'd allowed himself plenty of leeway to get to the marketplace on time, but the weather was slowing things down, not to mention the throngs of drivers and pedestrians heading toward what must have been some sort of festival. Children, bundled up for the cold, holding hands with parents and siblings, were everywhere. The sight made him think of his own family, crowded into a refugee camp somewhere in Turkey. At least they were no longer in Syria.

The van moved at a pedestrian pace as he tapped the horn to part the crowd. He jammed on the brakes and inhaled sharply as a little girl in a pink puffy jacket scurried across the road in his headlights. He turned left and entered the marketplace, stopping the van in front of the address that he'd been given at the garage and turning on the emergency flashers. His eyes strained as he looked through the frosted windows to confirm he was in the right spot, his bosses having been so adamant regarding the precise location of his unloading point.

From a bird's-eye view, the marketplace was the shape of a large triangle, wide at one end and narrow at the other. Ahmed's van sat idling at the base end of that triangle, unnoticed by the happy crowds attending the German Christmas market. The shopping district was busy on a normal evening but with the holiday event in full swing, it was packed. A recent online article had highlighted the quaint festival, and families from all over London and the surrounding suburbs had come to experience its wonders firsthand. Shoppers filled the storefronts, ate in the cafes and pubs, and strolled the booths selling everything from hats and scarves to hot spiced wine, warm pretzels, nutcrackers, candle arches, and traditional wooden ornaments. The already charming town market looked like an alpine village with snow-covered A-frame booths, strung with lights, punctuated by an enormous Christmas tree towering above it all.

Ahmed looked around and saw no sign of the men who were to unload the cargo.

All this congestion must have slowed them down, he thought as he dialed a number on his phone per his instructions and waited impatiently for an answer.

"'Allo."

"Ana hunak."

"Aintazar."

The line went dead. Ahmed looked at the LCD screen to see whether the call had dropped or if the other caller had simply hung up. He shrugged.

The explosion was deafening. The market's snowy cobblestone streets held thousands of shoppers and those closest to the van were simply vaporized by the detonation. They were the lucky ones. The steel shrapnel that had been embedded directionally into the explosive device raked into the crowd like a thousand claymore mines—killing, maiming, shredding, and amputating everything in its path, taking future generations before they even existed. A joyful Christmas gathering was now a twisted war zone. Scattered among the wreckage of charred wooden shopping booths, broken glass, tangles of hanging lights, and broken tables were scores of the dead and dying.

Those who could move and who weren't totally dazed from the shock wave surged toward the apex of the triangular market, rushing to escape the carnage. That end narrowed significantly and was now strewn with the remains of the festival, forced there by the power of the high-explosive charge. The debris-choked street was constricted even further by cars parked illegally at the mouth of the triangle. The human wave jammed to a stop in the narrow bottleneck of buildings, cars, and rubble, the panicked mob pushing, shoving, and heaving like stampeding cattle. The young were trampled underneath the old, the weak forsaken by the powerful. The confusing scene was such that, at first, few even noticed the gunfire.

Two men wielding Soviet-made PKM belt-fed machine guns opened up on the crowd from the flat third-story rooftops above, one on either side of the bottleneck. Several 7.62x54mmR rounds tore through the mass of humanity, shredding bodies in their path. Those below, many already wounded from the van's deadly blast, had no chance for escape. The crowd was packed together so tightly that even the dead did not fall to the ground, but rather were held up like sticks in a bundle by the unrelenting human wave. The shooters had each linked multiple belts of ammunition together to prevent having to reload and the steel rain fell until each man's belt ran dry. The firing lasted over a minute. The men dropped the empty weapons, barrels glowing white-hot from their sustained fire, and made their way down into the chaos below. The market's gutters ran red with blood as they stepped onto what had moments before been a street filled with the joy of the season.

Surveillance footage would later show the two men move to opposite ends of the outdoor market and find positions on the street that would be the most likely routes that first responders would take to treat the wounded. Blending in with the dead, they waited more than an hour to detonate the suicide vests strapped to their bodies, murdering police officers, firefighters, medical personnel, and journalists, and creating a new level of terror for twenty-first-century Europe.

. . .

Four hundred and forty miles to the southeast, Vasili Andrenov looked at the bank of four giant flat-screen monitors in front of him and admired the turmoil. It was being reported that this was the deadliest terror attack in England's history. Not since the height of the Blitz in 1940 had this many Londoners been killed in a single event. That casualty figures were cresting three hundred and expected to climb did not appear to bother him. That half of those killed were children and that there were not enough trauma centers in all of London to deal with the number of wounded bothered him even less.

The room was completely silent. Andrenov preferred it that way. He read the news tickers across the bottom of each screen and sipped his vodka. The media was on the scene before many of the wounded could even be evacuated; their satellite trucks added to the traffic gridlock and slowed the progress of the steady stream of ambulances dispatched from all over London under the city's emergency response plan.

While viewers from around the world watched in shock and horror at what the media quickly termed "Britain's 9/11," the Russian's expression never changed, nor did his breathing rate increase or his blood pressure rise. His eyes simply moved from screen to screen, processing information in much the same way the powerful computer on the desk before him processed data. This would not have been overly remarkable except for the fact that Vasili Andrenov was responsible for the carnage in the streets of London that December evening.

Shifting his gaze from the spectacle of violence radiating from the wall of his own personal command center down to his computer, Andrenov checked to ensure the correct stocks were set to automatically begin trading as markets opened across the globe on Monday morning. Satisfied that everything was in order, he took one last long look at the new London he had created, before turning in for an early night's sleep. Come Monday, Vasili Andrenov would be an extremely rich man.

PART ONE

ESCAPE

PART ONE

CHAPTER 1

THERE'S A REASON THAT recreational sailors don't cross the Atlantic as winter advances from the north: it's a rough ride. Lieutenant Commander James Reece found some amusement in the fact that as a naval officer he had minimal experience actually sailing a boat on the open water. The bad news was that the rough seas made the crossing both dangerous and physically exhausting. The good news was that the strong winds cut considerable time off the trip and lessened his chances of discovery. Within a few days of leaving Fishers Island, off the coast of Connecticut, Reece was getting the hang of sailing the forty-eight-foot Beneteau Oceanis, christened *Bitter Harvest* by the family from whom he had liberated it, and the tasks of managing the yacht had become more or less routine. The boat's AIS Transponder had been turned off by its owners to make him harder to find, if in fact anyone was looking for him in the mid-Atlantic, and he still had his Garmin 401 GPS that had been attached to the stock of his M4. He used it sparingly to conserve battery power, and in conjunction with the onboard charts and compass he was able to track his progress.

It wasn't perfect, but it gave him a good idea of his location and was better than trying to use the stars, because of the frequent cloud cover. The yacht had a small nautical library aboard along with a modern sextant, and Reece spent his downtime teaching himself a new skill. He didn't have a precise destination in mind, nor did he think he needed one: the terminal brain tumor he had recently been diagnosed with was sure to deliver him to the afterlife before long.

Just a few months ago, Reece had been a troop commander leading an element from SEAL Team Seven on a mission in Afghanistan that ended in disaster. Reece and his Team were deliberately sent into an ambush set by corrupt officials within his own chain of command. His men, and later his pregnant wife and daughter, were murdered to cover up the side effects of an experimental drug with a financial forecast that created a widespread conspiracy leading to the highest echelons of the Washington, D.C., power establishment. Those side effects were brain tumors, just like the one growing inside Reece. In revenge, he had embarked on a one-man mission of retribution that left a swath of bodies from coast to coast. Reece now found himself on the open ocean, a world away from the death and destruction he'd wrought on U.S. soil.

The interior of the *Bitter Harvest* was intended for far more hands than Reece's solo crew, which left him plenty of room belowdecks. The boat was provisioned with massive stocks of food, which filled much of the galley and nearly the entire second stateroom. The scene reminded him of the few times he'd been on fast-attack submarines during training missions. Those boats could make their own clean air and water; their only limitation was food. The submariners literally walked on top of their food stocks as they ate their way through the supplies. His fifty-three-gallon fuel capacity was supplemented by plastic fuel containers strapped to the deck railing. Even so, Reece was careful to keep his consumption to a minimum.

The wind howled topside and Reece bundled in his warmest layers as he steered the vessel day and night. Even after studying the instructions, Reece had a hard time trusting the NKE Marine Electronics autopilot. It still required him to be on deck every twenty minutes, its manual reminding sailors that in fair conditions at five knots one had twenty minutes to the horizon. What lay just beyond that was unknown. He wasn't sure how long he'd live but he preferred not to die in the cold, so he took a southerly course toward Bermuda. The headaches came and went at random intervals: but for the lack of a good night's sleep, he still felt better than he had in some time. Alone at sea, he couldn't help but reflect upon the past few months, the violent path that had led him to this relatively peaceful location in the Atlantic. The blanket of stars at night reminded him of his daughter Lucy and the endless sea reminded him of Lauren. Lucy was fascinated with the night sky during the times they'd escaped the light pollution of Southern California, and Lauren had always loved the water. He tried to focus on the good times with the two people he loved most in this world, but with the joy of his memories came moments of unbearable pain. He was haunted by visions of their untimely and bloody deaths at the muzzle of an AK meant for him, set up by a financial and political machine that Reece had then dismantled piece by piece.

With a tinge of guilt, he thought of Katie. Fate, or a divine force, had brought investigative journalist Katie Buranek into his life at precisely the right time to help him unravel the conspiracy that had led to the deaths of his Team and family. They had endured a lot during their brief friendship, but it was how he had left her that tore at him, his last actions and words. He wondered if she understood, or if she saw him as a monster, hell-bent on revenge with no regard for those left in his bloody wake.

Brotherhood was an often-used term in the Teams, a concept that had been tested to its limits as Reece's life had come apart in the preceding months. He had lost his brothers in arms when his troop was ambushed on a dark Afghan mountain, and he'd been betrayed by one of his closest friends on the home front. With his troop and family dead, and with death whispering in his ear, Reece had become the insurgent he'd been fighting for the past sixteen years; he had become his own enemy. Like any insurgent, he needed a safe haven in which to regroup, reequip, and plan his next move. He needed to go back to his roots.

. . .

His closest friend had recently come through when Reece needed him most, aiding Reece's escape from New York and inserting him on his over-the-beach mission onto Fishers Island to kill the last conspirators on his list. Raife Hastings hadn't hesitated when Reece requested assistance, risking everything for his former teammate without asking for anything in return.

They'd met on the rugby pitch at the University of Montana in the fall of 1995, Reece playing outside center and Raife as the number eight, by far the most skilled competitor on the team. Rugby was an obscure sport to most Americans in the early 1990s, so the community and the culture it fostered was a tight one. The running joke was that they were a drinking team with a rugby problem.

A year ahead of Reece in school, Raife had the serious demeanor of someone twice their age. The hint of an accent that Reece couldn't quite place suggested a history beyond the borders of North America. As Reece quickly tired of the traditional party scene associated with college life, he noted that Raife spent his free time either studying wildlife management in the library or taking off alone in his Jeep Scrambler to explore the Montana backcountry.

When Reece figured he had reached the point where his prowess on the pitch had earned him some time with the team captain, he decided to pry. At one of the famed rugby team parties at Raife's off-campus house, Reece made his approach.

"Beer?" Reece asked over the music, holding out a red Solo cup recently topped off from the keg outside.

"Naw, I'm good, mate," Raife responded, holding up a glass with what Reece assumed was whiskey.

"Nice muley," Reece commented, nodding at a shoulder mount of a mule deer measuring what Reece figured to be over two hundred inches.

"Ah, that was a great hunt. Back the Breaks. A wise old deer, that one."

"Is that where you're from?"

"Yeah, Winifred would be the closest town."

"Incredible country up there, but it's not really known for its rugby. Where were you from before that?"

Raife hesitated, took a sip of his drink, and replied, "Rhodesia."

"Rhodesia? You mean Zimbabwe?"

Raife shook his head. "I can't bring myself to call her that."

"Why's that?"

"The Marxist *government* is stealing the farms that have been in families for generations. It's the reason we came to the U.S., but that was when I was just a kid."

"Oh, man, we don't hear much about that over here. My dad spent some time in Africa before I was born. He doesn't talk about it, but he had a book on the Selous Scouts on the shelf in his study that I read in high school. Those guys were hard-core."

"You know about the Scouts?" Raife looked up, surprised.

"Yeah, my dad was in the military, a frogman in Vietnam. I've read about every military book on special operations I could get my hands on."

"My dad was in the Scouts, back when I was young," Raife offered. "We barely ever saw him until the war was over."

"Really? Wow! My dad was gone a lot, too. He went to work at the State Department after the Navy."

Raife looked at his younger teammate suspiciously. "You mentioned the muley. You a hunter?"

"I'd go out with my dad every chance we got."

"Well, we might as well do this right, then. Finish that beer," he said, pulling out a bottle of whiskey with a label Reece was unfamiliar with and pouring them both a couple of fingers.

"What should we drink to?" Reece asked.

"My dad would always say 'To the lads,' which was something from his time in the Scouts."

"Well, that's certainly good enough for me. 'To the lads,' then."

"To the lads." Raife nodded.

"What is this?" Reece asked, surprised by how smoothly it had gone down.

"It's something my dad gave me before I drove down. 'Three Ships,' it's called. From South Africa. I don't think you can get it here."

Encouraged by what seemed to be the start of a new friendship and by the lubrication of the whiskey, the normally stoic Raife began talking about his upbringing in Africa, their farm in what was then Rhodesia, their move to South Africa after the war, and their eventual immigration into the United States.

"I'm headed out to Block Four tomorrow morning, early. I have an elk tag. You want to go?"

"I'm in," Reece responded without hesitation.

The two were on the road at 0430 the next morning. It became obvious to Reece that his rugby team captain was a serious hunter who pursued mule deer and elk with the same dedication that he applied in the classroom and on the pitch. Reece had never met anyone with Raife's instincts for the natural world; it was as if he were part of it.

As fall turned to winter, they would set out following class Thursday afternoons and hunt dawn to dusk, carrying their compound bows and minimalist camping gear on their backs. Raife was always pushing farther from the trailhead, deeper into the timber, higher up the mountain. They would barely speak, so as not to disturb the heightened senses of their quarry, and were soon able to read each other's thoughts by body language, hand signals, and subtle changes in facial expression.

During one of their trips that fall, Reece shot a massive bull elk at the bottom of a canyon at last light. It was Sunday evening, and they both had classes the next morning that could not be missed. They worked quickly to butcher the bull by headlamp and carried him out on their backs, their packs laden with nearly one hundred pounds of meat per trip. It took them three hours to hike out of the bottom and back to the trailhead, where they hung the meat and headed back for more. They worked all night to recover the bull and hadn't had a second's sleep when they stumbled into class, their clothing caked with dried sweat and elk blood. Even in Montana, this drew strange looks from their professors and classmates. Their appearance that morning earned them the nickname the "Blood Brothers," and the moniker stuck with them through the remainder of their college years.

To store the massive amount of meat they'd packed out of the wilderness during the season, Raife added an additional chest freezer to his garage. During colder days of winter, they honed the art of preparing wild game. Their "beast feasts" became potluck events, with fellow students bringing their own side items and desserts to accompany the elk tender-loin, deer roast, or duck breast that the Blood Brothers had painstakingly prepared. Reports of homemade liquor being served were never fully sub-stantiated.

Reece visited Raife's family ranch outside Winifred that next spring and was amazed at the sprawling property. It wasn't over-the-top, by any means, but it was obvious that the Hastingses had done well. It explained Raife's Jeep and off-campus house. Mr. Hastings conveyed to Reece that he'd brought with him to Montana the techniques he'd learned ranching in Rhodesia. Back in Africa they didn't always have the option to bid on expensive, well-bred cows at auction and often found themselves nurs-ing weak or even sick cattle back to health. While others in the Montana ranching community continued to pay high prices for registered cows at auction, only to be caught off guard when the market shifted, the Hastingses bought the less desirable cattle and built them up, in essence buying low and selling high. When other ranchers had to sell parts of their property, the Hastingses were on solid financial ground and could purchase additional property at rock-bottom prices, not so much to run more cattle, but to diversify their assets. That newly acquired land al-lowed them to add hunting leases and operations to their portfolio while those same lands appreciated in value. They built a solid reputation as a family that knew the business and knew the land.

For the next three years, the Blood Brothers were inseparable, hunt-ing in the fall, backcountry skiing in the winter, rock climbing and kayak-ing in the spring. It was during a visit with the Reece family in California that Raife made the decision to join the Navy. His own father had instilled in him a deep sense of appreciation for their adopted country, and his family's military service in the Rhodesian Bush War made it seem like a mandatory family obligation. When Mr. Reece told him that SEAL train-ing was some of the toughest ever devised by a modern military, Raife made his decision to test himself in the crucible known as BUD/S.

The Blood Brothers' only separation was during the summers, when Raife would travel to work on the family farm in Zimbabwe. His father wanted him to maintain the connection with his roots working for his uncle's hunting outfit back in the old country. Raife felt most at home alongside the trackers, whose skill and instinct for reading animal signs bordered on supernatural. With them Raife was able to hone his skills in the African wilderness and perfect his command of the local Shona language.

Reece traveled to Zimbabwe during one college summer and spent a month working in the bush alongside his friend. They were the junior men in camp, and so their work wasn't very glamorous: changing tires, maintaining the safari trucks, helping in the skinning shed. Just before the final week of Reece's visit, Raife's uncle approached them after a particularly hard day in the field. He handed them a piece of yellow legal paper. It was their leftover quota, animals that they were required to harvest by the biologists who managed the game in their conservancy but that hadn't been hunted successfully by clients during the season. It was time for the boys from Montana to hunt and deliver the meat to the walk-in coolers that supplied food to the hundreds of workers employed by the Hastingses tobacco farming, cattle ranching, and safari operations.

"Take a Cruiser and a tracker. You have the run of the place. Just don't bugger it up, eh?"

. . .

Reece's reminiscing was broken by a cold breeze blowing across his face. He looked up to the sight of a front on the skyline, moving rapidly in his direction. *Was it a red sky this morning?* Something about the look of this storm unnerved him. It might even be more powerful than the one he'd sailed through when his journey began. He put on his raingear and made sure that everything on the deck was secure. He'd made a habit of wearing a safety line when topside and he checked to ensure that it was connected at both ends. When it hit, he would lower the sails to ride out the storm, but for now he took a tack to take full advantage of the wind, then headed below to make coffee; this would be a long night.

When the front hit, it did so with a vengeance. The cabin top kept the bulk of the rain out of the cockpit, but it was impossible to stay dry. Reece had lowered and stowed the sails to protect them from the ravaging winds, so the boat now moved under diesel power. An experienced sailor would be able to harness the power of the storm, but Reece didn't feel the risk was worth the potential speed reward. He wasn't worried so much about navigation at this point; his goal was to make it through the storm without sustaining any significant damage to the boat. He would figure out where he was if he survived. The sky had darkened and the seas churned ferociously; not being able to anticipate the next big wave was the most unnerving part.

Reece couldn't help but remember his last time in rough seas years earlier, speeding toward a class 3 tanker in the northern Arabian Gulf. It had been dark then, too, just after midnight as the combatant craft-assault driven by the experienced boat drivers of Special Boat Team 12 pursued their quarry while it made a beeline for Iranian waters. That was a few years back and Reece had been surrounded by a team, by the best in the business. Now he was all alone.

Though his family lineage dated back to the Vikings of ancient Denmark, Reece decided if there had ever been a genetic aptitude for seafaring pursuits, it had certainly been diluted since the ninth century. Water washed steadily over the starboard bow, but the bilge pumps did their duty and the *Bitter Harvest* stayed dry belowdecks. The boat bobbed like a toy in the maelstrom of wind and water, Reece's life totally at the mercy of the elements and the skill of the boat's builders. Even with a modern craft, the conditions were terrifying. Reece pictured his Nordic ancestors making such crossings in open wooden boats and decided that they were far more skilled than he. With his longish hair and beard soaked in rain and seawater, though, he didn't think he'd look too out of place on one of their longboats. He wondered what offering they would make at this moment to stay in the good graces of Aegir, the Norse sea deity fond of dragging men and their ships into the depths.

Just when Reece was sure that the seas couldn't get any rougher, the storm dialed up its intensity. The craft surged upward as a flash of lightning illuminated the ocean, and for a split second Reece was sure it wasn't the tumor that was going to kill him; he was riding directly toward the crest of a wave that towered above the boat's mast.

Like a roller coaster, the vessel paused at the peak of the wave before surging downward toward the black sea below. Reece felt weightless as he gripped the stainless-steel wheel with both hands and braced for impact, screaming an animal roar at the top of his lungs. All thirty thousand pounds of the *Bitter Harvest* careened into the trough in a deafening crash, Reece's body slamming into the wheel with the force of a driver in a head-on collision, knocking him into darkness.

A cold wave washing over the gunwale shocked Reece into consciousness. He found himself lying on the deck between the steering stations, his face throbbing from its meeting with the boat's wheel. His hand instinctively went to his face and came away wet with blood that washed translucent almost instantly in the downpour. His head was gashed open and his nose felt broken, but he was alive; the boat's keel had held. Using the wheel to pull himself to his feet, he reclaimed his place at the helm. Blood ran into his eyes, not that he could see much anyway. He focused on keeping the compass oriented south so he would pass through the storm as quickly as possible. Things didn't improve much, but they didn't seem to get worse. He hoped that the massive wave he'd ridden was the climax of the storm. Perhaps he was just adapting, but it seemed as though the weather was easing a bit. Over the next few hours Reece would wipe the blood from his eyes, check the heading, adjust the rigging, and wipe the blood away again. His nose throbbed and the open wound on his forehead stung in the salty spray of the unforgiving Atlantic winds.

CHAPTER 2

Save Valley
Zimbabwe, Africa
August 1998

REECE HAD SHOT A very impressive kudu bull that morning, a spiral-horned antelope known by many as the "gray ghost" due to its elusiveness. He, Raife, and the trackers had pursued the animal since dawn, and the old bull finally made the mistake of stopping to take a peek at whatever was tracking him. Loading the nearly six-hundred-pound animal into the bed of the small pickup had been a challenge, but between the ingenuity of the trackers and the Cruiser's winch, they had made it happen. They wore the carefree smiles of youth as they approached the ranch house. Raife drove with Gona, the junior tracker, riding shotgun, while Reece and the senior tracker rode in the high seat welded to the bed of the truck, sipping beers and enjoying the beautiful countryside.

As they turned the corner where the house came into view, Raife could tell instantly that something wasn't right. Three battered pickup trucks were parked haphazardly on the manicured lawn of the main house and a group of about a dozen men were scattered around the yard, most of them visibly armed. Raife drove straight toward the trucks and stopped just short of the crowd.

Feeling very exposed in the back of the truck, Reece eyed the group, whose demeanor was clearly hostile, and wondered what was going on. He counted the men, taking note of how many were displaying weapons, and glanced down at the .375 H&H rifle sitting horizontally in the rack that ran just in front of his knees. The math wasn't good.

Raife said something to the intruders in Shona, but they ignored him. The trackers hunched down in their seats like scolded dogs, their eyes fixed on their feet. Reece had learned to trust their judgment over the past month and decided that eye contact with their visitors was not a good idea.

Their dress ranged from soccer jerseys to threadbare dress shirts. Their only uniform seemed to be a lack of uniformity. Most appeared to be in their teens or early twenties, and the weapons they carried were a mix of AKs, shotguns, machete-like *panga*s, and battered old hunting rifles. Reece had no idea who these guys were, but he could tell that they weren't happy. After a few moments, Raife's uncle emerged from the house shadowed by a man roughly the same age. Unlike the others, this man was overweight and well dressed. He wore Ray-Ban aviator sunglasses and a purple silk button-down shirt with short sleeves. A thick gold chain hung at his neck and he sported what looked like crocodile-skin loafers on his feet. His swollen fingers removed a half-smoked cigarette from his mouth, which he flicked aside before strolling slowly across the Hastingses' veranda as if it were his own. Clearly, this man was the boss.

The younger men perked up when he appeared, their confidence and aggressiveness boosted. He was the alpha and they were the pack. He strode directly toward the white pickup with his gang falling in behind him. He ignored Reece and walked to the driver's-side window, saying something in Shona that Reece couldn't understand. At Raife's deliberate response in his native tongue, the fat man jerked a cocked and locked handgun from the back of his waistband. Reece's dad had the same one in his collection, a Browning Hi-Power 9mm. He held the muzzle to Raife's head with his finger resting lazily on the trigger. Reece glanced down at his rifle, knowing that he could never get to it in time. He had seldom felt so helpless in his life and made up his mind that, if Raife were shot, his killer would die soon afterward.

The man held the pistol for what seemed like an eternity, a gold bracelet dangling loosely from his sweaty wrist, the entire episode going into what felt like slow motion in Reece's mind. The tracker next to him murmured a hushed prayer and Reece found himself wondering what religion he followed. Raife's uncle stood ten yards away, unable to act against these armed tormenters.

Finally, the man leaned in close to Raife's face, an evil glimmer in his eye, before whispering "pow" as he raised the muzzle in feigned recoil. He laughed a deep-throated laugh, his belly shaking against his expensive shirt, turning to face his men. They responded with laughs of their own, and those who carried weapons fired shots of intimidation into the clear blue sky. He motioned them toward their vehicles with his handgun and they all crowded quickly aboard, one man holding the passenger door for the boss to drag his considerable bulk into the seat.

The trucks' wheels spun as they accelerated away, tearing deep red ruts into the lawn. Rich Hastings shook his head as he cursed the armed rabble.

"Bloody bastards!"

Raife opened the truck door and walked to his uncle's side, seemingly unfazed by his own brush with death. "Who in the hell were they, Uncle Rich?"

"War vets." He pronounced it as a single word, *warvits*.

"*War vets?* Those guys look too young to have even been born when the war ended."

"That's just what they call themselves. They have nothing to do with the war. Mugabe and his people keep up the revolutionary rhetoric, so no one notices they're stealing the country blind. They're a gang of thieves, plain and simple. *Extortionists*."

"What did they want?"

"Money, of course. Eventually they'll want the whole farm but right now they'll settle for a payoff. I'd love to shoot the bastards but that's what the government is hoping for. They send these gangs out to harass the landowners, knowing that if we fight back, they can run to the international media with cries of colonialism. Besides, if I fight back the army would seize this place by nightfall."

"What about the police?" Reece chimed in, his American-born mind shocked at the injustice.

"The police? The police probably told them how to get here. No, boys, there's not much we can do except pay their tribute and hang on as long as we can. I could move to the U.S. and go work for your father tomorrow, Raife, but what would happen to this place? This farm has been in our family for one hundred and fifty years. I'm not going to abandon it. We employ over a hundred people here. You think those bastards are going to take care of them? We run our own school here, for Christ's sake."

As a twenty-year-old, Reece wasn't sure what to think, though he did recognize he was from a vastly different culture. On one hand, you had indigenous people who had elected a leader viewed by much of the world as legitimate, though there were already rumblings about the disappearances and murders of those who opposed the now-entrenched dictator. On the other, you had the established property rights of families who had homesteaded their farms with the approval of the British Crown and lived on them legally for more than a century. Both sides believed that they were in the right and neither was willing to budge. To the young American, it looked like conditions were ripe for war.

CHAPTER 3

Aboard the Bitter Harvest
Atlantic Ocean
November

REECE WAS ON THE back side of the storm now, the seas having calmed from deadly to merely rough. He powered up the GPS and took note of his location. The storm had pushed him quite a bit south, which was good news, so he decided to put up the sails to conserve fuel. With things more or less under control, Reece set the analog autopilot and went below for the first time in what felt like days. He looked in the mirror and couldn't help but laugh at the disheveled figure that returned his gaze. The gash on his forehead had stopped bleeding but probably needed stitches; a few butterflies would have to do. Both eye sockets were swollen from the broken nose and were on their way to turning black. His hair was soaked and hung well below his collar. He washed his face in the sink, wrung his hair out, and stripped down so that he could put on dry clothes. He dug through the medical supplies and found what he was looking for: bandages and ibuprofen.

Hunger hit next. His food stocks would in all likelihood outlive him, but he was already growing tired of frozen and canned food. Reece opened a Tupperware container of Oreos and stuffed two into his mouth for a quick sugar fix. He couldn't muster the energy to do any serious cooking, so he grabbed a bag of ramen noodles and nuked them in the microwave. Shoving a forkful of noodles down his throat was an action that he regretted instantly. The hot food seared the roof of his mouth and he exhaled several quick breaths in an attempt to cool the scorching sustenance. He poked around the bowl with his fork, his exhausted brain debating between satisfying his hunger and the fear of burning his mouth again. Hunger won out and he blew furiously on a second bite before placing it gingerly on his tongue. By the time the noodles had cooled to a palatable temperature, the bowl was empty.

Reece drank some water and went back topside to give things a look. Satisfied that all was as it should be, he set the timer on his watch for two hours and fell face-first onto the bed in the main stateroom.

. . .

Reece was steering the boat on a calm sea as Lauren sunned herself on the deck, a precious moment of relaxation for the busy mother of a three-year-old. He took in the increasingly rare family time with a smile, consciously aware of his happiness in the moment. Lucy sat on Reece's lap and helped steer, taking serious interest in the letters on the floating compass.

"*S* is for Sisi!" Lucy announced, referring to her pet name for her maternal grandmother.

"That's right, pretty girl. You're so smart! What starts with an *E*?"

"Elmo!"

"That's right, Lucy!"

"What's that, Daddy?"

"What, baby?"

Reece turned his head to see what his daughter was pointing at off the stern. A massive wave crested above the sailboat as if in slow motion.

Reece yelled for Lauren to hold on, but he couldn't make her hear him. The rogue wave crashed over the stern, swamping the boat and tearing Lucy from his grasp. She looked pleadingly into his eyes as she reached for his outstretched hand, the water dragging her ever farther away. He kicked his legs, but it was like running in wet concrete. Gasping for breath and redemption, with seawater filling his lungs, he descended into the depths, away from his family, away from life.

. . .

A horrible beeping sound grew louder and louder, jolting Reece awake. He sat up, drenched in sweat, blinking his eyes and looking at the unfamiliar surroundings. It took him a few moments to get his bearings. He swung his feet to the floor and ran the fingers of both hands through his hair. *It won't be long, girls. I'll be with you soon. Maybe today.*

He fished around with his feet until they found his flip-flops, then stood and stretched until his hands hit the ceiling. He walked slowly through the galley and salon, grabbing his sunglasses from a table before heading up to the deck to face his demons.

CHAPTER 4

Al-Hasakah, Syria
November

ROJAVA, BETTER KNOWN AS the Democratic Federation of Northern Syria, occupied the northwestern corner of the embattled nation. This multi-ethnic confederation had seceded from the central government with relative success and operated as an autonomous nation with its own constitution. After expelling ISIS, known there as *Daesh*, from the area, the local residents and refugees from the south enjoyed reasonable living conditions. In Rojava, equal rights for both genders, freedom of religion, and individual property rights were all enshrined in the founding document. These principles of secular democracy had united Arabs, Kurds, and Turks into relative peace and stability and had the potential to spread across the rest of Syria. To most this would seem to be good progress. To others it was a threat to their power. The Interior Ministry of Syria had dispatched a sniper named Nizar Kattan to cut the head off the snake.

The federation and its nearly five million residents were led by co-presidents: an Arab, Masour Hadad, and a female Kurd, Hediya Fatah. Nizar was not a particularly devout Muslim, but he was an Arab and found the concept of a woman running a nation offensive. However, given the freedom to choose which of the copresidents to target, Nizar decided upon the male. As much as he would love to teach this Kurd bitch a lesson, leaving a woman in charge would actually help unravel this little fiefdom even more.

President Hadad's home sat in one of the better neighborhoods of Al-Hasakah, a large city that sat geographically near the nation's borders with both Turkey and Iraq. Hasakah was urban, crowded, and flat, making a long-range shot difficult to plan and execute. Though taking out the target at close range would make Nizar's escape more difficult, he'd planned for that contingency. He had examined the aerial photographs as well as the intelligence provided by regime assets operating in the city, but he could not locate an appropriate hide site. One of the older men in his unit mentioned a technique used by the "D.C. snipers," a pair of criminals who had terrorized the Americans' capital city over a period of weeks just a year after 9/11. Nizar was too young to have remembered the attacks, but an online article gave him all the inspiration he needed to create his own rolling hide.

The battered white Kia Frontier truck looked to be of similar vintage as most of the other vehicles parked on the street, and local plates had been secured so as not to arouse any suspicion from the Asayish, the local security forces. The truck's bed was piled with building materials covered by a plastic tarp and so looked like one of the many vehicles connected with a nearby construction site.

Just after 9:00 p.m., Nizar pulled the truck up against the curb, with the bed facing the target's home. The street was deserted but he went through the motions of pretending to look for something among the concrete blocks and lumber in the back of the truck, ultimately crawling into the hollow space he'd built and pulling a block into place behind him. He wasn't a tall man, but Nizar wished that the truck bed had been longer when he had to bend his knees to fit into the space. The night air was cool; he pulled up a woolen blanket, adding warmth and an additional layer of concealment to his prone form.

. . .

Nizar had dozed off on a thin foam mattress but was jolted awake by the sensation of the truck's movement. The Kia bounced on its worn shocks as someone pushed down on the rear bumper. He heard the rustling of the tarp and the scraping sound of blocks being moved against one another. His heart began to race, his hand finding the plastic pistol grip of his rifle.

Am I compromised?

He slowly moved the selector switch to semiauto, making far more noise than he'd hoped, but whoever it was didn't seem to notice as the scraping of the concrete continued. The blocks were a façade stacked on top of wooden slats just above Nizar's head, and removing one or two would surely reveal his position; in a matter of seconds, his mission could be over.

"What are you doing?" an authoritative voice cried out in Arabic from what sounded like ten or twenty meters away.

The movement of the blocks came to an abrupt halt.

"I am just looking at these blocks, these are good blocks," the nearby man responded.

"Those blocks are not yours, old man. Get away from that truck before I have to arrest you."

"I was only looking."

Nizar felt the man step down from the bumper.

"I am sorry, sir."

"Go now!"

"Yes, sir, thank you, sir."

Nizar could hear the man scurry away on sandaled feet. Heavier steps approached and a bright light blazed through the cracks between the blocks. Nizar put his head down and closed his eyes, not even daring to breathe, hiding from the police officer's flashlight like a child under sheets. The seconds ticked by slowly before he heard the light click off, and, after a pause, the boots moved away. The sniper audibly exhaled; no more sleep would come this night.

His thoughts wandered to memories from his youth, his father teaching him the virtue of patience under the thin metal roof of their family's farmhouse. Their perch in the loft was not much different than this one, cramped and dank but comfortable on a cushion of hay. The muted form of the golden jackal circled the goats' pen, but Nizar couldn't see the sights in the predawn light. The old British rifle felt huge in his hands and his neck craned forward uncomfortably due to the length of the stock. He could hold it only by resting the long wooden fore end on a rolled-up blanket. He could smell the tobacco on his father's breath as he whispered to him to stay calm. Nizar shook with excitement but his father's voice slowed his breathing and steadied the tremor of the iron sights. When the jackal circled again, the gray light had turned pink and he could make out the rectangular post through the rear notch. His father's repeated words became almost a hum as he began to squeeze the World War I rifle's heavy trigger. *Calm*...

As dawn broke, the city began to come alive: engines coughed, dogs barked, birds chirped, and children shrieked with laughter. Even during war, life went on. Among the many sounds of urban life, one stood out for Nizar: the ringing of church bells. Al-Hasakah was home to Christian churches as well as mosques, and, instead of the call to morning prayer echoing from a minaret tower, the bells of the Syrian Orthodox church clanged in the distance.

Under the cover of darkness, Nizar had rotated the concrete block in front of him so that he could see through the hollow end; he had broken the center section out so that neither his suppressed muzzle nor scope would be obstructed. He observed the increasingly bright area around Hadad's front door through the 4x magnification of the Russian PSO-1 scope mounted to the side of his VSK-94 rifle. It was an ugly black thing that looked like the stepchild of the ubiquitous AK-47, with half a meter of tubular suppressor in the front and a boxy stock to the rear. Nizar cared nothing about its odd looks. Instead, he found beauty in its function.

The home was surprisingly modest. The one-story structure was surrounded by a low stone wall topped with an iron fence that extended eight feet above street level. There was no sign of guards, armed or otherwise, though Nizar assumed that the gate was at least locked.

The sloping range estimator engraved into the scope's reticle allowed the user to bracket a man's height and establish an approximate distance to the target. No one moved within Nizar's field of view, but he could see the front door, which he used for the same purpose, taking into account that the door aperture would be slightly taller than the average male figure for which the reticle was calibrated. The range was just over one hundred meters, which was an incredibly short shot for a sniper of Nizar's talents, particularly from this stable shooting position. This rifle and its cartridge were engineered for maximum stealth: the suppressor masking the report of the shot and the bullet flying at less than the speed of sound so as not to create a sonic "crack" on its way to the target. As a result, the 16.8-gram subsonic bullet dropped like a rock, which made knowing the range to the objective critical.

Nizar had to piss but he dared not move since the target could appear at any moment; he hadn't come this far to be caught with his dick in his hand. With the rising sun came the encroaching heat, violating his confined space, his cloth head scarf quickly soaking through, sweat stinging his eyes. The waiting was always uncomfortable, but that was the job of a sniper.

CHAPTER 5

Aboard the Bitter Harvest
Atlantic Ocean
November

THE DAYS FOLLOWING THE storm allowed Reece time to think. One beautiful sunrise followed another as he sailed onward. The headaches he knew would eventually kill him came and went. They felt like a million small shards of glass grinding together inside his brain. There was no rhyme or reason to when they would hit, so there was nothing Reece could do to prevent them. He thought of his family, his beautiful wife and daughter. He thought of all those who had helped him over the preceding months in his quest for vengeance, particularly his friends Marco del Toro and Liz Riley. He hoped they were okay. He thought of Katie and his last words to her. And he thought of Raife Hastings . . .

During his last year of college, Raife began looking seriously into fulfilling his dream of becoming a SEAL. Reece still had another year of school but trained hard with his friend to get him ready for the rigors ahead. Raife's father was a bit hesitant about the prospect of his only son following in his footsteps to life as a commando and gave his blessing on the condition that he start in the enlisted ranks before becoming a commissioned officer.

Reece decided to go the enlisted route a year later, as he wanted to focus on building his tactical skills before assuming a leadership role. In today's Navy, there are programs that allow aspiring SEALs to enlist with the specific purpose of attending BUD/S, the brutal six-month selection and training program with 80 percent attrition. Things were different in the late 1990s. SEAL recruits would attend Basic Training at Great Lakes, Illinois, before attending an "A school," which Reece always thought stood for "apprentice school," before going to BUD/S. Reece's enlisted rate was Intelligence Specialist. His sixteen weeks of training took place in Virginia following boot camp. He had to complete the school for a job that he never intended to do before he could even attempt to become a SEAL. The thinking from senior-level military bureaucrats was that if only 20 percent were going to graduate BUD/S, they had better train up the other 80 percent ahead of time in occupational specialties needed by the big blue Navy.

The result was that Reece and Raife took similar paths but were separated by a year. Reece arrived at Coronado to begin BUD/S just as Raife was completing his SEAL Qualification Training course, and he was able to attend his friend's graduation. As he watched the man whom he considered a brother shake hands with the commanding officer, he knew that he wouldn't quit until he too was standing at that ceremony. If the instructors didn't want him to become a SEAL, they were going to have to kill him.

After the stories they had heard from Reece's dad about the SEAL Teams in Vietnam, Reece and Raife both thought they would be off on secret missions as soon as they crossed the quarterdecks into their first Teams. The reality was different: no secret missions to hunt down terrorist leaders and rescue hostages. This was peacetime, and peacetime meant a lot of training. That, they quickly discovered, was their job. To train. To be prepared. To always be ready for the call. Then, on a sunny Tuesday morning in September 2001, that call came in.

Raife had made it through the vaunted Green Team and had multiple deployments under his belt as an assaulter at Naval Special Warfare Development Group, when a master chief convinced him to become an officer. That meant attending Officer Candidate School (OCS) at Naval Station Newport, Rhode Island, where the Navy turned civilian candidates and enlisted sailors into butter-bar ensigns in a matter of weeks—

expertise in folding underwear and T-shirts somehow qualifying one to lead men into battle.

Reece had spent a few years in the enlisted ranks learning the trade, gaining tactical experience and earning a reputation as one of the most competent snipers in the Teams before going to Officer Candidate School, mostly due to Raife's influence.

It took a few years for their paths to realign, and when they did, they found themselves on the same battlefield during the height of the war as platoon commanders in a SEAL task unit in Ramadi, Iraq.

The fighting was hot and dirty that summer as a civil war erupted across Iraq. The Sunni-Shia rift that traced its roots back to the death of the prophet Muhammad in AD 632 was playing out in its modern incarnation. Throw in al-Qaeda in Iraq, tribal loyalties, Iranian influence, and a dysfunctional government propped up by a foreign military and political machine, and you had all the ingredients for a caustic cocktail of violence. When their task unit lost two men to a roadside bomb, they pulled out all the stops to dismantle the threat network, eventually finding the cell leader, Hakim Al-Maliki, through a tactical HUMINT collection effort that Raife spearheaded. Just prior to launch, a mission to capture/kill the cell leader responsible for the deaths of their teammates was called off by senior-level military leaders. The Blood Brothers dug until they found out that Al-Maliki was a CIA asset, part of a long-term deep penetration program of AQI. The Agency wanted him alive and working his way up to a position that would give them actionable intelligence on Abu Musab al-Zarqawi, the radical jihadist leader who rose to prominence as the leader of AQI after the U.S. invasion of Iraq and was currently public enemy number one.

Feeling responsible for the deaths of his teammates and knowing where the CIA-protected cell leader would be for the next two nights, Raife went off the reservation. He used the tactical HUMINT network to deliver a package to the AQI safe house. That package mirrored the IED profile common in Ramadi at the time. A backpack containing a device consisting of a fertilizer-based main charge with commercial detonators from Pakistan sent Hakim Al-Maliki to his seventy-two virgins.

When the CIA accused him of taking out their prized asset, Raife neither confirmed nor denied it. The CIA wanted him prosecuted for murder. They put the screws to the one officer rumored to have been in the source meeting where details of the assassination were discussed, but James Reece didn't say a word that could help convict his friend. Without Reece's testimony there wasn't enough evidence to take Raife to court-martial, and doing so would have exposed CIA sources and methods that they preferred to keep quiet. But to appease what had by that time become known as the interagency, Raife was removed from the country, pending the outcome of an official investigation. He was sick of seeing his men die in what he saw as a war without end due to the blunders and missteps of senior military and political leaders. Tired of a bureaucracy that tied their hands with absurd rules of engagement and a system that, as Lieutenant Colonel Paul Yingling famously noted, imposed harsher punishments on privates who lost rifles than on generals who lost wars, Raife didn't look back. He left the SEAL side of his life behind and dropped off the radar.

. . .

He saw the birds first. You wouldn't expect to see a massive clump of birds out in the middle of the ocean, but here they were. They circled and dove like a flight of Stukas, scores of them. Anglers paid tens of thousands of dollars in sophisticated marine electronics to locate bird activity of this kind. Stumbling upon it "blind" was more than a bit of luck. The turbulence on the water was visible from hundreds of yards away and Reece jumped to the wheel, steering toward it. Dashing below, he retrieved a rod stowed in clamps on the ceiling of the boat's salon. As he approached the churning water, he jerked the main line to leave the sail flapping in the breeze, the boat's progress creeping to a mere drift. From the bow, Reece bent backward before snapping the rod forward over his shoulder, flinging the free-spooling Rapala into the wad of baitfish. *Good cast.*

Flipping the bail back over on the big Penn, he began to reel briskly with his rod tip pointed toward the top water frenzy. It took thirty seconds to reel the lure all the way back to the boat and he quickly made a second cast. The line snapped taut and nearly jerked the rod out of his hands, and Reece eased back on the drag so as not to break the line. He let the fish take it, not being able to power the boat in its direction to take up any slack.

Reece could almost hear his father coaching him through it. *Let him get tired, son, just be patient.* This reel held a ton of line, so he let the fish wear itself out stripping most of it. When the fish turned or otherwise gave him a chance, Reece pumped the rod upward and reeled as he let the tip down. This dance lasted for at least a half hour, the fish stripping line, Reece fighting it back with increasing force. The muscles in his arms and shoulders burned and his lower back ached but he could sense his quarry's exhaustion. He couldn't help but think of Hemingway in his current plight: *You are killing me, fish.*

Reece reeled harder as the fish began to give up ground, bringing him closer to both the boat and the surface. He saw a flash of silver as the fish streaked by the bow, the sight of the white hull sending it surging away. *Nice tuna.* He walked slowly toward the transom as he reeled, bringing the line to a position where he could land his catch. Holding the rod in his left hand, he worked with his right hand to lower the folding swim platform. Stepping onto the teak decking, he felt the cold ocean waves splash onto his bare feet. He didn't want to fall in, but if he did, at least the boat wasn't moving. Ten more minutes passed as he fought the tuna. At this point he was pumping and reeling aggressively to capitalize on the fish's fatigue. He reached with one hand to grab the gaff, his wet hand slipping as he worked to remove the rubber tubing that was protecting the razor-sharp hook.

This sure would be easier with two people.

When the thick monofilament leader broke the surface of the water, he reached up and grabbed it, wrapping it in loops around his left hand. He swung the gaff hard and missed, cursing himself. The fish swung around in a small circle and he swung again, burying the hook into its shining flesh. He jerked upward and fell backward in one motion, dragging the eighty- or ninety-pound fish onto the swim platform. With one hand on the leader and one on the gaff, he hoisted the flapping yellowfin up onto the aft deck between the two steering wheels. He held on to the leader and gaff like a man possessed, determined not to let this fresh source of protein fall back into the sea. The tuna writhed and gasped, then went still, seemingly as exhausted as the mariner foe who had landed him, its massive unblinking eye staring skyward. Grabbing a towel that was hanging on the rail to dry, Reece threw it over the fish, covering its eyes to prevent it from finding that last primal reserve of fight that all living creatures possess as part of their being.

Reece stood over his bounty from the depths of the Atlantic, reflecting on an irony he'd often pondered when afield hunting and angling; why did taking the life of a wild creature always give him pause? Maybe it was because there was time; time to stalk, time to choose, time to contemplate the impact of removing an animal from the ecosystem to nourish his family. Life begets life, and death is a natural part of the cycle. In combat one kills as quickly and efficiently as possible and then moves on to the next target. Killing his fellow man was not something that gave Reece pause. One was to provide sustenance while the other was to protect the tribe. Both required skill in the act of killing, a capability in which Reece was exceptionally well versed. Now was not the time for introspection. It was time to eat.

Reece caught his breath and walked below, retrieving a filet knife from a magnetic butcher block in the galley and a small bottle of soy sauce from the refrigerator. The long slender knife pierced the gills, quickly draining its life, before cutting through the tuna's tough skin to reveal the bright red meat beneath. Reece carved himself a chunk the size of his thumb and doused it with sauce before dropping it into his mouth, the salty meat triggering a pleasure center deep within his brain. Sounds of primitive gratification escaped his lips as he chewed, closing his eyes and saying a silent prayer of thanks to the fish that sustained him.

Reece must have eaten two pounds of the fish before his hunger was satisfied. He began the slow work of slicing the yellowfin tuna into thick steaks, putting each into a Ziploc bag destined for either the refrigerator or the freezer. The intake of real food changed his dark mood dramatically; all he needed now was a night of solid sleep undisturbed by the nightmares that tortured his soul.

Reece took a deep breath and took stock of his surroundings. He sat barefoot on the deck of an expensive sailboat on the open ocean with nowhere to be and no one to answer to. The sun was shining; a steady breeze was blowing and he had enough food to sail anywhere. He was back on course and both sheets were tight and clean. Most people trapped in cubicles would cut off their big toes to trade places with him right now. If only his family were here to enjoy it with him.

With varying degrees of success, he'd managed to suppress the memory, but in this moment of introspection he thought of Katie. He remembered her bound and beaten on the floor of the secretary of defense's Fishers Island mansion, his old friend and teammate, Ben Edwards, standing over her with a detonator in his hand, det cord wrapped around her neck.

Reece had shot and killed the SECDEF and her financial sector benefactor before turning to Ben and putting a 5.56 round into his face, taking the last names off his list. Those responsible for the deaths of his SEALs on a remote Afghan mountain and the murder of his wife and child in their Coronado, California, home were now in the ground.

You need to find Katie and explain it. You knew that Ben hadn't primed that det cord, didn't you? Didn't you?

He closed his eyes and heard her last words to him before he headed for the secondary extract alone:

"Reece, how did you know Ben didn't have that detonator connected? How did you know he wouldn't blow my head off?"

He remembered the pleading, almost confused look in her eyes, the rain pelting down around them, wind howling, the Pilatus aircraft engine ready to propel her down the runway to safety as he told her the truth— *or did he?*

"I didn't," he'd said, shutting the door and sprinting toward the marina.

I didn't.

CHAPTER 6

Al-Hasakah, Syria
November

A NEW DATSUN HATCHBACK stopped at the curb in front of President Hadad's home, and two camouflage-clad figures holding Kalashnikovs climbed out while a third stayed behind the wheel of the idling car. The one closest to Nizar's sniper hide was a female, her dark hair hanging down the back of her uniform in a neat ponytail. He had planned on shooting only the president but then decided that it was her day to die as well. Despite carrying assault rifles made in Eastern Europe, the president's bodyguards wore surplus American chest rigs to hold their ammunition, no doubt provided by the CIA. Neither the male nor female YPG troops wore any headgear and there was no sign of body armor.

The male soldier stopped in front of the iron gate and turned to cover the road while the female was buzzed through and approached the home's front door. Within moments, a man in his sixties wearing a tan business suit stepped from the home and nodded to the female bodyguard. He was balding with white hair and a beard that he wore neatly trimmed. He looked like many other men in this city of nearly a quarter million, but Nizar had been studying his photo and recognized the face immediately as that of President Masour Hadad. His finger moved to the curved steel trigger.

Nizar's view of the target was obscured by the female soldier who walked directly in front of Hadad. Both she and the closer guard searched for threats as their principal crossed his small front yard toward the gate. They were well trained and dedicated but oblivious to the deadly sniper poised to strike. The female opened the gate and stood aside to let Hadad pass through, giving Nizar a clear shot. He reacted quickly, firing a 9x39mm round as soon as the scope's reticle settled on the president's face.

Even suppressed and subsonic, the shot was loud inside the confined space of the truck. Because Nizar didn't want the muzzle of his rifle to be visible from the outside, he kept it well behind the opening in the block, which contained most of the sound inside his makeshift hide. The soldiers one hundred meters away heard nothing but the sickening sound of a heavy bullet slapping flesh as Nizar's shot found its mark. The full-metal-jacket SP-5 bullet passed through President Hadad's eye and exited the back of his skull, taking a sizable amount of brain matter with it.

Nizar didn't pause to admire his shot, since he knew where it had gone the moment the trigger broke. He moved the selector switch on the odd-looking rifle to full auto and put a burst of rounds into the female soldier before moving to engage the male. The president was barely on the ground before his loyal bodyguards joined him, both writhing in agony as they quickly bled to death from the significant trauma to their vital organs. Nizar shifted his body to the right to allow him a better angle on the driver, who was stepping out of the Datsun to help his wounded comrades and their principal. Another suppressed full-auto burst from the Russian weapon put him down, too, though he was able to crawl behind his vehicle before drowning in his own blood.

Nizar repeated a command three times into the Russian-made R-187P1 handheld radio. Communications were shit in most of Syria but the Interior Ministry saw to it that his unit had the finest gear that their benefactor nation could provide. Seconds later, he heard a series of violent explosions. Assets had driven car bombs to strategic locations around the city and detonated them on his command. Not only had these explosions caused significant casualties among both the local civilian and military populations, but they also would provide a chaotic diversion and give Nizar a chance to escape the city.

He pushed his way through the false wall at the back of the truck, sending concrete blocks tumbling to the ground in front of him. He had loaded a fresh magazine into his rifle and held it at the ready as he climbed from the truck and moved toward the cab. With blasts still rocking the city around him, Nizar unlocked the truck, stashed his rifle muzzle down on the seat next to him, and fired up the Kia.

He watched Al-Hasakah erupt from peace into panic in real time, like a beehive that had been poked. Sirens wailed, cars honked and drove wildly both toward and away from the blasts, and pedestrians, many of them refugees from embattled cities to the south, darted in every direction. Their little democratic utopia had been shattered.

Nizar steered around the cars and crowds carefully, not because he cared for them, but so as not to disable his only means of transportation. The farther he moved from the center of the city, where the blasts were concentrated, the calmer the situation became, people's faces expressing more curiosity than fear by the time he reached the roundabout that connected to the highway. He tensed up as he saw what looked like a military roadblock ahead, but he relaxed once he saw that they were only stopping traffic heading into the city.

Leaving the narrow streets behind, he accelerated past the roadblock on the No. 7 highway, and drove south, out of town.

CHAPTER 7

Basel, Switzerland
November

FEW MEN ADDRESSED VASILI ANDRENOV by his given name. Almost everyone addressed him as "Colonel," the highest rank he'd achieved before the Soviet Union collapsed. To the intelligence services who were aware of his existence, he was known as *Кукольный мастер*, "Puppet Master." This apt description was the result of his years of service in Russia's Main Intelligence Directorate, better known as the GRU. If there was a Soviet-backed revolution, insurrection, assassination, or coup in the 1970s or '80s, chances were that Puppet Master was the one pulling the strings. Nicaragua, Afghanistan, Angola, and Mozambique all carried his fingerprints and those of his team of "advisors."

Unfortunately for Andrenov, he was not in the good graces of the current Russian regime and was forced to live as an expat due to unproven suspicions concerning his involvement in the assassination of a former defense minister. Basel had been Andrenov's home for the past decade, ideally located to maximize access to the power centers of Western Europe while taking advantage of the privacy and nonextradition practices of the Swiss Federation.

Andrenov also liked to be close to his considerable wealth, all of which was tucked into the world's most secure banking system, just down the road. His line of work had left him with numerous enemies, both state and nonstate, so he kept travel to an absolute minimum. When someone as wealthy as the Colonel needed to see a physician, banker, or prostitute, they came to him.

However, despite a lifetime of sin, depravity, and merciless violence, Andrenov saw himself as a devout Orthodox Christian, and the traditions of his faith did not make house calls. When he left his embassy-like walled compound in the Dalbe neighborhood, it was to visit St. Nicolas Orthodox Church on Amerbachstrasse, something he did like clockwork the one Sunday each month when services were held there.

The Colonel's devotion to the church had not prevented him from masterminding the assassination of Catholic archbishop Óscar Romero in 1980 or the subsequent massacre at his funeral; those events served the greater good of delegitimizing the government of El Salvador, which in turn served Mother Russia. Andrenov's religious dedication was more nationalistic than spiritual in nature. He saw the Russian Orthodox Church as the core of Russian culture, without which the nation would still be factions of warring tribes riding the steppe. Who else could have defeated the mongrels to the east, the Nazis to the west, the Japanese on the seas, and the mighty United States in the third-world battlefields of the Cold War? Inept government, rampant corruption, and an ethnic death spiral of low birth rates and short life expectancies had brought the tide of Russia's greatness to an ebb. Andrenov's calling was to see that greatness wash back over its banks from Istanbul to Paris.

Andrenov folded his coat collar upward to protect him from the bitter cold and nodded to Yuri Vatutin to open the door. Another man, part of the very capable security detail comprised of former members of the FSB's Alpha Group that Yuri led, opened the back door of the armored Mercedes S600 Guard idling its 530-horsepower V-12 in the gated circular driveway. Andrenov lowered himself into the heated leather seat as the door closed behind him. Yuri took his spot in the passenger seat, his suppressed AK-9 between his knees, and spoke into the microphone at his wrist to alert the men in the lead and chase vehicles that it was time to move. The wrought-iron gates opened, the vehicle barrier was lowered, and the well-armed and armored motorcade sped toward Sunday mass.

CHAPTER 8

Aboard the Bitter Harvest
Atlantic Ocean
November

MOST CITY-DWELLERS HAVE NO concept of what the night sky really looks like, as much of the sea of stars and planets above is obscured to the point of invisibility by the lights and distractions of civilization. On a cloudless night in the middle of the Atlantic, the light show was spectacular. Reece had always been fascinated with the heavens, particularly the fact that tens of thousands of years ago, humans would have looked up with the same sense of wonder. Through centuries of change and progress, the skies were a constant. He'd told his daughter Lucy to look at the sky at night and pick out the brightest star when he was away, telling her he would be looking at the same one so they would always be together. He looked up toward Sirius, the brightest in a brilliant array of stars that spanned the sky from horizon to horizon. *Daddy's here, baby girl.*

He wondered about Liz, whether she'd taken the escape plan he'd set up for her. He hoped she had but also knew that she might be stubborn enough to stick it out in the States. Liz wasn't the running-away type. He knew Marco was fine; guys like Marco find a way to dance between the raindrops. He assumed that Katie's status as a journalist, along with the hard evidence he'd given her, would keep her out of jail, though he was still worried about her. She had come into his life like a guardian angel sent by his father. In another time, under different circumstances, he would have liked to know her better. Too bad he was a grieving widower, too bad he was a domestic terrorist, too bad he was terminally ill.

Reece's thoughts were broken by a set of bright lights on the horizon. The object was on an angular path that brought it closer and closer to the boat; whatever it was looked massive and was lit up like something out of a space movie. With his binoculars, Reece confirmed it was a cruise ship—hundreds of passengers enjoying a break from reality. *Wonder where they are going?*

Sailing solo across the open ocean was an incredibly lonely experience, only compounded by the turmoil and loss of the previous few months. In spite of the circumstances, Reece also felt an undeniable sense of freedom. In this moment, fueled by the wind and guided by the stars, he could command his own destiny. There were no schedules; there was no destination; he had no responsibilities to anyone. For the first time in as long as he could remember, there was no mission.

Though it was liberating to not have a plan of any kind, he couldn't just bob around in the ocean forever under the specter of impending death. With the end of his life looming, he still felt compelled to keep moving forward. *Frogmen don't quit. Never ring the bell.*

Well, where to then, Reece?

There was a place, though the odds of making it there were slim. It would at least give him something to do while he waited to pass over to Valhalla. Reece had never paid much attention to the odds. *Why start now?*

It was a destination that was about as far off the grid as a human could venture—a leftover culture, a human time capsule, from a time and place that the West had long since moved past. An embarrassing relic of what Europe used to be, excommunicated like a relative who'd committed an unspeakable crime. No one would think to search for him there.

What's the worst that can happen? You could die. You're already dead, Reece.

He went below to the small bookshelf in the boat's salon and took down a copy of *World Cruising Routes*, by Jimmy Cornell. Spreading the boat's charts on the table, he began studying possible routes and grinned to himself when he read that the best time to make this journey was between May and June. It was November. *So much for good timing.*

According to his GPS, he was currently halfway between Bermuda and the Azores on what was listed as route AN125. At five knots it should take an average sailor just over eighteen days to reach the Azores. A professional could push the Beneteau at an ideal wind angle of eleven knots. Reece considered himself more of a wayward mariner than a sailor, but he was learning quickly. How long had he been at sea? He'd lost track in the storms and emotions after departing Fishers. Was it possible he'd only been at sea for two weeks? Depending on the weather and his ever-improving skills, he estimated he would reach landfall in ten to twelve days. The Azores would allow him to rest up, make any necessary repairs to the boat, and, in an emergency, possibly even resupply.

The dilemma was what route to take after the Azores. He could catch the winds to Gibraltar, enter the Med, and eventually head down the Suez Canal and into the Indian Ocean. That would be the most direct route, but it would leave him the most exposed to immigration and customs agencies from legitimate governments, many of which had close ties to the security apparatus of the United States. Gibraltar was covered with British intelligence assets and the U.S. enjoyed close relations with nearly every country that touched the Med, save for Libya, which was a country in name only at this point. Reece had no idea what kind of screening took place at the mouth of the Suez, but he had to assume they didn't just wave boats through such a strategically important waterway.

No, the direct route wouldn't do at all. He'd have to take it the long way around the continent. It was summer below the equator, which meant the winds were mostly favorable. From his reading, it was actually the ideal time of year to make that journey, but it was a long way to sail solo. It would be tough but not impossible. Besides, it would give him an objective to focus on, something that always helped him make it through hard times. The key was to keep your eye on the ball and take it one event, one day, one run at a time. *Just make it to breakfast. Then to lunch. Keep moving forward.*

Reece's study of the *Routes* book established he had already erred by taking too far south a course. Though he missed out on more favorable winds by steering the course he chose, he did have better weather. The temperatures were relatively warm and the high-pressure system gave him clear skies. He found himself using the motor more than he would have liked, thanks to intermittent headwinds and calms, but he was confident that he'd have sufficient fuel to make it through this stretch of ocean.

Don't get too comfortable, Reece. You'll probably die en route anyway.

CHAPTER 9

Essex County
Southern England
December

WITH ITS 2ND BATTALION of the Parachute Regiment back from its most recent deployment to Afghanistan, the 16 Air Assault Brigade had nearly all its troops at Colchester Garrison in time for the Christmas holiday. Several members of 2 PARA were receiving awards for valor, and the ceremony, with all the pomp and circumstance that the British Army has to offer, had been celebrated in the local media.

The garrison was on a heightened state of alert due to the recent terrorist attack in London. Barricades slowed approaching vehicles, giving base security cameras additional time to evaluate the passengers. Scales determined if a car or truck was unusually heavy and might be loaded down with explosives. Multipurpose canine teams patrolled between vehicles as they waited patiently to show the guards their identification cards.

The entire battalion, along with numerous other units from the brigade, formed up on the asphalt parade ground off Roman Way. Dressed in MultiCam fatigues and sporting their trademark maroon berets, the Paras were the pride of the British Army. On this special occasion, the Parachute Regiment's colonel-in-chief, His Royal Highness the Prince of Wales, would be attending the ceremony and decorating the troops.

The prince's motorcade had been slowed by uncharacteristically bad traffic, delaying the start time, so the troops stood shivering in formation as the band played every patriotic tune they could muster to pass the time for the visiting dignitaries. To a man, the Paras were anxious to put the ceremony behind them. Their holiday leave would begin upon the conclusion of the events and, after a long overseas deployment, they were looking forward to spending time with their wives, girlfriends, mates, or favorite bartenders.

The band's proximity to the troop formation made it impossible for the soldiers to hear anything but the music as they passed the time until His Majesty's arrival. As the minutes ticked by, even the senior noncommissioned officers began to grow impatient.

· · ·

The Al-Jaleel is an Iraqi copy of the Yugoslavian-made M69A 82mm mortar. Three of them had been placed in a triangular formation in the small backyard of a home on Wickham Road just north of Colchester Garrison. The crew was highly experienced, having fired similar weapons on hundreds of occasions on both sides of the Syrian conflict. Their leader, whom they knew only as Hayyan, had been an artillery officer in Assad's army before switching sides and eventually migrating through Greece and into mainland Europe. He had been recruited for this job months earlier and had spent long hours training his team, supervising daily rehearsals, and reconnoitering the target once it was established.

A woman with a sweet English voice had reserved the home for the week, sight unseen, under the auspices of a golf escape for her husband and a few of his friends from London. Google Maps and a close target reconnaissance had confirmed it as an ideal location. They had moved into the rental house the evening prior and painstakingly positioned their weapons inside a shed in the backyard to conceal them from nosy neighbors and overhead surveillance. If their golf bags and luggage were heavier than normal, no one seemed to notice.

Now it was time to execute the mission for which they had so carefully trained. The flimsy corrugated tin roof of the shed was pushed aside, having been detached from its screws the night before, sight blocks were double- and triple-checked, and ammunition was laid out for fast access.

Hayyan told the men to take their positions and watched the minute hand on his watch tick toward the time they'd been given by their handler.

"*Thalaatha, Ithnaan, Wahid . . . Nar!*" The men responded instantly to his command, releasing the high-explosive rounds into the tubes before ducking out of the way as each weapon fired.

Because the target was far closer than the maximum range of 4,900 meters, the tubes were placed at a high angle, which meant that the second and third volleys had been fired before the first rounds impacted.

The first three rounds landed simultaneously, with each round carrying a kilogram of explosive and accompanying shrapnel. Two of the rounds impacted within the close ranks of the troop formation, obliterating those in the immediate blast area and maiming dozens nearby. The third round impacted the parade deck in front of the troops and actually caused more wounded, the shrapnel dispersing over a wider spectrum. Those men not killed or wounded by the first volley were saved by the instincts that were still sharp from their time overseas. They hit the deck, almost in unison, the call of "Incoming!" echoing across the parade ground. The members of the band had no such survival instincts and stood in shock as the second volley landed in and around their formation.

As the second volley found its mark, the regimental sergeant major took action.

"Three o'clock, three hundred meters!" yelled the veteran of three wars, dating back to his first taste of combat at Goose Green in the Falkland Islands.

The troops responded without hesitation, sprinting from the kill zone and doing their best to drag their wounded comrades with them. Dignitaries dove under the bleachers and band members scattered in every direction as the third and fourth volleys landed. The Paras grabbed every piece of cover that they could find and immediately began treating the wounded. Belts became tourniquets and uniform jackets became pressure dressings as they fought to save their dying mates. While the men lay bleeding and screaming, the final volley impacted the parade ground. Second Battalion, which had survived the rigors of nine months in Afghanistan without losing a soul, had just been decimated on home soil. By the time the echoes from the explosions faded, the mortar crew had already piled into vans and were driving toward London.

CHAPTER 10

Basel, Switzerland
December

THE LONDON FINANCIAL MARKETS, barely recovering from the sell-off that followed the attack at Kingston Market, plunged deeper into recession on the news of the second terrorist attack in the span of a few days. The hysteria of fear affected holiday shopping across Europe and even in the United States, with nearly every Western market plunging deeper into the red.

Vasili Andrenov had learned early in his career that access to information meant access to wealth and he parlayed the strategic information at his fingertips into financial power. When a Marxist revolution was planned in a key oil-producing nation, he had surreptitiously invested in oil futures, knowing that the price of crude would soon spike. As he rose in rank and influence, he moved on to crafting specific intelligence operations for their potential market impact. The Colonel had built a fortune creating chaos, prolonging conflicts, and disrupting regional commerce. If the world economy demanded lithium, Andrenov would use his men to stoke the flames of hatred among the tribes that occupied areas rich in that resource. Drop in some Soviet-made weapons on either side and sit back and watch the prices rise.

Commodities and currencies were his focus in those days, but now, unable to manipulate the strategic assets of a superpower, he'd shifted his focus to more basic events. Nothing spooked investors like terrorism and, after the fall of the Soviet Union, it had become his bread and butter. The Islamists were easy to influence and, with an investment of a few hundred thousand dollars and a few martyrs, he could move markets single-handedly. The latest string of attacks in Great Britain had earned him hundreds of millions of pounds, euros, and dollars while serving the greater purpose of keeping the Western leaders and their budgets focused on chasing Muslim ghosts at home instead of pursuing worthwhile strategic goals abroad.

At age sixty-seven, Andrenov had a level of prosperity that ensured his fortune would outlive him, and without a wife or children to inherit the fruits of his labor or a business that would move forward bearing his name, he would be a mere footnote outside classified channels. That wasn't *entirely* true. He did have one illegitimate son in Russia that he knew of and probably a few more from postings around the globe that he didn't. He kept tabs on his son, more for the security implications to Andrenov's organization than out of any real concern for his well-being. His legacy wasn't flesh and blood, though; it was Russia. The moderates were killing his homeland and he was finally in a position to do something about it. It was time to start investing in Russia, investing in her people. He would continue to profit, of course, as that gave him freedom, but he would use his puppet strings to move his motherland back to its rightful place in history. Just as he'd single-handedly built and destroyed nations and economies, he would now rebuild imperial Russia.

CHAPTER 11

Langley, Virginia
December

OLIVER GREY GLANCED AT the battered 1960s-vintage Rolex Submariner on his wrist for the fifth time in as many minutes. Almost 5:00 p.m. Time to go. He removed his access card from the card reader on his desk, leaving the computer on so it could automatically update with any security patches overnight. It was a far cry from the old days of locking paper files in safes, or the more recent days of pulling hard drives and locking those in the same safes that once held the paper files. He did miss those paper files, though. So many more precautions were required now that it almost took the fun out of it. *Almost.*

He slid his desk chair into his cubicle and said good-bye to his section chief, a woman much younger than his fifty-eight years, almost forgetting his charcoal-gray overcoat. Virginia was cold this time of year.

The beauty of the building was completely lost on him as he wove his way through the halls past men and women walking with purpose, some just starting their day. If any of the attractive females who seemed to appear from around every corner paid him any unlikely attention, he didn't notice.

Logging out through the security checkpoint between him and the parking lot was a mundane matter, something he had done almost every day for the past thirty years. He nodded at one of the uniformed security guards who seemed to look right through him. It didn't bother Oliver. He was accustomed to being overlooked; his puffy white skin, plain off-the-rack suit, and comb-over hair made him essentially invisible among the younger, fitter, better-dressed staffers he passed on his way out.

Oliver didn't have an assigned parking space, even with so much time invested with the Company, and he briefly found himself turned around in the massive lot before realizing he had parked on the other side. He trudged his way there, got into his car, and lit a pipe with a wooden match. He had started smoking a pipe because he thought it less vulgar than the cigarettes that were smoked in abundance by many of his colleagues back when he started. To the new generation, smoking was seen as a weakness rather than an activity to be enjoyed or a tool to start casual conversations that were anything but. Still, the tobacco warmed his lungs and filled the car with the aroma he so loved. Putting it in drive, he moved slowly through the parking lot of the Central Intelligence Agency and out onto George Washington Memorial Parkway.

Grey didn't drive the 1987 VW Jetta because he couldn't afford a newer car. He kept it because it was the only purchase he had made with his first payment as a spy for what was then the Soviet Union.

A long time ago, Grey remembered. *Before the wall came down. Before the world changed.*

He'd bought the car used so as not to arouse suspicion, mindful of the Jaguar that Aldrich Ames had driven before the FBI had tightened their noose. Even then, large purchases were flagged by the counterintelligence division, and though the James Angleton era had long since passed, the spy hunter's specter still haunted the halls of his former agency.

Oliver's great-grandparents had immigrated to the United States from Russia following the chaos of the October Revolution and settled in Penn Wynne, Pennsylvania. They insisted on always speaking Russian in the home to preserve and pass on what was left of their heritage. Oliver's mother, Veronika, continued the tradition, albeit a bit diluted, giving her son the gift of understanding the intricacies of another language and culture. What memories Grey had of his father were now the type that made him wonder if they were real, or figments of his imagination.

As a traveling salesman, Oliver's father was rarely home: always on the road peddling encyclopedias, kitchen utensils, laundry soap, coupon booklets, and anything else that might keep his family clothed and fed. It was while selling bath bars during one of those trips that he met a widow in Philadelphia. As his trips to the big city became more frequent, their duration increased as well, until one fall day he packed a bag and never returned. Keeping two families had turned out to be more difficult than he'd imagined, and he chose the one that did not include his son. Oliver was six years old and never saw his father again.

Isolated and alone, Oliver and his mother moved in with her parents. Veronika took a job at the Pennsylvania Department of Motor Vehicles, leaving Oliver in the care of his grandparents. Though his Russian improved under their roof, his social skills stagnated. To his classmates he was the quiet kid with no friends, and to his teachers he was the perfect student.

He found kinship, not with other kids his age, but with the camera. He was fascinated with taking photographs, snapshots of others engaging in lives he could only dream about. With his mother working to provide for them all, Oliver found himself increasingly caring for his aging grandparents. Their deaths within days of one another during his sophomore year at Penn hit him hard. Two of the three people that he cared about were gone.

Even living in the dorms as a resident advisor and working for the university as part of a Russian cultural studies scholarship program he still compiled enormous student debt, which he offset with a part-time job in a small camera shop surrounded by the Nikons, Canons, and Leicas he couldn't afford. He sent his mother any additional money he made doing research projects and writing term papers for the students who had time only to chase girls and drink.

Grey was in his first job as an accountant at Arthur Andersen when the Agency came knocking. The nation's intelligence agencies kept close tabs on students taking a Russian track in college, and they continued to watch Grey as he began his professional career. They were looking for Russian linguists to be case officers and thought they had struck gold with the young accountant. It was during a meeting with a new client who turned out to be a recruiter for the CIA that he saw his first glimpse of glory. No longer would he be the awkward kid from the broken home whom no one remembered. He could be James Bond, the American version, anyway.

He wasn't even through the first set of interviews, though, when he was diverted from case officer to analyst, setting him on a different journey. The Agency was just as in need of fluent Russian desk analysts as they were of case officers, and Oliver's evaluator placed him unambiguously in the analyst category. Dashed were his dreams of playing the main character in a spy novel. Once again, he was not picked for the varsity team.

He found the training to be easy and sailed through without a hitch. When asked about Grey on peer reviews, his classmates had nothing remarkable to say. He rarely joined them for beers after class and kept mainly to himself, going home every weekend to care for his mother, who seemed to grow increasingly frail with each visit.

In those early years, Grey had worried about his annual lifestyle polygraph tests. He didn't think he was homosexual. In truth, he didn't know what he was. He seemed almost asexual to his acquaintances at school and work, though he never got close enough to anyone to know anything for sure. He had a hard time deciphering his feelings and used his studies and then his occupation as an accountant to stay too busy to deal with his sexual identity or lack thereof. One drunken escapade with a girl in college had ended in embarrassment. She was nice enough about the incident and tried to leave him with a bit of his dignity. That was the last time Grey had attempted intimacy of any sort.

During his first assignment in Central America, he'd asked a coworker out on a date not because he was attracted to her but because that was what he thought he was supposed to do. It ended in humiliation when she'd indicated she was not interested with an uncomfortable "no." While other men focused their youthful efforts pursuing their sexual desires, Grey had consumed himself with work, unaware that a master in the dark art of espionage had other plans for him.

CHAPTER 12

Managua, Nicaragua
October 1991

ANDRENOV HAD BEEN WATCHING Oliver Grey for several weeks. The report from the psychologists back in Moscow was on his desk, but he merely skimmed it. He knew how to read people and how to exploit their weaknesses, their egos, and their desires; it was all about finding just the right button to push. For some it was money, pure greed. For others, it was sex: the honey trap was so successful that the KGB actually had schools where men and women were taught to seduce their prey. Individuals whose sexual preferences deviated from the mainstream made the juiciest targets; the more perverse the fetish, the easier the sell. For the Boy Scout types who didn't have any overt vulnerabilities, blackmail was always an option. Drug a diplomat's drink and take compromising photos with a young boy or girl, and you had them on the hook for life.

For Grey, though, Andrenov would need none of these techniques. All Grey needed was to be wanted. Andrenov would give him the missions that the Americans wouldn't, give him the respect that his colleagues denied him, and become the father that he never had. He knew how he would recruit him, but at first, Andrenov couldn't decide how to make his initial contact. Grey's work rarely took him to the field, and he had the social life of a monk, so there weren't many circumstances where an introduction would be natural. He decided on a "bump." What would look to Grey like a chance encounter would actually be a well-orchestrated interaction.

Grey was an avid photographer, and Andrenov knew that he often took to the streets in the mornings or evenings, when the light was best, to photograph the city and its people. He had a man watching Grey's apartment near the embassy, waiting for the perfect moment.

His phone rang before dawn one morning with word that his subject was on the move. Andrenov quickly dressed and headed out, steering the Mercedes sedan north on 35a Avenida. He assumed that Grey was headed for the nearby coast. You had to be careful about radio communications, particularly in Russian, since the Americans were able to monitor almost everything. Andrenov's team had devised a way around this problem, and it had cost only a few thousand córdobas.

The taxi driver following Grey's Volvo would radio his location, at reasonable intervals, back to his dispatcher. Andrenov's radio was on the same frequency as that of the cab company and he spoke fluent Spanish, though the local dialect was a challenge. With so few vehicles on the road this early, Grey was easy to follow at a distance that wouldn't expose the tail, and Andrenov would need only rough vectors to find his parked car. Sure enough, the cabbie reported that the station wagon pulled off the road's shoulder near the beach. Andrenov drove another half kilometer down the beach before he parked, removed his shoes, and retrieved his camera bag from the seat.

The warm surf felt good on his feet as he walked along the hard-packed sand at the high-tide line. He could just make out the figure of Grey sitting on the beach in the predawn darkness, waiting for enough light to shoot. As he drew even closer, he discovered the likely subject of Grey's photographic journey—a group of men working on a pair of wooden fishing boats on the beach, preparing them for a long day at sea. By the time that Andrenov reached Grey, the men were heaving the first boat down the beach and into the water. Grey was wearing a pair of jeans and a light sweater, kneeling in the sand so he could frame the shot he was looking for. He took several photos as the men dragged, carried, and shoved the boat into the surf. When they walked back up the beach to work on the second boat, Grey immersed himself in the controls of his Minolta SRT-101.

"May I join you?" Andrenov asked in Russian.

Grey turned, startled by the man who had invaded his solitude without a sound and immediately aware that this was the situation the CIA counterintelligence division had warned their employees about.

"Umm, sure. By all means. How did you know I speak Russian?"

Andrenov just shrugged. "What are you shooting?"

Grey looked at his camera as if it were a foreign object: "It's, um, a Minolta. I bought it in Japan."

"Very nice. I've this old German thing," Andrenov said, pulling the olive-green Leica M4 from his bag. He grinned to himself as he saw Oliver Grey's reaction.

"Oh, wow, that's one of the Leicas made for the German army! Where did you get it?"

"The owner no longer had any use for it. Let's not miss our shot here, my friend."

Andrenov nodded toward the men dragging the second boat and raised the rangefinder camera to his eye. Each man snapped a handful of photos of the local fishermen at work. When they were done, Andrenov walked toward Grey and extended his hand.

"Sorry if I was abrupt, but when we rise this early, we may as well get what we came for. I'm Vasili."

"I'm Oliver."

"Pleasure to meet you, Oliver. Are you a photojournalist?"

"Me? No, I work for the U.S. government."

"Ah, an American. Diplomat?"

"I work for the State Department. Nothing exciting. How about you? Are you a diplomat?"

"Me? No, Oliver, I am a soldier."

CHAPTER 13

Aboard the Bitter Harvest
Atlantic Ocean
December

THE AZORES ARE A volcanic archipelago consisting of nine islands clustered into three groups in a nearly four-hundred-mile stretch along the Mid-Atlantic Ridge. Though the islands are located 850 miles from the continent, they are autonomous regions of Portugal and, therefore, represent European soil. Flores, named for its lush vegetation, is the westernmost island in the chain and is one of the least populated. With its high peaks, sharp cliffs, and towering waterfalls, its landscape could easily be mistaken for one of the Hawaiian Islands, with a temperate climate to match. The sight of so much lush greenery after weeks of blue seas and gray skies was startling to the senses. To Reece, it looked like Eden.

The northwest quadrant of the island between Ponta Delgada and Fajã Grande was virtually uninhabited, which is why Reece made his approach from that direction. The *World Cruising Routes* book, coupled with the boat's charts and the small GPS, had allowed Reece to make it this far. An unnamed island sat just off the west coast, forming a small cay that was protected from the winds and waves of the Atlantic. Reece steered the *Bitter Harvest* into the protected waters, lowered the sail, and dropped anchors fore and aft to secure the boat. Despite the strong desire to swim to the nearby beach and walk on solid earth, he resisted temptation and stayed aboard the boat. He wasn't sure whether anchoring in such an area would prompt a visit from the coast guard or other authorities, and at this point he just needed sleep.

He secured the deck and headed to the main stateroom, where he closed the curtains to block out the afternoon sun. Climbing into bed, he let himself fully relax for the first time since leaving the United States. Sleep came almost instantly and lasted fifteen uninterrupted hours. His bladder forced him awake, and he glanced at his watch as he made his way topside, confused as to whether it was six in the morning or six at night. After drinking from a water bottle on the bedside table, he went back to sleep for another four hours before finally waking refreshed and starving.

Emerging onto the deck, Reece marveled at the tenacity of the trees and bushes that found purchase, and therefore life, on the steep cliffs that ultimately met the white sand of the deserted beach at their base. He turned into the light breeze and closed his eyes, the familiar smell and taste of the sea soothing and calm, as if telling him he had been tested and found worthy. After ensuring all was in order and that he was still securely anchored, he headed down to the galley to make a proper breakfast. He cooked a half-dozen eggs, an entire package of bacon, and four frozen waffles and made a pot of coffee. Finishing every bite, he stripped down and took a shower. Clean, with a full stomach, a good sleep, and dry clothes, Reece took stock of the situation. He made up a checklist of duties and went about the process of confirming that everything on the boat was in working order. He inspected the sails and lines for signs of chafing, replenished the onboard fuel tank using some of the cans strapped to the deck railing, and confirmed that the bilge pumps were functioning.

A severe headache forced him to retreat to his bunk for a few hours, and again he found himself wondering if this was the one that would reunite him with his wife and daughter, but it passed as had all the others. He quickly grew hungry again and grilled himself a large tuna steak, which he ate along with two microwave bags of rice that he found in the freezer. An entire bottle of South African Cabernet Franc helped him go back to sleep, and he logged another solid night's rest, uninterrupted by nightmares emanating from the repressed emotions of his subconscious.

Reece cooked another big breakfast before consulting the *Routes* book and studying his charts. His final destination lay across a continent, 6,985 nautical miles away. If he could maintain an average of five knots, he had a fifty-eight-day voyage ahead. If his sailing proficiency allowed only for four knots, he was looking at closer to seventy-three days at sea. He was pushing his luck by sitting close to land for this long; it was time to make some forward progress. The seas were relatively calm as he steered south to clear the island and then east toward São Miguel. From there, Reece would head southeast to the Canary Islands before continuing on toward the Cape Verdes. Then the real voyage would begin.

CHAPTER 14

Brussels, Belgium
December

GENERAL CURTIS ALEXANDER FINISHED his breakfast of poached eggs and a side of American bacon, a delicacy hard to come by in Brussels, but being the Supreme Allied Commander of NATO came with a couple of perks. Putting down the local paper and taking a sip of espresso, he shifted his gaze across the table to his wife.

Even closing in on forty years of marriage, he still marveled at how beautiful she was. He couldn't help looking at her like it was their first date back when he was a junior at West Point and she was what was referred to as "the Supe's Daughter." Back then, some cadets looked to the daughters of senior generals as a good career choice, a practice that often led to failed expectations and even more failed marriages. Cadet Alexander could not have cared less about Sara's military lineage. She captured his heart the second he saw her and he knew he wanted to spend the rest of his life making her the happiest woman on earth. Today, thirty-seven years later, she would still blush when she caught his loving glance.

"What?" she said with a knowing smile.

"Oh, nothing," the four-star general replied, "just admiring."

"Stop it, Curtis," said Sara Alexander, playfully tossing a dish towel across the table at one of the most senior officers in the U.S. military.

She was the only person who still called him Curtis. To everyone else he was General or Sir. His close friends called him Curt. Their kids called him Dad. Curtis was reserved for Sara.

At sixty-one years old, the *old man* was at the end of a very long and distinguished Army career. His change of command and follow-on retirement ceremony were two weeks away. Technically he was still turning over his duties as Supreme Allied Commander Europe, but for all practical purposes he was done. His replacement was already in the seat, and it was time for General Alexander to step aside; the incoming commander needed to build rapport and set his priorities for his new command.

Supreme Allied Commander, Curt thought with a sigh. *Who would have thought? Well, probably a few people*, he admitted to himself.

His father had been a lieutenant colonel in Vietnam, shot down in a helicopter while leading an air assault on a VC-controlled hamlet in Tay Ninh Province. Having never shown any interest in following in his father's footsteps, Curtis Alexander surprised everyone when he turned down his acceptance to Yale and instead used his stellar grades and promising football skills to attain an appointment to West Point. That his father's side of the family could trace their military history to a captain who served in Washington's Continental Army played more than a small role in Curtis's decision. He found it slightly humorous now that, even with his family's military tradition, he had never intended to spend more than a few years in the Army before moving on.

Curtis never quite understood why he made the decision to attend the United States Military Academy, stumbling along blindly through his first two years until he met Sara. Then it all became clear. He was meant to go to the college with the cold, gray, imposing architecture that defines the Army post overlooking the Hudson. He was meant to be there to meet Sara.

Their first duty stations were a test of their marriage even back when the deployments mostly revolved around alliances and treaties born out of the ashes of World War II. Cramped housing, foreign cultures, long absences, and uncertainty with the added stresses of raising young children with a father bound by duty to another family, the U.S. Army, forged their marriage the way a fire hardens steel. Through it all, they persevered and became a team, defying the odds and becoming a rock for other families to lean against. Looking back, General Alexander felt more than a little guilt that he had never been in actual combat. The late 1970s, '80s, and '90s were marked by violent flashpoints rather than sustained combat operations, and Curt had missed them all, until September 11, 2001. He had just made colonel, which in the modern Army means not leading troops from the front as in centuries past. As with everything else in life, the newly minted full bird accepted his assignments in Afghanistan and Iraq with grace and distinction.

Sending young men off to fight from the security of a Forward Operating Base had always made him uncomfortable. Without any past special operations assignments or ground combat experience, Curtis Alexander felt he might not be able to measure up to the demands of a new war. He made up for that lack of experience through a personal devotion to servant leadership. The way he looked at things, he was serving the men under his command, rather than the other way around. He also made it a personal policy to never let anyone in or out of the military think he had accomplished tactical feats of brilliance on the battlefield. He preferred to shift that honor and those accolades toward the enlisted and junior officers out there at the tip of the spear doing the fighting and the dying. Curtis Alexander was a different kind of officer, something that did not go unnoticed by those he chose to serve.

General Alexander had been shaped by the Army of the 1980s, one still recovering from the wounds of Vietnam. He had entered a military focused on the Soviet threat so masterfully met and countered by the policies and relationships of the Reagan administration. He often wondered which world he would have rather passed on to his children and now two grandchildren: a world with an easily identifiable enemy with victories won at the negotiating table, or today's asymmetrical threat, where nonstate actors and terrorists focused their ideology of hate and violence on the weakest among us—women, children, citizens going about their daily lives? He almost longed for the days when their biggest concern was that the Soviets were going to invade West Germany by marching through the Fulda Gap.

Every time he thought he was ready to retire, the Army would promote him. Having grown up in a military family, Sara was well acquainted with Army life. She also knew the hold the Army could have on some. Curtis was different from every other officer she had known. The career just happened to him. He didn't pursue it; it was quite the opposite: the career seemed to pursue him. She had never met an officer who cared less about his rank than Curtis Alexander. By nature, he saw his job as taking care of his men and he took genuine pleasure in seeing them succeed. He always told Sara that they would get out after this "next assignment" and now joked that, after thirty-nine years, he was going to finally keep his promise.

It was a different world today, and the general was ready to turn over defense of the nation to a new generation, one that included their only son. He had just completed the Army's Ranger Assessment and Selection Program on his first attempt and was excited about his assignment to lead a company in the 75th Ranger Regiment. Curt and Sara's two daughters wanted a different life. One had married a doctor and the other an attorney. By happenstance, both had settled in Northern Virginia. Curt and Sara planned to reoccupy the home they had purchased and subsequently rented out in Alexandria during one of the general's Pentagon tours. They loved the Washington, D.C., area, and having their daughters and grandchildren living there made the decision to retire close by a relatively easy one.

The soon-to-be-retired general had accepted a position as president general of the Society of Cincinnati, the oldest patriotic group in the United States. The society had been founded in 1783 and was headquartered in Washington, D.C. Its namesake came from George Washington's admiration for the ancient Roman hero Lucius Quinctius Cincinnatus, who resigned his commission, returned power to the Senate, and retired to his farm after leading the Roman Army to victory defending the republic from foreign invasion. Often referred to as the American Cincinnatus, General Washington followed in the Roman leader's footsteps, in no small measure giving Americans the freedoms most take for granted today. The society is now dedicated to preserving the memory of those who sacrificed their lives in the War for Independence, standing up to the world's greatest superpower and creating a republic based upon freedom and liberty. Much like the Army he thought would hold him for only a few years, the Society of Cincinnati was a natural home for Curt and Sara. That posting, along with a few board positions, would see them into their retirement years as they enjoyed the perks of living just minutes from their grandkids.

"I have to make an appearance today," said Curtis, "sign a few papers, and say a few early good-byes. At 1400, er, uh, I mean, two o'clock this afternoon for us *almost* civilian types, I get to present a kid from the 82nd Airborne with a Purple Heart and Silver Star. He's been on the staff for a year due to a shrapnel injury he sustained in Afghanistan. Great kid. His award finally came in and he asked me to present it to him. I could hardly keep my eyes from watering up when he asked me."

"Oh, sweetie, you ol' softie."

"Well, I'm honored to do it and I'm certainly looking much more forward to that than to my change of command and retirement ceremony."

"I know you've never liked those things."

"I *despise* those things. Regardless of the job you did, they always make it seem like you single-handedly turned the tide of evil and saved the planet. It's ridiculous. They never tell the truth. It's all military pomp-and-circumstance bullshit."

"Curtis! The language," Sara joked.

"We are almost there. Just a couple more weeks and then home."

"That soldier will never forget receiving his medals from you," Sara remarked proudly.

"Nor I presenting them to him. So humbling. These kids today, they are something else, honey. They are the most well-educated, capable soldiers our country has ever produced. I just wish we could make better strategic decisions worthy of their sacrifice."

Sara nodded. She had heard those words from him more times than she could count throughout their married life. It was one of the reasons she loved him. He couldn't hide how much he cared for his troops. He could make hard decisions, but they were always tempered by his practice of never forgetting the human ramifications.

"I have to go, sweetie. I want to get this admin handled before the award ceremony."

Standing, he made an attempt to straighten the tie on his Army service uniform.

"Let me help you," his wife said, rising from her chair.

"Thank you, my dear," Curtis said, leaning down to kiss her good-bye. "See you later this afternoon. Let's grab a nice dinner and talk about the D.C. house. I think it might need an upgrade or two."

They still called it "the D.C. house" even though it was technically in Virginia.

"Perfect. See you tonight."

Sara watched as Curtis descended the steps of the quarters they had made their home for the past three years. It was a far cry from the junior officer housing they had endured in the late 1970s, though she knew theirs had been a large step up from what the junior enlisted families were provided.

Major Paul Reed met General Alexander at the door to the white Suburban parked in front of the general's home.

"Morning, General," he said, opening the rear passenger door.

"Morning, Paul. Don't get used to this sleeping-in business. You still have a career ahead."

"I won't, sir. Don't worry. What's on our agenda today?"

Paul had been the general's aide for the better part of two years and usually met him at the office well before sunup, sending a new officer or midlevel enlisted soldier to pick him up. When the general arrived, Paul would be ready with an agenda and schedule prepared for a full day leading NATO. Now it was all about helping the general through the administrative hurdles of a change of command, and Paul was enjoying a more relaxed schedule as well as some of the last days he would spend with a man he looked up to both personally and professionally.

"Let's sign those supply papers and the rest of those evaluation reports so we can get that off our plate. Then I want to prep for the award ceremony. You will be back to your wife and kids by four o'clock at the latest."

"You mean 1600, sir?" Paul smiled.

"However you best remember it, son," the general replied, smiling back.

Sara waved from the doorway and turned away to close the door. *What was that?* Stopping suddenly, she sensed rather than heard an unfamiliar buzzing that brought her attention back outside. Instinct based on the primal need to protect the one you love caused her to throw open the door and sprint for the Suburban, screaming Curtis's name at the top of her lungs.

She wasn't fast enough.

The buzzing came from a small drone. It dropped almost as quickly as it appeared onto the roof of the parked SUV, settling above the right rear passenger seat.

The small charge it carried was tamped to focus the blast downward, sending a molten copper slug through the armored roof and through the devoted husband, father, and Army officer inside, removing the left side of his brain, then carving its way through his lungs, heart, and bowels, and finally cutting his upper body in two before cratering into the pavement below.

Sara was thrown to the ground by the blast, her ears and nose dripping blood as she crawled toward the now-burning wreck. The passenger-side door had been blown off by the overpressure, half of Curtis Alexander's body slipping from the remarkably still-secured seat belt and sliding to the ground.

By the time Major Reed had regained consciousness, Sara had locked herself in an embrace of what was left of her husband, her screams echoing around the nearby buildings long after the reverberations of the explosion had dissipated.

CHAPTER 15

VASILI ANDRENOV STOOD BEFORE the photo on a credenza in his office having just received confirmation of the terrorist attack targeting the NATO commander. The faded black-and-white picture captured a man in a military uniform standing by his young son in a matching uniform sewn for him by his grandmother from surplus fabric. The young boy was Vasili, and the man in uniform was his father. Andrenov's father had been a high-ranking military official in the Soviet Union; men did not become officers in the GRU on merit alone. His father's service as a commissar at the Battle of Stalingrad during the Great Patriotic War had brought distinction to the entire family, and his subsequent political rise provided them with a lifestyle far above that of the average Soviet citizen. His life changed when his father disappeared while in Southeast Asia in 1971. His father's remains were eventually returned, but he and his mother were never given any information on the nature of his passing. As much as Andrenov missed his father's presence and guidance, he was glad that the old warrior hadn't lived to see the fall of his beloved socialist republic. A devout communist, his father probably wouldn't have approved of Andrenov's capitalistic tendencies.

Andrenov had been quietly profiting from overseas investments more than a decade before the Iron Curtain fell. When Russia became a Wild West of free markets, his experience put him far ahead of the game.

Within a few years, he had turned $2 million in seed money into hundreds of millions of dollars. Andrenov could have used this considerable wealth to retire in anonymity anywhere he desired. Instead, he used significant sums of money to invest in the future of his cause.

In 1997, Andrenov founded the ARO Foundation, a global charity focused on providing critical infrastructure to the most underdeveloped communities on the planet. His foundation showered dollars on high-profile causes and entertained some of the most influential leaders in the first world at lavish and exclusive fund-raisers in Moscow, New York, Paris, and London. He even supported the pet causes of members of the United States Congress, particularly those with committee assignments that aligned with his needs. With all the goodwill being spread by the foundation, no one seemed to notice that the overwhelming majority of the organization's staff were former intelligence officers from Eastern Bloc countries.

Had anyone paid close attention, they may have also noticed that the "most underdeveloped communities on the planet" were nearly all either in key strategic locations or were rich in some desirable natural resource. "Need" seemed to overlap perfectly with gold, oil, natural gas, lithium, and copper deposits. While performing token charity work such as providing vaccinations or digging wells, Andrenov's teams were bribing local officials for extraction rights or key information. When base metal prices skyrocketed, his mining contracts made tens of millions of dollars. When the demand for lithium exploded to feed the mobile-device battery market, the former GRU agent's wealth increased exponentially.

As that wealth grew, so did his global profile and influence. The foundation's political dealings didn't just grease the skids in places like Africa or Southeast Asia, it bought influence from Whitehall to Washington. This influence, and the lobbyists who wielded it, meant no heat, no investigations, no prying eyes; it meant insurance against the West.

CHAPTER 16

REECE HAD STAYED ANCHORED south of Pemba, Mozambique, for four days, waiting impatiently for the new moon. His journey from Cape Verde had taken him down the western coast of Africa and around the Cape of Good Hope; ninety-six days at sea. He had risked going ashore for supplies only twice, in Nigeria and Namibia. He treated each like an over-the-beach operation with an offset infiltration to a local village, where he played the part of a wayward traveler stocking up on a few supplies before disappearing as quickly as he had appeared.

His maritime skills had matured over the course of his voyage. The *Bitter Harvest* had kept her end of the bargain and delivered him safely halfway around the world. He was thankful for the boat's faithful service and felt a bit sad to be scuttling the Hastingses' beautiful blue-water voyager that had been his home for so long, but it was time for him to get back on terra firma.

With thunderstorms blocking the usually dazzling starlight above, the only light visible was from a handful of structures, miles away on the horizon. Using the subdued illumination from the red LEDs on his headlamp, he double-checked his bags, packed with clothing and what was left of his gear and cash. Cash opened doors and closed mouths; with cash and a bit of luck, *maybe* he could get where he was going.

Confident he was ready to make a hasty exit, Reece went belowdecks and found the thru-puts in the bottom of the hull. He'd never sunk a sailboat from the inside before and did his best to remember what they had taught him in the low-vis sailing course he'd taken in the Teams years ago. He located the macerate pump and outboard dump handle, turned it ninety degrees, and opened it to the outside elements. He loosened the hose clamp to ensure that the first big wave the yacht hit would free the hose completely, which meant the craft would start taking on water and begin her journey to the bottom of the ocean. He made his way to the circuit breaker and flipped the one labeled BILGE to prevent the bilge pump from pumping water. With a nonfloatable hull it was unlikely to pump water out faster than the forty-eight-foot craft would take it on, but Reece wanted to be sure. He then unscrewed the thru-put and scampered topside.

Reece killed the red light and pulled the elastic strap on the headlamp so it dangled around his neck. The inflatable launch was tied along the port side of the *Bitter Harvest*, protecting it from the prevailing winds and mild seas that lapped along the starboard edge of the hull. He shouldered his pack and secured the bump helmet to his head, lowering the dual lenses of his NODs; the world turned green and the immediate space brightened significantly. He lowered his Sitka Gear duffel into the launch and took one last look around the deck before swinging himself over the railing, his bare feet landing on the rigid deck of the Zodiac MK2 GR below.

Reece pumped the primer bulb and set the choke before cranking the motor. It took three tries before it caught, and he let it idle for a full minute to warm it up. Satisfied that it wasn't going to stall at the wrong moment, he untied the bow and stern lines from the *Bitter Harvest*'s cleats and drifted away from the boat that had been his only home for the past fourteen weeks. As he advanced the throttle, the bow lurched skyward, obscuring his view of the shoreline in the distance. He kept the speed to a minimum, just enough to stay on plane. He wasn't in a rush and there was no sense in making any unnecessary engine noise. He assumed it was too early to encounter any fishing vessels, and he didn't know if his destination nation had a navy or even a coast guard patrolling its waters. After sixteen years in the Teams, Reece felt perfectly comfortable in a small boat headed toward the coastline of a foreign land that wasn't expecting his arrival, though he did silently long for a couple of armed teammates, some fresh intel, and perhaps a map.

He had debated whether to steer the *Bitter Harvest* to within a mile of shore and simply swim in from that distance, but given that his only exercise over the past several weeks had been operating the sailboat, he wasn't sure he was physically up for it. Also, given the lack of intel about potential coastal patrols, he preferred the decreased signature that the Zodiac gave him. As he steered the boat and scanned the horizon, he inflated the small dive vest around his neck using the plastic tube attached to the front. The spray of salt water that soaked him felt good against his skin in the warm night air. It took twenty minutes to close the distance to where Reece planned to make his approach, approximately five hundred meters offshore. He carefully scanned the sandy beach and dark waters for any sign of activity.

Seeing nothing concerning, he swung his legs over the side and entered the eighty-degree water while keeping a firm grip on the inflatable hull, his vest helping support his head above the waves. He had lined the inside of his duffel with garbage bags to render it effectively waterproof, which also made it buoyant. His NODs quickly fogged thanks to the water, body heat, and humidity, and he pushed them up onto the helmet and out of his way. He didn't need to see much other than the white sand of the beach at this point, anyway. He unclipped the Winkler folding knife from the waistband of his board shorts with his right hand, locking the blade with a flick of his thumb before methodically stabbing each section of the sponson tubes, turning the workhorse craft into a flooded mess. Weighed down by the thirty-five-horsepower outboard motor, the craft quickly sank into the black water. Pushing his floating duffel ahead of him, Reece kicked toward Mozambique.

. . .

The beach was deserted. Reece had aimed for the darkest spot on the horizon during his approach and, as his feet made landfall for the first time in ages, he made his way onto a stretch of coastline devoid of structures. He paused in chest-deep water, slowly scanning the shoreline in front of him with his NODs, looking for any movement, the glow of an ill-timed cigarette break, or sharp edges to shapes that might signify something man-made. Satisfied his approach was clear, he waded ashore. He had thought he might feel an urge to kneel in thanks like some conquistador who had just discovered the New World, but, oddly enough, he felt like he was coming home.

Reece moved as quickly as the soft white sand would allow toward the tree line ahead. As he entered the scrub vegetation, he opened the duffel and reached into the back pocket of his pack to remove his Glock from the freezer bag that had protected it during his one-man over-the-beach operation. He then sat quietly, pistol in hand, for ten minutes, letting his senses get in tune with his new terrestrial environment. It took about thirty seconds for the mosquitos to discover his presence and he endured scores of bites as he struggled not to move.

Satisfied that no one was aware of his arrival, he reached back into his duffel and tore through the garbage-bag liner. He stripped off his vest and traded his soaked T-shirt for a dry one, using his wet shirt to clean the sand from his feet before putting on socks and lightweight Salomon trail runners. SEAL or not, Reece was not a fan of sandy feet. Digging a hole with the help of a nearby rock as a spade, he dropped in his vest and dirty wet shirt. He then removed his NODs and helmet, giving them one last look. He needed to travel light, and being caught with ITAR-restricted night vision might complicate his story as just another backpacker wandering the earth in search of the meaning of life. Not the greatest backstory, and not much to support it except for the long hair, beard, and lack of personal hygiene, which just might be enough.

Looking down at his M4, he whispered a quick good-bye as he wrapped it and his NODs in trash bags from the boat and cached them as best he could in the ground, brushing over the area with a dry limb. Though it didn't fit his thin backstory, he couldn't bring himself to cache his Glock. It wouldn't do much against many of the larger animals of the African bush, but it would be more than sufficient against the two-legged variety. *Be prepared.* Noting the exact position of the cache on his GPS, Reece stood and began the next phase of his journey.

CHAPTER 17

OVER THE ENSUING WEEKS since their unlikely encounter on the beach, Grey and Andrenov met regularly. Their photographic journeys took them away from the city and into the villages and hinterlands of this nation not far removed from the conflict between the Sandinistas and Contras. There was still a sizable U.S. presence in Nicaragua, but engagement was cautious at best after the fallout from the Iran-Contra affair. It was no coincidence that these remote locations kept them from the prying eyes of U.S. counterintelligence agents and chance encounters with other embassy personnel that would require explanation. Grey enjoyed the companionship and the ability to speak freely in his mother's native tongue. He knew he was being assessed and recruited, of course, but like a lonely spouse who wasn't getting enough attention at home, he enjoyed being on the receiving end of the chase. For the first time in his life, he felt *wanted*. Andrenov *believed* in him and trusted him to be the spy the CIA didn't think he could be.

When the ask came, there was no great philosophical pitch or movie theatrics; it was simply a favor from one friend to another. Grey was scheduled to return to Langley and Andrenov asked if he might be able to look up something for him in the archives, something personal. As a token of their friendship, Andrenov also gave Grey a gift just before he departed: his olive-green Bundeswehr-marked Leica M4. To a layperson, the camera looked like something one might pick up at a garage sale, but to a photography buff like Grey, or any auction house, it was a priceless treasure. That it was a fake, a Leica painted and engraved by the technical division of the GRU to mimic the famed collector's piece, was a fact that Grey would never discover.

Upon his return to the States, Grey set about returning the favor to his newly adopted Soviet father. He found Andrenov's first request to be an odd one. He didn't ask for details of a classified weapons program or even the identities of any U.S. intelligence assets working in Russia. His request was ancient history by Agency standards: the identities of the MACV-SOG team members who ambushed and killed a group of Soviet military advisors in Laos in 1971. It took some digging, but Grey found the after-action report of Reconnaissance Team Ozark, a mixed U.S. and South Vietnamese special operations unit attached to the Phoenix Program. Led by a U.S. Navy chief petty officer, Team Ozark had been tasked with a series of cross-border missions to interdict communist supply lines along the Ho Chi Minh Trail.

The team's report was among the records from the CCN Compound near Da Nang, where Agency and SOG personnel based many of their classified operations. Though the paper reports had been converted to microfiche and were cumbersome to sift through, Grey did his research the way he lived and worked, unnoticed by anyone. RT Ozark reported executing a near ambush on a three-vehicle convoy on the Laotian side of the border, killing all the enemy troops with a combination of claymore mines, 40mm grenades, and small-arms fire. Among the dead was a Caucasian male dressed in the uniform of a Soviet army officer.

CHAPTER 18

Pemba, Mozambique
March

AT FIRST LIGHT, REECE found himself walking westward on a dirt road that ran toward the city of Pemba. The shacks and homes that lined the roadside became more frequent as he traveled, confirming that he was moving in the right direction. Within minutes of sunrise, Reece began seeing other pedestrians along his route, no doubt headed to work. Many stared wide-eyed at the strange-looking white man who'd trespassed on their morning commute, while others paid him no mind, having seen many of his adventure-seeking backpacker brethren wander through over the years.

Even this early, the salty air was warm and damp and Reece slowed his pace so as not to soak through his clothing. He'd lost so much weight during his months at sea that he had to safety-pin the excess waistband of his board shorts so they didn't slide off his hips. Still, he had to pull them up every few minutes as he walked. His uphill path took him by an abandoned-looking sports complex complete with faded tennis courts and an empty soccer stadium, artifacts from the nation's colonial past. Reaching a paved two-lane road, he followed it for close to a mile until it intersected with a four-lane highway. Across the intersection was the Pemba airport, a relatively small facility with commercial service to larger sub-Saharan locations such as Dar es Salaam and Johannesburg. Where was Liz Riley and her plane when he needed her?

He had no idea of the day's flight schedule but expected that the early morning departures from the major destinations would be arriving shortly, with taxis likely to be queuing up to meet the passengers. Even a remote third-world airport such as this might have surveillance cameras and would definitely have a police presence. Reece had to assume that his face was plastered on every television in the world, so contact with law enforcement had to be avoided. He crossed the four lanes of traffic and began walking on a shaded path that paralleled the road toward any cabs that would be approaching the airport from the city center. Unlike in some African nations, drivers in Mozambique used the right-hand side of the road.

The morning traffic mostly consisted of flatbed and stake-bodied delivery trucks, but within ten minutes of walking, Reece saw what he was looking for. He stepped into the edge of the oncoming lane and waved his hand at the white compact sedan. The Toyota slowed, put on its turn signal, and drove slightly past him before pulling onto the road's shoulder. The driver of the King Cab Radio Taxi Toyota, a thin black man dressed in penny loafers, dark dress pants, and a threadbare button-down, stepped out to help Reece with his bags. He was obviously uncomfortable with his car's position and moved quickly to open the hatchback. Reece loaded his duffel but kept his pack as he climbed into the small backseat.

Feigning an Australian accent rather poorly, Reece asked the driver to take him to an Internet café. Reece hadn't spoken to another human since he'd left Katie and Liz on the runway at Fishers Island. He couldn't help but wonder where they were now and if they were all right.

The cab's path took it back toward the airport, where the driver made a U-turn to head toward Pemba proper.

Pemba had a reputation as a refuge for mercenaries, spies, and criminals due to its remote location and minimal connection with the inept national government. The city, known as Porto Amelia during Portuguese colonial rule, was both decrepit and beautiful at the same time. In some ways it reminded Reece of the many Caribbean islands he'd visited where locals scratched out a destitute existence adjacent to the walls of luxury resorts catering to families who never ventured beyond their secure boundaries. The beaches here were as beautiful as anywhere on earth and were virtually undeveloped; no skyscraper condos, just a scattering of thatched roofs along the white sand. The city sat on a peninsula and would be an ideal deepwater port if Mozambique had an economy to support it. The architecture was a mix of utilitarian concrete residences, shacks, and aging Portuguese structures that highlighted the dominant influences of the world's first colonial empire; churches represented an expeditious religious footprint to win the hearts of the indigenous population, along with the accompanying military fortifications required to win their minds.

Following the high ground on the bay side of the peninsula, the driver's path into the city led them through streets crowded with more pedestrian than automotive traffic. People and vehicles moved at a laid-back pace; no one seemed to be in much of a hurry. After spending so much time alone on the open seas, he felt a bit claustrophobic in the crowded street, but a few deep breaths got things under control. The taxi stopped in front of a building in what appeared to be a shopping district and the driver pointed to the meter, which read 462.25 MZN.

"How much U.S., mate?"

The driver smiled and held up seven fingers. *Everybody likes dollars.* Reece peeled a ten-dollar bill from a wad of cash in the top pocket of his pack and handed it to the driver, who nodded enthusiastically. He stepped out of the cab as the driver moved to unload his duffel from the back, pointing at a storefront. Reece nodded, looked around at his new surroundings, and headed through the propped-open double doors of the café.

Inside, a tired-looking employee manned the desk, and a handful of young men occupied seats in front of a row of ancient computer terminals. The room was dimly lit, with much of the illumination coming from the computer screens. There were no overt signs of surveillance cameras. A price list in what must have been the local language and what looked like Portuguese specified the rates. *Hora* was surely hour and, based on the cab fare, that much time was around five dollars. Reece handed the man behind the counter a five-dollar bill. He studied it carefully before putting it into his shirt pocket, then waved his arm toward the computers and said something that Reece couldn't understand.

The other patrons were glued to their screens and paid Reece no attention as he moved to the computer closest to the wall. The machine was ancient, one of those Dell desktop tower PCs from the late 1990s that cost $3,000 and, a few months later, were worth about $100. The browser was an old, unsupported version of Google Chrome and it took a full minute of clicking and whirring for the program to open after Reece double-clicked on it.

He had a strong urge to look up a few news stories related to his last days in the United States and an even stronger inclination to do a Google search for Liz and Katie, but, knowing that the long arm of the NSA was likely on the lookout for just such an event, he resisted. He typed "Richard Hastings safari operator" into the browser and waited an eternity for the response. The first hit was a Web page for RH Safaris and he clicked on the link. It was obvious from the "About Us" section of the site that he had found the correct Richard Hastings, so he clicked on the "Our Areas" page. A map of the safari area eventually loaded and he took a small notebook and pencil from his pack to take note of the location.

The area was in one of the hunting blocks that bordered the Niassa National Reserve, a vast wilderness area in northern Mozambique along the border with Tanzania. The map wasn't interactive, so Reece made a sketch of its proximity to terrain features, including the river that bordered the safari area and the closest town of Montepuez, which is where the paved roads ended. After waiting painfully for Google Maps to load, he found the approximate location of the safari area, and instead of dropping a pin, he used the scale in the bottom right-hand corner to estimate distance. The camp was at least five hours from Pemba by car, and that was being generous considering the likely condition of the roads. It was probably more like an eight-hour trip during this, the rainy season. Besides, he didn't have a car, so the point was moot. He did a search for RH Safaris and, among various links and junk results, found a trip report from a previous safari client on a hunting message board. The report described the hunter's trip down to the most minute of details, including his clothing and ammunition choices. Fortunately, this attention to detail also described the air charter service he'd used.

Pemba Air Charters listed an address on Avenue de Marginal near the airport, meaning that he had walked directly past it this morning. Given the remote location of the safari area, Reece figured the charter service likely served as a regular shuttle to and from the camp and that the individuals involved would have a strong working relationship. Rather than trying to buy a truck or motorcycle to navigate his way to the camp while avoiding police and military, chartering a plane was course of action one. He wrote down the address and phone number before deleting the browser history and heading for the door. He nodded at the attendant and went back out into the slow-motion hustle and bustle of the coastal African city.

The same Toyota taxi that had dropped Reece off was still waiting, and the driver treated him like a long-lost brother. *Currency breeds loyalty in certain parts of the world, well, most of them anyway.* Reece handed the address to the driver, who nodded and steered the car back into traffic. A few minutes later, they were at their destination. Reece gave the driver another ten and this time the man handed him a business card and pointed at the phone number. *Call me if you need me again.* Reece nodded in understanding.

The world headquarters of Pemba Air Charters was a faded baby blue single-family home, surrounded by an iron gate with brick columns. The windows of the building were covered with burglar bars and an older Suzuki minivan parked just inside the gate had a magnetic "Pemba Air Charters" logo on the door. Reece pressed the doorbell button on the brick column and put on his best smile.

The front door of the house opened and a short, broad-chested white man wearing sandals, blue athletic shorts, and a faded olive T-shirt stepped out, squinting his eyes in the bright sunlight. He walked half the distance between the house and the gate.

"Can I help you?" he asked in the heavily accented English of East Africa.

"I'm looking for Pemba Air Charters; am I in the right place?"

"You are. We just don't get many walk-ins." He walked to the gate, fishing a key ring out of his pocket, and extended his hand. "I'm Geoff."

"Richard Connell, nice to meet you," Reece improvised.

"Come on in, Mr. Connell. It's bloody hot out here, eh?"

"Thanks, I appreciate it." Reece followed Geoff inside. What would have been the family room of the house was set up as an office with a desk, an office chair, and a sofa in the center of the room. He assumed that Geoff both worked out of and lived here.

"Set your bags down anywhere. Can I get you anything? A beer?"

"No, I'm fine, thanks."

"Have a seat." Geoff pointed at the couch as he made his way around the desk and took a seat behind it.

"American, eh?"

"More of a world traveler."

"I guess so, if you're walking around Pemba. What can we do for you?"

"I'm looking to charter a flight to the RH Safaris camp near Niassa."

"Ah, yes, we do a good bit of work with them. You realize that it's not the hunting season, though, right?"

"I do. I'm not headed there to hunt. I am a friend of the Hastings family and thought I would visit Mr. Hastings since I was in this part of the world."

"Right." Geoff nodded skeptically. "We can help with that for sure, eh. I need to call them and make sure that someone is in camp before we put in a flight plan."

"I completely understand. You can tell him that *Utilivu*'s friend from college wants to visit."

"Right. Let's give him a call then, eh?" Geoff picked up a desk phone and dialed a number from memory. Ten seconds later, the call was answered on the other end. "Hey, bro, it's Geoff. I've got an oak here who wants to visit you. Says he's a college friend of *Utilivu*, whoever the fuck that is." Geoff winked at Reece to let him know that he was joking. "Right, okay then, let me take a look at the weather. See you soon. Need me to bring you anything? Right."

Geoff hung up the phone and looked up at Reece. "He said to bring you in as soon as possible. I'll check the weather and we'll see about getting you there today."

"That's great, thanks, Geoff. How much do I owe you?"

"You must be a good friend of Rich. He said to add it to his tab."

Within an hour they were loading Reece's bags into a small truck and backing through the driveway gate. Geoff had changed into his pilot uniform and carried a black chart case, identical to the ones used by commercial pilots the world over. It took them three minutes to drive onto the airport grounds and, much to Reece's relief, Geoff drove around the terminal and directly onto the tarmac and stopped next to a high-wing single-engine turboprop aircraft. The Cessna 208 Caravan could hold up to nine passengers, but Geoff and Reece would be the only occupants on this trip.

Reece loaded his bags while Geoff went to handle some business with the aviation authorities. It was too hot to sit in the plane, so Reece took a seat on the door's step and rested in the shade of the wing. Geoff returned after a few minutes and began preflighting the plane, instructing Reece to sit in the right seat of the cockpit. There was no sign of police or military activity at the field, but nonetheless, Reece breathed a silent sigh of relief when they were finally airborne.

CHAPTER 19

Niassa Game Reserve
Mozambique, Africa
March

THE FLIGHT TO CAMP took them an hour and a half, with Geoff playing the part of tour guide over the headsets as they flew. He pointed out rivers, towns, and villages along the green and brown landscape, giving Reece the lay of the land. The last town of any size before camp was Montepuez, but from the air it looked to be nothing more than a few buildings. Geoff indicated the river that formed the boundary of the hunting area as they passed it, and it still took ten minutes of flying to reach the runway. He had certainly chosen one of the most remote spots on the globe to come to die.

Reece noticed a white pickup parked alongside the red dirt runway, which Geoff circled to approach into the wind. The pilot lowered the flaps and eased back on the throttle, dropping the Cessna on a glide path toward the earth below. The plane touched down gently and bounced along the runway until it slowed to a stop in front of the vehicle. Through the plane's windshield, Reece immediately recognized the man standing by the white Land Cruiser as Rich Hastings, Raife's uncle and the owner of RH Safaris.

He had aged quite a bit since Reece had seen him last; it was hard to believe that almost twenty years had passed since that summer in Zimbabwe. His short hair was stark white, which contrasted drastically with his deeply tanned skin. He stood more than six feet tall and had the lean build of an endurance athlete, the ropy veins of his muscled forearms visible below the rolled-up sleeves of his starched green safari-style shirt. He wore short shorts and sandals without socks. His face broke into a wide smile when he saw Reece descend from the plane's cabin and walked forward to meet him.

"James, good to see you, young man!" He shook Reece's hand with an iron grip and slapped him on the back with his other hand, greeting him as he would a long-lost nephew.

"Great to see you, Mr. Hastings. Thank you so much for, well, uh . . . for not turning me away."

"Of course, James, you are like family. Family is always welcome, especially when they are in need." The twinkle in his blue eyes told Reece that Mr. Hastings was well aware of his fugitive status. "Do you have any bags I can help you with?"

"I can get them, thanks." Reece climbed into the Cessna's cabin and handed his duffel down to Richard, who was standing in the doorway. He slung his pack over one shoulder and approached the cabin to thank Geoff for the ride.

"Thanks so much for getting me here, Geoff. I really appreciate it."

"No worries, eh, mate. Hopefully I'll see you again. If you need a ride anywhere, Rich knows how to get hold of me. Best of luck to you."

"Thanks."

The men shook hands and Reece climbed down the steps to the dirt runway. His bag was already loaded into the bed of the Land Cruiser and Rich Hastings motioned for him to get on the passenger side. The older man started the truck and pulled onto a track that led away from the runway. Reece was taking in the landscape in silence when Hastings spoke.

"I'm only going to mention this once, James. Bloody awful business about your family. I read up on it. A young reporter seemed to have the inside scoop. I tried asking Raife about it, but you know him, elusive bastard," Hastings said with a smile while shifting gears. "The reports mentioned something about brain tumors in your men?"

Reece remained silent.

"Well, you'll let me know if you need a doctor, eh? And you're welcome to stay here as long as you'd like. I'd say the chances of them finding you in Mozambique are pretty slim so long as you don't stick your head up too high."

"I appreciate it, sir. I really do."

"We don't get much in the way of outside news here, James. Our focus is the land and its game. I guess that's why we're all out here. The camp doesn't even have Internet. All our bookings come through a hunting concierge service out of Georgia, and they call us the old-fashioned way, on the telephone. There's only one in camp and it's in the main office. That's a big attraction for clients, actually. Here they can forget about the modern world that has them constantly connected. No choice out here. If you want to be off the grid, this is your place."

"Thank you. That suits me just fine."

"You struck me as a good lad when you were here last. We won't speak of it again," Hastings declared, pulling into the safari camp. "You look like a bloody skeleton. We've got a big dinner cooking. We'll see if we can put some meat back on those bones."

"I can't wait. It has been a long time since I've had a decent meal, or a beer."

"We'll get you caught up on both then. You can get washed up, and then we'll eat."

Camp was a series of structures made of stone, timber, mud, and thatch. There was a massive barnlike common building with an open-air dining room, bar, and seating area. A detached kitchen building sat nearby and a series of guest cottages were strung laterally along the ridge that faced the river below. There was also a shop for maintaining the vehicles, a skinning shed, walk-in refrigerated storage, and staff quarters. Hastings led Reece down a stone path to one of the guest cottages and showed him the amenities. It was basic, but it was clean and well maintained, and the view was amazing. *Home sweet African home.*

Reece had just enough time to get his bags situated when a polite female voice from outside his hooch told him that it was time for dinner.

He headed for the bathroom to clean himself up and barely recognized the man who stared back at him in the mirror: long sun-bleached hair, bronze skin framing the pale white where his sunglasses had blocked the rays, a visibly broken nose from its meeting with the ship's wheel, and a beard that nearly touched his chest. His eyes were set deep by the drastic loss of body weight, the rest of his face obscured by his gray-streaked facial hair. He didn't figure on dinner being too formal in this corner of the world, but the last thing he wanted to do was offend his generous hosts.

He turned on the shower and dropped his clothes to the stone floor before stepping into the stream of warm water. Nothing in his life had ever felt better. Standing still for what seemed like an eternity, he let the water wash the salt and grime from his matted hair. There was shampoo and a bar of soap on a shelf cut into the stone wall and he lathered himself carefully, making sure to hit every inch. He stepped out of the shower feeling more human than beast and toweled dry. Using his fingers, he worked the tangles out of his wet hair, slicking it back as best he could without the benefit of a comb or brush. A toothbrush and toothpaste had been laid out for him, and after rationing toothpaste throughout his transoceanic voyage, he enjoyed the luxury of squirting a giant dollop onto his brush and scrubbing away.

He found a short-sleeved white polo shirt and a pair of lightweight pants that looked to be about his size laid out on his bed when he emerged from the shower. Obviously, Rich had canvassed the camp for clothes that might fit his guest. Donning his new apparel, Reece declared himself as presentable as possible and exited into the cool evening air.

He assumed that dinner would be served in the open-air dining room he'd seen on the way in, so he followed the stone path in that direction. Sure enough, he entered the massive thatched-roof living and dining area to find Hastings standing by a small bar with three younger men. Despite Reece's visions of colonial Africa, none of the men were dressed any more formally than he was. Hastings spotted Reece as he entered the room and waved him over.

"James, come, come." He motioned toward the younger men. "James, this is Louie, Mike, and Darren. They are my PHs here in this concession."

Anywhere else in the world they would be known as hunting guides, but in Africa they are known as *professional hunters* and are subject to various licensing standards. To be a PH in Mozambique you have to meet the requirements of neighboring Zimbabwe, which had the toughest PH standards in all of Africa. These men knew their business.

The three men, each at least as tall as Reece, extended their hands and greeted him warmly and politely. They looked to be in their late twenties or early thirties and all had the same long and lean build as Hastings. They were deeply tanned, with sun-beaten skin that gave them the faces of men in their forties or fifties. These were hard men.

"What are you drinking, James? We have plenty of booze, beer, wine?"

"A beer would be great, thanks."

Richard motioned to the youngest looking of the men. "Mike, get Mr. Reece here a beer, please."

What little alcohol had been on the sailboat had been consumed in the Azores, and Reece hadn't had a drink in what seemed like an eternity. The young man handed him an ice-cold can of beer.

"Cheers, mate."

Reece took a long drink that disappeared at least half the can. He couldn't remember a better-tasting beer in his life.

"First sip is the best, eh?" Hastings said, smiling. "James here has had a long trip. He is a friend of my nephew Raife, whom you all know, and he is going to be spending as much time with us as he likes. He needs to keep a bit of a low profile, though, so he will stay out of sight when we have clients in camp, eh? I know that each of you will respect that."

Each man nodded soberly at his boss's request.

"James, it's our honor to have you here but we're going to put you to work. I want you to rest up and eat for the next few days. Then you can go out scouting with Louie and we'll make a plan from there."

"I appreciate it, Mr. Hastings."

"Rich, please call me Rich. You ready for another beer?"

Reece had been around Australians and New Zealanders on multiple deployments and had come to respect their ability to consume quanti-

ties of alcohol that would put most men in the hospital. It became immediately apparent that this was a talent shared by his new African friends.

After a few minutes, dinner was served for the five men at a dining
table that looked like it could hold at least twenty. This camp was primitive, but Rich made sure that it maintained an air of first-world civility
complete with white tablecloths, linen napkins, and crystal wineglasses
that were kept full with a seemingly endless flow of South African *pino-
tage*. A salad of fresh vegetables was served along with a medium-rare
filet of some of the best meat Reece had ever tasted, which turned out
to be eland.

After surviving on a small supply of canned goods and fresh-caught
fish for weeks, Reece's body was starving for vegetables and red meat. The
food was amazing, and not just due to Reece's hunger. His host served
him seconds and thirds from the family-style platter until Reece could
not eat another bite. A waiter then brought out heaping portions of bread
pudding, which he somehow found room to devour.

The mood at dinner was laid-back and friendly. The men whom
Reece had just met treated him like an old friend and put him immediately at ease. The reserved confidence of those around the table reminded
Reece of the men he'd worked with in the SEAL Teams, a fact that helped
dispel any nervous feelings regarding his new surroundings. As odd as it
was, Reece felt more at home in this faraway corner of the world than he
had since before his last disastrous deployment and the events that followed. As it turned out, the PHs were natives of bordering Zimbabwe, a
country that Reece knew had a turbulent history.

Rather than talking politics, they focused on the rivers, the terrain
features, and the game of Niassa, casually briefing Reece on what to expect during his time on the reserve. They didn't ask any personal questions, though Reece assumed that they already knew exactly who he was.
Men like these were the last of the cowboys. They believed in personal
freedom and had no desire to complicate their lives or anyone else's by
reporting the surprise guest, a friend of their employer, to the authorities.

"Let's have a drink and talk, James," said Hastings, handing the
younger man a glass of brown liquid, neat.

The PHs bid them both good night as Rich motioned for Reece to follow him into the darkness outside the dining area. He led Reece down a series of stone steps toward a small sitting area, illuminated by the dancing light of a blazing fire pit. The men took adjacent seats and stared silently at the fire for a moment.

"Africa Channel One, we call it."

As Reece's eyes adjusted to the darkness, he could see the reflection of the full moon on a river below. The sitting area was situated on a high bluff overlooking the river. He thought maybe he'd had too much to drink when he saw the silhouettes of elephants bathing in the reflective waters.

"Are those elephants down there?"

"Yeah, cows and calves."

"Do you guys hunt them here?"

"We hunt a few old bulls, but we don't do any hunting within a mile of camp. This area is safe for them, and they know it. Have you spent much time in the bush, James?"

"I did a lot of hunting with my dad and grandfather when I was a kid, but haven't done much lately. Raife and I hunted as much as we could in college in Montana, deer and elk mainly. We obviously hunted with you in Zim that time I came to visit. I also spent some time up in Kodiak, Alaska, in the Navy and hunted every chance I got. I loved it up there."

Rich nodded. "It's tough to find the time when you're busy doing what you and Raife were doing for the past decade."

"Did you fight with Raife's dad?"

"Not together, no. His dad, Johnathan, was my older brother. He was the reason that I became a soldier. He was eight years older and joined the army before the war really got kicking. Our father had served in the Long-Range Desert Group in the war and later in C Squadron in Malaya. I guess he was our inspiration to join the regiment."

"So, you were SAS? I thought Raife's dad was a Selous Scout?"

"Oh, he was. We both were, actually, though he was in longer."

"I studied the Scouts when we were deep into our counterinsurgency efforts in Iraq. What an incredible time in special operations history."

"Ah, it was bloody fun, eh. We'd go out dressed like the enemy and trick them into thinking we were insurgents traveling into the area. 'Pseudo-operations,' we called them. We had all of the passwords and knew their SOPs, so we could talk the talk. I obviously couldn't get too close no matter how much face paint I put on. They'd show us where all of the *terrs* were hiding and then we'd call in the Saints."

"They the cavalry?"

"Indeed. The RLI, the Rhodesian Light Infantry. They'd parachute or chopper in and sweep up the enemy in fire-force ops. I'd be on the high ground with a radio guiding them in. It was tremendously effective."

Reece was too young to have had any real perspective on the politics of the Rhodesian Bush War, but there was no doubt that it involved some of the most effective counterinsurgency efforts the world had ever seen. He hoped that history would remember his own men's bravery and tactical acumen rather than whether they fought for Iraq's oil or Afghanistan's lithium. He also knew what it was like to fight an enemy whose PR machine was agile and relentless.

"We fought hard but, in the end, it came down to politics. I still think about the boys we lost, both white and black. What do you say we drink one for those boys and their widows?"

Reece looked Rich in the eye and extended his glass. "To them. The brave ones."

Both warriors sat in silence for several minutes, each paying respect to their fallen brothers.

Reece cleared his throat and said, "How did you end up here in Mozambique, Rich?"

"Well, you were there in Zim. You saw them harass us."

"I remember it well. Did that start as soon as Mugabe took over?"

"Not right away, no. It was all pretty civilized at first. Bob and his crew were stealing everything they could, of course, but they left us alone for a while. Mugabe sent his Fifth Brigade, men trained by the North Koreans, to slaughter his rival tribe the Ndebele, and the world paid no attention. They tortured, starved, and shot them by the thousands. No one even knows how many they killed, but it was something upwards of twenty thousand people. All civilians, men, women, children, and all because they belonged to the wrong tribe. Where was the international outrage then? Anyway, once they realized that no one gave a shit about what happened inside Zimbabwe, they started taking our farms and anything else that had any value. My brother was smart: he left as soon as the war was over and took his family to the Cape. He started with fuck-all and made himself a bloody fortune. When things started to turn in South Africa, he did the smart thing again and moved to the U.S."

"Yeah, I met Raife not long after that."

"That's about right. What year was it that you visited us?"

"Nineteen ninety-eight. It was the summer before my senior year in college. I'll never forget it. That place was so beautiful."

"It was that. Anyway, I stayed on the farm as long as I could. My family had spent decades building it, and I wasn't about to let the 'War Vets' poach all of those animals. I stayed for them, really. It got bad for a couple years after your visit, so I sent the family down south to live to get them away from the violence. They'd seen enough of that. When our farm was burned in 2000, I knew it was over. I took what I could and bid on a concession in Botswana, where we hunted for about ten years. After they shut down hunting there, we found this place. Pretty damn ironic to be back in Moz, where I did so much fighting."

"So, you're a man without a country?"

"You know how that feels, don't you, James?"

Reece paused. Staring into the fire, he nodded and took another long sip of his drink.

CHAPTER 20

REECE WAS WALKING IN downtown Coronado when he saw Lauren and Lucy shopping on the opposite side of the street. Lauren was combing the sidewalk sale rack of a boutique for bargains and Lucy stood next to her, holding on to the strap of her purse. Turning, she saw Reece across the street, her face lighting up with joy. He waved and began to make his way between two parked cars to cross the street. Lucy let go of Lauren's purse and began to run in his direction. Then everything went into slow motion. Reece could see the taxi and knew that the driver wouldn't see Lucy until it was too late. Lucy's path and speed put them on a perfect collision course. Reece yelled at the top of his lungs for her to stop but no one could hear him: not Lucy, not Lauren, not the cabdriver. Lucy kept coming, as did the taxi. Reece began to run toward her but his legs felt like they were mired in concrete; he'd never get there in time. He looked at the taxi driver and recognized the face of a man he'd last seen before putting two bullets into his brain on the streets of LA. *It can't be*. When he turned his head, Lucy's smile was the last thing he saw as the cab accelerated to make impact.

Soaked in sweat, Reece shot up in bed and looked at his strange surroundings.

A tiny voice came through the thatched wall to his right. "Morning, morning, sir."

"Um, yep, I'm up . . ." was all Reece could muster in response, remembering that he was thousands of miles from Coronado and that Lauren and Lucy were gone forever.

The hangover hit him like a sledgehammer. There was no tumor to blame for this one, just too many beers, a lot of red wine, and more than a few whiskeys. He flung the blanket off his legs and swung his legs over to the floor. Struggling to find his balance, he stumbled into the bathroom. The figure that gazed back at him from the bathroom mirror looked like a homeless guy selling drugs at a music festival.

He wasn't sure about drinking the water, so he threw on a pair of shorts and a T-shirt along with some flip-flops and staggered toward the dining area in search of coffee. Even in his current state, he was struck by the beauty of the African sunrise. The orange ball emerging over the treetops bathed the entire scene in a warm glow. The green forest was broken by the deep, sandy riverbed below, where he could see Cape buffalo and what looked like kudu drinking. He assumed correctly that giant crocodiles were somewhere in the water below, waiting patiently for one of the mammals to venture too close.

"How's it?"

Reece turned to see Louie, walking diagonally toward the common area.

"Hope Rich didn't bore you with too many of his stories from the good old days?" Louie smiled.

"No, no, it was great. Just wish I'd drank less."

"Ah, join the club. Let's get you some coffee."

Reece followed Louie toward what would likely be a steady stream of caffeine consumed over many hours. Hastings was already seated at the breakfast table when they entered, a coffee mug in his hand and a large topographical map spread before him. "Good morning, James. What are you doing up? I thought you'd sleep for days."

This guy is pretty cheery for as much as we drank last night. "Yes, sir, good morning to you as well. I'm good, but I'll be better as soon as I get some coffee in me. Thank you again for last night. Dinner was great and I enjoyed our talk."

"Ah, I get carried away with the bloody politics. Get some coffee and rest up today."

"If it's all the same with you, I think it would be good for me to get out and about."

"Understood. Then come have a look at the map. I'll give you the lay of the land."

Reece filled a mug from an old-fashioned urn and added some sugar and cream, a bit disappointed that there was no sign of honey. He took a seat next to Rich and tried to focus his blurry vision on the map in front of him.

"This, as you know, is the Niassa Reserve. We hunt this block here." Hastings outlined the boundaries with his thick, tanned finger. "We just finished the paperwork to take over this neighboring block, which will more than double the size of our concession. We are going to be busy with clients over the next few months and we need you to help scout the new block, if you're up for it."

"Sure, I'd be happy to. I can't promise that I'll know what I'm looking for, but I'll give it a shot."

"You'll have a couple of trackers with you. They know the game better than anyone; they just don't have a sense of the big picture. Neither of them can read or write very well, either, so I can't rely on them to give me much of a report. There's an old camp here on this river; check it out and let me know what kind of shape it's in. After that, the three of you can spend a few weeks seeing what we've got for animals out there. Just having you moving around will help with the poaching. You'll probably run across some snares and you may even bump into some poachers in the block. I know you can handle yourself if that's the case. We'll give you a vehicle and you'll need a proper rifle, which I've got for you."

"Check. What can you tell me about the poachers?"

"Ah, yes. Two lots of them, really. The first are after bush meat. They put out wire snares, thousands of the bloody things. Some are looking for meat to sell in the villages, but a large number of them are conscripted to feed the Chinese mining and lumber operations that are popping up all over the country. The damn snares don't know the difference between an impala ewe and a lion. We counter them in two ways: one, we patrol constantly and pick up every snare we see and destroy it; we even pay bounties for them. The other way we do it is outreach: we try to employ as many locals as we can here in the camp or out in the field and we distribute a good bit of meat to the villages. The staple of their diet is mealie meal; you'd call it grits, ground-up corn that they cook into a slop. They are all protein starved, so we make sure that everyone gets a piece of what we shoot in the unit. If they help protect the game, the game can provide for them. *Sustainable* is such a bloody greenie word, but that's what this is if we do it right."

"Sounds like everyone wins that way," Reece said. "What about the second group of poachers? Guessing they feed the Asian black market?"

"Exactly. The Chinese are raping Africa blind for her resources. They come in and make deals with the corrupt officials and mine whatever they want. It's all economic for them; there's zero return for the communities. Where's Jimmy Carter now? Sorry, I'm getting political again. As part of that Chinese presence, the demand for ivory and rhino horn has a direct line to the source. We've seen sophisticated poaching syndicates, often in bed with the game departments, all over Africa. We don't have any rhino here, so they're mainly after elephants. You won't see any Chinese in the field but they're pulling the strings. The ivory gets smuggled out along with all of the other resources to feed the demand back in Asia."

"Sounds similar to the drug problem in the U.S. As long as there is a demand, the cartels will provide the supply. With the demand from Asia, turning the tide on the supply side will be tough."

"Right you are, James. Unfortunately, right you are."

CHAPTER 21

Basel, Switzerland
March

COLONEL ANDRENOV REVIEWED THE spreadsheets on his screens and offered a rare smile. The string of terrorist attacks and his investment strategies in advance of them had been far more successful than even he could have imagined. He knew, of course, that the retail markets would decline sharply out of consumers' fear of terrorism, timed perfectly with the holiday shopping season. His problem was spreading that fear and panic to the United States, where no kinetic attacks had taken place.

His solution came thanks to a group that called itself the "Syrian Electronic Army." This group of pro-Assad hackers took over the Associated Press's Twitter account in June 2013 and posted an erroneous "Breaking News" headline about an explosion at the White House that had wounded the president. Despite the lack of an explosion, the U.S. stock market lost $136 billion in equity value in just five minutes.

As a Russian national with plenty of capital, Andrenov had access to his choice of hackers and "bot" accounts. For a few thousand euros' worth of cryptocurrency, his hackers had been carefully coordinating false reports of terrorist attacks at shopping malls and other retail locations across North America and Europe, keeping the Western world constantly on edge.

As shoppers stayed home, brick-and-mortar stores had lost out on the holiday income that usually put them in the black for the year. The ordinarily chaotic shopping scenes on the Friday after Thanksgiving had been replaced by empty retailers whose shelves stood piled with unsold merchandise. Instead of flocking to movie theaters and restaurants over the holidays, consumers sat at home and fed on the fear stoked by the twenty-four-hour news media. The ripple effect was felt across nearly all sectors of the economy as demand fell.

This was all a predictable result of Andrenov's carefully planned operations, but the second element was pure luck. Over the past two decades, investors had exponentially increased their use of exchange-traded funds (ETFs). These securities offer investors a vehicle by which to profit from commodities, currencies, futures, and other "goods" without actually owning or taking possession of those items. For example, a gold ETF allows an investor to profit from an increase in the price of gold without buying actual gold.

When the stock markets in New York, London, and across the globe declined sharply after the Kingston Market attack, it set off a demand for cash. The problem was that many of the ETFs that had become so popular lacked any true liquidity. They were built on investor confidence rather than actual value. As that confidence shattered, so did the value of the funds. A gold ETF that owned very little actual gold bullion became a nearly worthless investment as institutions and individuals scrambled to cash out. The "ETF bubble" took the market by surprise, just as the housing bubble had done a decade earlier. The entire system collapsed like a trillion-dollar house of cards, catalyzing what would have been a small recession into an event that surpassed the 2008 financial crisis in terms of lost wealth.

Hardworking people saw their 401(k)s evaporate and their pension plans become nearly insolvent. Retailers, who were already teetering on bankruptcy thanks to online sales, shut their doors and laid off tens of thousands of workers. There was a worldwide contraction of credit that stifled growth to a standstill.

Everyone, wealthy and poor, suffered. Everyone, that is, but Vasili Andrenov. He had shorted the equity markets in the United States, the United Kingdom, and across the European Union months before the attacks. That news alone had caused some uncertainty in the market since he was viewed as such a savvy, if shadowy, investor. Instead of looking to the world like the profiteering terrorist mastermind that he was, he came out looking like an oracle, the kind of mind that could lead a nation out of decline.

Andrenov pulled a tattered volume from the vast collection of first editions in his opulent library. Published in Russian, it was known to most of the world as *The Protocols of the Elders of Zion*. It was the only relic of the life of his maternal grandfather, a man he'd never met. His mother spoke of her father with awe, influencing young Vasili deeply with the political beliefs of a generation past. Unlike Andrenov's father and grandfather, who were devout communists, his mother's father had been an outspoken supporter of imperial Russia. He was a member of the Black Hundreds, an ultranationalist society that espoused a motto of "Orthodoxy, Autocracy, and Nationality." The Black Hundreds despised anything and anyone who would challenge the House of Romanov: communists, Jews, and Ukrainian nationalists. The Black Hundreds had fought to suppress Ukrainian language and culture in Odessa, of all places, a feat that Andrenov planned to repeat. Capitalism had defeated the communists, Andrenov's attack on the world economies had punished the international bankers, and the next phase of his plan would finish the Ukrainians for good. A century after the fall of the empire, Andrenov would rebuild what his grandfather fought so hard to protect.

CHAPTER 22

Niassa Game Reserve
Mozambique, Africa
March

AFTER A HEARTY BREAKFAST and three cups of coffee to get Reece's brain back in gear, he followed Rich toward the parking area. Rich reached behind the seat of his safari vehicle and retrieved a battered canvas rifle case that he handed to the new arrival. "You can use this rifle. It's old but it works."

Reece unzipped the case and pulled the big-bore rifle out to inspect it. It was an old Mauser sporting rifle that looked like it had been carried to the moon and back. The bluing was worn from every visible surface from years of honest use, leaving the steel a burnished silver. The scarred walnut stock was the color of dark chocolate, and only small areas of the checkering at both the grip and forend remained visible. There wasn't a speck of rust or dirt, though, making it obvious that the rifle was heavily used but never abused. Reece noticed some lettering at the top of the barrel that read "W. J. Jeffery & Co, 60 Queen Victoria Street, London." It wore several proof marks, presumably from a house in England, and was marked "404 EX Cordite." He slowly cycled the bolt, which was as smooth as glass, pushing a cigar-sized round into the chamber.

"How many does it hold?"

"Three down, one up the pipe. The .404s are too bloody wide for the standard Mauser but this one feeds like a charm. A gunsmith down in Pretoria took the sides out of the mag box to give it more room so the rounds actually ride on the wood. I've got a couple of extra boxes of ammo for you, along with a pouch for your belt." Rich dug around behind the seat and handed Reece a handful of battered yellow and red cardboard boxes with "KYNOCH .404 JEFFERY 400 gr. Solid" printed on the front.

"All solid bullets?" Reece asked.

"Yeah. If you shoot this thing, it means that something is trying to stomp you into jelly. A solid is what you'll want; the softs won't penetrate on something like an ele. If you shoot an impala or wartie for the pot, the solid will wreck less of the meat."

Reece nodded in understanding.

"Carry this thing everywhere when you're not in camp, eh? You go off to have a shite and a dagga boy with a snare around his leg might decide to have a go at you, right?" Hastings laughed.

"No sling?"

"When bad things happen out here, they happen fast. You want your rifle in your hands, not on your back."

"Understood. How's the recoil?"

"Ah, not bad. The bloody English knew how to shape a stock, which helps. It's like a heavy shotgun load, nothing a big, tough frogman can't handle."

"Is there somewhere I can test fire it?"

"Sure, Louie will stop outside of camp on the way out this morning and you can have a go with it. Grab whatever you need from your room; he's gassing up the truck and will be ready to go in a bit. He'll have a cold box with food and drinks. Just take whatever you need for the day."

"Got it. Thanks, Rich. I really appreciate this." Reece held up the rifle and nodded toward it.

"No worries, eh? Can't have our new friend getting stomped on his first day. Take the case, too; you'll want it for the truck."

Back in his room, Reece searched through his duffel to find the items he thought he'd need as a professional . . . well, whatever he was now. The temperatures were already rising to the point of being uncomfortable, so he wouldn't need much in the way of clothing. He found a tan ball cap with an old platoon logo on it and traded his flip-flops for socks and his Salomon hiking boots, which admirably looked none the worse for wear considering what they'd been through. He clipped a folding knife onto the pocket of his shorts and put his backpack on the bed to take inventory of what was inside. He pulled out several items that he wouldn't need for this excursion and made sure that both his binoculars and camera were packed. He slipped the boxes of .404 ammunition into an outside pocket and zipped up the bag. Grabbing his Gatorz sunglasses from the small bedside table, Reece picked up his rifle and headed toward the parking area.

Louie was standing by a white Toyota Land Cruiser pickup, the workhorse vehicle for most of the underdeveloped world, supervising the loading of supplies while he smoked a cigarette. He spotted Reece approaching with his gear and nodded.

"Mind if I throw my stuff in the back?"

"Just hand it to Muzi, eh? You can put it up front if you'd prefer. Hand him your rifle, too, and he'll put it up in the rack."

Reece handed his cased rifle to the thin black man in coveralls, who appeared to be in his fifties. Muzi placed the rifle in the rack behind the rear window with deliberate respect.

"Do I need to get some water?" Reece inquired, still suffering a bit from last night's bender.

"No, we've got plenty in the cold box. Muzi, *ipa iye diridza.*"

Muzi opened the cooler and handed down a one-liter bottle of water. Reece nodded and thanked him. "What language is that?"

"It's Shona. Muzi is from Zim; he's been my tracker as long as I can remember. He's like an uncle to me. He understands English well but it's more efficient for us to speak in Shona. Most of the workers in camp speak the local tribal language as well as Swahili and a little English or Portuguese."

Reece nodded.

"Okay, looks like we're packed up, eh. You can jump up front with me. Muzi will ride in the back."

Reece noticed a padded seat mounted behind the cab of the truck that would give the tracker a bird's-eye view as they drove. The Land Cruiser was a left-hand-drive pickup with a standard floor shift. Though it was probably only a few years old, judging by the appearance, its lack of modern features made it appear to be from the 1970s. These stripped-down utility vehicles were virtually indestructible but were also all but unobtainable in the United States. Reece had always loved using them overseas due to their dependability.

Muzi tapped on the sheet metal roof and Louie started the motor, slipping the truck into gear. Three thin black men in the olive-green coveralls were walking toward the camp on the narrow dirt track as the truck left the parking area. Louie steered the truck toward them and slammed on the accelerator. The men laughed and feigned fear as they scattered over the rocks that bordered the road. Louie waved and said something that Reece couldn't understand as they passed. They drove with the windows down, fresh air filling the cab.

"All right, you've seen the camp, and Rich gave you the lay of the land on the map this morning. Today we're going to take a bit of a drive to the new block and check out some spots for buffalo, so you can start to learn your way around the concession."

"Sounds good. This place is beautiful."

"It really is special. Moz is backward as hell, but there's so much potential. The wilderness areas are huge and the animals are really starting to recover from the war. If we can keep the poaching under control, this place will be paradise."

"What do you do with poachers?"

"Well, half the time you run into a couple of guys that you know are up to no good but you can't prove anything. We try to catch them with snares or guns but if we don't, we basically try to scare them. We tell them that we know what they're doing and if we catch them out here again, they're going to jail. If we catch anyone in the act, we call in the game scout and let him handle it. Rich wants to build a dedicated antipoaching unit, but that's expensive and we'd have to fund it ourselves. It'll be worth it but after buying this new block, I think it's a matter of resources. Maybe if you stick around long enough you can help us train them, eh?"

"Happy to help if I can. Who do the game scouts work for?"

"They work for the government, for the game department. In most of Africa, you have to have a game scout with you when you hunt with clients. They make sure that the laws are followed and all of that. A good one is a real blessing, eh, but a bad one can fuck up a hunt right quick."

"So, it's like taking the game warden hunting with you?"

"Exactly. We pay for them, of course, but we don't pay them directly because they don't want them to have a conflict of interest. They take tips from the clients, though, so it's not exactly perfect in that regard."

"Are they competent?"

"Ha! This is Africa, James. You never know what you'll get. Some of them are as good as the trackers but some come straight out of the cities and you have to keep them from getting lost. They're given AK-47s but no training, so you just hope they don't shoot you in the bloody back by mistake when you're on a track."

"Sounds like half of the Iraqi Army."

"I bet. Speaking of that, I hope Rich didn't talk your bloody ears off about the Bush War last night."

"Not at all. I'd never heard most of that before."

"Did he tell you about his sister?"

"No, he didn't mention her. I thought it was just Rich and his brother?"

"It is now. They had a sister, she'd be Raife's aunt. I never knew her, but I know the story. She was an air hostess for Air Rhodesia. The terrorists shot down two flights back in the late 1970s using Russian missiles; she was on one of them. They killed something like forty people when the plane went down, then they hunted down the survivors and killed them on the ground: all civilians, women, kids. They bragged about it on TV afterward, sick bastards."

"No wonder he's bitter."

"Yeah, those guys fought a tough fight but it's over and some of them have a hard time letting go. It's never going to be like the old days no matter how much they complain. Rich is a *lekker* bloke but sometimes he lives in the past. It's an African thing, I guess." Louie's eyes narrowed as he took a long drag on his smoke.

"In Afghanistan, they're still using us to settle centuries-old grievances every chance they get."

"Well, perhaps it's a human thing then, eh?"

Louie took his foot off the accelerator and slowed the truck as they approached a wide spot in the dirt road. He turned off the track and steered the truck so it was perpendicular across the red dirt path.

"Looks like a good spot to test that new rifle of yours."

"Let's do it."

Reece opened his door and Muzi passed the .404 down from the bed. Louie said something in Shona, and Muzi climbed down from the truck holding a *panga*, a utilitarian blade that was the African version of the machete. Reece retrieved his pack and laid it on top of the hood so that he could use it as a rifle rest. Louie handed him a rolled-up jacket to support the butt end.

Muzi had walked fifty or so yards down the road and looked back toward them for approval. Louie flashed a thumbs-up, and Muzi used his *panga* to slash the bark away from a tree along the roadside, exposing the light-colored wood underneath. Reece now had a target. Reece expected Muzi would retreat to their position for safety, but instead he walked a few yards off to the side and stopped.

"Go ahead and give it a go," Louie said, his binoculars already focused on the makeshift target.

When in Rome, I guess.

Reece checked to ensure that a round was chambered and arranged Louie's jacket underneath the toe of the stock before leaning across the hood with the rifle. The back of his hand that gripped the forend rested on his pack. He moved the safety to FIRE, found the silver front bead, and began to control his breathing. It occurred to him that the past weeks had been the longest period in two decades that he'd gone without firing a weapon either in training or in combat. He centered the bead in the express-style rear notch and arranged the sights on the target downrange, his eyes dancing between the three visual planes. He transitioned his focus to the front sight, exhaled slowly, and began to apply pressure on the trigger.

BOOM.

The recoil was significant, as was the noise, and Reece was instantly reminded of his lack of hearing protection by the report of the elephant gun. He worked the bolt as the recoil pushed him rearward and chambered a new round as he returned his sights to the target. He saw Muzi move toward the tree and he moved his finger away from the trigger. Muzi used the tip of his *panga* as a pointer and indicated the bullet's point of impact like the judge at a turkey shoot. The rifle's sights were zeroed perfectly.

"Good shot. You want to give it another one?"

"Sure, can't hurt. You have any earmuffs, by any chance?"

"Ha, yes, mate. Loud, eh?"

Louie dug around behind the seat and returned with a pair of red earmuffs that he handed to Reece. He put them on and settled back in for a second shot, one that landed less than two inches from the first. Satisfied, Reece reloaded the rifle from the box of ammo in his pack. Muzi nodded at Reece approvingly as he took the rifle, returning it to the truck's rack.

They drove on through miles of dense *miombo* forests broken occasionally by rivers or open savannas, with giant stone monoliths towering upward from the otherwise gentle terrain. Reece took it all in, awed by its savage beauty. The game appeared to be plentiful: small groups of giraffes could be seen close to the road, their necks towering above the tree line like periscopes.

Ever the guide, Louie would stop the truck and allow Reece to take in the scene while he passed along some knowledge about the species in question.

"You can tell a male from a female by looking at the antenna up top, eh. Like a human, the bulls go bald on top and sometimes you can see where they've bent them from fighting. See how the antenna are crooked on the dark one on the left?"

Reece found the correct bull in his binoculars and took note of the askew headgear.

"I see what you're talking about. Why is that?"

"They fight for dominance by banging their heads together sideways. When they do it, they'll often break something on the skull and those things get crooked. Must give them a headache, eh?"

After a few moments, Louie started the truck again and continued on their journey. Similar stops were made to observe groups of impala, zebra, and a small herd of Cape buffalo. Unlike in the touristy photo safari camps that Reece had seen on television, these animals didn't stand around very long once the vehicle stopped. It reminded him of the difference in animal behavior in places like Yellowstone versus the backcountry wilderness areas where he'd hunted during his college days in Montana. About two hours into the drive, Reece heard a tapping sound on the truck's roof and Louie brought the truck to a halt. He exchanged words with Muzi in Shona for a moment before opening the door.

"Muzi sees big bull tracks, elephant. Let's go have a look."

By the time Reece was out of the truck, Muzi was already handing Louie his weapon, a massive double-barreled express rifle with bores that looked at least a half inch wide. Muzi handed Reece his rifle next before climbing down from the truck's bed.

Louie and Muzi stood over a large circular track on the dirt road, Muzi pointing at it while speaking rather animatedly in his native tongue. The PH knelt by the footprint and pointed out the various characteristics to Reece.

"This is from a bull's front foot; we can tell because it's round. The rear track is more of an oval. These wrinkles are like a fingerprint; every ele is different. This smooth spot here comes from the back of his foot, so we know which direction he's moving. See how worn this track is? This is an old bull, probably a big one, definitely worth having a look at."

Reece nodded as he took mental note of Louie's explanation.

"Muzi will lead the way. Just stay behind me. Stop if I stop and if I run, run like hell?" He smiled.

Muzi took off in the direction of the elephant's travel, his eyes focused on the ground. Reece was surprised at the pace they kept and struggled to keep up while staying quiet. Reece's eyes were mainly focused on the ground, looking for places to put his feet with minimal noise. He considered himself a decent tracker but could see no sign of the trail they were following. The fact that his hosts could do it at a near jog was amazing.

Reece quickly established that spending months on a small sailboat was not a great way to maintain cardiovascular endurance. The temperature was in the low hundreds with plenty of humidity and he was quickly covered in sweat. They traveled in silence for roughly thirty minutes before Muzi brought the trio to a halt. Louie motioned Reece in close and whispered quietly.

"He's slowed down now and has been eating a bit. He'll probably find some nice shade to rest in and that's where we'll catch him." Reece nodded and reached into his pack for the water bottle. Despite his desire to drink the entire liter, he rationed it on the assumption that this little walk could last the rest of the day. While he drank, Louie took what looked like a baby's sock from his hip pocket. He shook it, and talc-like dust billowed out and floated to their right, indicating the direction and speed of the wind. He nodded at Muzi and they resumed their tracking, this time at a much slower and more careful pace. They encountered a massive pile of green dung that Louie tested with the sole of his boot. He turned to Reece. "Very fresh, eh."

Every fifty or so yards, Muzi would stop and listen while Louie tested the wind with the ash bag. Reece's heart raced as he knew they were nearing one of the largest animals on the planet. The pace finally slowed to a creep, with each of them paying painful attention to every step. The air was hot and musty with the smell of decomposing vegetation, any breeze blocked by the thick bush they'd entered. The massive elephant had cleared a discernible path through the tangled *jesse*, which made their passage easier and stealthier. Suddenly, Muzi froze. Reece strained his eyes for any sign of the animal but all he could see were trees. Louie lifted his binoculars and looked into the bush before motioning Reece to move up alongside him.

Louie nodded and whispered as quietly as he could, "Do you see him, James?"

Reece shook his head, indicating that he could not. Louie raised his arm and pointed toward the trunk of a tree just ahead of Muzi.

"Do you see that big tree, eh? Just to the right of it is his leg."

Reece saw nothing but trees and shadows. He blinked his eyes and visually traced the trunk of the tree from the ground upward. Then he saw it, so close that he'd been looking past it, thinking that it was a shadow. The sight of a massive bull elephant mere yards away overcame him; it was like one of those hidden images inside a picture that, once seen, become obvious. He couldn't see the entire animal, only bits and pieces of wrinkled gray skin: a leg, a piece of shoulder, the curve of the belly, the twitch of the fanning ear. The bull appeared to be napping in the shade of the thick forest as an escape from the midday heat.

Louie whispered again, "Let's get a look at his ivory; move to your right a bit if you can."

Reece stepped as if he were in the middle of a minefield and moved a few feet to his right to give them both a better vantage point on the bull's face. He saw a filthy tusk the size of a man's leg extend from the skin of the elephant's lip, the tooth sweeping forward in a graceful arch. Louie shook the ash bag and motioned for Reece to keep moving to their right. Out of the corner of his eye Reece saw Muzi retreating the way they'd come. Reece moved until he could see the other tusk; it was a mirror image of the right one but for a flat spot worn on the inside edge of the tip. Louie and Reece stood there, admiring the animal for what must have been five minutes before Louie motioned for them to back away from the sleeping pachyderm. Reece's heart was beating so fast he was afraid that the bull would hear it.

"Pretty close, eh?" Louie whispered when they'd put a hundred yards between themselves and the bull.

"Wow!" Reece replied, the wide smile beaming across his face. "That was amazing!"

"Not something you do every day, eh? Even when you do, it's still exciting. Come, let's go to the truck and have some lunch."

Louie took off at a pace that required Reece to nearly jog to keep up. Adrenaline flowed through his veins as they walked; he couldn't remember when he'd felt so alive. It also struck him that he was smiling and had actually felt real happiness through the experience rather than the pain that had filled the past few months of his life.

Could I learn to live again here?

CHAPTER 23

Capitol Hill
Washington, D.C.
March

NOT COUNTING THE TIME spent on the San Francisco City Council and the state assembly, it had taken Senator Lisa Ann Bolls more than two decades to become the chair of the Senate Armed Services Committee. Though it had taken the support of countless political allies to get her there, the true author of her success was Stewart McGovern. McGovern had served briefly in the Senate as well, appointed to finish out the remainder of the term for a member from his home state of Nevada who had passed away while in office. When he was defeated in the next primary election by the state's popular attorney general, he took his talents to K Street, where he was quickly able to monetize his relationships with his former colleagues.

After thirty-five years as an attorney and lobbyist, there was not a door that McGovern could not open, or an ear into which he could not whisper. His social skills helped, no doubt, but the real source of his influence had nothing to do with his personality. Thanks to a client list that would make any D.C. lobbying firm envious, Stewart McGovern could raise staggering amounts of money. Campaign dollars were the lifeblood upon which politicians fed, and McGovern kept members of both parties in ample supply.

There is a $117,000 limit on the amount of direct federal campaign contributions that each U.S. citizen can make. Stewart McGovern's personal contributions hit that numerical ceiling every year and he made sure that each of the other twenty-nine attorneys and lobbyists in his firm did the same. His firm alone handed out $3.5 million in perfectly legal, reported campaign contributions to member and leadership political action committees. Add in ancillary contributions to national and state political parties as well as members' pet charities that often employed the members' spouses or children, and one would start to get a picture of how much influence can be legally obtained in Washington. Each of Stewart's clients in the defense, energy, insurance, and health care industries and their respective executives took his direction on where to make their own political contributions; the aggregate was a staggering amount of money. According to reports of the Federal Election Commission, McGovern & Davis LP took in just under $40 million per year in lobbying revenue, in addition to the nonreportable money they made doing legal work.

Senator Bolls was the number one recipient of campaign dollars from the clients of McGovern & Davis LP, thanks no doubt to her committee's jurisdiction over vast segments of the United States government and their corresponding budgets. So, when McGovern wanted to see Senator Bolls, he didn't call her scheduler or the staff member responsible for the subject matter of his request; he simply strolled through her doorway in the Hart Senate Office Building. He walked past the receptionist, past the row of Senator Bolls's constituents waiting to meet with her or her staff, and to the open doorway of Becca Callen, the senator's chief of staff.

"Can I get in to see her? I just need a minute."

Becca Callen hadn't heard him walk into her office, thanks to the soft carpeted floor, but she was accustomed to constant interruptions and instantly recognized the voice of her boss's confidant and benefactor.

"Oh, hey, Stewart. Let me pull up her schedule," she said, minimizing a Word document on her computer screen.

Two clicks later, she was looking at her boss's calendar, which was booked solid from a breakfast speech at 8:00 a.m. to a dinner that would last until nearly midnight. Like them or not, you couldn't say that Senate members didn't stay busy.

"She's wrapping up a meeting now. I can fit you in before her next appointment," she said, leading him to the senator's door.

Even at his age, McGovern liked to eye the often-attractive congressional staff members, but Callen was a bit too "granola" for his tastes. She was competent and smart, though, and knew better than to give him any trouble when it came to granting access to her boss. She knocked on the door and didn't wait for a response before opening it and sticking her head in.

"Madam Chair, Mr. McGovern is here to see you."

"Thank you, Becca."

Senator Bolls rose, signaling the end of the meeting. She shook hands with two lobbyists whom McGovern knew by face if not name. He nodded and graciously stepped aside as they and two staff members in their twenties quickly filed out of the office. Senator Bolls walked from behind her desk to greet her closest political ally and gave him a genuinely warm hug.

"How are you, Stewart?"

"I'm great; we just got back from our place in Naples. I couldn't stand the thought of coming back to this weather, but duty calls and Pam was dying to get home and see the grandkids."

"I bet she was. Have a seat. What can I do for you?"

"This won't take long. I have a little export issue that I need resolved. One of my clients, as you know, is the Republic of Turkey. They are fighting ISIS and are looking to upgrade some of their weapons. Their military wants to purchase a couple of sample rifles and scopes along with some ammunition so that they can try them out. The U.S. companies that make the rifles and scopes can't export them without an ITAR permit, and State is going to take forever on this," he explained, referencing the export control regulations designed to prevent weapons from being transferred to foreign entities without the approval of the U.S. government. "Think you could make a call or two?"

Bolls frowned. "This isn't something I'm going to regret, is it, Stewart? I don't want to end up like Leland Yee," she said, referring to a California state senator who was convicted and imprisoned for trafficking in arms despite a long history of support for stronger gun control laws.

"Ha, you know I would never ask you to do anything that would put you at risk, Lisa. We're talking about two rifles going to a NATO country in the fight against a terrorist organization. This is mom-and-apple-pie stuff."

"What do you need me to do?"

"Well, here's the deal: SOCOM has the most flexibility when it comes to procurement. Do you think you could call a general down in Tampa and get them to take delivery? Then they can ship the rifles to their counterparts in Turkey and everything is aboveboard."

"Aboveboard?"

"How about 'legal'?"

The senator hesitated but Stewart flashed her that look. *Damn him.* "Fine. Give the details to Becca and I'll see what I can do. Anything else?"

"Can I get another hug?"

CHAPTER 24

Niassa Game Reserve
Mozambique, Africa
March

THE HEAT OF MIDDAY was intense and Reece's clothing was soaked from the fast-paced hike. Louie began to off-load gear from the Cruiser, directing Muzi to hand him this or that item from the bed. Reece lent a hand with the unloading but felt very much in the way of what was obviously a well-oiled team. Within minutes, a mini-campsite had been erected in the shade of a giant baobab tree complete with a small folding table and chairs. The top of the cooler had been covered with a cloth and converted into a small buffet table of Tupperware containers. Reece couldn't help but marvel at the dedication to tradition. It was almost as if Europe's sons in the colonies had maintained their proud customs long after they'd been abandoned in the Old World. The ex-British in Africa seemed more "British" than those in Great Britain. Reece wondered whether the separation from the European aftermath of World War II had something to do with it.

Louie motioned for Reece to fill his plate at the buffet. There appeared to be enough food for a dozen men and Reece piled his plate high, still feeling the effects of the beer, wine, and liquor consumed the previous evening. Reece took a seat and noticed that there were only two chairs arranged at the table. Muzi stood at the truck, his coverall top tied at the waist as a break from the heat, watching with interest as Louie made himself a plate. Reece put his fork down and watched curiously to see what would happen. When Louie sat down to eat, Muzi approached the table and picked up two of the food containers, which he carried to the base of a tree some twenty yards away, then sat. Reece had worked with enough indigenous troops in various corners of the world to understand that not everyone shared the West's view of equality. Regardless, caste systems always made him uncomfortable. He decided not to make an issue of it on his first day, but it nagged at him as he ate.

Though the SEAL Teams were predominantly Caucasian, they were color-blind as a culture. The military was, in many ways, far ahead of the rest of American society in terms of racial equality. While elements of segregation existed in the United States well into the 1960s, the military was integrated by Harry Truman soon after World War II. In the military, particularly in the special operations community, no one cared what color you were or what neighborhood you grew up in so long as you added value to the Team; it was always about the Team.

Reece was in the difficult position of not wanting to offend his hosts while at the same time wanting to treat everyone on the team equally. These were the cultural issues that often made training foreign militaries difficult. The reason that the Army's Special Forces ODAs were so good was that they trained specifically to deal with these cultural challenges. Reece was more comfortable kicking in doors. *Baby steps.*

They ate ravenously, and mostly in silence. After the morning's quiet stalking, it almost seemed like a sin to speak loudly in the bush. The heat had silenced most of the animal sounds as well; the cacophony of bird noises that had filled the morning air had quieted to a few faint calls in the distance. Reece watched a butterfly land on a nearby branch and thought of Lucy. She would have called it a "lellow flutterby," most likely. *She would have loved it here.*

Louie finished his plate, stretched his feet out in front of him, and shifted his wide-brimmed bush hat forward to shield his face from the daylight. Reece looked to Muzi and saw that he was in a similar posture. Apparently, it was nap time for humans as well as animals and it didn't take long for Reece to join them in slumber.

. . .

The sound of movement broke Reece from his sleep. He lifted the cap from his eyes and saw Louie and Muzi quietly loading their makeshift camp back into the truck. He rubbed his eyes and looked down at his watch.

"Good nap, eh?" Louie asked in a low voice.

"Oh yeah," Reece said with a yawn. "I could get used to this."

"It's not a bad life, is it?"

Reece had always relished the clarity of his combat deployments. The distractions of daily life were pushed aside to focus solely on the objective of finding and killing the enemy. His short time in Africa connected him with that clarity, but without the responsibility of leading men into battle or dealing with a chain of command. There was something primal about this existence. It struck him that his nap had been free of the nightmares that had plagued him of late. He was beginning to feel human again.

"We're going to head west and check things out along the river, make sure the roads are getting to be passable," Louie announced.

Reece appreciated being kept in the loop, which made him feel less like a mere observer and more like an active participant learning the ropes. Muzi returned to his perch in the bed of the truck while Louie and Reece climbed inside. Louie lit a cigarette before cranking the motor, offering the pack to Reece, who shook his head.

They had barely traveled a mile down the bumpy track when Muzi began to tap on the roof. Louie stopped the Cruiser and listened as the tracker spoke in hushed Shona. He put the truck in reverse and backed up twenty or so yards before killing the engine, grabbing his binoculars from the dashboard, and peering into the mopane scrub to the right of the vehicle. Reece raised his own binoculars and leaned forward to get a glimpse of what had caught their attention.

"Bastards," Louie hissed as he opened the driver's-side door. "Let's go, grab your rifle from Muzi."

Reece quietly opened his door and found the stock of his borrowed

.404 already extended in his direction. He accepted the rifle and pulled the bolt back to confirm its condition. He walked carefully around the front of the truck and joined Louie, who was standing on the sandy road.

"Eland," Louie said as he lowered his binoculars and pointed into the trees. Reece followed his extended finger and could just make out the tawny hide of a giant antelope through the brush. Louie kicked at the sand with the toe of his suede Veldskoen ankle boot to test the wind, the dust blowing perpendicular to the antelope's direction.

"He's hurt. Probably caught in a snare. Let's go have a look."

Reece nodded and took his place in line as they moved off the trail. They stalked quietly, taking their time as they closed the distance with the wounded antelope. At fifty yards, Muzi halted and took a knee. Louie and Reece raised their binoculars and took in the gruesome sight. The ordinarily massive eland bull was skin and bones, the sun filtering through the forest and shining on the corners of his hips, ribs, and spine. There was something embedded in his haunches. If the bull was aware of their presence, he didn't show it. Louie leaned back to whisper in Reece's ear.

"He needs to be put down. Are you comfortable with that?"

Don't take him before it's his time, Reece. His father's words echoed the wisdom of generations past.

It's past his time, Reece thought, sidestepping to the right and bracing his left hand against the trunk of a small tree. He moved the flag-type safety with his thumb and exhaled slowly. His finger touched the trigger as the front sight found the bull's shoulder and he began to increase pressure. Reece's shoulder absorbed the recoil as the sights rocked skyward. Without taking the butt from his shoulder, he cycled the action and reacquired his sight picture.

"Nice shot. He's down," Louie said as he patted Reece on the shoulder. Muzi began walking directly toward the fallen animal and the other two men followed. Reece never took pleasure in the killing of an animal. Though putting finger to trigger or nocking an arrow and bringing a bow to full draw was the culmination of one's training and preparation, it wasn't something Reece celebrated. Instead, after sending his bullet or releasing his arrow, he'd approach the animal quietly, kneel, and place his hand on the creature he'd taken to provide for his family. He respected the wild others, much more so than the men he'd put in the ground.

Flies were everywhere. A wire snare had entangled the eland's leg, just above the hoof, and the wound had festered for weeks. The hoof itself had been severed, leaving nothing for the animal to walk on but a horribly infected stump covered in maggots. A homemade ax was embedded in its back between the hips, and a massive gash on the bull's face was probably made with the same weapon. A big eland bull in prime condition can weigh close to a ton; this one wouldn't weigh half that.

The law of club and fang, Reece thought, remembering a classic novel from his youth.

Whatever poacher had trapped the eland indiscriminately with the wire snare had attempted, unsuccessfully, to kill it with the ax. The bull's flesh would have brought a significant sum in the local bush meat trade. The skin and horns had value as well. Nature is a cruel place, but this animal's suffering was purely man-made. Reece was enraged at the poachers' callous disregard for the suffering of their quarry. He was just beginning to learn about life in the African bush, but he knew more than a little about hunting men and he was about to apply those ample skills to a new cause.

As Reece stared at the gruesome scene, Louie retrieved a small pack and a jerry can from the Cruiser. He took a notebook from the bag and made some notes, glancing at his watch as well as a small GPS unit. When he was finished, he took detailed photos with a digital camera to document the atrocity. His documentation of the scene complete, he nodded to Muzi, who cleared the brush around the carcass with his *panga*. Louie doused the eland with diesel fuel and flicked his cigarette toward the bluish fluid, the smell of burning hair and flesh bringing Reece back to dark places in his past.

. . .

After dinner that night, Rich Hastings invited Reece back to the fire pit for a drink.

"Nasty business today, eh?"

"The total disregard for suffering reminded me of Iraq at the height of the war."

"They're the same kind of people. They don't care about anything or anyone but themselves. For some of these blokes it's just a way to make a living, but that doesn't excuse the suffering. We provide jobs and meat to the surrounding villages, so most of the poaching is to feed the Chinese camps that are exploiting the natural resources of this country with only the politicians that made the deals getting rich on the take. Now I'm starting to talk like a greenie."

Rich shook his head, staring into the burning embers. "The real bad actors are the men at the top. They profit, while those doing the killing take all the risk. Sound familiar, James? The general public in Europe and the States don't see the difference between what we do and what the poachers do. Without us here, the game would be gone. We're out there protecting it because it has value to our business, sure, but we also love this place and these animals. We manage and conserve it for the next generation. The poachers, on the other hand, would wipe the game out in a year or two if we let them have their go. Look at what happened in Kenya in '77. They banned hunting because the poaching was out of control. With the hunters out of the field, it was open season for the poaching syndicates. They killed half a million elephants in no time at all. We'll lose out in the end and that will be that. The game will be left to the poachers."

"How can I help, Rich? I think I could be an asset if we put some thought into it." *Before I die*, he almost added before thinking better of it.

"The boys and I have done our best to keep the poachers in check but we all have other jobs to do. I don't know what your long-term plans are, but you should consider studying to be a PH. It takes a few years but with your background I'm sure you'll pick it up quickly."

"To be honest, I haven't been thinking long-term," Reece replied, remembering his brain tumor.

"Well, let me do that for you. Tomorrow you'll start working for us as an appy. You can run our antipoaching efforts. I'll give you two good trackers. They'll at least keep you from getting lost. Learn everything you

can from them. They're uneducated in the formal sense but they are professors of the bush."

"I'll do what I can, Rich."

"I know you will, son. I know you will."

. . .

Reece set his alarm to wake him before dawn; he had a job to do. Despite
a long career in the military, Reece wasn't an early riser by nature. Whenever he did wake up early, he felt like he was in on a secret, one that those
still in bed would never know.

Though it was before 6:00 a.m., he could already hear the hum of the
diesel generators powering the camp so the cooks could perform their
morning rituals. *Just like overseas.*

It was time to gear up for work. He turned on the small lamp on
the bedside table and once again laid out the gear that he'd taken from
the boat, this time with more focus. He had his Glock 19, its holster, and
three spare magazines. There was a SureFire flashlight, a Petzl headlamp,
a folding knife, and a Gerber multitool. He had his watch, his small Garmin, boots, and new clothing thanks to Richard Hastings. He picked up
his Winkler-Sayoc tomahawk and examined the curved edge, remembering when he'd used it last to remove the head of the man who had
arranged the ambush of his SEAL troop in Afghanistan. All told, it was
less than he was used to working with, but it was enough. He thought of
World War II UDTs like his grandfather, who got it done with little more
than a mask, swim fins, a knife, and maybe an M3 "grease gun."

Reece dressed for the field in his boots, shorts, and an olive button-
down shirt. He picked up his Glock from the bed and released the magazine to ensure that it was loaded with fifteen rounds. Reinserting the
mag, he pulled back the slide far enough to confirm that a 9mm round
was in the chamber before stuffing it under his pillow. None of the other
PHs wore sidearms, and if he wanted to blend in he was going to have
to leave his pistol behind. The remainder of the gear went into his backpack, which he slung over a shoulder as he headed off in search of cof-

fee, his rifle in one hand like a suitcase, binoculars in a harness around his neck.

The dining area was empty in the predawn darkness, but he found fresh coffee and poured himself a cup. The cook had already taken note that Reece liked to add honey to his coffee and had placed a jar beside the cream on the buffet table. Say what you want about the journey to get to this place, at least the service was good.

As if on cue, the cook appeared carrying a plate of toast.

"Good morning, *Patrão.*" The cook smiled broadly, genuinely happy to see him.

"Good morning."

"Eggs for you?"

"Sure, eggs would be great. Thank you."

"Right away, *Patrão.*" The cook bowed his head slightly and headed back toward the kitchen.

Reece was somewhat embarrassed by being waited on hand and foot but he figured he could get used to it. He took a seat at the table and enjoyed the solitude as he drank his coffee. He was halfway done with his eggs and toast by the time the rest of the camp made their way, one by one, to the table. They all ate in relative silence. The work was hard and the hours long, with few breaks during the season.

Rich Hastings finished his breakfast and addressed Reece.

"James, today you'll go out with your trackers. They are good men, Solomon and Gona. They came with me from Zimbabwe but they know this place as well as anyone and won't steer you wrong."

"Thanks, Rich."

Reece rose from the table and followed Hastings toward the white Toyota Land Cruiser. The sun was starting to rise and the camp was bathed in the pinkish-gray light of the African dawn. The two men loading the truck stopped when they saw Hastings and Reece approach and stood next to each other alongside the truck with their hands at their sides in a relaxed version of the military position of attention. The taller of the two men was also the youngest. He appeared to be in his twenties, thin and muscular. He wore olive-green coveralls and a British desert camouflage boonie hat with the sides turned up. He was good-looking and carried himself with an air of confidence that set him apart from the other trackers Reece had met.

"Reece, this is Solomon."

The young man smiled warmly and extended his hand to Reece, who shook it firmly. "Nice to meet you, Solomon."

"Very nice to meet you, Mr. Reece," he said in perfect, though accented, English.

"You can just call me Reece."

Reece wasn't worried about using his real name among the workers. If anyone was looking for him, he'd be dead and buried from the tumor long before anyone questioned a game tracker in East Africa about a man last seen on an affluent island off the east coast of the United States.

"Yes, sir."

The second man was smaller and older, probably closer to Reece's age. His skin was very dark, which contrasted sharply with his tan coveralls and ball cap. A skinning knife hung from the fabric belt around his waist.

"This is Gona."

"Very nice to meet you as well, Gona."

Gona's face remained stoic as Reece shook the man's hand.

"Gona, Mr. Reece is a good friend of *Utilivu.*"

Suddenly, the tracker's eyes brightened.

"Mr. James! You remember me, you remember Gona?"

"Gona! Of course! Great to see you again!" Reece said in the midst of an enthusiastic handshake, remembering the tracker from his trip to Zimbabwe with Raife all those years ago.

"How is *Utilivu?*"

"Raife is great, Gona. He's really doing well. I know he misses tracking with you."

Hastings bid them good luck as they loaded up. Solomon drove, Reece sat in the passenger seat, and Gona rode on the high seat in the bed. They mostly worked the perimeter roads that bordered the concession, looking for signs that poachers had crossed onto the property.

There has to be a more effective and efficient way to do this, Reece thought.

It was past noon when Reece's stomach began to protest. He'd become accustomed to his hosts dictating the schedule and it struck him that his men were waiting for him to tell them it was time to eat.

"Let's stop somewhere for lunch, Solomon."

"Yes, there is a good place just ahead." Solomon's mood brightened at the mention of food.

When the truck stopped, Reece climbed into the bed and helped the men unload the chairs, cooler, and other assorted gear that made up the lunchtime spread. He made sure that he was the one setting up the folding camp chairs, setting three of them in a triangle under the shade of the tree that they'd parked under. This drew strange looks from Solomon and Gona as they wondered who else might be joining them. When the food containers were opened on the table, Reece motioned for the men to make their plates.

"No, no. You eat, Mr. Reece."

"We are changing things up. You guys eat first."

The two trackers exchanged puzzled looks.

"Go on, make your plates, guys." Reece motioned toward the food.

The men shrugged and moved toward the table. Solomon went first, making a plate for himself, and then walking toward the base of the tree to sit.

"No, no. Sit in the chair. You guys are eating with me. If we're going to be a team, we'll eat together, at least out here."

Solomon hesitated for a minute and then broke into a smile and took his place in one of the chairs. Reece was building a team, and in the close-knit world of special operations, where officers and enlisted men trained, fought, slept, and bled in the same mud, leaders ate last. Reece thought of his SEAL Teams, the skills developed and honed through the hunting of men as they dismantled and destroyed terrorist networks across the globe. Reece was adapting those skills to a different battlefield against a new adversary. It was time to hunt again.

CHAPTER 25

MacDill Air Force Base
Tampa, Florida
March

GETTING UP FROM HIS office chair was painful for Sergeant Major Jeff Otaktay, thanks to the 7.62mm bullet that had shattered his femur in Sadr City a decade earlier. That bullet had turned the 3rd Special Forces Group's most promising sniper into a deskbound staff NCO. He could have retired medically thanks to the plates and screws that held his leg together, but he felt a duty to train and mentor the soldiers who came after him, passing along his knowledge to the next generation of Special Forces operators. That path led him to an instructor slot at the Special Forces Sniper Course at Fort Bragg's Range 37, a job for which he was perfectly suited.

His current position was not so stimulating. As the senior noncommissioned officer of the SOF Warrior Acquisition Office at SOCOM, which was part of the Special Operations Force Acquisition and Logistics office, the once-proud warrior now spent his days going over gear requests instead of teaching snipers to stalk and kill their prey. He'd resigned himself to his fate and dedicated his efforts to putting the best equipment available in the hands of the special operations soldiers, sailors, airmen, and Marines still working downrange. He worked long hours to shuttle requests through the acquisition process as quickly as possible and had learned to navigate this new battlefield nearly as effectively as he'd done in the streets of Iraq. He was still able to contribute at the tactical level by spending much of his free time training SWAT snipers from all over Florida's Gulf Coast.

It was his overseas battlefield experience that made the current request on his desk seem unusual. Someone was requesting a pair of CheyTac M200 sniper rifles with high-end Nightforce optics and a large amount of match ammunition for a joint U.S.-NATO sniper program in Turkey. Relations with Turkey had become increasingly strained as of late, and it struck Otaktay as strange that the United States would be urgently shipping them high-end sniper weapon systems. This wasn't a rifle that fit into the traditional military arsenal of either the Americans or Turks. As a sniper, he was very familiar with its extreme long-range capability and this wasn't something he wanted in the hands of the bad guys on his watch. Trusting his instincts had kept his men alive on the battlefield, and those same instincts were now sounding the administrative alarm.

The sergeant major made a few calls to his contacts in the special operations community, and thanks to a friend in the military deputy's office, he was able to trace the request to a call placed from a Senate staffer a week earlier. It wasn't totally out of the ordinary for someone on the Hill to carry water for a weapons manufacturer constituent, but it was rarely for something so specific. Having done his due diligence, it was time to go see the boss.

As he pushed himself up from his chair, he took a moment to steady himself before making his way into the glass-paneled hallway that led to the program executive officer's domain. Otaktay had encountered a few good officers during his military career, but his current boss was not one of them. Major Charlie Serko was a logistician, and not a particularly good one. He had been a mediocre Field Artillery officer before transitioning to the Acquisition Corps, where he did nothing but hone his skill for managing his career up the chain of command. The NCOs on his staff were all convinced that his regulation-length brown mustache was the result of the time he spent crawling up the SOCOM acquisition director's ass. This, along with his rodentlike face, led to his nickname: Gerbil.

Otaktay's limp became less noticeable as his leg muscles loosened with each step. Exhaling deeply, he knocked on the Gerbil's open door frame.

"Sir, do you have a moment?"

Major Serko looked up, surprised to see the hulking and heavily tattooed Native American NCO in his doorway. The man's camouflage uniform was covered with badges and patches that were a testament to his career in special operations. The major stared at the Combat Infantryman's badge, Master Rated Parachutist badge, HALO wings, and Special Operations Diver badges that decorated the NCO's chest, tangible reminders of a life spent running toward the sound of gunfire. The major's own uniform was almost bare but for his rank, name badges, and single row of administrative ribbons. The Special Forces Group combat patch, Ranger tab, and Presidents Hundred tab on Otaktay's sleeve only added insult to the major's injury.

"Umm, sure, yeah, Sergeant Major," he said, glancing at his watch. "Can you make it quick?"

The walls of the office were covered with photographs and mementos from the major's single deployment to Afghanistan. There was a traditional Afghan *pakol* wool hat on the shelf, a decommissioned Chinese hand grenade on his desk, and a seemingly endless array of photos depicting the Gerbil holding various weapons. Otaktay was amused by the fact that all the photos appeared to have been taken inside the walls of the sprawling Forward Operating Base that the major likely never left.

"Sir, I need you to take a look at this." Otaktay slid the request across the major's desk. "Something's not right about it. I checked with some of the guys overseas and they haven't heard anything about this program. We appear to be exporting weapons to an unknown entity."

Serko glanced at the form and frowned. "Where did this request come from?"

"That's why I came to see you, sir. It came from Colonel Fenson's office. Someone in D.C. asked him for a favor, from what I hear."

"The deputy? You expect me to question a request that came down from an 0-6?"

"Sir, I don't really give a shit who it came from. I'm trying to prevent sniper weapons systems from being used against U.S. forces overseas."

Major Serko paused and chose his next words deliberately. "You think you're still a sniper, don't you? Better get used to the fact that you're not. You are just another staff NCO."

Otaktay's hands balled into fists as he suppressed the urge to pull the Gerbil's spine out through his throat. He took a breath and pressed on in a professional but measured tone: "Sir, this isn't about me, this is about keeping weapons out of the hands of our enemies. This request is highly abnormal. No one that I've spoken to has ever heard of a combined U.S. sniper program with Turkey. At best, these rifles are going to be used by the Turks against the Peshmerga."

"And what, precisely, do you expect me to do about it, Sergeant Major?"

"Sir, perhaps you could reach out to someone on Colonel Fenson's staff and dig a bit deeper. Once these weapons ship, there's no getting them back. Remember all of the weapons we sent to Afghanistan in the eighties?"

"Sergeant Major, have you ever heard the phrase 'the nail that sticks up gets hammered down?' The chain of command exists for precisely this reason. We must all do our part to keep the machine moving. These rifles need to ship as expeditiously as possible."

Serko signed each page of the form and placed it in the outbox on his desk.

"Anything else, Sergeant Major?"

"Negative, sir." Otaktay turned to leave and then stopped. "Sir, you don't have to lead men in combat to show courage."

"What are you talking about, Sergeant Major?"

"It's a pity you don't know," Otaktay replied, leaving the office with no sign of his limp.

CHAPTER 26

Niassa Game Reserve
Mozambique, Africa
March

REECE SET HIS MIND to developing a strategy to better address the poaching problem. He had his mission. Now it was time to gather intel.

Rich Hastings was delighted to have a seasoned combat leader dedicated to antipoaching, and he offered him every resource available. Reece's first request was a wall-sized map of the area and all the reports of poaching activities they'd collected. Within minutes, Reece was staring at a pile of notes an inch thick. Hastings's team had been diligent about compiling the raw data from the field but hadn't had the resources to apply it tactically.

Reece had seen the same thing happen in the early days of the counterinsurgency effort in Iraq. Teams would gather laptops, cell phones, and written materials from raids on high-value targets, only to see those intelligence gold mines go stale without procedures in place to exploit and analyze them effectively. Once they understood the benefits of sensitive site exploitation and coordinated with the intelligence analysts waiting back at base, their effectiveness in dismantling the enemy network increased exponentially.

It was important that the PHs remain in the field scouting and interdicting the poachers, so Rich and Reece remained in camp, compiling the reports and developing a plan. Reece was amazed that many of the targeting techniques employed by the Rhodesian SAS in the 1970s were the same ones developed by him and his contemporaries three decades later; too bad they hadn't consulted with guys like Hastings back in 2003.

Hastings's command of the local geography was essential in locating each poaching event, which was marked on the oversize map. As they pinned each poaching site on the map, patterns began to emerge; the poachers used two main travel corridors, the roads and rivers. The hunting blocks themselves were essentially devoid of human population, so the poachers had to come from somewhere. Movement on roads would be risky, especially during the day, but would be faster and safer than overland travel. After the poachers infiltrated the game-rich reserve and bordering hunting blocks, they would have the logistical problem of moving the meat, hides, or ivory back to their point of sale. It is roughly fifteen times more efficient to move goods by water than by land under the best conditions, and the roads in this part of the world were less than ideal. Those same rivers that flowed rapidly during the wet season turned into sand pits in the dry winters. Reece's theory was that the poachers moved by water during the wet months and reverted to land travel only when the rivers ran dry.

"That's about right," Hastings agreed. "We've always suspected that the local fishermen were in on it. The bulk of the poaching takes place during the wet season. Part of that is the ability to use rivers and the other reason is that we are not in the field as actively during the wet months because many of the roads are impassable. When we're out there scouting and hunting, we're a big deterrent. During the wet months, our PHs are usually back in Zim or South Africa visiting their families, which limits our presence. The poachers know this and work around it. Even if we could afford to run antipoaching patrols all year, we couldn't get around without a helicopter."

"Too bad you don't have a UAV."

"What's a UAV?"

"Unmanned aerial vehicle. A drone."

"Hell, we've got a *bloody* drone. None of us know how to fly the thing, but we've got it."

"What?"

"Some Russian client brought it with him last season along with some old Soviet-era night vision that looks like it belongs in a museum. He wanted to use it to find game. We told him it was bloody unethical. He could hunt the way we do or find another outfitter. He got pissed and spent the rest of his trip drinking in camp and shacking up with his twenty-year-old supermodel 'translator'. He left the drone and night vision as a tip, kind of a joke, really. We were pissed because none of us had any use for it. We attempted to use the night vision scouting for cats, but the batteries ran out, so it's sitting in the shed with the drone."

"So, you still have it?"

"Of course; it looked expensive, but we didn't have anyone to sell it to."

"Can we check it out?"

"Sure, come with me."

Hastings led Reece out of the dining area and toward what looked like a small thatched storage building. The building was dark inside and it took a few moments for Reece's eyes to adjust after being in the bright sunlight. Rich Hastings pointed to the back corner of the structure. Reece couldn't help but smile at the sight of the dust-covered quadcopter-style video drone sitting on the concrete slab. It was an Inspire 2 drone, complete with a Forward-Looking InfraRed (FLIR) camera and an iPad Mini-equipped remote control. The instruction manual was still in the plastic wrap. Reece brought it back to his makeshift headquarters in the dining area.

"Think you can fly this thing?" Rich asked.

"Maybe. Where's the night vision?"

"I'll get it."

According to the specs, the drone had a flight time of almost a half hour and could travel at 58 miles per hour. The maximum operating temperature was 102 degrees, which meant he couldn't fly it in the heat of the day here. That wasn't a problem, though, as Reece planned to use it at night. He began charging the batteries as he read over the instructions, hoping to give it a test flight once the air cooled down that evening. The misconception about drones was that you could have eyes in the sky everywhere at once. They had one drone and its range and flight time were fairly limited, meaning that they would still have to develop a plan as to where best to deploy it. The drone was a game-changing asset, but not a magic wand.

That evening, Reece was ready to give the drone its maiden flight. All the PHs were back from the field and they gathered around, beers in hand, to watch Reece crash the expensive-looking flying machine. The camp staff weren't exactly sure what was about to happen, but they soon joined the crowd to see the spectacle. Reece feigned confidence as he carried the drone down to the fire pit area overlooking the river. The camp staff murmured in a collection of languages at the sight of the alien contraption. Reece activated the motor and the drone rocketed skyward. The joyful reaction of the native camp staff drowned out the whir of the four small rotors and Reece couldn't suppress his grin. As the device held a hover, the iPad displayed a bird's-eye view of the camp and surrounding landscape. Carefully, Reece steered the drone over the river and eased up to its maximum speed. The flowing river and its banks were thick with animals at this hour, and the view from above was like something on a nature show as Reece steered the craft. He got the hang of flying it quickly and brought it around for a low pass over the camp. The staff cheered and the PHs raised their beers in a salute to their new friend's flying skills.

Reece toggled the display to activate the FLIR camera and the scene was converted instantly to blacks and grays highlighted by the heat displays of the wildlife below. Elephants, giraffes, impala, and even crocodiles showed up in fiery reds and oranges. The craft stopped and hovered over a lioness stalking through the riverine grasses in search of prey, invisible to the naked eye but clear as day on the screen. The camp staff were bewildered and amazed at what they saw, unsure whether this visitor in camp was a genius or some kind of magician. After twenty minutes of flying, Reece brought the drone in for a landing to the cheers of the staff and applause of the PHs, who were relieved that their new reconnaissance asset had not crashed. He smiled at the prospect of using it in operations against his new enemy.

CHAPTER 27

Niassa Game Reserve
Mozambique, Africa
April

REECE HAD OUTLINED A basic campaign plan and was feeling increasingly confident in his ability to operate the drone, but he lacked a ground force to physically interdict the poachers. His research indicated that the poachers were part of a larger syndicate as vast and complex as the terrorist organizations he'd targeted in the military. Endemic corruption at all levels of government, low socioeconomic conditions, and high demand in Asia were fueling an illicit trade that generated more money than the illegal trafficking of small arms, gold, diamonds, or oil. There wasn't much Reece could do about the demand, but he could impact the supply.

Reece was in Mozambique to keep a low profile, not to end up in what he assumed would be one of the worst prisons on earth. That meant he couldn't lead the antipoaching teams themselves, as doing so would require interaction with authorities, something that he intended to avoid. He ran the dilemma by Rich Hastings and the two of them came up with a plan. Rich would use the resources of the safari company to beef up the capability and number of their game scouts, and Reece would act as their eyes and ears. Rich would assign experienced trackers to work with Reece and, once they got "eyes on" the poachers, they'd call in the game scouts.

The government-provided game scouts were mostly good men with the right intentions, but they lacked any real training or experience when it came to weapons and tactics. Rich and his PHs, most of them ex-military and all of them highly competent in the field, could act as advisors to the game scouts when it came to larger operations. They would scale up their antipoaching efforts during the off-season when the activity was at its peak and scale it back during the hunting season when the PHs and game scouts had traditional duties to attend to, the ones that actually paid the bills. Reece would focus most of his time on coordinating the antipoaching efforts while doing some general scouting for the safari operations as an apprentice or "appy" PH.

Special Reconnaissance (SR) was a core SEAL mission during much of Reece's time in the Teams. More recently, the SR role was spun off to specialized teams on each coast that performed highly technical surveillance operations in support of direct-action elements like Reece's troop. Even though Reece hadn't done an SR-only mission since his first deployment to Afghanistan shortly after 9/11, it was something that he and his men had trained to do for years. In his war against the poachers, Reece would shift back to the SR role full-time. It would take some adjustment not to be the one leading the strike force onto the objective, but it was the smart play. Instead of being the quarterback on the field, Reece would become the offensive coordinator calling the plays from the skybox.

. . .

The fisherman steered the dugout canoe carefully to avoid the boulders at the river's bend. Without a moon the stars still gave the older man enough illumination to navigate the waters he knew so well. The light reflecting off the calm surface made steering the boat as easy as navigating a modern highway, not that he'd ever seen one. He used his hand-hewn steering pole to stop the craft, listening intently for any sign of movement on the nearby bank. All he could hear were the normal forest sounds: a steady hum of birds and insects interrupted by the occasional bark of a baboon. Satisfied that he was alone, he poled the canoe toward the shoreline.

"Okay, he's moving again," Reece said quietly into the Motorola handheld radio, staring intently at the IR image on the iPad tethered to his drone's controls. "He's ten meters out from the bank, one hundred meters south of the scouts."

He heard Hastings's radio break squelch twice, indicating that he'd understood.

Reece was sitting on the tailgate of his Land Cruiser, on the opposite side of the river from the action, coordinating the events as they played out before him on the screen.

"Land-based guys are moving toward the bank with the cargo. Let's wait until he gets out of the boat to intercept. He's five meters out. He's beached. He's out of the boat, time to move."

Reece could see the six game scouts move forward in a line formation with Hastings at their center, keeping them moving in the right direction. When the scouts were thirty yards from the bank, the two land-based poachers dropped their cargo and fled to the east.

"Coming your way, Louie," Reece advised.

The PHs and their trackers were waiting in a blocking position directly in line with the poachers' escape path. Louie waited until they were ten yards out before he fired a round from his massive .500 Nitro over their heads. The fireball and concussion from the express rifle left the poachers in shock as they dove to the ground at the feet of the blocking force. Louie and the other PHs quickly pounced on the men and secured their hands with thin rope as they searched them for weapons. The main force of game scouts tackled the fisherman as he tried to climb back into his beached canoe.

The lead game scout placed the three men under arrest, carefully inventorying their contraband from the scene, with everything cataloged and photographed for use during prosecution. All told, the men seized a .375 H&H magazine rifle along with ten rounds of ammunition, a Chinese-made single-shot shotgun with two shells, two axes, three *pangas*, and a tireless bicycle loaded down with 150 pounds of elephant ivory from what looked to be nine different elephants, all of whom were young bulls and cows. The three men were a sight to behold: barefoot and dressed in hand-me-down clothes from Western tourists, including, ironically, the Dartmouth Crew jersey worn by the getaway canoe driver. The men were separated and questioned, with audio recordings made of each interrogation. They had no idea that their apprehension had been guided by one of the most wanted men in the world, aided by technology they didn't know existed.

Reece sat back and smiled. This was their third interdiction operation in two weeks and the men were really getting the hang of it. They'd taken thirteen poachers into custody and seized guns, ammo, ivory, meat, hides, and a truckload of wire snares. In this little corner of Africa, they were beginning to make a difference. Reece shook hands with Muzi and Gona and thanked them for the great job they'd done in helping him track the poachers to their point of exfil. It was after midnight. Reece and his team would be back at it in the morning.

. . .

Without the wartime stress of preparing for and leading men into combat that had preoccupied him in the SEAL Teams, Reece's mind was clear and calm. He rose with the sun, pushed himself hard all day, and slept soundly at night. He'd found peace here in the primal rhythm of the wild. He had a mission, an enemy, and was part of a team he trusted—he had purpose.

His sun-streaked hair hung to his shoulders and his beard nearly touched his chest. His skin was burned to a shade of walnut from his time at sea and from the relentless African sun. The simple but nutritious diet of game meat and vegetables coupled with the nearly constant physical activity had made his body lean and hard. The chiseled separation between his muscles was visible, as were the thick veins on his arms; his body fat hadn't been this low since he completed BUD/S nearly two decades earlier. He wore khaki shorts and an olive-green cotton safari-style shirt with the RH Safaris logo embroidered above his chest pocket. His boots were locally made buffalo hide *veldskoen* and he wore a wide-brimmed slouch hat. The old .404 rifle had become a trusted friend that was never more than an arm's length away and he wore its thick cartridges on his belt like a gunfighter. He looked far less like a fugitive naval officer from California and more like an African-born professional hunter.

. . .

After two months of antipoaching operations, Reece and his team had taken a serious toll on the opposition. They'd arrested three dozen men, both local bush meat poachers as well as those working under professional poaching syndicates, burned numerous camps, and seized three pickup-truck loads of wire snares. Word had gotten out that this was no longer a good place to be if you weren't respecting the game laws. Rich was confident that they would see game numbers rise sharply in the concession as a result.

With the change in season, hunters from the United States and Europe had begun to arrive, and the PHs shifted their focus to the day-to-day operations of the safaris while Reece continued to scout for poaching activity. The bush pilot who brought the hunters into and out of the camp's airstrip would sit idly in camp during safaris, keeping the plane ready in case of a medical emergency that would require an air evacuation. He was bored to death waiting for the call that never came, so Reece put him to work. For major operations, he became the drone pilot and Reece became the ground force commander for the game scouts. The antipoaching force was competent and capable, and Reece provided tactical leadership while staying in the shadows. All the poachers knew was that the game scouts had gotten really good at their jobs; none were aware of the trained commando leader quietly pulling the strings.

CHAPTER 28

Niassa Game Reserve
Mozambique, Africa
May

FLAT TIRES WERE AN everyday occurrence, so common that Reece and his two trackers acted like a NASCAR pit crew as soon as they felt the tire go. The Land Cruiser pickup carried two spares mounted on each side of the tubular safari rack above the truck's bed, and they were about to use the second spare of the day. Reece glanced at his watch and gave both men the "go." They seemed to understand far more English than they spoke, and, though they'd probably never seen an auto race, they quickly caught on to the fact that Reece had turned this mundane exercise into a game.

Reece retrieved the Hi-Lift farm jack from the front bumper while Solomon loosened the lug nuts on the flat and Gona wrestled the spare wheel down from the rack. Reece got the jack in place on top of a flat rock and began pumping the wounded pickup skyward. The tire had barely cleared the ground when the flat was removed and the fresh wheel was mounted. The three men labored swiftly and without words, teamwork born of several months working together closely in this remote wilderness.

Reece lowered the jack and the tire hit the ground, calling out the time: "Two minutes, forty-five seconds. A new record."

Both trackers beamed as they all shook hands.

Their celebration was broken by the sound of gunfire, a three-round burst that, to Reece, had the unmistakable report of an AKM. The only

AKs in the block belonged to the government game scouts who accompanied the hunting parties, and they would be dozens of miles from Reece's location according to their last radio call. The shots could have come from only one source—poachers. Reece reached into the rack behind the cab of the pickup and slid his rifle out of the soft zippered case that protected it from the elements. He retracted the bolt slightly and confirmed that a round was in the chamber before closing the bolt and checking the safety. He opened the flap on his leather belt pouch and was satisfied to see the five massive brass cartridges gleaming in the East African sunlight. He took the Motorola two-way radio from his belt and attempted to call back to base camp.

"Base, this is James, over. Base, this is James, do you read me?" No response, just static. *Shit.*

"Base, this is James. If you can hear me we've got full-auto gunfire just south of the Lugenda River near the boulders, moving to take a look." Reece turned down the volume on his radio and took a deep breath.

He nodded to his trackers and pointed toward the sound of the shots. Without hesitation, all three men moved at a light jog down the red dirt track. Even after working with them for months, Reece was constantly in awe of their tracking skills. Not only could they follow a track over hard ground, they could often do it at a running pace. Solomon's finger pointed toward the ground, and he took a left turn into the *miombo* forest. As they entered the bush, they slowed to a walking pace and moved as stealthily as possible. No words were spoken. Reece could read the men's body language at this point, and hand signals would cover any needed communication. They moved in single file down a narrow game path, Solomon in the lead, Gona behind him, and Reece taking up the rear.

They worked just as they had when scouting game animals for their outfitter: each man had specific responsibilities. Solomon was the point man who led the way and kept an eye out for any sign on the ground; his eyes were primarily directed downward. Gona kept his head up and searched for any visual sign of life, animal or human. Reece supervised the tracking, provided cover, handled communications with their base camp, and made the command decisions when necessary. It was just like the old days back in the Teams.

Solomon slowed the pace and all three men crouched as they walked to lower their profile. He stopped and squatted at the edge of a clearing, and Reece moved up quietly to kneel beside him. The tracker nodded toward the source of the gunfire: four poachers, two of them armed with AKs and the other two with small axes. All four were surrounding the blood-soaked carcass of an elephant on its side, a cow from the looks of it. The men were close to eighty yards away, too far away to hear any voices, but their body language told the tale. One of the men wielding a rifle was motioning toward the ax men, letting them know how he wanted the ivory cut loose. Reece's plan was to observe the crime and keep track of the poachers while he worked to gain radio contact and wait for the game scouts. Getting into a gunfight in a third-world country as a wanted man was not part of the plan.

Reece retrieved a small digital camera from the pocket of his shorts and extended the optical zoom as far as possible. He was too far away to get any good facial shots, but any photos would be better than nothing when it came to building a criminal case. He took a few pictures and was putting the camera back in his pocket when he heard a crashing sound to his left. He turned in time to see a gray blur coming toward them along with a loud screaming sound. *Calf!*

The dead cow obviously had a young calf and the little guy was doing his best to avenge his mother's death. The calf, which easily weighed five hundred pounds, was heading directly for Gona. The three men scattered to avoid the charging animal, their movement catching the attention of the poachers. Gunfire erupted across the clearing and Reece heard the unmistakable crack of high-velocity rifle rounds passing just over his head.

"Get down!" he yelled, diving to the ground and flipping the safety catch on his .404 to FIRE. Lying on his side, he put the silver sight bead on the closest poacher and pressed the trigger without conscious thought. The big bullet found its mark with an audible slap and Reece rolled to his right while working the bolt to reload. He made his way to his feet and, in a crouch, ran to his right to flank the remaining gunman, who he could still hear firing in long bursts. Taking cover six feet behind the trunk of a large tree, Reece worked to get a visual angle on his next target. He saw a lone figure kneeling near the elephant's head, struggling to change magazines on his rifle. Reece dropped down to one knee, took an extra second to be sure of his aim, and sent a 400-grain solid through the man's chest. The man dropped instantly, his rifle and magazine falling into the dust in front of him. Reece saw no sign of the two men armed with axes but could see both AKs on the ground, so he was reasonably sure that they hadn't armed themselves to mount a counterattack. *Head count*, he thought, racing back toward where he'd last seen his trackers.

His heart sank when he saw Gona leaning over Solomon, who was covered in blood. Reece unzipped the wounded man's olive jumpsuit and quickly identified two bullet wounds, one to the upper chest and one to the abdomen. He gently rolled him over and determined that there was an exit wound on his back from the chest wound, but not one from the abdominal hit. Solomon was conscious but obviously struggling to breathe.

"Gona, run back to the truck and get the aid kit. The red bag, hurry!"

Gona took off at a dead run toward the truck as Reece tried to calm his wounded friend.

"You're gonna be fine, buddy. We'll get you to a doctor."

Reece grabbed the Motorola and turned the volume up before keying the mic. "Base, this is James, over!" Nothing. "Base, this is James. Solomon has been shot. I say again, Solomon has been shot, over!" No response. "Breathe, buddy, relax and breathe."

Solomon's eyes were wide as he struggled for breath. Reece knew that he needed to get the wound sealed up fast. On a deployment, he would have had the tools to provide immediate aid with a blowout kit secured to his gear, but here he had to wait for Gona to return with the bag, wasting precious seconds. Rifle in hand, Reece rose to a squat to peek above the low brush where Solomon was lying and confirmed that the clearing was still devoid of life. He heard movement behind him and spun his muzzle around to see Gona sprinting through the brush with the aid bag, dropping it at Reece's feet. Reece handed him the rifle; Gona couldn't drive but he was good with a gun. Without saying a word, the man took off at a jog, skirting the woods on the right side of the clearing to locate the two surviving poachers.

"Stay with me, Solomon. This is going to help you breathe."

Reece unzipped the aid bag and dug around until he found an Asherman Chest Seal. He wiped Solomon's chest with a gauze pad before tearing open the package and placing the adhesive seal on his chest. He rolled his tracker and repeated the process on the exit wound. Reece found a 2.5-inch needle and laid it on top of the Asherman on Solomon's chest. Then, locating a spot above the wound, between the first and second rib, Reece held his left finger on the spot and, with the needle held in his right fist, stabbed it into the chest cavity. He heard a hissing sound and watched with relief as Solomon was able to take a breath. When the hissing stopped, he removed the needle and laid it back on the bandage.

The breathing situation handled for now, Reece searched the bag until he found a large dressing. There was a small section of bowel herniating out of the abdominal wound that needed to be addressed. Reece used his fingers to spread the wound and moved the abdomen from side to side as he gently eased the exposed intestine back inside. The wound wasn't bleeding much, so Reece was hopeful that the bullet hadn't hit the liver. He covered it with the large dressing and wrapped the attached Ace-style bandage around Solomon's body until the dressing was secure.

"How's your breathing?" Reece asked.

"Water, *Shamwari*. I must have water."

Reece knew that putting fluid into the man's body could blow out any clots that were forming on his abdominal wound.

"I can't give you water right now. We've got to get you to a hospital."

Reece tried the radio again, without success. *Damn it.*

The closest medical facility was the clinic at Montepuez. They were two hours from the clinic and two hours from the airstrip at base camp. With solid comms, Reece could call back to the camp manager and have a MARS flight on its way to meet them, but, as it was, he couldn't be certain that taking Solomon back to base wouldn't add hours before treatment. Reece speculated that Solomon would survive the two-hour ride to the hospital, but he wasn't sure that he'd survive waiting around for a plane that might take all day to arrive. With Gona unable to drive, Reece would have to deliver him to the hospital, which meant he'd be seen. Gunshot wounds meant police, and police meant questions. Still, there wasn't even a choice; Solomon was a good man. They'd become teammates, and Reece wasn't going to let one of his men die to protect his cover.

He whistled to Gona, and they prepared Solomon for travel.

CHAPTER 29

BLOWING THROUGH SMALL VILLAGES and towns with Solomon slowly bleeding out in the back of the Land Cruiser, Reece did his best to avoid major bumps that would cause his wounded teammate any additional suffering, but he was also more than aware of the "golden hour" and that time waits for no one, least of all someone with a gunshot wound to the chest.

Reece sped around women carrying goods on their heads, boys in donkey carts made from old cars and pickup trucks, and the occasional automobile. He certainly wasn't winning any hearts and minds. He didn't dwell on the men he'd just killed in the African bush. He was back in operator mode, doing what he did best. He was protecting his team, and to Reece, that was as natural as breathing.

No more than a gas station with a few small stores, the tiny enclave of Montepuez was also home to a small medical clinic. It was located adjacent to an old Portuguese mission, the stone walls still dotted with bullet strikes from the civil war decades earlier.

Reece pulled the Cruiser to a stop in front of the building and sprinted through the front doors. A queue of locals, mostly elderly men and women and mothers holding their children, waited in the room that served as the lobby. Rushing past the line and ignoring the young female aid worker who tried to block his path, he ran through a hallway that opened into a large room filled with two dozen mosquito-netted cots where a tall white man in scrubs with a stethoscope was attending to a patient.

"Are you the doctor? I need your help right now."

The man turned and faced him, unfazed by his sense of urgency.

"You'll have to wait your turn, sir," he said with an obvious British accent. "There are a great number of people here that need our help."

"I have a critical patient. Gunshot wound to the chest, he's bleeding out in the back of my truck!"

The doctor's demeanor shifted instantly. "Drop everything and let's get this man in here right now," he ordered his staffers.

Reece led the way back out front as the doctor and four other individuals in scrubs followed him carrying an old-fashioned canvas stretcher. They placed the stretcher on the open tailgate and eased Solomon onto it, Gona looking over their shoulders like a worried father.

Reece kept pace with the physician as they made their way back inside.

"He's got a 7.62 round through the chest that exited and a second round to the abdomen that's still in there. I put an Asherman on his chest and dressed the abdominal wound. The bowel was herniated, so I tucked it back in. He hasn't had any fluids."

"How long ago was he shot?"

Reece glanced at the watch on his wrist. "Just over two hours ago."

"You've done well. Now I need you to step aside while we get him ready for surgery."

The medical team carried Solomon into a smaller room, where they placed him on a table and began to examine him. Someone closed a curtain to block Reece's view, signaling it was time to let the professionals take over.

Leaving the clinic, Reece looked up at Gona staring down at him from the truck's bed. "I think he's going to make it. We got him here in time."

Gona nodded and sat down on the tailgate. Reece sat next to him, waiting in silence.

• • •

Reece was asleep in the bed of the truck, his legs dangling from the tailgate, when he felt someone grab his leg.

"Sir, excuse me, sir. Your friend, your friend is going to survive."

"Huh?" Reece bolted upright and found the British physician standing by the truck.

"Your friend's doing better. He's stable, and the prognosis is optimistic. Barring any infection, he will be ready to move tomorrow. We should arrange to get him to a hospital, where he can receive more advanced care."

"Great. Can I see him?"

"Certainly. He will be groggy from the anesthesia, but you can visit with him."

"Thank you so much, Doctor. I can't thank you enough for saving his life." Reece shook the physician's hand.

"You saved his life, Mr.———"

"Bucklew, Phil Bucklew," Reece said, conjuring up a name from the past. He trusted the team at Hastings's concession but not an unfamiliar European working in a medical clinic.

"Where did you receive your training, Mr. Bucklew? Clearly this isn't your first time treating a gunshot wound."

"I was a medic in the army."

"The U.S. Army?"

"Canadian."

"Ah, I see. Well, you may see your mate now."

Reece headed for the door and looked back at Gona, who sat timidly on the truck's roof. He waved for Gona to follow him and went inside.

Solomon was lying on a cot on top of a metal table, his chest and abdomen wrapped in bandages. An IV ran to his arm and an oxygen line wrapped below his nostrils. His face had a grayish hue and his ordinarily fit body hung limp. Reece stood by his side and put his hand on the man's forearm. Gona entered the room slowly and stood in the corner, clearly uncomfortable.

"It's okay, Gona, doctor says he'll make it. We'll get him moved to a hospital and he'll be back on his feet in no time."

Gona nodded, concerned for his close friend, but reassured by Reece's words.

Reece didn't want Solomon to wake up alone, but he also knew that he needed to coordinate his transfer to a more advanced medical facility. They were out of radio range, so he decided it was best to head back to camp to get the ball rolling on the medevac. He took the cap from his head and placed it on the cot next to his tracker. Patting him on the arm, Reece headed out the door. Gona leaned close to Solomon's ear and spoke to him in Shona before following.

Reece found the doctor attending to a baby in her mother's arms.

"Hey, Doc, we're going to head back to Rich Hastings's camp and arrange to have him transported to a hospital. Where does he need to go?"

"Well, if you have the funds, I would highly recommend getting him to Johannesburg or the private clinic in Pemba. There's an airstrip three kilometers from here; we have an ambulance that can transport him there for the flight. The nurse in the lobby can give you a card with our phone number and you can call us from the camp to coordinate."

"Thanks, Doc."

"There's one more thing, Mr. Bucklew, is it?"

"What's that?"

"We run on a shoestring budget here, Mr. Bucklew. We are happy to help your friend, but we are perilously low on resources. A donation would be quite helpful."

"Understood. I'll talk to Mr. Hastings about it."

"Very kind of you, Mr. Bucklew."

• • •

The camp had received a broken transmission from Reece just after Solomon was shot. The game scouts were sent to investigate and found the elephant carcass along with the two dead poachers. They also found the wrapper for the chest seal and bandages but weren't sure whether someone on Reece's team was wounded or if he had wounded and then treated a third poacher. As soon as Reece was back in radio range, he heard Hastings frantically calling for him on their main channel.

"Go for Reece."

"James, what's going on? What's your status, over?"

"We encountered a group of elephant poachers and were compromised. Two enemy KIA and two squirters. Solomon was hit, but he's stable at the clinic. Need you to arrange moving him to a real hospital, over."

"Roger that, James. Confirm that he is stable and at the clinic at Montepuez, over."

"Affirmative."

"We will get to work on that immediately. You headed back to camp, over?"

"Roger that, I'm an hour out."

Hastings and his team worked quickly and efficiently. Every man on the team, black or white, was seen as part of the family and no expense or effort would be spared to ensure Solomon's survival and recovery. The pilot, still waiting for a commercial flight to arrive in Pemba, was dispatched to Montepuez to pick up their wounded man. As soon as he was airborne, Hastings called the clinic to let them know that the plane was on its way. Solomon was loaded into the clinic's humble ambulance and transported the short distance to the airstrip. Within three hours of Reece's radio call, Solomon was being treated at the private hospital in Pemba.

CHAPTER 30

Tirana, Albania
May

AMIN NAWAZ SLID HIS aging fingers from one prayer bead to the next as he recited the *Dhikr*. This was his third location in as many nights, which is how he had lived into his fiftieth year, an old man in a profession where men died young.

> *La ilaha illa'llah*
> There is no god but God.

To an outsider it would look like contemplation or meditation, which in a sense it was. In what had become a lifetime of war, the *Dhikr* had been a constant. An escape. The one place Nawaz found peace. *The one place I can go to remember.*

The war against the West had entered a new phase. Nawaz had been at it long enough to recognize that. Today he was having a tougher time concentrating than usual. His collaboration with the Russian, a man exiled from the country that Nawaz had traveled so far to defeat in the Afghanistan of the 1980s, was a necessary evil. This time of war, terror, and treachery made for more than a few strange bedfellows, just as it had decades earlier when the United States and Saudi Arabia had collaborated to fund the mujahideen with money and weapons to turn against their common enemy. Little did they know they were sowing the seeds of a new battle in an ancient war.

Nawaz was nothing if not a pragmatist. The Americans had been very successful in shutting down the flow of money that had once run so freely through Saudi Arabia. If the former Russian GRU colonel wanted to finance the al-Qaeda operation in Europe, so be it. That he understood *hawala* from his time in the waning days of the Soviets' misadventure in Afghanistan allowed them to conduct business off the radar of the NSA, whose analysts fought their war with algorithms from climate-controlled offices in Fort Meade, Maryland. Nawaz would use the Russian until his usefulness expired. Then he would kill him.

astaġfiru llāh
I seek forgiveness from Allah.

Performing the *Dhikr* never failed to transport Nawaz back to the humble home in the Kingdom he had shared with his mother, father, and two sisters. With the glow of an early morning dawn just beginning to illuminate his bedroom window, he had felt a presence. At first he had been startled, thinking it was a messenger of Allah, but then he smiled when he recognized the familiar shape of his father. His eyes were closed and he had rested his hand on his son's head. His lips were moving, yet only slightly, and the young Nawaz strained to hear his words.

Laa ilaaha illal laahu wahdahoo laa sharikalahoo lahul mulku wa lahul hamdu wa huwa 'alaa kulli shai'in qadeer

There is No God But Allah Alone, who has no partner. His is the dominion and His is the praise, and He is Able to do all things.

His father slowly removed his hand from his son's head and pressed a set of beads into Amin's smaller hand. Then, like an apparition you convince yourself didn't exist, his father was gone. Amin was puzzled, as his father had never visited him in the night. He rubbed the beads of the *misbaha* between his fingers as he had seen his father do many times. The prayer beads symbolizing the ninety-nine names of Allah were never far from his father's grasp. The young boy curled back into a ball to ward off the early morning chill, the beads clutched tightly against his chest.

The date was indelibly etched into his mind: November 20, 1979. A lifetime later Nawaz recognized his father's visit for what it was: a good-bye given in the way of one who is not coming back.

bi-smi llāhi r-raḥmāni r-raḥīm
In the name of God, the gracious, the merciful.

Had the West known the chain of events that would be set in motion that early November morning, they might not have sent the GIGN French commandos to help quell the two-week seizure of the Grand Mosque in Mecca. They might not have killed more than two hundred of the devoted rebels who had seized it, or publicly beheaded sixty-seven of the captured Wahhabist insurgents in the weeks that followed. The House of Saud might not have capitulated to the terrorists' demands and reversed their progressive policies, adding fuel to the tactic of terror.

Amin Nawaz was not the only one who lost a father that day. The Muslim clerics recognized this pool of new recruits, young fertile minds primed for indoctrination and ready to do battle with the West. The principles of Islam would guide them. Experience on the battlefield of Afghanistan against the Soviet invaders would hone them into mujahideen.

Audhubillah
I seek refuge in Allah.

Nawaz first met Osama bin Laden in 1988 as a twenty-year-old Arab Afghan in the same mountains where he would return to fight the Americans in 2001. He had been one of al-Qaeda's first recruits and had been with Sheik Osama at one of his last sightings before that Tuesday in September that changed the world forever. It had been at the wedding of one of his most trusted bodyguards where bin Laden had quoted the Holy Quran: *"Wherever you are, death will find you, even if you are in lofty towers."* Only Nawaz and a few select others understood the significance of that remark.

Now, after a lifetime of struggle, spent planning the attacks that would be precursors to what the Americans called the Global War on Terror and fighting in the Hindu Kush, Iraq, and Syria, he was now the head of al-Qaeda operations in Europe and was close to striking their most devastating blow to date.

Sheik Osama had bunkered down after his escape from Tora Bora, and had been rendered relatively ineffective in hiding. He had kept the Western forces at bay, but they had eventually found him. The Americans had slain their dragon. The SEAL commando pigs who shot him down would pay. *The defenders of the faith have long memories.*

Nawaz chose the opposite approach, emulating the security protocols of Yasser Arafat. Well, the Arafat of the Fatah days anyway; before he grew soft and capitulated to negotiations with the Israelis. Nawaz preferred to stay highly mobile, rarely spending the night in the same place twice, often changing plans and spreading disinformation among his own people. While the U.S. intelligence apparatus sifted through Google and Facebook accounts, Nawaz and the new al-Qaeda he commanded communicated via courier and used the movement of funds via the ancient system of *hawala*. Systems born of the Silk Road still worked in modern times. *The Great Game continues.*

The refugees pouring into Europe provided the conduit; more than enough of his fighters had made it into Europe as part of the mass influx of migrants. The very people the West spent such vast sums trying to destroy in foreign lands had been welcomed right into the heart of Europe, *into the belly of the beast.*

Say what one would of the Israelis, they were smart enough to understand the essence of the conflict. They understood. Had the Americans been surrounded by their enemies instead of protected by vast oceans, they might have understood it, too, instead of opening their borders to let in the very people bent on destroying them.

Though Ayman al-Zawahiri had thus far evaded the special operations teams and drone strikes favored by the enemy, he remained in hiding. As the worldwide leader of al-Qaeda, he had sent Nawaz from Afghanistan first to Iraq and then to Syria to lead Jabhat al-Nusra, al-Qaeda's operation in the Levant. A brilliant man who had lived for the cause, al-Zawahiri was now entering the twilight of his life. Nawaz had the drive and the energy to be the architect of al-Qaeda's next evolution. While ISIS had captured the headlines and distracted the American military and political machines, Nawaz had patiently built his network, not in the Middle East and Central Asia, but in Europe. America was next.

He was proud to have led a group with so many veterans of the wars in Iraq and Afghanistan. That experience had filled the ranks of Jabhat al-Nusra. The West had built their army for them, and then opened the doors into Europe. That would be the next battleground. America would follow, but that duty would fall to the next generation of jihadis, just now finding their voice. The death of the West was not a fantasy, it was an inevitability.

SubhanAllahi wa biHamdihi, Subhan-Allahi 'l-`adheem
Glory be to Allah, and Praise Him, Glory be to Allah, the Supreme.

It had been close to forty years since his father had last placed his hand on Nawaz's head, and it had been not quite twenty years since the lofty towers had been brought down by Allah.

Stupid Americans. Didn't they comprehend what was happening? They were killing themselves. While they foolishly spent their treasure and spilled their blood in Iraq, Afghanistan, and Yemen, the very ideology they were fighting to defeat was moving into their cities, their schools, their very government. The freedoms the West championed so proudly would be their ultimate downfall. Those freedoms would be targeted and exploited. Their freedoms were their weakness. *Know thy enemy.*

Didn't they realize that 9/11 hadn't been planned in the caves of Afghanistan? The idea had been approved there, but the foot soldiers had done their work in Hamburg, Germany, and in the United States itself. They had learned to fly and blended into communities in California, Arizona, Florida, Virginia, and New Jersey. September 11 had been planned right under the nose of the most powerful nation the world had ever known.

Though they had doomed themselves through their culture of political correctness and open borders in the strategic sense, you had to be extremely wary of their tactical acumen. At that level the Americans could be exceedingly dangerous.

lā ḥawla wa lā quwwata illā billāh
There is no might nor power except in Allah.

Nawaz knew he would not live to see the sword of Islam sweep across the Americas. This was a generational conflict. Just as the Mongols had altered the ethnic identity of Eurasia, Islam would change the very fabric of Europe and America; instead of invading on horseback, they would legally immigrate, build their political bases, and incrementally defeat their enemy from within.

The very countries whose policies had helped create the refugee crisis were welcoming the enemy with open arms. They were sowing the seeds of their defeat, spurred on by politicians pandering to a new constituency.

The mujahideen of the new millennium didn't need territory to plan and train. The new jihadis could adapt within the very countries they targeted. The Americans projected strength with their tanks and bombers, but they had a soft underbelly. Their comforts and entitlement culture were breeding a weakness. He could prey on their fears; he could inflict further damage to their economy. Even the attacks that failed caused a reaction from the West that continued to cripple their markets.

What had been their greatest strength and brought them abundant prosperity was a soft target ripe for exploitation. *Death by a thousand cuts.*

Nawaz hesitated on the final bead of the *misbaha.*

Lā ilāha illā-llāh
There is no god but Allah.

"Tariq!" he called, summoning the courier who would make contact with a series of what he had learned the West called "cutouts." The message would eventually find its way to the man who could decipher it, a man who had been trained by the CIA but who had proven himself in Syria as a most valuable asset to the cause. He would be the instrument of yet another cut into the soft fabric of Europe.

Pressing the encoded note into his courier's willing palm, Nawaz set his hand on Tariq's head and closed his eyes.

"Allāhu'akbar."

CHAPTER 31

Niassa Game Reserve
Mozambique, Africa
July

"BASE TO REECE," THE Motorola radio lying on the seat next to him squawked with Rich Hastings's voice.

"Go for Reece."

"There's a man here to see you. A Yank, over."

Shit.

It had been two months since Solomon's encounter with the poacher's bullet, and it would be another month until he was back in the field. It was also Reece's first exposure to anyone outside the hunting concession since his arrival.

Had to happen sooner or later.

"Check. Did he say who he was?"

"Negative. He was polite but firm, eh. One of us from the looks of him. I tried to run him off, but he knows you're here, over."

"Roger that. I'll be there in an hour. Reece out."

Reece stopped the Cruiser and explained to Gona that he needed to head back to camp. Gona nodded down from the high seat and didn't ask any questions. Reece did a three-point turn in an open area and began making his way back, though he wasn't exactly in a rush to see whoever it was who was waiting for him. If they knew he was here, there was no sense trying to make a run for it, they'd have UAVs or other assets on him, and Reece had done enough running.

He saw a lone black Land Rover Defender 110 parked in front of the lodge as he pulled into camp. At least whoever had come for him had good taste in vehicles. Instead of pulling around to the back, he stopped the truck next to the Defender and walked up the path toward the broad veranda. The door opened and a man his own age and height stepped out. Sandy hair fell below his battered Florida Gators ball cap and his reddish beard betrayed a few flecks of gray. He was dressed in a short-sleeved plaid shirt and jeans and wore Salomon hiking boots. Though he didn't see a handgun, Reece knew there would be one concealed on his right side at the four-o'clock position or possibly in an appendix rig just beneath his shirt. His eyes narrowed in recognition as Reece approached the stone steps. Reece stopped and looked up at his old friend, Navy SEAL Senior Chief Freddy Strain.

"I guess you didn't come all this way just to kill me."

"Nah, Reece. If they wanted you dead they would have droned your ass weeks ago."

The men stood five yards from each other, Strain looking down at Reece from the elevated deck. The last time Reece had seen him was months ago, when elements of the United States government had ordered Strain's SEAL Team to hunt down and capture or kill their former teammate before he eliminated any more of the conspirators who had planned the killing of his family and SEAL troop. Strain had maneuvered right into Reece's ambush and Reece had let him live. Neither man spoke for what seemed like an eternity; this time it was Strain who broke the silence.

"Speaking of killing, thanks for not blowing those claymores. I should have known better than to have rolled in there like we owned the place. You had us dead to rights."

"You weren't on my list."

"Thank God for that. It's good to see you, brother." Strain's stoic expression broke into a wide grin.

"You too, Senior." Reece smiled, climbing the steps to shake Freddy's outstretched hand before embracing him in a hug.

"Damn, Reece, you going for the Jesus look?" Strain pointed at his friend's shoulder-length sun-bleached hair and scraggly beard.

"Something like that. Grooming hasn't been a high priority lately."

"I wouldn't think so. Reece, I'm really sorry about Lauren and Lucy. I don't even know what to say to you other than that."

There was an uncomfortable pause as each man considered how to transition to the meat of the conversation.

Finally, Reece simply nodded. "So, how'd you find me?"

"Well, it certainly took some doing," Freddy answered, relieved to be moving on.

"Let's grab a drink," Reece said, nodding toward the main lodge.

"I think I need one," Freddy said, and smiled. "You might too, when I tell you why I'm here. Any Basil Hayden's?"

"I might be able to scrounge some up," Reece said. "We are fairly well provisioned in that department."

The two frogmen moved through the lodge, where Strain stopped to pick up his backpack, and out into the dining area. Reece poured two fingers of the brown liquid for his friend and opened himself a can of MacMahon beer, known locally as 2M. Taking a seat at the bar that overlooked the river below, he motioned for his former teammate to join him.

"If someone had to find me, I'm glad it was you," Reece offered as they touched drinks.

"So," Reece led off again, "how did you do it?"

"Well, the working theory was that Liz dropped you off somewhere after you took care of Horn, Hartley, and Ben on Fishers Island. We couldn't confirm that since she's still on a nice estate in Mexico protected by an army of lawyers, courtesy of your buddy Marco."

"He's a good one, that Marco," Reece said, taking another sip of Mozambique's finest.

"Turns out he's a little more than just a good businessman, and even I'm not cleared to know exactly what he's involved with, but my guess would be he's a highly placed DEA asset. I don't have a 'need to know,' so that really is just a guess."

"I'd bet it's a good guess," Reece confirmed.

"Well, we would never have figured out that you liberated the Hastingses' boat if a few other pieces hadn't fallen into place. Even if we had, we would have assumed you were killed at sea in the storm the night of your escape. Never in a million years would we have thought to look for you here," Fred continued, gesturing at the surrounding wilderness.

"It was a bit of a trek," Reece admitted with a smile.

"I'll say. I'd love to hear how you did it at some point."

"Trade secrets, my friend."

"And maybe a bit of luck."

"To be honest, it was a lot of luck."

"They say it's better to be lucky than good, Reece."

"Isn't that the truth? But you didn't find me because some yacht club finally noticed a boat went missing."

"True. It started with the East African desk at the Agency coordinating with the NSA on Chinese interests in Mozambique. The signals guys intercepted a series of Chinese intelligence reports detailing a major shift in antipoaching efforts on this particular concession. The meat poachers feed the workers the Chinese use to support their mining and logging operations, and it was beginning to impact their productivity."

"It's nice to know it was working."

"Yeah, enough for them to mention it to higher. Now that alone would never have raised any eyebrows, but when a white guy with an American accent claiming to be a former Canadian army medic brings a wounded tracker into an East African medical clinic without a good explanation as to why he knows how to do a tension pneumothorax and apply an Asherman Chest Seal, well, that's not something they see every day. Unfortunately for you, the doctor that you encountered is an MI6 asset."

"Are you kidding me? Is there anyone in this country who isn't some kind of spook?"

"You would have gotten away clean not very long ago, but our intelligence collection capability has grown exponentially over the years. That, along with our ability to sift through mountains of information, can now be done at speeds unheard of in the past."

"I still don't see how a cable saying the Chinese have some hungry workers coupled with a stitched-up game reserve tracker led them to believe I somehow made it from New York to Moz when they weren't looking for me here to begin with."

"It wasn't *them*, Reece. It was *me*."

Reece looked quizzically at his former sniper school spotter.

"I know you, remember? And I know Raife. And I know that you two spent time at Raife's uncle's hunting operation in Africa when you were in college together."

"Thanks for remembering," Reece said sarcastically, taking another long drink.

"Africa got me thinking, so I checked on all Raife's family's East Coast–based planes and boats. Guess which one disappeared the same night you did?"

"You missed your calling, Freddy; you should have been a detective."

"Maybe in my next life. And Reece, next time you kill the secretary of defense and unravel the biggest government conspiracy in modern history, you might not want to give your name as Phil Bucklew to a British spy at an East African medical clinic."

Reece shook his head. "Yeah, using the name of one of the legends of Naval Special Warfare was probably not the best move."

"After that, we put up a UAV and have had you under surveillance for the past couple weeks. Facial recognition works, even from fifteen thousand feet."

"Lucky me."

Freddy paused. "I guess you know I didn't come all the way here to go hunting with you."

"I figured you were here to kill me or arrest me. I'm guessing arrest me."

"That's where this gets complicated. I'm leaving here as soon as we're done but I'm not dragging you out against your will. Let me run this by you and you can make the call. You'll want to hear it all, though."

"Doesn't seem like I have much of a choice."

"I have something I need you to see," Freddy said, sliding off his bar stool and motioning for Reece to follow him. "Might want to snag a couple more drinks."

Strain pulled a tin of Copenhagen from the pocket of his jeans and packed it with several flicks of his wrist. He opened the tin and put a pinch of tobacco between his lip and gum before offering the can to Reece, who shook his head.

"When did you start dipping?"

"When the wife made me quit drinking," Fred responded, motioning to the bourbon in his hand with a gleam in his eye. "I think she meant only in the States, though."

"I'm absolutely sure that's what she meant. How is Joanie?"

"She's good, man. She never really loved Virginia Beach, so she was happy when I got out and could live wherever she wanted. We're down in South Carolina, near her family."

"So, you're not at the Command?"

"No, I got out a few months back. Things got really weird after you skipped town. Your friend Katie's reporting put the spotlight on all of the Hartleys' shenanigans and the shit rolled downhill pretty hard. I don't blame you for what you did, Reece. If we had had any idea what the real story was, we'd have helped you knock those bastards off instead of targeting you."

Reece nodded. "So, I guess I'm public enemy number one?"

"Yes and no. When the whole story came out, it certainly eased up the pressure to find you or confirm your death at sea. The conversation shifted to the Hartleys, the Capstone finance operation, and all that. Even the conspiracy theory people started looking mainstream. You became a little bit of a Robin Hood type. There were James Reece sightings everywhere. You were like Elvis for a while."

"What about my friends?" Reece asked, not mentioning names.

"The reporter, Katie? She's untouchable, at least for now. No one would go near her with a ten-foot pole. She had the best law firms in the country lining up to insulate her from questioning by any government investigators. DOJ is ready to go after your friend Liz Riley and have her extradited to the U.S., but the president has them at bay for now."

"Why would the president do that? Wasn't he part of Hartley's bunch?"

"Jesus, you don't know, do you?" Strain looked bewildered.

"Know what?"

"That the president resigned over this whole thing."

"*What?* That's crazy!"

"Yep. The fact that he was letting the SECDEF run DOD like it was her own kingdom and piggy bank was too much for even the media. How could you not have heard about that?"

"Guess I just wasn't looking. You can really lose yourself out here," Reece said, gesturing to their surroundings. "The only news comes in over a radio in the main office, and most all of that is local. This is the land that time forgot."

"Well, the long and the short of it is the media loved a good story even more than they loved the administration. The Republicans in Congress had all of the wives and kids of the dead guys from your troop on TV demanding his resignation, and it worked. He stepped down and Roger Grimes, the VP, took over to finish out his term. He's a good guy, old Army O-6 that they put on the ticket to keep Middle America happy. He never really fit in with the old boss, and he's already said he's not running for reelection. The parties are going nuts. Hartley was the Dems' chosen one and, with her gone, they're slashing each other's throats trying to posture for the job. The Republicans smell blood and half the governors in the country are now looking to run. It will be a crazy primary on both sides—anybody could win. Fun to watch for a political junkie like me. I still can't believe you haven't heard any of this."

"Look around," Reece said. "No Internet, no newspapers. Main concerns here are the environment, the animals, and poaching."

"Well, whether you wanted to or not, you changed the course of U.S. political history."

"I wasn't trying to take down the system. They just needed to pay for what they did to my troop and my family. They got what they deserved."

"I agree. We were part of the investigation, since they had us out looking for you on domestic soil. The entire Command had to stand down. I had twenty-two years in and the option to take this job, so I made the leap."

"So, you're with the Agency now?"

"Yep. And that's why I'm here, even though I'm kind of a new guy. You ready to hear my sales pitch?"

Reece nodded. Strain took an iPad from his backpack, entered a long passcode, and selected an icon on the screen.

"You came to Mozambique to show me a PowerPoint?"

Strain laughed. "High-tech, Reece. Our manila envelope days are over."

Strain held the screen so that Reece could see it. It was a file image of Kingston Market, fully decorated for Christmas. Strain swiped the surface to advance to the next photo and a close-up picture of a deceased eight-year-old girl in a pink winter coat filled the screen. The next image was an aerial view of the market post-attack.

"Kingston Market on the outskirts of London. They hit a Christmas event with a VBIED and bottlenecked the crowd here at the other end. Two guys with PKMs opened up on the survivors from these two rooftops and then blew themselves up with s-vests. It was bad, really bad. They killed close to three hundred people outright, with more dying later in the hospitals. Total dead was three hundred and seventy-eight. Hundreds more were wounded. A lot of amputations. More than half of the victims were kids."

Reece looked away from the screen.

"Yeah, man, bad stuff," Strain continued. "Not only did they kill and wound all those innocent people, they crippled the brick-and-mortar retail economy all over the West. People were scared to go Christmas shopping. The malls were empty despite tons of beefed-up security. The stock markets got spooked. The global impact of these attacks was enormous."

"I'm honestly surprised that we don't see this kind of attack more often," Reece said solemnly.

"I agree with you."

"Who's behind it? ISIS?"

"They took credit, of course, but every jihadist organization in the book is calling themselves ISIS now. This is actually a little more organized than the typical ISIS-inspired attack by a bunch of lone-wolf types affiliated through social media. This is a real network—AQ in Europe. Check this one out." Strain moved to another series of images. "Right after the market attack, they hit a formation of British Paras with a mortar barrage during an awards ceremony. Poor guys had just returned from Afghanistan and got ripped up right before their Christmas leave. Only reason they didn't kill the Prince of Wales is that his motorcade arrived late."

"So this isn't a one-off."

"No, as a matter of fact, they just killed the NATO commander in Brussels. An Army four-star. They blew him up in front of his wife. He was all set to retire, too. Good guy, from what I understand."

"Bastards," Reece said, shaking his head, "but what does this have to do with me?"

"The charge that killed the general, it was delivered via drone."

"What?"

"That's right. Defeated the armor in his vehicle by putting a drone on the roof with a shaped charge. An EFP sliced him in two. Same way you killed that Jaysh al-Mahdi lieutenant in Iraq back in '06."

"That was an Agency deal, buddy. And that drone was huge. Experimental CIA bird, if I remember correctly."

"You're right. Technology has come a long way since then. UAVs are smaller, more powerful, GPS programmable, but the idea is the same, so we started tracking down everyone involved in your op in Baghdad. We think you know the cell leader responsible for the NATO attack." Strain swiped to display an image, obviously taken by a surveillance team with a long telephoto lens.

"No way! Is that Mo?" Reece asked, unable to contain his surprise at the photo of his old comrade.

"That's right, your buddy Mohammed Farooq from Baghdad. The Agency trained him to build mini-EFPs and taught him how to fly a drone to deliver an explosive payload. He fell off the radar back in the summer of 2014 when ISIS started sweeping across Iraq. He'd worked with the Coalition and would be a dead man if they caught him, probably tortured first. He was rumored to be in Syria working with the al-Nusra Front, an anti-Assad group now called Jabhat Fatah al-Sham. Next thing you know, AISI spots him in Italy, which is where this photo came from. They lost track of him after that and no one thought much of it until these attacks."

"What makes you think he was involved? Why wouldn't he just disappear? Mo's no terrorist."

"MI5's assets point to a network that is pulling the strings on a lot of the radical elements that have come in as asylum seekers. There are so many newly arrived refugees from Muslim countries that all the European security agencies are overwhelmed chasing down jihadi elements. We think they're hiding in plain sight."

Strain advanced to a new image. "This is Amin Nawaz. He's a Saudi but hasn't set foot in the Kingdom for close to twenty years. He's original *muj*: Afghanistan, Iraq, Syria, and now Europe. He's running the show while UBL's son Hamza bin Laden prepares to take the reins."

"Wasn't bin Laden's son killed in the raid in 2011?"

"That was a different son. Hamza was off at a terrorist training camp studying the family business, so he lived to fight another day. Until he's ready, Nawaz is the number one terrorist on our list and the mastermind of these recent attacks in Europe. Multiple independent sources with reliable reporting histories confirm that Mohammed Farooq and Amin Nawaz worked together in Syria. We think that your buddy Mo runs one of his cells in Europe. He would be highly trained courtesy of the program you ran with the CIA in Iraq and his follow-on experience in Syria with Nawaz."

Reece shook his head. "I can't believe Mo is involved, but nothing out of Iraq should surprise me, I guess. Still don't understand what this has to do with me. Mo and I were friends but that was a long time ago. I haven't seen or spoken to him in at least ten years."

"We know. I'm here because you are the only one, as far as we can tell, left alive who worked with him."

"How can that be?" Reece asked. "A lot of SEALs rotated through that position over the years, not to mention the scores of Agency people."

"It's really not as many people as you think. I've been through the documents. Brent got killed in Khost, and Eckert had a heart attack in freaking Vegas, of all places. He was at SHOT and somebody joked that the president had signed an executive order banning ARs and thirty-round mags; he just fell over dead. *Weirdest thing.* The last guy is Landry, who just also happened to be working with you and Mo on the drone op in Iraq. No one knows where he is."

"That's probably for the best. I had a run-in with him in Iraq when we were both working with Mo. He liked the interrogations a little too much. Caught him going off the reservation on the Iraqi side of camp. I reported it up the CIA chain. Never heard anything after that and I was rotated out soon afterward. I never liked that guy. But I don't think he's bright enough to build an EFP without blowing himself up."

"That very well may be. The Agency is trying to track him down. They have some questions for him."

"Why do you need somebody who knows Mo to take him out? Can't the Brits just pick him up? They're great at this sort of thing."

"That's the catch: we don't want him dead. We want someone that he knows and trusts to flip him, use him to track down Amin Nawaz and dismantle the network. If he's already swapped sides once, we know he's not an idealist. We just need to make him an offer he can't refuse. We need Nawaz's head on a spike, Reece. It's kinda like a shark attack; the public isn't going back into the water until we show them a dead shark."

"You're not going to start playing Lee Greenwood and tell me that my country needs me, are you?"

"Nope, you only fall for that once."

Reece sat in silence, staring past Strain. Then, "You know I'm dying, right? The tumors that the Hartleys' medical experiment gave me and my Team, they're terminal."

Fred grinned. "Funny that you mention that. You are going to want to hear this."

He closed the slide show and selected an audio player icon, tapping it twice to make it play.

A voice from the past filled the African air.

"Um, hello, Mr. Reece, this is Dr. German. We've been trying to get in

touch with you. We usually don't leave messages like this but I wanted you to hear this as soon as possible. Your biopsy came back and, under the circumstances, it is the best news that we could expect. Your tumor is what's called a cerebral convexity meningioma, which is a very common and slow-growing lesion. Based on the type and location of the mass, I am very confident that I can remove it surgically. We are talking a seventy-five percent or better survival rate. It could be causing you headaches, which is nothing to be alarmed about. Please call us back and my assistant will schedule you an appointment for a follow-up. We can speak in more detail at my office. Again, sorry to have to leave this on your voicemail but I didn't want you to worry needlessly. Have a great day, and enjoy your new lease on life, Commander."

Reece's entire body flushed. Whatever Freddy said next came through as complete nonsense, like he was underwater.

"It's real, Reece. You're going to be fine, bro. Welcome back to the world of the living."

"What the . . . how did you . . . where did you get that?"

"It was on your voicemail, man. It was just sitting on your voicemail."

Reece stood and walked away from the table, fighting a sudden smothering sensation. He found himself by the stone fire pit, overlooking the river below. Was it possible for him to live again after all he had done? His family was still dead. Dead because of a conspiracy to monetize a war by those who had never spent a day in combat, content to sit back immune to the consequences of their vile decisions. *Or so they believed.* He stood there alone for several minutes until he heard Strain's footsteps behind him.

"I'm done working for the government, Freddy. I'm done with that life."

"I understand, Reece, and I know this is a lot to process. It's not just about you, though. I'm not even gonna lay the line on you about protecting civilians and all that, even though it's true. Remember what I said about DOJ being ready to prosecute Liz?"

"Yeah." Reece's jaw tightened in anger.

"That's the stick, Reece. If you don't play ball they'll go after her: aiding and abetting, conspiracy. They'll try to ruin her. Raife and his sister, too . . .

Marco, if they can find him . . . Clint . . . everyone they can find who helped you. When the government sets its sights on destroying you, all the lawyers in the world won't stop them. Might slow them down but that's it."

Fuck. Nothing in Reece's makeup would allow him to stand by while those who stepped up for him had their lives destroyed by a vindictive government. *The Agency sure knows what buttons to press.*

"So, what's the carrot?"

"You get your life back. You and all your accomplices will be given presidential pardons. Little-known fact: you don't need to be convicted of anything to be pardoned. It's like immunity, but it's preemptively coming from the president. All is forgiven. Flip Mo, take out his boss, and go on with your life."

"What life? Go back and pretend that my wife and daughter weren't murdered in our home? Will the president bring them back, too?"

"I'm sorry, man, I didn't mean it like that. All I'm saying is that you won't be a wanted man."

"And Mo? What happens to him?"

"He goes down, buddy. After what he did to those kids in London? He goes down, and he goes down hard."

Reece shook his head. "There has got to be something we can offer to make him flip. The way this is set up, he gets the same deal regardless if he helps us or not."

"What are you saying, Reece?"

"I'm saying I'll need leverage. Unless you have his family in Gitmo, we are going to need to offer an option. Maybe take the death penalty off the table and offer up life in something other than solitary confinement."

"I'll take that back to the bosses."

Reece paused again, looking out toward what was turning into a beautiful African sunset and thinking of those he had put in the ground on his crusade to avenge his family and the lives of the men killed under his command in the mountains of Afghanistan.

"Why would they let me go free after all I did?"

"Two reasons, I think. First of all, there's a sizable chunk of the American public that thinks you're a hero. No one is looking to keep this story going any longer, especially with the election coming up. Second, and this may be the bigger reason, the U.S. and Eurozone economies are in the toilet with a new terror threat on the horizon. You've got retailers about to go under en masse. They were just coming out of the recession and now the public and the markets are scared shitless. The EU is on the verge of breaking up. This mass influx of refugees certainly hiding a percentage of current and would-be terrorists is part of that instability. The whole system is a house of cards that relies on the public trust, and right now we're losing that. We need a dead terrorist, and we need him now."

Reece sighed. "So who's my handler?"

"You're looking at him."

"Could be worse, I guess." Reece smiled. "How does this work logistics-wise?"

"Pretty simple, really. Your early retirement from the Navy will be approved instantly. You were never indicted or arrested, so there are no actual charges to worry about. DOJ has made it clear to all of the state and local agencies that this is their show, so you won't have to worry about any local DAs deciding to make a name for themselves. You'll come to work for us as a contractor, which will give you and the Agency maximum flexibility."

"Terrific," Reece said sarcastically.

"It's a contracted position. You won't pay taxes on most of it as long as you're working overseas. Added to your retirement pay and benefits and it's better than the dollar a day you'd earn making license plates in prison."

"That does sound a bit better. Where does the brain surgery fit into all this?"

"That's a bit of a catch. As soon as we can, we are going to scan your brain and compare it with the scans you had done at the clinic in La Jolla to give us a better idea of what we're dealing with. With the latest three attacks in Europe, this thing is time sensitive. We'll do a quick work-up before attempting to make contact with Mo. Unless things have taken a drastic turn for the worse, the surgery will have to wait until he's been flipped and Nawaz is in the ground."

"That's the government I know. Where are Mo and Nawaz now?"

"We're not sure. The analysts are working it. In the meantime, we've got to get you tuned back up. There's a compound in Morocoo where we can train and plan. You're still a recognizable face, so we need to keep you off the grid until this op kicks off. Once we know where Mo is, you and I will move in and get to work."

"The government sure knows how to make you an offer you can't refuse."

"Art of the deal, buddy," Freddy said with a smile.

"When do we leave?"

"As soon as I make the call."

"Any chance we can take off in the morning? I have to settle up around here."

"Yeah, we can make that happen."

"Thanks, Freddy."

Strain rose to retrieve his Iridium satellite phone and placed a call to Langley, letting them know he had successfully recruited America's most-wanted domestic terrorist.

CHAPTER 32

Niassa Game Reserve
Mozambique, Africa
July

RICH TOOK THE NEWS like a man who knew it was coming. Though he obviously wasn't surprised, he was visibly saddened. Hastings had come to look at Reece less like his nephew's friend and more like his own blood. With little family left in Africa, it pained him to see Reece leaving. He could see that Reece had found both peace and purpose here in Mozambique, and he was worried that with the appearance of the new American in camp he was now destined for neither.

Though Rich understood Reece's reasons for leaving, he was inflexible on one point: ever the gracious host, he insisted that Reece and Freddy join the camp in a final farewell dinner. Reece gave his friend a tour of the camp before watching a breathtaking sunset over the river. Beer was flowing by the time Rich Hastings made his appearance at the lodge, leaning his heavy double rifle against a chair and hanging his worn leather ammunition belt next to it.

"Rich, this is my buddy Freddy Strain. We go back a long way."

"How's it, Freddy?" Reece could sense the reservation in Hastings's voice.

"Pleasure to meet you, Mr. Hastings. I know your nephew. He's a good man."

"Rich, don't hold it against Freddy that I have to go. He's just the messenger."

"Mr. Hastings, is that a Westley Richards droplock?" Freddy motioned toward Rich's rifle nearby.

Reece grinned.

"You know your guns, Freddy. Please call me Rich."

Hastings walked toward the rifle and broke open the action, slipping the panatela-sized cartridges into his hip pocket. He offered the gun to Freddy, who set down his drink and wiped his hands on his pants to ensure that they were dry. He took the rifle as if it were the queen's scepter, eyes wide.

To the casual observer, the rifle looked a lot like a double-barrel shotgun; it was, in fact, a massive rifle with juxtaposed bores larger than a half inch in diameter. Often referred to as an "elephant gun," its 750-grain bullets would stop a charging Tyrannosaurus. This particular model was crafted by one of the gun trade's most prestigious makers in Birmingham, England, during what is widely regarded as the golden age of gunmaking. A new one would run the buyer about as much as a Range Rover, and even one with this many miles on it would fetch a workingman's annual salary at auction.

"Five Seventy-Seven, wow. Westley hasn't made a hundred of these," Freddy said as much to himself as those around him.

"That one is number twenty-five," Hastings proclaimed with pride.

"That would make it between the wars, would it not?"

"Indeed it would, lad. This rifle belonged to my father and his father before him."

Even Hastings couldn't help but smile now. He looked on as his new guest slowly turned the gun to admire the exquisite rose and scroll engraving, the swirling grays, blues, and purples of the faded case-colored frame, and the rich marbling of the reddish walnut stock. Though the gun was close to one hundred years old and had been carried for countless miles in the bush, it was in surprisingly good condition. Every ding in the stock, every tiny scratch in the metal told a story. The most prominent sign of wear on the gun came near the twin muzzles of the thick barrels, where the deep blued finish was worn silver like the pale skin under a man's wristwatch. Rich had carried the rifle over his shoulder with his right hand gripping the barrels in the "African style." Over the decades, the sweat and friction from Hastings's hand had worn completely through the finish.

"Why is it called a 'droplock'?" Reece asked, baiting Freddy into showing his encyclopedic knowledge of firearms.

"May I?" Freddy looked at Hastings with hesitation.

"Please do."

Strain snapped the barrels shut, turned over the rifle, and removed the checkered walnut forend. He lifted a hinged plate on the bottom side of the rifle's action and removed a jeweled metal part.

"This is one of the locks." Freddy held the Victorian-looking steel object in his palm. "These guns were designed to be used in places like this where there were no gunsmiths to be found for hundreds of miles and where sending the rifle back to England meant weeks of sea travel. The best of them came with a spare set of locks that the hunter could carry in his gear and replace in the field if something broke. As you can see, these locks drop right out of the bottom of the action, hence 'the droplock,'" Freddy concluded, winning Rich over with his knowledge and enthusiasm for the classic rifle.

Throughout dinner, Rich captivated Strain with war stories from the Rhodesia days. Reece couldn't recall an instance when Freddy had stayed quiet for so long. As they finished the feast of Cape buffalo filet and fresh vegetables, Rich took a more serious tone.

"I won't pretend that I don't know who you two blokes will be working for, but let me explain my reservations. When our prime minister agreed to end the Bush War and turn the country over to majority rule, a man named Abel Muzorewa was elected prime minister and led the interim government. He was a good man, a bishop of all things. The war didn't stop, though, because the bloody communists didn't control Parliament. Those pulling the strings in Washington and London felt that the new government was too cozy with the European settlers, so they sent in the CIA to disrupt things. We caught them red-handed, meddling in our constitutional process, and we rounded up the entire ring. In exchange for their agents' return, the U.S. government agreed to drop their sanctions and recognize the interim government. Like fools, we took the deal and Carter and his people stabbed us in the back, pretending it never happened. Now, I don't blame the CIA men. They were following orders. They were tools, though, pawns of a government that would break any agreement to get what they wanted. The CIA actually had the gall to try to recruit me to bury weapons caches and mark coordinates for possible runways, DZs and LZs, ah, but that's a story for another day. Don't forget what I told you, boys. You are good blokes. Be wary of politicians meddling in the affairs of other nations, ordering young men like you to their deaths in exchange for reelection."

After an uncomfortable pause, Louie made a toast to Reece, which broke the tension and effectively ended the dinner. It was time to say good-bye to the camp staff—the trackers, the cooks, the skinners, the maids—the people whom Reece had grown to know like family over the past four months. They stood single file in the main lodge, with hats in hand as a sign of respect. One by one, they approached Reece and either hugged him or shook his hand. Reece had a gift for each of them: a headlamp, a knife, a pair of boots that looked as though they might fit. He gave away virtually all his possessions. These seemingly ordinary items were treated as treasures by the staff. Finally, the procession thinned out, leaving only Gona and Solomon. Gona, a man of few words, said nothing lest the tears that filled his eyes spill down his cheeks.

"*Sara mushe*, Gona," said Reece.

Gona merely nodded in response, gripping Reece's hand tightly before half-hugging him and turning quickly away.

Solomon stood alone in his olive coveralls, looking none the worse for wear despite having been recently on the brink of death.

"You saved my life, Mr. James. I cannot thank you . . ."

"You've been a great friend, Solomon. That's thanks enough. Take care of yourself, and take care of Gona, too. I'll come back one day."

That brought a wide smile to Solomon's face. He pulled an object from his pocket that looked like black wire wrapped in a small circle and handed it to Reece, who recognized it as a traditional elephant-hair bracelet, woven from the thick hair of the tail with four rectangular knots spaced equally around the circumference.

"This is from the cow, Mr. James, where I was shot. I hope that she brings you luck."

Now it was Reece's turn to choke up, knowing that Solomon had walked miles to the site of his own near-death shooting to recover the slain animal's tail and weave it into a bracelet for the man who saved his life.

Reece spent one final night in his open hooch, listening to the sounds of the hippos and elephants in the river below, a lion roaring somewhere to the west. He slept little, his thoughts racing to process the news that he wasn't dying after all. *Are they really going to pardon me? Pardon my friends? Is this a trap? How could Mo be working for ISIS?*

His last thought as he finally drifted off to sleep was of an explosives-laden drone settling onto the roof of an SUV in Baghdad.

. . .

At dawn, a Pilatus landed on the strip where Reece had first arrived many weeks ago. Reece caught a look at the pilot through the Plexiglas window, secretly hoping to see his friend Liz Riley. Unless she'd grown a beard, it wasn't her. The two passengers disembarked: a junior case officer from the Tanzanian embassy and an interpreter to drive Strain's Defender 110 back to Dar es Salaam. Strain shook Rich Hastings's hand and climbed aboard the idling aircraft, leaving Reece and Hastings to say their good-byes.

"I can't thank you enough for all that you've done for me, Rich."

"You would have done the same for me, James. Family looks after one another."

"Here, take this, you never know when you may need it." Hastings handed Reece a small sheath knife, its handle made from smooth ebony.

Reece pulled the blade from the leather scabbard and saw a stylized osprey engraved on the side, perched on a rocker that read *Pamwe Chete*, the motto of the famed Selous Scouts, meaning *all together*.

"I can't accept this, Rich."

"My fight is over, James. Yours has just begun. Take it and be well."

Reece reached into his bag and brought out his Winkler-Sayoc tomahawk, handing it to the man he now saw as family.

"Thank you. Thank you for showing me how to live again."

Before the older man could protest, Reece turned and boarded the plane.

As they lifted off, he saw Hastings standing beside his white Land Cruiser, watching yet another son depart Old Africa.

PART TWO

TRANSFORMATIONS

CHAPTER 33

South of Fes, Morocco
July

THE FLIGHT TO MOROCCO was uneventful. A bird from a covered air program run by the Agency delivered them to Fes Air Base. Reece remained quiet most of the trip, reflecting on his last few months in the bush and processing the news that Freddy had brought him from halfway around the world. *I am going to live.* That meant he had to live with the pain, the pain of losing his wife, daughter, and unborn son. He also had to make peace with the fact that he was going to work for the same government that had tried to destroy him. He was being given a second chance—just one last mission and he was free. *Free to do what?* That was a question he needed some time to work out. Reece had been prepared for death for so long, ready to join his wife and daughter, had he forgotten how to live?

"Nice truck," Reece commented, gesturing toward the beige Toyota Hilux waiting on the tarmac.

"I know. These things are great. Too bad you can't get them in the States. You don't still have that old Land Cruiser, do you?"

"Ha! Well, I did until a few months ago. Had I known I wasn't dying, I might have stashed her away for a rainy day." Reece smiled, climbing into the passenger seat as Freddy put the truck in gear and began to weave his way toward the exit.

Reece had first met Freddy Strain when they were both enlisted

SEALs just prior to 9/11. Fred had enlisted a year after Reece. He had a reputation as a smart guy and a capable operator. They were in the same sniper school class and were assigned as shooting partners, which meant they were more or less married for the duration of the school.

"What are we listening to? Is this Waylon Jennings?" Reece asked as a pseudo-psychedelic country rock melody floated into the air.

"This is Sturgill Simpson, man. Great sound. Reminds me of the country my dad would play back in the seventies."

Freddy had grown up in Stuart, Florida, which is just south of Fort Pierce, where the original Navy frogmen were trained during World War II. When Freddy should have been studying, he was fishing and diving off the nearby Atlantic coast or swatting mosquitoes while working on old cars in his family's garage. He came from a blue-collar family in a very white-collar town and had a bit of a chip on his shoulder when it came to others' expectations of him. He was an avid reader and scored highly on all the aptitude tests, but he just couldn't make himself care about high school. Other than a few history courses that piqued his interest, the only A's on his report cards came from the multiple shop classes that he took each semester.

On Veterans Day of his senior year, his dad took him to the annual muster at the UDT/SEAL Museum in Fort Pierce; the site of the old training grounds. Freddy watched in awe as active-duty SEALs performed live demonstrations of raids and ambushes complete with blank-firing machine guns and demolitions, scaled the sides of the museum building without ropes, and parachuted onto the museum grounds from aircraft circling high above. The following Monday, he was in the recruiting office signing delayed enlistment papers.

Freddy was living proof that not all stereotypes are true. In the Hollywood version, the sniper is always a quiet loner who lives for the solitude of the stalk. Freddy Strain was the opposite; he basically never stopped talking unless silence was absolutely necessary. Even then, Reece was sure he was thinking about what to say next. Freddy made up for not studying in high school by reading about subjects that interested him.

He could talk about anything: arcane historical information, Keynesian economics, Nietzschean philosophy, his family, or the ignition timing of a 1956 Ford, but he especially loved to talk about guns. While Reece believed guns were tools of the trade and that armorers and gunsmiths existed for a reason, Freddy was obsessed with every single moving part. He constantly debated the best weapon, best optic, best bullet, and made modifications to nearly every piece of equipment he carried. His team-mates used to joke that, if anyone ever broke into Freddy's house, they'd get away before he decided which gun to use on them. His biggest con-cern was always having the perfect setup for any contingency. When the operators at his most recent command went for beers after work, Freddy would be in the armory tweaking his weapons.

"Reece, you missed some of the latest SEAL drama while you were away."

"What do you mean?"

"Remember that fucker Martell?"

"Oh yeah. What an asshole! Elitist snob, if I remember correctly."

"Yep. Total hypocrite. Turns out that as commanding officer of the training center, just as we are about to welcome our first BUD/S class with females, he gets caught sending pictures of his crank to female sub-ordinate sailors in his chain of command. Turns out he was a total perv the whole time he's playing the 'holier than thou' role as CO. Unbeliev-able. Some reporter got wind of it and started asking questions, but the Navy used the 'ongoing investigation' garbage to conceal it while Martell quickly and quietly retired."

"The ol' dick pic. Always a hit with the ladies. Couldn't have hap-pened to a nicer guy."

"Agreed. Wonder how having women come through the program is going to change things? I mean, you want your daughter to have all the opportunities that men have and feel like they can do anything they . . ." Freddy's voice trailed off. "I'm sorry, Reece. I didn't mean 'your daughter.' I just meant in general. Sorry, buddy."

"That's okay," Reece responded, attempting to hide the hurt in his eyes. "I'll never get over losing them. Now that I'm not dying, I guess I just keep moving forward. I thought I was done, buddy. My grave was already dug. Not sure if that makes it easier or harder to live with what I did."

"Well, you certainly improved on the old 'before embarking on a journey of revenge, dig two graves, one for yourself' proverb," Freddy said smiling, trying to lighten the mood. "I think you did a bit more digging than the original author had in mind."

"They had it coming."

"Don't we all?" Freddy asked, suddenly serious again.

Seeing the conversation as an opening into his friend's well-being, Freddy ventured, "Think you can move on without Lauren?"

Reece paused, unsure not only of how to respond to his old sniper school buddy but also of how he actually felt.

"I don't know, brother. Seems almost sacrilegious to even talk about it. Lauren and Lucy were my life. I felt this devotion to country that kept me in the Teams. It's funny, had the war not happened I probably would have gotten out long ago, and Lauren and Lucy would still be alive."

"You're out now."

"Yeah, I keep forgetting. Seems like I'm back on the USG leash," Reece said, using the abbreviation for United States government.

"True. Almost like the old days." Freddy grinned.

"You want to tell me where we're going?"

"Not much longer now. I've only been here once before. It's a former black site where we used to bring suspected terrorists when we wanted another country to do our dirty work for us. Part of the extraordinary rendition program started after 9/11."

"I remember," Reece affirmed. "Fairly effective from what I can recall, that is until the media and the enemy figured it out."

"Exactly. Just finding out we had black sites was a big PR win for them. Kind of like the very existence of Guantanamo. I'm not sure how we measure the ROI, but the law of diminishing returns would indicate that at some point the enemy got more out of those from a recruitment and world sentiment standpoint than the value of the actual intel we got from using them."

"Such a tough call, and another reason we have civilian control of the military," said Reece.

"Yeah, on a certain level it almost condoned certain behaviors that we ended up having a lot of trouble with at my former command and in the military in general: desecrating bodies, tactical interrogations that went too far." Freddy paused. "It was interesting, though, Reece. Everyone who came from working with you always was a bit more thoughtful about it. They said you talked about the importance of maintaining the moral high ground to differentiate us from our enemies. I don't think they got that from many others."

Reece shook his head. "I threw that right out the window when they killed my family."

"No, you didn't, Reece. Never think that. You just went to war. Plain and simple. They killed Lauren and Lucy. They killed your entire troop. Tried to kill you. You held them accountable. Just because you broke a few laws doesn't mean you lost the moral high ground. You always held that territory."

"Thanks, Freddy," Reece said, looking out at the desolate yet beautiful desert scenery.

"You ever do any of those 'diaper runs'?" Reece asked his friend, using the Agency slang for the kinetic side of extraordinary rendition due to the use of diapers on terrorists snatched off the street in country X on the way to country Y as both a means of humiliation and practicality.

"No. By the time I got to the Agency that program was pretty much over. Too much controversy. Though what we're about to do sure comes close. And besides, I came on just to find you." Freddy smiled again.

"Gee, thanks," Reece responded, not attempting to hide his sarcasm.

"No problem, and thanks again for not putting me in one of those revenge graves," Freddy said, thinking of everyone Reece had put in the ground avenging his family and SEAL Troop.

"You're welcome," Reece returned with just the slightest hint of a smile before shaking his head and continuing more to himself than to his friend. "I just couldn't do it, man. I saw you down there in the kill zone, and suddenly everyone down there became a version of you. Guys with families, kids, dogs, aspirations, dreams. Not only did you save everyone's lives that day, you probably saved mine. I'm not sure I could live with myself had I followed through with it. I was just so blinded by what I needed to do that I almost ambushed a troop, just like the SECDEF and Admiral Pilsner ambushed mine. I should be the one thanking you for saving my life."

"Whatever you say, brother. Let's call it even."

"Freddy, you didn't get out *just* to find me, did you?"

Freddy glanced at his friend and then back to the road. "Well, not *just* to find you, although that's what sealed the deal on going to the Agency and, in all honesty, was a huge part of it. I had to find out why you didn't kill us all that day when you had us in a textbook ambush. I looked at the claymore set up after we assaulted Ben's cabin, came up empty, and patrolled back to the trailhead. I sent some of the reconnaissance guys out to locate possible hide sites, and sure enough they found where you had set up. Looks like you had most of the Team Seven armory laid out up there: LAWs, an AT-4, an Mk 48."

"It was a good position."

"Yeah, well, thanks again." Freddy paused. "But like I said, that wasn't the *only* reason I left."

"Really? I thought you loved the Teams."

"I did. Remember the witch hunts that went down in the wake of the 'tell-all' book on the big mish?" Freddy asked, referencing one of the many nonfiction books on the Osama bin Laden mission.

"I remember. What a shit show. The same people that gave the green light to that Hollywood movie starring active-duty SEALs and benefited more than a little bit from BUD/S tours they gave wealthy donors to the different SEAL foundations suddenly got convenient cases of amnesia. They fried a bunch of guys for off-duty employment, from what I remember."

"Yeah, that's about the gist of it. Years before I had done some teaching at a hunter's marksmanship program in Texas called Bladelands Ranch."

"That place is amazing," Reece said in acknowledgment. "I took my snipers out there before our last deployment to Iraq. Beautiful facility in the Hill Country. Guy that started it made a fortune selling a microbrewery to Coors or Budweiser or something, right?"

"That's right, Blackbuck Brewery. Great stuff! Anyway, some of us in our off time would go out there on leave to pick up a few extra dollars helping people prepare for hunts in Africa or Alaska, getting their rifles dialed in, teaching them how to dial and hold, that sort of thing. Well, after the tipping point of the UBL books, they came after everybody doing outside employment. They said we were teaching 'sniper' tactics and giving away TTPs. Of course, that wasn't even close to what we were doing. I learned that the justice system is not always out to do what's right. They are out for the win. It was an eye-opener."

"Sounds like I should have added a few people to my list," Reece offered with a slight smile.

"Ha! I have a few names for you, for next time."

"So, what happened?"

"They took a bunch of us to mast. You wouldn't have believed it, Reece: standing right next to the CO was the CMC who'd taught tactics and CQC out at Blackwater in North Carolina for years to make extra money on the weekends. Guess he just forgot."

"You didn't bring that up?"

"Reece, you know me better than that. Not my style. Besides, he has to live with it. And if I remember correctly, his wife had more platoon hats than he did."

"Karma's a bitch sometimes."

"You actually already took care of one of them: Admiral Pilsner. Turns out he was even dirtier than we thought. His wife was funneling money from one of the SEAL-oriented foundations into an offshore account and selling influence through guided tours and access. Emails proved Pilsner knew all about it. If you hadn't killed him he would have gone to jail for a long time. I think ol' Mrs. Pilsner got six years in the federal penitentiary. Probably be out in four, I'd imagine."

Looking out the window as the desert started to turn rocky and the Atlas Mountains began to take shape in the distance, Reece swallowed and asked, "How's your son?"

Freddy's son, Sam, had been born with a rare genetic disorder and would require full-time care for life. Reece remembered Freddy and his wife, Joan, putting on brave fronts as they dealt with the situation. Reece always had the highest respect for how they handled what had to be one of the toughest situations imaginable.

Taking a breath, Freddy kept his eyes on the road. "He's okay, Reece. Thank you for asking. It's a lifelong journey. Our mission is to help him reach his full potential, regardless of what it is."

"Was there ever a final diagnosis?"

"Raife didn't tell you?"

"What do you mean?" Reece asked, puzzled.

"He's the only reason we have a diagnosis."

"He never mentioned it, but our relationship was a bit strained after Iraq when he left the Teams. And," Reece remembered, "the last time we met up, we were a little busy."

"Yeah, well, we got the runaround from the Navy doctors for years. We almost went broke paying specialists from some private top-name hospitals for their opinion, hence the off-duty work at Bladelands. Nobody could figure it out. They kept trying to diagnose him with labels that just didn't fit. Joanie knew. She knew they didn't have it right."

"So, what happened?" Reece pressed.

"Somebody mentioned it to Raife. I always thought it was you."

"We discussed it, but only in terms of you having a lot to deal with, especially with multiple deployments and workups, which as we know are stressful enough on a family *without* a special needs kid. You and Joanie were an inspiration to everyone."

"Thanks, man. What happened between you and Raife, anyway? You guys were like brothers."

"Something happened in Iraq. Nothing you or I wouldn't have done in his shoes. So how did Raife help out?" Reece asked, clearly not wanting to discuss his old friend and getting the conversation back on track.

"He talked with his father-in-law about it. Must have been right about the time he was getting out. Next thing we know, Joanie is getting a call from the lead doctor at Southwestern Medical Center, just outside Dallas. Apparently Raife's father-in-law donated most of the money to build it. Anyway, about a month later we're getting picked up by a G550 private jet, complete with a nurse, and flown from Virginia Beach to Dallas. They assembled a team of genetic specialists from around the country, did a full workup of genetic tests on all of us, and sent our blood around the world to institutions doing similar research."

"That's incredible!"

"Yeah, we would never have gotten a legitimate diagnosis from the Navy."

"What did they find out?"

"A researcher in the Netherlands had discovered a rare genetic mutation of the NR2F1 gene. It helps form the brain. They didn't even have a name for it back then but now they call it Bosch-Boonstra-Schaaf after the team that discovered it. Sam was the thirteenth person ever diagnosed with it. There are more out there, they just don't know someone who can correctly diagnose it."

"How is Joanie doing?" Reece asked.

"She's the strong one, Reece. She dealt with it all while we were away doing the job, focused on the mission, on the Team. She did it all alone. I'm not sure I could have done it in her position. Sam is a sweet kid. He's nine now, but cognitively he's very young. He certainly keeps us on our toes."

"How is he with the other kids?"

"Ha! He's sandwiched in between an older sister and younger brother that are absolute rock stars. We have to believe that Sam came to us for a reason, and that reason is that God thought we were strong enough to love him while at the same time raising two other kids and giving them the attention and support they deserve."

"You guys are an amazing family, Freddy. Sam is certainly lucky he got you two as parents."

"Thanks, buddy."

Freddy nodded at the road ahead and changed subjects. "It will be a few miles off this main road back in those mountains. Not a bad place to spend a few months."

CHAPTER 34

■■■■ *Black Site*
Near Midelt, Morocco
July

WITH THE ATLAS MOUNTAINS visible to the north and the rocky terrain flanking each side of the road, the Sahara Desert looked like some of the Nevada training sites where Reece had learned to call in aircraft for bombing runs known as Close Air Support.

Strain slowed the Hilux as they approached a stone-walled compound surrounded by open fields. He tapped the horn and, a few seconds later, the corrugated metal gate was pushed open by a muscular Westerner wearing hiking boots, desert tiger-stripe pattern camouflage pants, and body armor over a brown T-shirt. Topped off with a thick reddish beard, Oakley sunglasses, and a battered ball cap, his appearance screamed "private security contractor." His Glock sidearm was visible in a holster at his waist and Reece was sure that a long gun was somewhere within arm's reach. The contractor returned Fred's wave as they rolled through the open gate.

"Welcome to Falcon Base, Reece."

Reece took stock of the compound and saw a large two-story stucco building at the center surrounded by several single-story concrete structures of various sizes.

Bringing the Hilux to a stop, Freddy said, "That main house is home base. We'll bunk in there. It also has a mission planning space and class-room where you'll have your lessons."

"Lessons?"

"Yeah, they've lined up an Islamic studies teacher to bring you up to speed on culture, language, all that. Make you stand out like less of an *infidel* when we get to work."

"Interesting. How long am I supposed to be here?"

"Not sure, buddy. As long as it takes for our intel guys to get a solid lo-cation on Mo. My guess would be anywhere from two weeks to a month, but you know how this stuff works. We could get a call to go tomorrow or it could be a few months."

"Wonderful."

"Over there is the arms room."

"You sleep in there with your toys?" Reece asked.

"No, but it's not a bad idea. The big barn-looking building is where we work out, keep our gear, all that kind of stuff."

"How's the gym?"

"Not bad. We've got a big Rogue rig with ropes, bumper plates, kettle bells, a rower, VersaClimber, assault bike, all that. We could start our own CrossFit box here. We have a couple of Woodway treadmills and some mats, so we can roll. I'm sure you can still kick my ass in jiujitsu, but I've been training, so we'll see."

"I'm pretty rusty, brother. You may have me."

"I'm not buying that, Reece, not at all."

"Ha! Guess we'll find out."

"We have a range a couple klicks south of here, but I put some steel out back so we can shoot handguns without going anywhere."

"Great. I haven't been shooting much, so I'll need the tune-up."

"We'll get you dialed back in."

Freddy pulled the pickup in front of the main structure and both men climbed out. Reece grabbed his duffel from the bed of the Toyota and followed his Agency handler toward the entrance.

Freddy stopped abruptly at the door. "I almost forgot, your name is

'James Donovan' while we're here. We'll get you a full identity worked up but that'll do for now."

"Donovan, huh? As in Wild Bill?"

"I don't know. The computer picks the names based on an algorithm that keeps your first name and doesn't repeat last names. It could be much worse, trust me. Some poor guy got 'John Holmes' recently."

Reece just shook his head.

As they entered, a slightly built man with dark features and a neatly cropped beard, wearing a clean white djellaba robe and red fez, greeted them politely in British-accented English.

"Welcome, gentlemen. You must be Mr. Donovan. I am Maajid Kifayat."

"*As-Salaam-Alaikum*, Maajid." Reece extended his hand.

"*Wa-Alaikum-Salaam*, Mr. Donovan. Please, come in."

Reece bent down and untied his boots, leaving them outside the door in the Islamic tradition. Maajid walked gracefully through the foyer of the large home, as if in deference to its grandeur. The z*ellij* mosaic tiles in bright blues and yellows, elaborate furnishings, and arched doorways represented classic Moorish architecture. Reece guessed that the home was hundreds of years old, or was at least designed to look that way. It was like a scaled-down version of the Alcázar palace in Seville, Spain, which was built during the days when the Moors occupied much of the Iberian Peninsula. "Not like the plywood shitholes we lived in in Afghanistan, is it?" Freddy quipped.

"I've stayed in worse."

"Let me give you a quick tour, and then we can get settled in."

Maajid faded off to another part of the house as Freddy led the way through the foyer, which opened to a large living area adjacent to a stone and grass courtyard. A second-floor balcony overlooked the enclosure on all four sides. Freddy showed Reece the common areas of the home—the kitchen, bathrooms, and study that would serve as a classroom—before heading up a marble staircase.

"Maajid is cleared TS/SCI, but even so, this is need-to-know and he is not on that list. Upstairs is off-limits to the rest of the staff, so all our planning will happen up here."

Strain hit a succession of numbers on a cypher lock to open a series of rooms along the balcony hallway. One had been converted into a
mini briefing room with a large LCD screen on the wall, while two other
adjoining rooms would be their sleeping quarters. They were small but
clean and had been retrofitted with LG mini-split air-conditioning units.
The last room was secured with a heavy wrought-iron gate as well as a
steel door that bolted shut from the inside.

"This is the Alamo; if any Benghazi-style shit goes down, this is our
fallback position."

"What's the threat environment?"

"Morocco's a stable country, at least for this part of the world, and
we have a good relationship with the DST, that's their secret police. We
keep a very low profile here. We're also a good distance from town and
the cover story for this place is that it's used by the Moroccan government to house visiting dignitaries. We built it under the guise of training
host nation counterterrorist units, which we'll end up doing eventually."

"Got it. How much security do we have?"

"We have four GRS guys assigned. They're all solid: three Rangers
and a Marine. All of them have multiple deployments. You and I can help
in a pinch. We're a long way from reinforcements if something really goes
sideways."

"Thanks, Freddy. This place will work just fine."

"Let's grab your stuff and get you squared away in your room. Then
I'll show you my toys."

. . .

Freddy led Reece to the padlocked storage building that would serve as
their small armory. Fluorescent lights hummed overhead in the long,
narrow room where he had arranged various weapons on a stout wooden
table. Reece recognized most of them, though a few were clearly more
exotic than what he'd been issued in the Teams. They were arranged from
smallest to largest, starting with handguns and ending with belt-fed machine guns. Most of them had been spray painted in mottled camouflage
patterns.

"Okay, here you've got handguns: even though you like the Glocks, I'd like you to try the new SIG 365, especially for work in low-vis environments. It holds more rounds than your 43."

"I heard a lot about this during development. I'll give it a run," Reece said, immediately impressed by the subcompact pistol.

While Reece loved his subcompact G43; the unprecedented 12+1 9mm capacity of the SIG 365 along with its surprisingly smooth striker-fire trigger and night sights made this one a winner right out of the box.

"And this is the SIG P320 with upgraded triggers by Bruce Gray," Freddy said, picking up the SIG's new 9mm pistol. "I think you'll like her."

"I like her already," Reece said with a smile.

SIG had recently won the highly sought-after, nearly decade-long process to replace the Beretta 92F and supply the U.S. armed forces with a new advanced pistol, a variant of the SIG 320, now adopted as the M17/M18.

"Is Mato still running training up at SIG?" Reece asked, referring to their old SEAL master chief who could probably still out-PT the newest BUD/S graduate.

"He sure is. They have an incredible facility up there. He's crushing it."

"Well, if we make it through the next few months and the tumor doesn't do me in, let's go pay him a visit."

"Done deal, brother."

Freddy motioned toward a small, blocky, futuristic-looking submachine gun that looked like something out of a science fiction movie. A curved magazine protruded out of the weapon's pistol grip and a smaller foregrip folded down from near the muzzle. A tubular suppressor extended its length, and the entire package was dappled with a brown and tan homemade camouflage scheme.

"Next, we've got some MP7s like we use at Dam Neck. You ever shot one?"

"I got to play around with one when I augmented you guys a few years back, but I didn't spend enough time on it to get proficient. We don't get that high-speed stuff on the West Coast."

"Roger, pretty slick little gun. Compact and has a really high rate of fire. Great for close-in stuff that needs to be done quietly. When you use the subsonic ammo you can hardly hear it. Easy to shoot with this Aimpoint Micro red dot. Just be aware that its terminal performance isn't what you're used to due to the little 4.6 cartridge."

"In English, Freddy, English."

Strain exhaled and feigned an eye roll. "It uses a *really* little bullet, so if you shoot a guy with it, put half a mag into him."

"That, I understand."

"Next, for rifles we've got HK416s that we'll use instead of the M4, both ten-inch and fourteen-inch models. It works just like an M4 but it's a lot less ammo sensitive and more reliable due to the piston system, especially when it gets dirty. We can mount whatever optic you want."

Reece could sense his new partner's excitement as he described the various weapons and their features: "Now I see why you really went over to the dark side."

Freddy smiled. "Dude, this is the coolest part of my job. I can pick any guns I want and trick them out to my heart's content. Kid in a candy store, bro."

"You're like a whiskey-tango version of 'Q' from James Bond," Reece joked.

Strain broke into his best English accent: "Double-oh-seven, here are your sniper options: a LaRue OBR in 5.56 and a gun that I built myself in .260," dropping the accent and continuing the description like a proud father. "It's got a carbon-fiber barrel from Proof, so it keeps cool and it's light. You'll notice that I put the same flash hiders on just about everything so we can mount the same suppressors across the board. The .30-cal cans work just fine on the 5.56 and the .260."

"Is the .260 like a .308?"

"Fills the same role but it's better in nearly every regard. It shoots faster, flatter, and with less recoil. Same mags as a 7.62, but has the dope of a .300. I've been trying to sell everyone on this round for years, but the military is slow to move on anything."

"I'll take your word for it."

"How did you ever make it through Sniper School?" Freddy asked in feigned astonishment.

"I must have had a good spotter." Reece smiled back.

"Must have," Freddy agreed. "Anyway, I doubt we'll do anything super long-range, but we have an Accuracy International in .300 Norma and even a Barrett M107 .50 if we need it. We've got some belt-feds as well as a bunch of anti-armor stuff. Plus we have demo." He pointed to a row of tubes leaning against the back wall of the room. "LAW rockets, AT-4s, even a Javelin in that case back there. Those things are like a quarter mil a pop but certainly do the job."

"Well, I'll be sure to use those sparingly."

Reece noticed a row of Ops-Core ballistic helmets fitted with L3 Technologies GPNVG-18 night observation devices hanging on the wall; the best NODs that money could buy. The devices were easily recognizable thanks to the four panoramic lenses that gave the user better peripheral vision than with other models.

"Four-bangers, huh? That's rich-kid shit."

"Taxpayer money spends easy, man. Those things are so much better than the stuff we used to use."

"You're kind of a gear snob, Freddy."

"I like nice stuff, man, what can I say?"

CHAPTER 35

IT WAS A TWENTY-MINUTE ride in the Hilux to the range, the wide-open landscape reminding Reece of being back at sea. The mostly flat, sometimes rolling, but always barren terrain made for a perfect training area. A local construction firm had used a bulldozer to create impact berms at various distances. There was a U-shaped berm, 100 meters deep, for short-range work, and beyond it was a rifle range for shots as far as 1,800 meters. A faded red shipping container served as a supply closet, and its roof gave them line of sight to the sniper targets. There were steel-plate targets of various sizes and shapes scattered across the landscape, allowing for shots at just about every conceivable distance. What looked to be an inoperable Mercedes sedan from the 1970s sat inside the perimeter.

"Let me guess, that's my ride?" Reece quipped.

"Yeah, man, sorry about the windshield. We'll have to get you some goggles."

As they parked, Freddy's usually casual tone and body language shifted to all business.

"Okay, we'll start with some handgun work, then get you going on the MP7 before moving to the 416s. We can mess with the long-range stuff another day."

"Sounds good, buddy."

Freddy unlocked the shipping container and swung open the heavy steel doors. Inside were cases of spray paint, assorted cardboard targets, additional steel plates, several cases of ammunition, and pieces of plywood cut into various shapes.

"Help me with this barricade." Freddy motioned to a vertical ply-wood façade with steps down one side and filled with holes of varying shapes and sizes. They carried the mock barricade to the center of the range and set it up next to the Mercedes.

"Go ahead and get the kinks out with your nine-mil while I get some of this other stuff set up. There's ammo in the back of the truck."

Reece nodded and walked toward a row of three steel silhouette tar-gets. It occurred to him that the last time he'd fired a handgun, it had been into the mouth of a federal agent responsible for killing his family. It was difficult for his mind to reconcile that act with the fact that he was back in the employ of the United States government. *Crazy world.*

Reece was wearing the SIG 320 in a holster on his belt rather than his usual BlackPoint Tactical Mini WING concealment rig; there was no reason to try to conceal a handgun while wearing full battle gear.

Skills such as shooting are highly perishable, and Reece hadn't done any serious firearms training in close to a year. Being an "expert" in any-thing means doing the basics exceptionally well, so Reece started with the fundamentals. Putting on his ear protection, he took a deep breath to focus. Then, standing ten yards from a steel plate, Reece drew the handgun from his holster, his left hand meeting the gun at his pectoral muscle as the muzzle rotated toward the target. He pushed the SIG out with both hands gripping firmly until his elbows nearly locked, pressing the trigger as he drove the gun swiftly toward the target. His eyes met the front sight just as the trigger broke and his brain recognized the instant gratification of a center-mass hit on the steel target as the gun recoiled slightly upward. Keeping his trigger finger on the trigger, he scanned to the left and right of his target before moving his finger to the frame to look behind him for threats before replacing the handgun in his holster. *Situational awareness.*

He drew again, a bit faster this time, and put two rounds into the tar-get in quick succession. He repeated the process until the magazine ran dry, performed a slide-lock reload, stepping to his left, and fired two more rounds. He moved farther from the targets and began engaging multiple plates in rapid succession, quickly transitioning from one to the next.

Speed came back quickly, thanks to hundreds of thousands of rounds fired over the past eighteen years during similar training sessions. He had burned his way through ten magazines when he saw Freddy watching him over his left shoulder during one of his post-target scans.

"Just like riding a bike. Looking sharp, Reece."

"Thanks. Feels good to be back at it."

"I bet. Let me paint these targets and we'll get dialed in on the fun gun."

Freddy shook a rattle can of spray paint as he approached the targets that were covered with the gray splatters of Reece's pistol rounds. He recoated them with glossy white paint and waved for Reece to follow him to a folding table with the suppressed MP7 and a row of loaded magazines. Freddy picked up the tan and brown camouflaged submachine gun and pointed the muzzle skyward.

"Okay, Reece, this will be a new toy for you. This thing shoots really fast and has almost no recoil. It's also exceptionally quiet with serious penetration, so if the bad guys are wearing armor it's a better choice than a handgun. We started using them at Dam Neck and a lot of guys fell in love with them."

Freddy retracted the small stock to its rear position and folded down a stubby grip below the barrel. "You can shoot it like a handgun in a pinch but you won't hit much. The mags go in the grip like an UZI and hold forty rounds. You cock it here and the selector is here." He demonstrated, handing the firearm to Reece. "It might look like it works like the old MP5 but that's just because it's an HK. It'll operate like an M4 from your perspective. Have at it. Slow is smooth, smooth is fast."

"I've heard that somewhere before," Reece said, remembering the old SEAL adage.

Reece loaded a magazine into the hollow grip and moved the safety/selector to semiauto. His eye quickly found the crisp red dot of the Aimpoint Micro sight and he pressed the trigger. The shot was totally underwhelming, with almost no discernible recoil and minimal report, reminding him of the pellet rifle his grandfather had given him as a kid. A single tiny speck of gray was visible at the center of the target thirty meters away. He flipped the selector to full auto and leaned a bit harder into the gun to control its rise. Reece tried for a short burst and five or six suppressed rounds spat from the muzzle, pinging against the steel target downrange. The gun barely moved. He fired a longer burst, ten or so rounds, and was amazed by how controllable the little gun was. He emptied the remainder of the magazine into the target in a longish string and all twenty-four rounds stayed in the eight-inch circle.

He turned to his friend, grinning ear to ear. "I like it."

"I knew you would. It has its limitations but it's definitely useful."

Reece spent a few minutes familiarizing himself with his new toy before Freddy began running him through some basic drills with it. He held an electronic shot timer that would measure Reece's reaction time from the buzzer to his first round on target. Freddy set up orange traffic cones on the range and had Reece navigate them in various ways as he engaged the targets: shooting while moving forward, backward, and laterally and ultimately shooting while weaving through the cones like a sports car on a slalom course. Gunfights aren't static events and perfecting the skill of shooting while moving could mean the difference between life and death. They fired from various positions over, under, and through the plywood barricade and practiced using the junk Mercedes for cover.

After hours of work with the handgun, MP7, and HK416 carbines, it was time for a breather. They broke for lunch and talked as they ate gyro-like sandwiches on the tailgate of the Hilux. Reece opened the paper wrapper and looked at the contents as if the food was booby-trapped.

"They put mayo on these things?" he asked in disgust.

"You and your mayo. I'd forgotten about that phobia. Wonder if there's a scientific name for it."

"It's so nasty."

"Fear not, Reece. No mayo. It's some kind of yogurt sauce."

Visibly relieved, Reece took a tentative bite. His face lit up in approval.

"You always were a natural, Reece. It kills me that I eat and sleep this stuff and you just stroll out here and shoot like a champ."

Reece shrugged as he chewed a bite full of lamb and pita. "Should I sandbag a little to make you feel better?"

"Ha! No, dude, keep it up. The sooner we get this done, the sooner we can get back to our families." Freddy paused for a second, catching himself. "Sorry, bro, didn't mean it like that, I forgot . . ."

"It's okay. Seriously, stop apologizing. You're a dear friend and a great dad. No need to apologize."

"I'm just sorry, man. With all of the challenges we have with Sam, at least I can hug him when I get home."

"I admire the hell out of you and Joanie. You guys never complain, never ask for anything. You just get it done."

"You play the cards you're dealt, Reece. That's all you can do. When you look at the statistics of families dealing with special needs kids, the odds are that the added stress breaks you apart. For some reason, it made us a closer, more compassionate family. It made us a team."

"Never look at the odds, buddy. My hat is off to you guys. Now, let's go train so you can get home to see them."

After lunch both men strapped on their heavy chest rigs, harnesses of nylon webbing laden with body armor, gear, and loaded magazines. They spent the afternoon working as a team, perfecting the choreography of shooting, moving, and communicating. They began at a walking pace and progressed rapidly to full speed. If one of them was moving or reloading, the other was putting rounds on the target. By day's end, they were doing it seamlessly and without words.

When the sun went below the horizon, they attached NODs to their helmets and repeated the drills in darkness, their infrared lasers painting the targets, invisible to the naked eye. The only sounds came from the hard ground crunching beneath their boots and the suppressed gunshots from their muzzles. To the two professional commandos, who had spent more than half of their lives working at night both in training and on combat deployments, their actions were as natural as breathing.

CHAPTER 36

Iraq-Syria Border
August

LIEUTENANT COLONEL SAEED HAD received the encrypted message on his phone the previous evening and had spent the day planning and coordinating. He'd picked fifteen of his best men and called it in as a training mission. An Mi-8 from their airwing, flown by Iraqi pilots trained to fly with NODs over the pine forests of the Florida Panhandle courtesy of the CIA, took off under the cover of darkness and flew them to this rendezvous site. As the men waited in the darkness, they smoked and checked weapons and gear, joking with one another, just like every group of soldiers in history. Saeed loved his men and observed them with both pride and sadness.

To many, it would seem odd for an Iraqi special operations commander to be handing his troops over to work under a former general in the Syrian Army but, to Saeed, nothing was strange anymore. Times were simpler under Saddam, when ruthless loyalty to the Ba'ath Party and its leaders was all that it took to thrive.

Following the 2003 invasion, Saeed had worked for the Americans and then the inept and corrupt government they'd left behind in their hasty departure. He'd fought ISIS as they swept across much of the only country he'd ever called home and watched with even more confusion as they were beaten back by the Iranian-influenced Shia militias and the Kurds, who were still allied with the Americans. Would he work for the

Turks next? The Iranians? Who knew? He would serve nearly any master, so long as they were in power. That's how you lived in a place like Iraq. It had always been all about survival for him and his family. Side jobs such as this one that had brought him to the middle of the desert would help ensure that he had the resources to someday move his family to a safer place.

One of his men spotted the trucks, driving in complete darkness across the flat desert terrain. This was his cue to leave. He hugged each one and bid them farewell, hopeful that he would see them again.

"Captain Daraji," Saeed said, motioning to the officer in charge.

"Yes, Colonel."

"You will be picking up two local assets when you land. Their handler will be briefing them up. For them it is about the cause. For us, it is about payment."

"Understood, Colonel," Daraji said, snapping a smart salute. *"Ma' al-salāmah."*

"Fī amān Allāh," Saeed responded, returning his subordinate's salute.

As Saeed boarded the now-empty cargo bay of the helicopter, he asked his Creator to watch over them. He didn't need to wait around to see what would happen next. His men would board the trucks and be driven into Syria to a military airfield under Assad's control, where they and their gear would be transferred to an AN-26 cargo aircraft. This twin-engine workhorse was built in the former Soviet Union and could serve as everything from a flying hospital to a bomber. It lacked the range to reach their destination on a single tank of fuel, so they would fly over the Mediterranean Sea until they refueled at a remote airstrip in the failed state of Libya. From then, God willing, it was on to the target.

CHAPTER 37

REECE KNEW HE WAS almost out of air. Despite his attempts to stay calm, his heart raced, eating up precious oxygen. His world had darkened at the edges of his vision due to the suffocation. He was in trouble, and he knew it.

He was suddenly with his father, hiking a steep muddy trail canopied by the thick vegetation of North Carolina's Nantahala National Forest. His father's career in what they thought was the foreign service meant long periods of separation, so Reece cherished the time they spent together. They'd walked down a twisting narrow path to a surging waterfall, hidden miles from the nearest highway. The steady rains in these mountains provided a constant source of creek water that had worn the rocky face so smooth that you could actually slide down part of the falls in the seated position and splash into the deep pool at the bottom. It was a place where people had gathered long before any Europeans had stepped ashore in the New World, and it was still special.

The heavens opened and within seconds they were drenched from an abrupt deluge of rain; their respite from the summer heat had become a shivering battle for warmth. His father took a look at his son, whose face was a mask of misery, and decided that they would hike back to the Wagoneer at the trailhead, which meant a steep and muddy climb in the torrential downpour. James's little legs powered along as best they could, attempting to match his father's long and powerful stride.

"C'mon, Jamesy, you can do it, buddy. Just put one foot in front of the other."

James wasn't about to let his father, or himself, down. He'd climb three steps forward and slide two steps back in the slick brown ooze that the trail had become but kept moving forward, his legs feeling like jelly.

Thomas Reece wiped the crystal of the faded steel dive watch on his wrist. "Twenty more minutes and we're back at the car, James. Just don't quit, buddy; life is hard sometimes, but if you stay with it and keep moving forward, you'll prevail . . . trust me."

Reece kept hiking, maintaining a stiff upper lip and a stride that mimicked his father's gait. He tripped over twisted roots on the trail, his muddy sneakers squished brown water with each step, but he pressed on.

"You've got it, son . . . Never quit!"

He wasn't going to quit.

Reece was suddenly back in the present, sweat stinging his eyes. He struggled to free himself, but the hold was too strong, the other man's legs locking his neck in a delta of flesh and muscle and restricting the flow of blood and oxygen to his brain. His opponent was on his back with one hand pulling Reece's right arm across his body and the other pulling downward on his head. The man's right thigh was pressed against one side of his neck and a bent leg hooked over the back of his head, compressing Reece's own shoulder into his throat. In jiujitsu terms, the man had Reece in what was known as a triangle choke. He had set the trap perfectly, and Reece had taken the bait. *Damn, this guy is strong.* Reece sucked oxygen and, for a moment, gained absolute clarity regarding his position. The proper technique for escape from a triangle had been drilled into him years before by sixth-degree Brazilian Jiu-Jitsu black belt Master Renzo Gracie at his academy in New York. Though they trained constantly in Virginia Beach, Reece and his platoon still made the six-hour pilgrimage to Manhattan to train with the grandson of legendary Gracie Jiu-Jitsu founder Carlos Gracie as often as they could.

With a surge of energy, Reece postured up, craning his neck upward in the process. The man saw his attempt to escape and increased the force upon Reece's neck. Using all his strength, he moved his hips as high as possible and began to move laterally, slowly turning his body at a right angle to that of his adversary. Like a coiled spring, Reece snapped his hip against the man's legs, breaking the choke. His lungs filled with air that, despite the heat and odor of sweat, was like a taste of paradise. Continuing his momentum, Reece worked quickly into side control, snaking one arm under the man's neck and one over his body, locking his hands into a Gable grip. It was a chance to suck in critical oxygen, clear his mind, and regain his composure after nearly blacking out only seconds earlier.

Taking the initiative brought by his position, Reece threw his leg over the man's body and climbed astride, putting him into mount—the most dominant position in ground fighting. He grasped the man's arm and pushed it to the ground, causing his rival to turn onto his side in defense against the shoulder lock. As he did so, Reece slid farther up his torso and took his adversary's exposed back. His opponent knew what Reece was trying to do and fought a "grip fight" to prevent Reece from getting his arm across his exposed throat. Reece used his legs like hooks, sliding them around the front of the man's body like a constricting snake. His arm slid past his opponent's sweat-soaked hand and wrapped over the neck. With his opposite hand, he locked it into the crook of his elbow, using it as a fulcrum against the throat and carotid artery. With a technically perfect rear naked choke, there is essentially no escape; the other fighter had three to five seconds before he would black out. Reece felt the tap on his forearm and released his grip. Freddy Strain gasped for air.

"*Shit*, I thought I had you with that triangle."

"You almost did," Reece admitted, sucking in precious oxygen.

"Thanks for not making eye contact."

Both men laughed at the tired jiujitsu joke.

Reece lay back onto the mats and took some deep breaths.

"I'm proud of you, James—you didn't quit." His father tousled his son's wet hair in the front seat of the faux-paneled Jeep back at the trailhead. "Remember, a fight isn't just about surviving, it's about prevailing. There's a difference."

These weeks of training in Morocco had hardened his resolve and cleared his mind; Reece had become a warrior again.

After their "rolling" session, Reece and Freddy ran a few laps around the inside wall of the compound before getting into their morning workout. Like most of the special operations community, their physical training centered on useful strength, cardiovascular endurance, and durability, which, as both of them were pushing age forty, was increasingly important. Looking like a steroid-fueled bodybuilder was not part of the equation and was a liability in terms of both physical performance and blending into civilian populations.

Their workouts pulled elements from various coaches and training programs, including CrossFit, Gym Jones, and StrongFirst. The idea wasn't to be able to compete with endurance athletes, power lifters, or alpinists, but to achieve a broad-based level of fitness that would allow them to perform well in each of those areas. After a series of warm-up exercises that most would consider a serious workout, they completed the strength and endurance Hero WOD "Murph," named in honor of Navy SEAL Lieutenant Mike Murphy. Wearing their body armor, they started with one hundred burpees followed by four one-hundred-yard buddy carries. Then it was right into a two-mile run, one hundred pull-ups, two hundred push-ups, three hundred air squats, followed by another two-mile run. Both men powered through, thinking of the scores of soldiers, sailors, airmen, and Marines who didn't make it home.

After a shower and lunch, it was off to school for Reece while Freddy caught up on whatever admin tasks Langley was sending his way. By dusk they'd be back on the range, which tonight meant long-distance precision shooting in low light. The rhythm of the training suited Reece well and reminded him of his days as a young enlisted SEAL in the pre-9/11 era, the lifestyle that led many to joke that the SEAL acronym stood for "Sleep, EAt, Lift," or as their Army brothers used to joke, "Sleep, EAt, and Lie around."

It felt good to be training alongside his old sniper buddy, honing his skills for the mission ahead.

"A file came in on Mo from Langley," Freddy said as they packed up their rifles under a beautiful starlit sky. "Makes for some interesting reading. I printed it and left it in the briefing room safe. Give it a look tonight. Might help shed some light on where he is and why he's turned."

Reece nodded. If his old friend really had switched sides after their time in Iraq and was now running a terrorist cell in Europe, Reece was going to have to be at the top of his game.

• • •

Later that night, Reece turned on a small lamp at his desk, opened the CIA's file on Mohammed Farooq, and began to read.

Mo's father had been an academic, educated first at the University of Baghdad, majoring in biology and then studying abroad, where he completed his Ph.D. in plant toxins from the University of East Anglia's School of Biological Sciences in Norwich, England. Returning to Iraq, he had found a home teaching and conducting research at his alma mater, eventually rising to chair the biological sciences department. Both of Mo's older sisters were studying at the university where their father taught and would sometimes stop by to visit him between classes. Mo had been blessed with his father's intellect and his mother's good looks, excelling in school and on the football pitch. He chased girls with his friends and ran a small black-market enterprise selling bootlegged CDs of American and European pop music that put some additional Iraqi dinar in his pocket. "Biology" and "plant toxins" didn't mean much to Mohammed. From his perspective, they were just something his dad lectured about in what seemed to be a fairly dull profession. Life was good for the popular young Iraqi, until his sisters did not return from university.

Pretending to be asleep that night, Mohammed strained to listen to his parents' hushed voices as they sat hunched around the small round dining table where they had all eaten together for as long as he could remember. From beneath the covers of his mat on the floor of the next room, Mo had risked a glance into the kitchen; the fear he saw etched across the faces of his mother and father would be forever imprinted on his memory. He distinctly heard his mother's strained voice whisper

"*Uday.*" It was just beginning to dawn on the young man that his sisters might never join them for dinner again.

His father had been a kind and thoughtful man, insisting on speaking and reading English and German in their house so that his children could live fuller, more prosperous lives. When he said goodbye to his only son the next morning, he did so in Arabic. That night, Mohammed and his mother waited up for a man who would never return. In the days of Saddam, one did not ask questions, particularly when those questions involved one of the president's sons.

Inquiries at the university went unanswered. Mo and his mother attempted to meet with school officials, only to be kept waiting indefinitely in the reception area. Dr. Farooq's name had been removed from his office door, and the entire room was empty, except for a desk and chair. It was as if he had never existed. Both mother and son knew better than to go to the authorities.

Six months later, his mother passed away in her sleep, and sixteen-year-old Mohammed was alone.

But Mohammed had a plan. He had learned patience from his parents and knew enough to realize that he needed training, intelligence, and access if he was to avenge them.

Even in a police state, there were ways to go unnoticed. As in most countries around the world, there was a subset of the population in Iraq's capital city that went almost ignored among its eight million inhabitants. The homeless were invisible, and Mohammed became one of them, joining the ranks of the unwanted, sleeping in the streets, learning to subsist from the alcoholics, drug abusers, criminals, and the mentally ill. Out of necessity, he learned to fight, to defend what was his, but more important, he learned how to think like a criminal, like a survivor. The logic he had learned from his father was applied practically in the back alleys of the ancient city. Under the constant threat of government sweeps and forced disappearances, Mohammed's black-market CD money provided just enough cash for meals, which he shared with those who passed along their knowledge.

When the kid known simply as Mo vanished, the rhythm of the dusty streets continued unabated. But Mohammed wasn't imprisoned by the secret police, nor was his body bloating in the Tigris. He was on his way north. North to those who lived in the mountains along the Turkish border. North to be either killed or accepted by the Kurdish Peshmerga, the military wing of Iraq's largest ethnic minority group. The Kurdish people had known nothing but war for centuries; rebellion was in their blood. Blurring the lines between a guerrilla force and standing army, Peshmerga translates as "those who face death," and Mohammed was ready to do just that. Exhausted and near death himself on arrival, he was at first a curiosity until his value was recognized by senior Peshmerga leaders. They decided he could be useful. Training began in earnest, and the boy from Baghdad started his formal education in irregular warfare.

When the CIA reactivated their network in Northern Iraq before the 2003 invasion, they were surprised to find a young Iraqi, fluent in English, German, Arabic, and Kurdish. Not yet in his midtwenties, Mohammed had trained and fought alongside his adopted Kurdish brothers and sisters, distinguishing himself in battle, and had been hardened by the atrocities of the Iraqi government. That government was not merely quelling an uprising, it was systematically conducting a campaign of genocide against the Kurdish people. From the CIA's perspective, Mohammed Farooq had all the qualities and attributes required of a deep-penetration agent in what would be the new Iraqi government. Unbeknownst to them at the time, Mohammed had another, more personal agenda.

As part of the CIA support of Peshmerga forces, Mohammed was released into the custody of his new masters. At a base in Jordan, he began a training program with U.S. Army Special Forces, building on his experience in Northern Iraq. The Agency had assembled a group of Iraqi exiles and selected Kurds for special operations training by two Army ODAs for what the trainees were told were leadership positions in the post-invasion Iraqi Army. As with most undertakings in the intelligence world, that was true only on the surface. At its heart, it was a selection process. Aptitude with firearms and explosives were tested, along with close-quarters combat and decision making under the stressors of urban combat simulations. The Agency's best polygraphers and psychologists were flown in from Northern Virginia to administer their exams, both to assess loyalties and establish a baseline for future scrutiny. Those who excelled eventually boarded a C17 that touched down sixteen hours later at Hurlburt Field, Florida. From there, they were driven in windowless vans to a classified CIA facility for indoctrination, further assessment, and doctorates in the darker arts of espionage under the expert tutelage of the Agency's Special Activities Division. The small group that graduated became known as the Scorpions, and in early 2003 they returned to Jordan, where they staged for war. Led by the CIA's Ground Branch, the Scorpions infiltrated Iraq prior to the official invasion to coordinate precision air strikes, incite rebellion to overthrow the regime, and assassinate high-ranking members of the Iraqi government. Of the fifty-two high-value targets on his issued deck of cards, Mohammed kept only one in his pocket: the ace of hearts, Uday Hussein.

A knock on the door pulled Reece out of the past.

"Yeah," he called out flipping the page.

The door opened, and Freddy leaned against the doorjamb, a bottle of water in his hand.

"Water?"

"Sure," Reece replied, turning in his chair to catch the toss from his friend.

"I told you it was interesting reading. Did you know all that?"

"Mo told me some of it but not in the detail here. This thing reads like a novel."

"Well, as you can see, the Agency invested a lot of time, energy, and effort, not to mention money, on him. The psychologists and analysts did a thorough job. Want to see your file?" Freddy asked with a smile.

"Ha! Not tonight. The psychoanalysis might be a bit much."

"Good call."

"What I can't figure out is why he would switch sides. He seems like the perfect spook. The background and right motivators are there. I just don't see how or why he goes rogue."

"Obviously, the big brains at Langley couldn't figure it out either. Get some rest, buddy. And let me know if that file sparks any ideas."

Sleep did not come easily. Reece's thoughts kept returning to a young orphan, living in the treacherous streets of Baghdad, dreaming of revenge.

CHAPTER 38

"MR. DONOVAN, I FEAR if I do not know the nature of your mission, I will not be able to assist as readily as I might."

"Sorry, Maajid, I think the initial idea was to get me trained up enough to pass off as a disgruntled veteran who converted to Islam, but Freddy mentioned that now I might go in as an aspiring novelist doing research, so I'm not really sure. I did my best to study the enemy while in the military, but I fear I fell short, uh . . . I don't mean that all Muslims are the enemy . . . it just came out that way."

Maajid smiled, his wise professor's eyes betraying the fact that he genuinely liked his new pupil.

"Mr. Donovan, I . . ."

"Maajid, how many times do I have to tell you that it's okay to call me James?"

"Ah, yes, James. Part of this training is also to familiarize you with your new last name. Mr. Donovan it is."

Reece smiled. They'd had this conversation before. He'd come to thoroughly enjoy his time spent with Maajid and never tired of hearing him speak. Maajid had been put through the wringer by his native country of Great Britain and a foreign one: Egypt. After what Reece had suffered from elements of his own government, he felt a certain kinship with Maajid. If Maajid could forgive, maybe Reece could, too.

"As I was saying, Mr. Donovan, if you could tell me the country in which you were going to attempt this foolish stunt, I could be of more use."

"I honestly don't know exactly where I'm going. I need to make contact with an old friend through the Muslim community, somewhere in Europe I think."

Reece smiled at the man he now considered a friend.

"Maajid, I wish we'd had you around a few years back. Maybe we wouldn't be in this mess of a global insurgency."

"Unfortunately, I was on the other side then, Mr. Donovan, as you well know."

They had discussed this many times, but Reece kept coming back to it. How someone who had been through what Maajid had experienced could be so positive and energetic was inspiring beyond words.

"I guess we are all on our own path, huh?"

"I can certainly affirm that, Mr. Donovan. It took more years than I care to remember, but I am at that stage in life where I have taken accountability for my past actions. My only desire is to pass along my experience so that others can make more informed decisions that influence the narrative and counternarrative by extremists on *both* sides, though you know I dislike characterizing things in such polarizing terms. It's not as easy as a *clash of civilizations*; it's more nuanced than that, as we've discussed before. This is not about destroying infrastructure or assassinating various so-called *leaders*. This is a war of ideology, and it won't be won or lost on the battlefield."

"Agreed," Reece said, shaking his head. "We can hit them every night where they sleep in Afghanistan, Iraq, Yemen, Syria, wherever they seek refuge, and still not defeat the *idea* that is militant Islam."

"Have I ever told you what Dr. Muhammad Badee' told me when we were imprisoned together in Mazrah Tora prison?" Maajid asked his student, referring to Cairo's infamous prison where he had spent considerable time. "He said, 'Ideas are bulletproof.'"

"Yeah, I've heard something similar before. I think it was 'You can't kill an ideology.' Kind of reminds me of our response to that same ideology with a 'War on Terror.' We declared war on a tactic, while what we are really doing is countering an idea. Politicians thought we could kill our way out of it. Maybe they thought we'd kill our way to their next election victory."

"Perhaps, Mr. Donovan, perhaps, but I urge you not to be too hard on them. To borrow and paraphrase from your Bible, *'They know not what they do.'*"

"I understand, but we trusted our leaders both elected and uniformed to study and understand the conflict. We had let things fester for so long that any other response wasn't even on the radar. It was war."

"Yes, and that is why after all these years, I wish to share my journey with those who can make a difference for future generations. My son in London will be on his way to college soon. I missed most of his life and he's never forgiven me. I let my hate of 'the West' guide my every move. From the fights with skinheads in Essex to my recruitment by Hizb al-Tahrir. I bought into the *us versus them* narrative and truly believed that a global caliphate would right the wrongs I felt from the bullying and beatings by the white fascists who roamed Essex looking for smaller groups of 'Pakis' to torment and harass. Today I feel sorry for them, but more important, I *understand* them. They fell for the same narrative, albeit the other side, but the same narrative nonetheless."

"How did prison not turn you into a more hardened jihadi like we always hear about on the news?"

"I'm not saying that never happens, Mr. Donovan. I'm saying that it didn't happen in my case. And, strangely enough, had I *not* been imprisoned in Egypt in the same cell block as Dr. Badee', I might either still be in there or I might be planning the next 9/11."

"Well, I guess I'm glad?" Reece said with a semi-confused look on his face.

"Ha! As strange as it sounds to say, I would not change a thing. It was just happenstance that I ended up in Mazrah Tora. I picked the wrong day to fly to Egypt to start my graduate-level Islamic studies program. July 7, 2005. Of course, I knew nothing of the attacks, though at the time I was so consumed by hate that I would have gladly assisted. As fate and Allah would have it, I was known to authorities for my outspoken criticism of the British government for its treatment of the Muslim community, unlike the bombers that day who were *clean*, as they say in intelligence circles."

That July day was one Reece knew well. Four al-Qaeda operatives wearing s-vests killed fifty-two people and wounded more than seven hundred in coordinated bombings across London. It was the first suicide bombing to target Great Britain and their deadliest terrorist attack up to that point since Pan Am Flight 103 was brought down over Lockerbie, Scotland, in 1988.

"Departing on a flight to Egypt hours prior to the attack put me on the MI5 and MI6 radar. When I landed in Cairo I was immediately arrested by the state security apparatus, Aman al-Dawlah. I was handcuffed, blindfolded, stripped naked, and thrown into a van with a few other unfortunate souls whose only crime that day was flying to Egypt."

Reece was enthralled. In the SEAL Teams, the old and often-quoted Sun Tzu saying "Know thy enemy" was usually followed by a class on Islam, thereby grouping "enemy" and "Islam" together for a platoon or troop of young, hard-charging frogmen who would rather be out training than stuck in a classroom, listening to a lecture from the intel shop by someone who had probably looked up most of the brief on Wikipedia. He had made so many Muslim friends in his travels over the years, he always found it hard to listen to the intelligence briefings focused on Islam.

"Do you know the difference between Islam and Islamism, Mr. Donovan?"

"I thought Islamism is the same as Islamic fundamentalism."

"Not precisely. I know we've discussed the basics over the past weeks, like the difference between Sunni and Shia, the various calls to prayer, and the Five Pillars of Islam. It is important to understand this next point, Mr. Donovan, and it took me seven years in an Egyptian prison to grasp it. Islam is a religion, just as Christianity is a religion. Islamism is the idea that a certain interpretation, any interpretation, of Islam must be imposed on society at large. It's a *political* movement, a *totalitarian* movement, with Islam as its vehicle, with the goal of eventually creating the *Khilafah*. Submit to Islam and join the movement or be put to the sword. The minority has hijacked the narrative and is gaining momentum and followers. I was one of those followers, Mr. Donovan. I recruited impressionable young men just like me to the movement. I hijacked their lives.

This is how I atone. I share my story with the younger minds coming up through the ranks at MI5 and MI6, and have been fortunate enough to do the same at your CIA, FBI, and occasionally the Department of State."

"And it was Dr. Badee' that changed your outlook and understanding of your religion."

"Not of my religion, Mr. Donovan, but of the *movement*. Though he is very old now and has accepted that he will die in his prison cell, Dr. Badee' is the current leader of the Muslim Brotherhood. It was he who smuggled Sayyid Qutb's Islamist manifesto out of Mazrah Tora in the early sixties. It is ironic that that very text ignited an already simmering movement of militant Islamism and inspired Osama bin Laden and Ayman al-Zawahiri to form al-Qaeda."

"So, how did you get out? How did anyone even find out where you were?" Reece asked, fascinated by the story.

Maajid looked at his watch. "That, Mr. Donovan, is a tale for another day," he said with a twinkle in his eye. "I fear we have gone too late as it is, and it is almost time for evening prayer."

"Thank you, Maajid. I'd like to meet your son one day."

Maajid paused. "Yes, I'd like to meet him again, too," he said, his voice trailing off with more than a tinge of sadness.

"And, Mr. Donovan, I sense our time here is coming to a close. Remember, the United States is the most powerful nation on earth, just as Great Britain was before her. Rome and the Mongols held that title as well, but more formidable than the dominance of those empires has always been the power of an *idea*. As those great powers rose and fell, *ideas* remained. Never forget that, Mr. Donovan. And now it is time for prayer."

CHAPTER 39

REECE WAS AWAKE, STARING up into the darkness, when he heard the dog barking in the distance. You might have the best plan, the most high-tech equipment, and the best-trained operators but the dogs could always give you away. He wasn't wearing his watch, but he figured it was about 4 a.m. Sleep hadn't come easy since the death of his family and SEAL brothers; he'd spent many an hour listening to the rolling seas, the sounds of the African bush, and, here in Morocco, the hum of his room's AC unit.

The screaming of a vehicle engine at high RPMs and a handful of outgoing 5.56mm rounds sent him rolling off his bed and onto the floor before a massive shock wave blew the glass from his bedroom window.

Reece knew what it was immediately. *VBIED—just like in Iraq.*

Who the hell had found them out here? Not now, Reece. Win the fight.

A switch flipped in his mind. He was no longer at a safe house in Morocco. He was at war.

Wearing only boxers and a T-shirt, with no time to get fully suited up, Reece slid into his running shoes as he processed the situation. He was sure that the vehicle-borne explosion had breached the wall of the compound. If this was a coordinated attack, which he believed it was, whoever had targeted them would be surging in at any moment. He'd seen this tactic before.

A second blast hit the back side of the compound, near the buildings where the other occupants lived. As he crawled quickly across the room and felt for his plate carrier in the darkness, he could hear the unmistakable sound of suppressed rounds coming from the window of the room down the hall; Freddy Strain was already engaging targets.

Reece did a quick rundown of friendly forces: Freddy, four GRS security personnel, and his Islamic studies teacher, Maajid. He quickly pulled on his armor and helmet, less for protection than for the advantage of the NODs mounted to it. He found his MP7 leaning against the wall and pulled the two-point sling over his head as he activated the IR aiming laser. He wore Peltor tactical ear protection with a boom microphone integrated into his helmet but without a radio there was no way to communicate with the other friendlies. Knowing that Freddy was overwatch at the window, Reece cracked his door and peered into the hallway.

Whoever had planned this was following the now-familiar script from Iraq and Afghanistan of using a vehicle to breach the perimeter before flooding the compound with fanatical men armed with small arms and suicide vests. The lack of gunfire from the perimeter indicated that the GRS contractor who had fired at the approaching vehicle before it exploded had been either killed or seriously wounded by the blast.

The hallway was dark and quiet in the green glow of his NODs, only the popping of Freddy's outgoing rounds audible over the ringing in Reece's ears. Reece peered over the balcony railing and saw no sign of movement below. He crept slowly and quietly down the stairs, his lightweight running shoes masking his movement.

Close-quarters combat is a tricky game of angles, and Reece used his years of training and experience to his advantage as he made his way toward the front of the structure. As he "sliced the pie" of the corner that led into the home's grand entryway, incoming full-auto gunfire sprayed across the front of the building, shattering the windows. Those rounds sounded suppressed. *What the hell is going on?* He took a knee behind an antique bookshelf and could hear rounds impacting the building's thick stone walls. Fortunately, they did not penetrate. *Good cover.*

Reece rose to his feet and spotted muzzle flashes through the window's opening. A dozen-round burst from his submachine gun sent the shooter to the afterlife. He checked to ensure that no one had entered the room behind him and moved closer to the window to get a better angle on the area outside. He could see a ragged black hole in the perimeter wall forty yards away, the blinding flames of the burning vehicle casting strange shadows of twisted metal across the yard. Two men carrying M4s sprinted through the breach, running laterally across Reece's vantage point. He held his fire, confused by the sight of weapons and gear typically associated with friendlies. When they aimed their fully automatic fire at the upper level where Freddy held the high ground, he snapped out of his paralysis. He led the first man and put a burst into him that sent him tumbling forward onto the ground. The second runner tripped over the falling man, causing Reece to miss him high. He adjusted his aim and stitched the remainder of his magazine into him as he attempted to regain his feet. A head shot into the front of his face dropped him for good.

M4s. Why are we being attacked by a unit using M4s? Later, Reece. You know what to do.

Words from Reece's father came to him: *If something just doesn't look right, it's probably not.*

Reece took a moment to study the men he had put down and was surprised that one was attempting to regain his feet. Too many men to count had been killed by people they thought were dead.

Reece took carful aim, depressed the trigger, and sent a round through the PVS-15 night vision attached to a helmet similar to the one worn by Reece and into the left eye socket of his attacker.

Night vision? I need to see one of these guys closer up.

Reece stripped the empty magazine from the weapon and inserted a fresh one from a pouch on the front of his armor before hitting the slide release and sending the bolt home. A firefight erupted behind the main house, from the direction of the security contractors' building. The longer strings of fire were being answered by short bursts from what sounded like a belt-fed weapon, which let Reece know that at least one of the GRS contractors was alive and fighting.

As Reece scanned for targets, a window broke behind him and suppressed gunfire erupted into the room. An attacker had made his way to the back of the house and was firing his M4 with its muzzle stuck through the window. Reece dropped prone, behind a large sofa, effectively pinned down by the shooter.

Only concealment, not cover. Move, Reece!

The rounds blistered the wall above his head, filling the room with dust and sending tiny red-hot bullet fragments into Reece's exposed legs. He crawled toward the heavy wooden front door, thinking that he could head outside to maneuver behind the shooter. As he reached the door, two more M4-wielding attackers fired at the front of the house from the direction of the breach, their rounds thudding into the walls and door, leaving Reece with no means of escape.

The fully automatic fire from the rear of the house continued, chewing the room's fine furnishings into splinters. Reece had a fragmentation grenade in a pouch on his armor, but the window he'd have to throw it through was small and he couldn't risk the explosive bouncing off the wall back in his direction.

"Freddy! I'm pinned down here!" Reece yelled, hoping that his partner could hear him over the sounds of battle.

The firing resumed, his attackers unable to get a good angle on their target. Time slowed as muzzle flashes illuminated the smoke, airborne plaster and concrete dust filling the house, the entire room flashing like a strobe-lit nightclub through the green display of the NODs, a surreal and visceral assault on the senses.

Nothing back from Freddy, which meant he was in a fight of his own, or dead.

Reece had to move. He waited for the shooter to change magazines, then rose to his knees to unbolt the front door. As he did, he heard something thud onto the floor to his right and roll across the tile. The grenade spun like a top five yards away, its fuse burning rapidly toward the explosive charge and coiled wire concealed beneath the outside casing.

Reece yanked open the door and button-hooked through to escape the blast. His sudden emergence from the door surprised the man who had tossed the frag, stacked outside preparing to make entry following detonation. Reece couldn't stop his forward momentum and found himself crashing into the team who had moments before held the upper hand.

Speed. Surprise. Violence of action.

Forcing his attacker's rifle up and out of the way as he tumbled into the first man in the stack, the strong smell of sweat filling his nostrils, Reece drove the suppressed MP7 into his opponent's throat, zipping a burst of 4.6mm rounds through the enemy's neck and into the face of the man behind him.

The thunderous detonation of the grenade sent shards of the already shattered window into the side of Reece's head and shoulder as his momentum sent him into the last man in the stack. Momentarily confused by the two men in front of him dropping to the ground and from the dust and debris exploding through the open door and window, he was not ready for the full weight and fury of the man who had suddenly appeared like a vision of death from out of the chaos.

With his NODs dusted out from the explosion, Reece felt more than saw the man in full battle gear before him, his MP7 caught up in the collision of man and gear. Face-to-face with the enemy, his MP7 knocked to the side, Reece seamlessly transitioned to the knife on the front of his body armor, crashing the gap and indexing the chest plate on the man before him with his elbow, using it as a reference point to sink the blade into his throat. Quickly, Reece stepped left to sweep the man's leg and put his startled enemy on the ground.

A knife fight is not like it's portrayed in the movies. It's close. It's personal. It's visceral. It's the most primal and devastating thing one man can do to another, and sometimes men die hard. Reece did not shy from the task. From his dominant mount position, he drove his shoulder down and into the pommel of his blade, driving it deeper into the unprotected neck of his adversary, whose body, mind, and spirit were finding the reserve of strength and energy known only to those on the brink of death.

Reece grabbed his opponent's NODs, twisting them from his head, finding the carotid artery with the edge of his blade and trapping the arm while moving his blade just below the armpit and driving it into the lungs. Avoiding the body armor designed to protect, Reece used it as a guide. Sliding perpendicular to find the side control position, Reece transitioned his blade just below the body armor and above the pelvis, stabbing it in and ratcheting it back and forth to create a massive wound channel in the man's guts.

In the violence that is hand-to-hand combat, seconds seem like minutes and minutes seem like hours. Only five seconds had elapsed since Reece had connected with the man whose life he was now extinguishing. Even with the blood draining from his body, Reece's opponent fought on. Just like countless men over the centuries, he didn't yet know he was dead. Reece felt the man's hands flailing, reaching in adrenaline-fueled desperation for the grenade Reece wore on the left side of his armor. Moving immediately back to the mount, ripping his grenade from the dying man's grasp, Reece sank the blade into his opponent's left eye, before cutting down across the man's face to the back of his head toward the mandible. He worked his own left arm around the back of the enemy's head, where it met his other hand holding the blade. Reece's face was pressed against the side of his opponent's head as he worked the blade deeper and deeper into his brain stem until the thrashing body went limp. Reece held the deadly embrace for a moment, before disengaging the knife and sliding off the corpse beneath him.

Situational awareness, Reece.

Breathing heavily, Reece straightened his helmet and pushed himself back against the building that had minutes before been his sanctuary, scanning the compound before him as the discipline of his years of training took over. Resheathing the blade that had just saved his life, Reece caught a glimpse of the inscription. Interrupted by blood, bile, and sticky white slivers of bone and brain were the words *Pamwe Chete*; the gift from Rich Hastings had taken another soul.

Smoothly bringing his MP7 up into his workspace, Reece pulled a magazine from his armor and performed a tactical reload, retaining the partially spent one for later use. Without pockets to stow the magazine, he shoved it into the empty radio pouch on his rig. Seeing no sign of movement in his immediate vicinity, he knelt at the side of the man he had just killed and removed his helmet. The man's face was a bloody mess but something about it seemed vaguely familiar. *Do I know him?*

He wore desert boots, a chest rig over his body armor, and an older Kevlar helmet. But what really interested Reece were his NODs and uniform. PVS-15s meant one thing—they were U.S. backed. The desert tiger-stripe uniforms meant something else—CIA.

Later, Reece. Make sense of this later. Win the fight. Prioritize and execute. Where is the nearest threat?

Taking a wide angle, Reece moved around the side of the house. He was doing the most natural thing a man could do: he was hunting.

After the grenade blast, the firing coming from the back of the building had stopped, which meant that the shooter could be on the move. Reece crept quietly but quickly down the ten-foot-wide alley between the side of the house and the perimeter wall where there was no cover. He needed to get through the lethal funnel as fast as he could. He could still hear the pitched battle at the back of the compound, where things sounded like they had reached a stalemate.

As he approached the back of the house, Reece had the strong urge to toss a grenade around the corner, but, not knowing the location of the other friendlies, he held back. He eased around, step by step, and saw the bright streak of Freddy's IR laser coming from the upstairs window. Knowing the yard was covered, Reece rounded the corner to clear the area close to the house that would be below his partner's line of sight. Expecting to find his target directly behind the building, Reece was surprised when he saw no sign of movement. Assuming that the man had moved around the opposite side of the house, Reece checked back the way he had come to ensure that he wasn't being outmaneuvered.

Nothing. Where did he go?

Then he heard it: a scraping sound above him. He looked up to find a man, just ten feet away, scaling the side of the building using a water pipe as a ladder, with his weapon slung at his side. Ordinarily he would have seen him when he rounded the corner, but the narrow vertical view through his NODs prevented it. The climber was obviously planning to shoot through the window above to take out the SEAL sniper, who was firing from a few feet back in the room. Freddy would never see it coming. Reece calmly put his IR laser on the figure's backside and gave him a long burst. He could hear the hollow sound of the tiny suppressed rounds impacting flesh and a quiet yelp of pain. The impact of the body hitting the hard ground was louder than either, and Reece put two rounds into his head for good measure. Knowing the enemy had a similar technological advantage of NODs, he resisted the urge to make a circling motion in front of the window with his laser to let his partner know of his position.

"*Freddy,*" Reece whispered as loudly as he dared "*Freddy!*"

"Reece, that you?" came the response.

"Yeah, I'm down here."

"You okay?"

"I'm good. These guys have NODs."

"I know. What the *hell*?"

"I'm going to go help the boys out back."

"Roger that, I'm coming down."

A minute later the back door opened and Freddy, dressed identically to Reece except that he was wearing pants, emerged, carrying his HK416.

"Do you sleep in that gear?" Reece asked his buddy, half in jest.

"Says the guy with no pants. Hey, you recognize the uniforms?" Freddy asked.

"You know I do. Let's get this done and then figure it out. Try to take one alive to question."

"Hey, are you shot?" Freddy asked, reaching toward his friend.

"No. I'm good. It's not my blood."

"Roger that."

"Sounds like they breached the wall in two places with VBIEDs," Reece said.

"Yeah, I've taken out about a dozen guys back here. You?"

"Four dead guys out front and Spider-Man here who was coming to get you."

Freddy looked down at the body and then looked up at the water pipe, putting two and two together.

"*Shit*, thanks, bro."

"My pleasure."

"Let's move down the left side here, circle behind the barn, and see if we can get behind them. I couldn't see them from upstairs, but I could hear them."

"Let's do it."

No further conversation was needed as they moved toward the gunfight. Freddy led the way, since he had the more capable weapon in the open space of the compound. The little MP7 was great at close range, but Reece suddenly felt way undergunned in the open area between the buildings. They maintained laser discipline, knowing the lasers would be visible through the enemy's NODs. Luckily for them, the enemy was not as disciplined.

As they approached the large storage barn, they could see infrared beams darting around the courtyard. Freddy motioned upward, indicating that he would look for an elevated position. Reece gave him an exaggerated nod and continued along the backside of the building to flank their aggressors. Even though suppressed, the firing became louder as Reece approached the corner of the building. Suppressed meant just that: suppressed, not silent.

Reece worked his way around the corner and found six men twenty-five yards from his position, all facing away from him, using one of the compound's vehicles for cover as they fired toward the GRS building. He ducked back behind the barn and pulled the fragmentation grenade from his kit, removing the electrician's tape from the pull ring. He held the spoon between the web of his right-hand thumb and pointer finger, then yanked the pull ring clear of the device and tossed the baseball-sized bomb around the corner toward the cluster of combatants. The explosion was followed immediately by screams. Reece took a knee and methodically pumped rounds into the heads of each of the writhing bodies on the ground before him.

The GRS contractor who had been guarding the gate stopped fir-

ing, aware that friendlies had moved in among his targets. Still, Reece
sprinted across the open ground behind the now-burning truck and past
the six dead men so as not to be in his line of fire. He would sweep the
back corner of the perimeter and come in at the rear of the GRS building to ensure that no one was behind their position. He moved past one
of the two small staff houses and scanned for any sign of movement. He
heard a scuffle behind him and spun quickly to see two figures struggling
fifteen yards away. He took a step toward them when a white-hot explosion blew him from his feet.

CHAPTER 40

REECE WAS UNDERWATER. IT was pitch-dark. He put his hand in front of his face but couldn't see anything. He couldn't breathe but there was no panic, only peace. A tiny light, as if glowing through a pinhole, emerged in the depths below him. He swam toward it, the water thick as jelly; it was like trying to swim in winter clothing. He heard a faint voice that sounded like Lauren's; he swam harder downward toward it. The voice sounded garbled under the water, but became increasingly louder and clearer.

"James . . . James . . ."

He swam as hard as he could, the voice morphing from his late wife's voice to one with a tinge of an Eastern European accent. He felt himself floating toward the surface, an unseen force pulling him away from the light. Suddenly the light was blinding; he blinked away from it and turned his head to avoid it.

"James, James, you okay, buddy?" The red penlight shifted from his eyes to his chest and he felt a hand moving over his body, searching for wounds. As he regained his senses, he realized that he was on his back and one of the contractors was administering first aid. He pushed the man's hand away and sat up quickly, reaching around frantically until he found his weapon slung at his side.

"You good?"

"I think so," Reece responded in a hoarse tone.

The man kneeling in front of him was wearing black "Ranger panty" running shorts, flip-flops, and a plate carrier. His NODs were pushing upward on his helmet and his belt-fed MK46 machine gun was sitting nearby on its bipod, barrel a glowing white.

"You'll be okay, man. I like your outfit," he said, indicating Reece's boxers.

Freddy ran up and knelt beside the two men.

"Reece, you alive? That guy in an s-vest came out of nowhere. I was changing mags and couldn't get on him fast enough. Somebody tackled him right before he blew it."

"Yeah, man, I'm fine." Reece shook his head to clear the cobwebs.

"If you can watch this breach in the wall and make sure no one gets behind us, Brett and I can clear the rest of the place," Freddy said, nodding toward the GRS man.

"Check, I'm on it."

The sun rose an hour later, bathing the smoldering compound in the pink radiance of morning. Fires, big and small, were scattered about from the various explosions and bodies were strewn everywhere. All had been quiet since the last explosion that had almost killed Reece, and they had confirmed that the compound was secure, at least for now. One of the security contractors had been killed in the opening VBIED blast while another had been wounded shortly after the incursion began. By Freddy's count, there were at least twenty-three enemy dead. Reece was cut up and bruised and probably had a concussion but was fine otherwise.

He rose to his feet slowly and walked stiffly toward where the suicide bomber had detonated his vest, examining the grisly scene.

Pieces of human flesh and bone were scattered across the blackened ground. When he saw it, he froze; it was a foot, severed at the calf but unbloodied and still wearing a brown leather sandal. He recognized it immediately. It had belonged to Maajid, his teacher. The man who had taught him so much about his own beloved religion in hopes of stamping out the darkness within it had died protecting him. Reece knelt and prayed to his own God silently, an act of which he knew Maajid would approve.

Within an hour of daylight, a twelve-man Crisis Response Force from the 10th Special Forces Group was fast-roping into the compound from a pair of hovering MH-60 aircraft, the powerful rotor wash turning the entire area into a dust bowl. They had been working with government forces in nearby Mali when the emergency call went out from the GRS unit on-site. They were hours closer than other units of similar capabilities in Italy and Djibouti, and were routed directly to the emergency. Unlike the debacle in Benghazi, they had launched on very little information and headed toward the fight.

The MultiCam-clad Special Forces men fanned out as soon as they hit the ground, forming a defensive perimeter and deploying a sniper and machine gunner to the roof of the main house. The team's highly capable medic went to work on the wounded former Marine GRS contractor as the unit's commander approached the two SEALs, who were sitting on the tailgate of a pickup. He was five feet six and stocky with a face of dark stubble, full tattoo sleeves on both arms poking from below his Crye combat shirt. A 10.5-inch-barreled M4 hung across the front of his body armor. He looked too old for his rank, and Reece assumed that he was a fellow enlisted man turned officer.

"I'm Mack, team leader. You guys okay?"

"Thanks for coming, Mack. I'm Freddy." The exhausted operator shook the Army captain's extended hand.

Mack turned his gaze to Reece and his eyes widened. "I know you! You're James Reece!"

"No, I'm not . . . I get that all the time, though."

"Ah, yeah . . . well, let's just say that if you were James Reece I'd want to shake your hand."

"Well, in that case you'll just have to settle for mine." Reece took the man's hand and shook it warmly.

"You need the medic?" Mack asked, nodding toward Reece, who looked like he'd bathed in blood.

"I think I'm good. Just a little rattled from that s-vest."

"So, what in the hell happened here? What is this place? They told us it was a CIA compound."

"It's a training site," Strain responded. "They hit us in the middle of the night. Breached the wall with VBIEDs in two places. One of the GRS guys was killed immediately and another one was wounded, as you know. He and the other remaining contractor kept the bad guys busy back here while we fought them off the house."

"Looks like you guys kicked some ass. Sorry we couldn't get here in time to help."

"No worries, it didn't last very long. GRS took the brunt of it. They hit the wrong end of the compound in-force if they were trying to get us. You actually made it here faster than I thought."

"You can thank the 160th for that," Mack replied, referring to the Army's 160th Special Operations Aviation Regiment, which was widely regarded as having the best helicopter pilots in the world. "Any ideas on who they might be? Seems too coordinated for locals, and the gear is almost better than ours."

"I have an idea," Reece replied.

"Well, my team will run biometrics on them. If they're on any databases, we'll know ASAP."

"Sounds good. Thanks, Mack."

"I've got to check on my team. Holler if you need anything. We have a perimeter set up and there's a Pred on station, so rest easy."

Reece nodded as the Special Forces captain jogged off toward the main house.

"You know who they were, don't you, Freddy?"

"I do. But I can't bring myself to believe it."

"They were Agency trained, buddy. Someone at Langley wants us dead."

"We've trained and outfitted a few different units in this part of the world, Reece. Some of them are not under Agency control anymore, but they still have our weapons and haven't forgotten our training."

"Is it possible that someone inside doesn't want us to take down Nawaz? Even crazier, could Nawaz have someone in the CIA?" Reece asked.

"That doesn't seem possible, but stranger things have happened."

"Remember what Hastings told us the night before we left Moz?"

"Yeah, I remember," Freddy confirmed. "He told us not to trust the

CIA. More specifically, he warned us not to trust the politicians that control the CIA."

"Maybe he was right."

"I'm sure the DST is on their way," Freddy said, changing topics and referring to the Moroccan secret police. "We need to get you out of here. CRF can stay and secure the site while we drive to the embassy. We're obviously compromised."

"Roger that. I'll get packed up."

"Don't be a tough guy. Why don't you go see the Eighteen-Delta before that shit gets infected," the former SEAL Senior Chief said, using the military occupational shorthand used to classify Special Forces medics.

"I will. Freddy, who knew we were here?"

"It's a short list. And I'm going to find out everyone who was on it."

· · ·

They were halfway to Rabat when a call came through on the Sat phone. Freddy mostly listened, chiming in only occasionally in affirmation, then ended the call.

"Change of plans. We're headed to Istanbul."

"What's in Istanbul?"

"It's not 'what' but 'who.' Mo's in Istanbul, at least that's what the analysts think."

"Istanbul. Great place to go to ground."

"We need to hit the embassy in Rabat to pick up your passport and then we'll head straight to the airfield. They have a clean identity for you, and they've wiped your data off the facial recognition databases. You're still technically a wanted man. We don't want some cop in Turkey taking you down."

"Just like that?"

"Just like that, Reece."

CHAPTER 41

IN THE SPY NOVELS he'd read, the CIA always flew around in private jets, so Reece was a bit disappointed when their ride turned out to be a twin-turboprop MC-12W, a military version of the King Air 350ER. This particular model was set up for electronic surveillance missions and must have been the closest aircraft available. The plane's narrow cabin was packed with what looked to be complicated electronic warfare gear, making accommodations a bit cramped. As professional soldiers, both Reece and Freddy knew that you took sleep when you could and were out within twenty minutes of takeoff.

It was 10 p.m. local by the time they touched down at Istanbul Ataturk International, a smaller facility on the European side of the Bosphorus Strait. They were waved through Passport Control thanks to their black diplomatic passports, their gear bags and weapons cases sealed as diplomatic pouches, exempting them from inspection by customs officials. A fresh-faced kid who looked to be in his midtwenties met them just outside the secure area and led them to a nondescript white van in the loading area. Reece guessed that he was the junior man at the local CIA station, but he had the good sense to sit up front and not ask any questions of the shaggy-looking commandos in the backseat. Thanks to the late hour, the ride to the consulate took only thirty minutes. Reece shook his head in amusement when they passed a Burger King just before turning toward the American compound.

After a good night's sleep in small but modern rooms on the consulate grounds, Reece and Freddy were guided to the CIA section, which constituted an entire wing of the top floor of the building. Their escort left them in a secure conference room, where a coffee mess was set up on the long rectangular table. Reece was pleasantly surprised to see they had both honey and cream at the ready.

Five minutes later, the chief of station breezed into the room holding a tall cup of Starbucks. Kelly Hampden was forty-five but could probably pass herself off as being a decade younger. Those who met her professionally were often surprised to learn she was the ranking CIA officer in Turkey. She stood five feet eleven and still had the physique from her college days swimming for Princeton. She wore a simple blue pantsuit over a white silk blouse, and her light brown hair was still a bit damp from her shower. A mother of two small children, she carefully juggled her home life with her CIA career, as well as her "cover for status" position as a Deputy Political and Economic Affairs Officer for the Department of State. Reece liked her instantly.

"Good morning, gentlemen, I'm Kelly. Did you get coffee?"

"Yes, ma'am," both men said in unison.

"I'm Freddy Strain," the CIA man said, shaking her extended hand across the table. "And this is James Donovan."

"Nice to meet you both." She smiled warmly. "We have a video teleconference set up with Langley, so let's get this thing running."

She used a remote control to operate a large LCD screen on the wall at the end of the room. Within moments, the smiling face of an Asian female who looked like she belonged in a college sorority filled the screen.

"Good morning, guys! I'm Nicole Phan. I'm an analyst at the CTC," she said, referring to the CIA's Counterterrorism Center. "We have some exciting news: we believe with a high degree of certainty that Mohammed Farooq is in Turkey." The young analyst spoke with such enthusiasm, Reece could tell that she loved her job. "One of his lieutenants, Aadam el-Kader, was spotted on a surveillance camera outside a bank near the Arap Mosque in the Karaköy neighborhood and he pinged on the NSA's facial recognition database. Our data people dug into the mosque's computers and found a series of donations by a Waseef Hamade, which is a suspected alias of Mohammed. The most recent donation was made last week, so we assess there is a high likelihood that he's still in the area."

"That fits," Freddy responded. "Any idea where he's living, what he's driving, establishments he frequents?"

"I wish I had more on that front, but that's all we know for now. We'll keep working it. This all popped within the past forty-eight hours."

"Well, thanks so much for getting it to us so quickly. Anything new on Nawaz?"

"Unfortunately, no. He is notoriously cautious about communicating electronically. We believe all his planning is done in person or via courier. He's learned from watching us target his contemporaries."

"Well, keep us posted. If we are able to make contact with Mohammed, we'd sure like to be able to corroborate anything he tells us about Nawaz via technical means. Otherwise, this is all going to happen based off single-source HUMINT."

"We do have some other interesting information, though," Nicole continued. "The Special Forces team uploaded the fingerprints they scanned from the men who attacked your compound in Morocco. We ran them through BATS and AFIS, and it turns out that almost all were members of an Iraqi commando unit: Mohammed Farooq's former commando unit. As you both know, that was a CIA-run program. What you might not know is that when we withdrew from Iraq in 2011, we attempted to keep running them through Iraqi officers we'd recruited during the war, but in all the chaos of the drawdown and withdrawal of forces we lost control. It's been rumored that they have become a death squad of sorts and hire out as mercenaries if it's approved by their officers and the money is right."

"Did I help train any of them?" Reece asked.

"They ranged from 2007 to 2014 and were all still active on the unit's roster. One set of prints came back as a Captain Salih Daraji. His time overlaps with yours, Mr. Donovan."

Reece nodded, remembering the face he'd last seen covered in blood as he'd pulled his knife from Captain Daraji's brain stem in the dirt of the CIA compound.

"So, you're saying an active, CIA-trained Iraqi commando unit traveled to Morocco to attack a U.S. compound?" Freddy asked.

"That's exactly what I'm saying. Crazy, huh? Somebody doesn't like you boys very much."

"Solid assessment," Freddy acknowledged. "You said *almost all* were part of the STU. Who were the others?"

"The two suicide bombers were unidentifiable. What parts we could find didn't link to anyone in our databases. We do have a source in Libya who's reported that two recruits being developed as suicide bombers are missing. And get this, one was only sixteen."

"As horrible as that is, it makes sense," Freddy offered. "The STU is a direct-action-focused unit, not fanatical suicide bombers, but they wouldn't hesitate to use someone recruited to wear an s-vest to get the job done or place blame for an operation elsewhere. Thank you for your help, Langley."

"No worries, reach out if you need us!" Nicole smiled warmly as she ended the conference.

"She certainly was chipper," Reece said, sipping his coffee.

"If this station can support in any way, just let me know," Kelly said.

"What do you have on that mosque and neighborhood?" Reece asked. "Any assets inside?"

"I'll get you what we have. For now, I'll give you a quick lay of the land. Are you two familiar with the state of affairs here in Turkey?"

"We'd love a refresher," Freddy answered.

"Okay, well, as you may or may not know, Turkey is sliding quickly from a secular nation to an increasingly intolerant Islamic state. They've rediscovered their identity and are begging to flex their muscles. Things were already heading in that direction but, after the attempted coup in 2016, it's gone into overdrive. This is a country with eighty-five thousand mosques and they're building more every day. The imams are all government employees, so assume that when you step foot inside, everything you say will be reported to the MIT, the National Intelligence Organization. Hostility toward the West, and the U.S. specifically, is snowballing. The U.S. has over one thousand personnel at Incirlik Air Base, ████ ███████████████████████████. During the coup attempt, the Turks cut off power and the base was encircled by a mob incited by the government-controlled imams. Not usually how allies act. Ordinarily, I'd be hesitant to put an American into a mosque in this environment, but in this case, your status as a fugitive may be an asset."

"James Donovan is a wanted man? That's news to me, Ms. Hampden," Reece said.

"I'm sorry, you look so much like someone named James Reece who made the news last year."

"Honest mistake."

"We'll keep this between us girls. In all seriousness, though, this is an absolute priority mission, so you have our complete support. You can use this conference room as your office if you like. My extension is 5150. This line is secure," she said, motioning to a phone on a side table as she prepared to leave, "if you need to reach out to Langley. And gentlemen, good hunting."

. . .

"What are you thinking, Reece?" Freddy's tone turned all business.

"I'm wondering just what in the hell is going on here."

"You've got history with that Iraqi unit. Any theories?"

"I'm thinking Landry."

"What do you mean?"

"Think about it: He stayed on with that program after I left in '06 and continued to work with Mo and his squadron. Now he's disappeared and the men he trained show up at our door in the middle of the Moroccan desert? Too much of a coincidence for me."

"What was he like?" Freddy asked. "I never worked with him."

"Jules Landry is a shady character, the kind of guy that gives the Agency a bad reputation. He was a one-way street; he'd take whatever info you had but never show you his cards. I never really trusted him. He was a sick bastard, too."

"How so?"

"He'd get a few beers in him and then wander over to the Iraqi side of the compound where the detainees were kept. One night I couldn't sleep and was outside getting a late-night workout in to clear my head. I heard a scream coming from that direction, so I went over to investigate. He was alone in a cell with a detainee he had tied to a chair naked. He had a knife in one hand and a Taser in the other. I yanked him out of there and put him in the dirt. He was drunk, so it wasn't hard. Then I locked him in a cell and called my Agency contact at the embassy. I never saw Landry again."

"Surprised a guy like that made it through the psych eval. I'll call the counterintel guys and see if they have anything on him."

"That's a good place to start; in the meantime we have to figure out how to make contact with Mo."

• • •

Within an hour of his request to Langley, Strain had an initial counterintelligence report on Jules Landry emailed to him. Most of the materials were from his personnel file. Strain read them aloud: "Lafayette, Louisiana, native, came into the Agency as a contractor in 2003 after two deployments to Iraq as a Marine NCO. Assigned to the CIA's Special Tactics Unit, Baghdad, in 2005 and ran the program beginning in 2006. Rotated back and forth to Iraq and stayed on with the program when conventional forces were pulled out in late 2011. Requested emergency leave in June of 2013 and disappeared after his flight landed in Frankfurt. He went to ground and the Agency hasn't heard from him since. Passport hasn't been used. He was rumored to be working as a mercenary in Syria but that was never substantiated."

"Nothing about my report that he was torturing prisoners?"

"Nothing I can see."

"That's unbelievable! Sounds like they just reinserted him into the STU after I left. How does that make any sense?"

"I don't know, Reece. Maybe he has someone looking out for him?"

"Possibly. I'd like to know who that is. Hey, when did the Syrian Civil War start?"

"Middle of 2011, if I recall," Freddy answered.

"And ISIS swept Anbar in early 2014?"

"Yep. With Mo going missing in December of 2013."

Reece tilted his head back and exhaled, pausing for several seconds. "Who recruited Landry to the CIA?"

"It doesn't say but I'm sure I can find out."

. . .

There was a knock at the door and, almost immediately, the lock clicked open and Kelly Hampden's head poked into the room.

"Am I interrupting?"

"Not at all, please," Freddy responded.

She closed the door and took a seat.

"Here's what I have on the Arap Mosque: it's actually an old Catholic church that was taken over by the Ottomans. They call it the 'Arap Mosque' because after Spain exiled the Andalusian Arabs in 1492, that's where they settled—*arap* means 'Arab.' It's a relatively small mosque that serves the Beyoglu district. One of our local assets worships there. We didn't ask him about Mo because we didn't want to risk tipping him off, but he says that the imam is very moderate. He doesn't think there are any jihadi links with the mosque or its members. It's a Western, upscale part of the city, so that's not unusual."

"Mo can fit in anywhere," Reece said. "He also never struck me as deeply religious, so it sounds like his kind of place. He could go through the motions of looking like a young, progressive Muslim. Let's assume he's living nearby; any recommendations on how to get noticed in that community?"

"You'll be noticed all right. I'd recommend we put you up at the Tomtom Suites. I know, it sounds goofy, but it's the nicest spot in that area, really modern. It's about a mile from the mosque. We are putting you in as an aspiring novelist doing research on Islam's influence on Turkey. It gives you a reason to be there asking questions and taking notes. Make yourself seen in the hotel bar and the local cafés. My guess is that an operator like him is going to have a local network and, if we're lucky, he'll approach you rather than you having to work your way into the mosque.

I know you've been trained, but that's just really risky in my mind. So much can go wrong, especially in this climate."

Freddy turned to Reece. "Sounds like we need to get you some new clothes."

"May I also suggest a haircut and a beard trim?" Kelly Hampden said with apparent amusement. "Give me your sizes and I'll send someone shopping for you."

CHAPTER 42

BY EVENING, THEY HAD an initial plan in place, and Reece had a new wardrobe. It was a bit contemporary for his taste, but he convinced himself that it was a form of camouflage. Freddy had wandered down to the consulate's detachment of Marines and located a lance corporal who served as the de facto barber for the security element; nearly every military unit had someone who made a few extra bucks cutting hair. Reece was a bit nervous given the "high and tight" standards of the Corps, but the kid from Chicago did a great job. Reece emerged looking less like a biblical character and more like a dapper city dweller with collar-length hair and a neatly trimmed beard.

"You look like a hipster" was Freddy's only comment.

The next morning, Reece traded his faded T-shirt for a fitted blue oxford along with dark jeans, a tan linen sport coat, and brown leather boots. The remainder of his new wardrobe went into a nylon duffel along with some of his casual clothing and workout gear. A tan messenger bag contained various smaller items, including spare magazines and a suppressor for the SIG 365 concealed inside his waistband. A newly issued iPhone was equipped with various useful apps along with an extremely sophisticated VPN, which made his communications as secure as the NSA could make them.

When he climbed into the back of the Mercedes SUV alongside

Freddy in the underground parking garage, he made the conscious mental shift from James Reece: former SEAL commando and CIA contractor to James Donovan: aspiring novelist.

The driver, a local CIA case officer, took a circuitous route from the consulate to the Gayrettepe metro station, making frequent turns to ensure that they weren't being followed. Freddy bid Reece good luck as the SUV approached the curb.

"I'll see you when I see you."

He rode down the escalator into the modern subway station and made a show of examining the arrival and departure screens. He pulled his phone from his pocket and pretended to read a text message before taking the up escalator back to the street level among a gaggle of arriving passengers. A line of four yellow Hyundai taxis sat outside the station's entrance and Reece motioned for the lead driver to open his trunk. Stowing his duffel inside, he retained the smaller bag, showing the driver a printed reservation for the Tomtom Suites.

This was Reece's first time seeing Istanbul's grandeur in daylight. The historic city of seventeen million residents had been the seat of both the Byzantine and Ottoman empires, bridging the continents and thereby connecting the world. Their route took them from the modern neighborhood with towering high-rises, south until they turned to parallel the Bosphorus, connecting the Black Sea to the north with the Sea of Marmara to the south. This side of the water was Europe, the other Asia. They passed an arena on their right and massive cruise ship terminals on their left. Reece craned his neck like an excited tourist, which, fortunately for him, fit his cover story.

After a scenic twenty-minute drive, the cab stopped in front of an elegant white structure with black shutters. The Tomtom Suites, which was built into the steep slope of the hill on which it was constructed, looked more Dutch than Mediterranean in its architecture and reminded Reece of Cape Town. A young uniform-clad bellman opened the cab door and welcomed Reece to the property. Reece made a show of paying the driver in U.S. bills, leaving a hefty tip. The man smiled and thanked Reece in vastly improved English and, seeing the wad of cash, the bellman's eyes lit up too. He scurried to the open trunk to retrieve Reece's luggage and led him through the hotel's glass-canopied entrance. He stood aside as Reece approached the front desk, handing him a U.S. twenty-dollar bill. *There are few better ways to attract attention than by throwing money around.*

The hotel staff were efficient and courteous, obviously pleased by the ten-day reservation. When asked if he needed assistance with his bags, he almost spit out his default "no thank you" but decided that a guy like James Donovan wouldn't mind someone carrying his luggage for him. Another twenty dollars ensured that the staff would remain interested.

The spacious room was on the third floor with an amazing view of tiled rooftops, minaret towers, and the churning waters of the Bosphorus. The parquet wooden floors stretched the length of the suite, with a living area arranged at the foot of the king-sized bed. A large impressionistic painting that appeared to depict the city's skyline hung above the headboard and, through the sliding-glass wall that separated it from the living area, he could see that the bathroom was covered in dappled white marble from floor to ceiling. Reece much preferred his humble hooch in Mozambique.

The SEAL turned intelligence operative took a small device from his messenger bag that was disguised to look like an external hard drive. It was, in fact, a countersurveillance device designed to detect hidden listening devices and cameras. There was no reason to suspect that he was under surveillance, government or otherwise, but one didn't make assumptions in this line of work. After sweeping the room without any indication of an active bug, Reece returned the device to his bag. He entered the nine-digit passcode into his iPhone and sent Freddy a text message:

In room 307, view to the southeast. All good.

Within thirty seconds, his phone vibrated.

Good copy. 5 min out if you need me.

Freddy and the case officer who had driven them from the consulate were set up in a safe house several blocks to the northeast. From their position, they could act as backup in case Reece ran into trouble and could also feed him information as it came in from local sources and from the various information-gathering assets at the U.S. government's disposal. Their position was close enough to respond in case of an emergency but far away enough so as not to arouse suspicion. It was time to rely on the time-honored attribute for which snipers were known: patience.

CHAPTER 43

THE ARAP MOSQUE SITS in a cluttered neighborhood near the river, with multistory buildings of assorted vintages lining narrow streets. A wider, more modern four-lane thoroughfare runs two blocks to the west with a parking lane separated by a concrete curb in front of a shopping area that is more Middle Eastern than European.

An undeveloped lot sat between two apartment buildings and served as a park for the local residents; a direct path to the mosque would pass right through it. A glade of green grass added some color, and several towering trees provided shade from the midday sun. At 11:00 a.m., Reece found a bench facing the four-lane road, removed his sunglasses, and opened a copy of the *Times* of London.

Foot traffic was light, as most of the residents of this working-class neighborhood were busy working at this hour. A mother scrolled through her smartphone as her three-year-old daughter played nearby. The child quickly turned her interest to Reece, staring at him curiously through big brown eyes. He began to play "peekaboo" with his newspaper, her soft giggles evolving into belly laughs as the duration of his hides lengthened. The child's laughter brought a smile to his face but sadness to his heart as he thought of his own daughter, who had never tired of playing the game.

Focus, Reece.

By 11:30 a.m., the volume of traffic increased as men began making their way toward Jumu'ah. The oldest men arrived first; some traditions seem to transcend culture. As the noon hour approached, the crowds grew thicker and the worshippers younger. The men ranged from business suit–clad professionals to blue-collar workers in more modest dress. They converged on the steps of the mosque and made their way inside.

Nothing out of the ordinary.

An hour later the doors opened and the worshippers descended the steps, returning to the jobs and families awaiting them.

Reece stayed seated for another thirty minutes before heading back to the hotel. He spent the afternoon reading and rereading everything that the Agency had provided him on Mohammed, including the reports of all his unit's operations. Using an Agency VPN developed by a company called 7 Tunnels, he linked to a folder on Dropbox and accessed a seemingly benign music file hidden among thousands of similar files. Just as Freddy had trained him to do in Morocco, he used a VeraCrypt encrypted partition hidden within the music file and entered a twenty-six-character password. Nothing was ever downloaded to his computer.

Looking over the operations orders and after-action reports from the ten months that Reece had worked with Mo and his Special Tactics Unit brought back a flood of memories. Their operations had taken place at the height of the insurgency, in some of the worst neighborhoods in Baghdad. Working in conjunction with, and alongside, allied special operations units, Mo's STU team played a critical role in capturing high-value individuals and rapidly exploiting intelligence to dismantle enemy networks. They had the added benefit of being an entirely Iraqi unit, which gave them some of the best tactical-level intelligence in theater. They also worked for the Iraqi Ministry of the Interior, which put the fear of Allah into those they captured. Iraq's MOI did not give the Geneva and Hague Conventions the same weight as their American allies.

When Reece returned to the United States and the liaison role transitioned completely to Jules Landry, the scope of the operations shifted; retaliation seemed to be the motive rather than counterinsurgency. Why would the CIA have kept Landry on after Reece's report on his behavior in Iraq? In Reece's estimation, Landry was not a stable individual and had no business working sensitive intelligence operations.

Mo had been the one Iraqi commander who stood head and shoul-

ders above his peers. He excelled in both the planning and tactical ex-
ecution of direct-action missions, spoke English almost fluently, and had
the trust of both his men and the senior leadership of the MOI. After
Mo's disappearance, the references to his existence became few and far
between—all unconfirmed. A mention of one of his aliases on an intercepted phone call emanating from Syria, possible sightings in Greece,
and, of course, the intel that had brought Reece to Turkey. The only concrete proof that Mo had left Iraq alive was the photo taken in Italy that
Freddy had shown him back in Africa. *Are we chasing a ghost?*

• • •

A week had passed, and the routine was beginning to wear on him. At
least the hotel had a gym where Reece could crank out some brutal
CrossFit and Gym Jones workouts. Each day he followed the same pattern to make it easy for anyone wishing to make contact. He'd wake up,
work out, and have breakfast, taking his time to read the paper as he
finished his coffee. Then it was a leisurely stroll along the river, eventually ending up outside the Arap Mosque. *Still nothing.* He wanted to avoid
entering the mosque and having to use Maajid's lessons. He wasn't sure
he could pull it off even if he was going in under the guise of an author
doing research for a new novel. He'd give it one more day; if no one made
contact with him by then, he'd go the mosque route.

At ten to noon, he saw them. Three men, crossing the road toward
the park, their heads on swivels. *Predators.* Two of the men appeared to
be in their late twenties while the third was closer to Reece's age. They
each had the broad shoulders of athletes; all wore sunglasses, expensive
leather boots, and light jackets. They didn't wear rank or unit insignia,
but to Reece's trained eye, it was as if they were in uniform.

Reece lowered the newspaper to his lap and stared directly at them
as they approached. The older man noticed him as soon as he stepped
onto the sidewalk, and, by the time they were within twenty yards of the
bench, all three were staring holes in him. The posture of the younger
men changed from vigilant to combative as they neared Reece's position: chests thrust upward, a swagger in their step, heads held high. Their

physical behavior sent a primordial message: this was their territory and he was an intruder.

Could this be Mo's security detail?

Reece made sure to hold their stares until they walked completely past him. *Message sent.*

Reece lingered until quarter past noon to ensure that Mo wasn't coming and then walked toward the front of the mosque on his way back to the hotel, noticing a pair of ten-year-old boys tailing him from a block behind. *Perfect.* He kept a slow and easy pace to ensure they were able to follow him.

· · ·

Back in his room, Reece rechecked for listening devices before calling Freddy at the safe house. He answered immediately. "How'd it go?"

"It went. Three guys that looked like they could have been extras in a Chuck Norris movie walked right past me, eyeballing me the whole way. They had a couple of kids follow me home, so I think we set the hook."

"That's great, just be careful. Hopefully they *are* Mo's guys and not just some local thugs."

"They looked former military. I'll be careful."

"Good. I've got some news on Landry. A buddy in counterintelligence called and gave me some intel from their initial report. It seems as though young Mr. Landry had a criminal record that the Agency didn't know about when they hired him. Besides a couple of simple battery-type arrests as a juvenile, he was arrested for rape during his senior year of high school. Somehow the case went away. I'm guessing he cut a deal to join the Marines. The counterintelligence division and the IG's office are still looking into it, but the odd part is that someone made it disappear during his screening."

"It doesn't surprise me that he's a scumbag, but it is weird that he got in the door with that kind of record. See if you can find out who recruited him and who signed off on his background."

"I'm already on it."

"Thanks. I'll hit you up at our next comm window."

Reece cut the call and looked out his window over the city. Mo was out there somewhere, one of the most highly trained covert operatives in the world. He had become a terrorist, and somehow Landry was involved. Not long ago, they had all depended on one another to survive in battle. Reece couldn't help but think that the next time they met up, not all of them would be walking away.

CHAPTER 44

HOW WOULD MO MAKE contact? Reece knew the CIA had given him some of the same training they give the case officers, but Reece's experience with Mo and his unit in Iraq had been of a more kinetic nature. Reece still had a hard time believing that the Iraqi major he'd trusted with his life was now a terrorist, targeting the same Western nations he had fought alongside in the cradle of civilization.

Reece needed to get some air. The coffee bar downstairs had proven to be excellent, so he ordered a to-go cup of their lightest roast. After doctoring it with milk and honey, he nodded to the bellman, who held the door for him as he walked out into the afternoon sunshine.

The coffee was too hot to drink, so Reece removed the plastic lid and blew on it as he walked along the steep uphill path. With his subconscious mind occupied by the mountain of intelligence documents he'd read and his conscious focus on the coffee, Reece noticed and then dismissed the maintenance worker clad in bright coveralls as he walked past him. *Mistake.* Two seconds later, he heard the *pop* of the compressed nitrogen and immediately felt the sting of the metal barbs that penetrated his shirt and embedded themselves into the muscle of his upper back. His limbs instantaneously contracted and cramped as two thousand volts of electricity surged into his body, dropping him to the sidewalk, his entire body in taut agony in addition to being burned by the scalding-hot coffee.

The pain ended nearly as quickly as it began, and he found himself floating above the sidewalk, unable to move his limbs. As his chest hit the floorboard of the Transit Connect delivery van, he realized that he'd been flex-cuffed at both his wrists and ankles. A pillowcase was pulled over his head as the door slid to a close. In a moment of out-of-body clarity, he marveled at how quickly his abductors had planned and executed this operation.

It was hot inside the van and the floor smelled of grease and oil, mixing with the strong odor of the coffee that soaked his shirt. Reece lay still, conserving his energy in case it became necessary to run or fight later, though the objective of the mission was to do neither.

Strong hands frisked him from head to toe, covering every inch of his body with no regard for modesty. His subcompact SIG, spare magazine, knife, shoes, and iPhone were taken from him. He assumed that the phone was being placed inside a container that would prevent his location from being tracked. There was no talking among his captors, which made it nearly impossible for him to determine their exact numbers. The driver didn't speed or drive erratically. Instead he navigated the city's streets as part of the normal flow of traffic, making frequent turns. These men were pros.

After what seemed like an hour but was probably half that, the van stopped. The driver turned off the diesel motor and engaged the parking brake. He heard the sound of chains from outside the van and a steel service door rolled downward on its tracks. They'd pulled into a garage or warehouse, based on the echo of voices in what sounded like Arabic. The van door slid open quickly and what felt like three men dragged him out by his ankles and stood him upright, his stockinged feet landing on the cold concrete floor. Some type of motor hummed in the background.

"Walk," a voice from behind him said in accented English.

One man held each arm and a third had him by the top of the head, guiding him forward and away from the direction of the door. He walked twenty paces before his feet felt the threshold of a door and then thin carpeting. After a few more steps, he could hear the sound of a chair being dragged across the carpet behind him.

"Sit."

Footsteps shuffled away, and he heard the door shut behind him. He slowed his breathing, settled his heart rate, and concentrated on the plastic restraints that bound his wrists in front of him. In a move that he and his teammates had practiced dozens of times in various SERE courses, Reece pushed his arms up and away from his body, then snapped them down across his abdomen. The plastic gave way to freedom. He rubbed his wrists as the blood rushed into his tingling hands and pulled the cloth away from his head.

The room was dark. It was a small office, the kind attached to industrial spaces, with a desk, filing cabinets, and dusty stacks of books and papers on the floor. Ten feet away he saw a dark couch against the wall and a shot of adrenaline shot through his body as his brain registered a human figure seated on it. As he rose to his still-restrained feet, a flash of light illuminated the room. The flame burned brightly and, as the man inhaled on his cigarette, the light glowed against his bearded face.

"Mo!" Reece shouted.

"James Reece, what on earth are you doing here, my friend?" Mo said as he exhaled a cloud of gray smoke and extinguished his lighter. He turned on a lamp, and Reece saw him clearly for the first time. Dashing as ever, Mo's longish black hair was slicked back, his beard precisely cropped, and his clothing impeccable. He stowed the silver lighter into the pocket of his tailored sport coat, rose from his chair, and embraced Reece in a strong hug. Then, drawing an automatic knife from the pocket of his jeans, he dropped to one knee and swiftly cut the plastic binding from Reece's ankles.

"Sit down, sit down." Mo motioned Reece back into his chair as he turned back toward the couch. "Sorry about the way my men treated you, but I had to make sure it was really you."

"Well, you could have just called my room! No worries, though, no permanent damage except for the coffee stains."

"I have heard so much, Reece. I am so sorry for the loss of your family, may God watch over them. To lose loved ones in wartime is one thing, but to have the peace of one's home shattered is another altogether. I have some experience there, if you recall."

"I do. Thanks, Mo," Reece said, feeling the gut-wrenching pain at the thought of his wife and little girl riddled with bullets on the floor of their home.

"Why did you come to Istanbul? The way you put yourself directly in my sights, my guess is you came here to find me. I can help you, but if you are looking to hide, there are better places, my friend. The American intelligence services will find you here. You should not have come."

"I'm not on the run anymore, Mo. The government made me a deal."

"Why in the world would they do that?"

"Because they needed me to find you."

Mo's calm and composed demeanor changed perceptibly. He shifted forward with a puzzled look on his face. "What do you mean by that? They know exactly how to find me."

Now it was Reece's turn to look puzzled.

"What are you talking about, Mo? You're running a terrorist cell for Amin Nawaz. You're a wanted man with a price on your head."

"Reece, you don't understand. I work *for* the CIA. Remember Jules Landry? He's been my handler for years."

CHAPTER 45

Tomtom Suites
Istanbul, Turkey

"REECE, WHERE IN THE hell have you been? We lost track of you."

"I'm safe, Freddy. He made contact. We need to talk, ASAP," Reece responded.

Reece was back in his hotel room, personal possessions returned and none the worse for wear.

"Roger that. How do you want to do it?"

"I'm blown here, so it doesn't matter. I'll get cleaned up, grab my gear, and catch a ride back to the consulate. Meet you back there in an hour or so."

"If you're blown, we'll just pick you up."

"Check. Give me fifteen."

"You got it."

Reece changed and packed his bags. There was no sense staying at the hotel any longer. He was exposed here and, though he trusted Mo, he couldn't know whether someone in Mo's private army was playing both sides. An American intelligence officer would be a fat target to a jihadi looking to help the cause.

The Agency SUV was idling at the curb when Reece walked through the hotel's front door, the anxious bellman trailing behind him. Reece loaded his own bags and nodded to the confused employee as he handed him a twenty and climbed into the backseat.

Freddy turned around in his seat with an extremely worried expression on his face. "You okay, buddy?"

"Well, I can't exactly claim to be a superspy. Mo's guys Tased me and threw me into a van while I was sipping a latte."

"That would never have happened to Mitch Rapp or Scot Harvath."

"Hey, man, I'm just a vanilla frogman."

"I think the Hartleys would disagree, *if* they were still around. You want to give me the download?"

"Let me have a minute to stew on it. I think I have an idea."

"I don't know why that makes me nervous," Freddy replied with a shake of his head.

The case officer drove directly to the consulate and within a half hour they were inside a secure conference room. Reece began to go through the details of the meeting while Freddy scribbled notes on a yellow legal pad.

"Mo thinks he's still working for the Agency. He admitted to coordinating the mortar attack on the British Paras and taking out the NATO commander, but he swears he was following our orders."

"Who gave him the orders?"

"You ready for this?" Reece paused for effect. "Jules Landry. He's been handling Mo this entire time, first in Syria, then in Europe."

"You're shitting me," Freddy said in disbelief.

"Nope."

"And you believe him?"

"He was genuinely shocked when I told him Landry had gone rogue. I could tell he felt betrayed. Remember, I've been in combat with Mo. We've trusted each other with our lives. I don't think he'd lie to me."

"Why would the CIA be running a pseudoterrorist to hit our allies? That doesn't make any sense."

"I know," Reece said. "He's been thinking that Landry was running him *against* Nawaz, getting him close, having him gather intel, and that Landry gave him CIA-approved targets to hit in order to prove his worth to Nawaz. Kind of like how the DEA assets operate in the cartels. They pass information to their DEA handler, who lets the majority of drug shipments continue into the U.S. to not blow their asset's cover as they continue to move up in the organization. Same thing here."

"Jesus."

"And think about where he comes from: Iraq. He grew up under Saddam Hussein, who did the unspeakable to keep his people living in fear and in line. He told me Landry was specific with him about hitting military targets. Mo actually thought the supporting effort was to keep our allies involved in the GWOT and ensure they had the public support to do so. He admitted to organizing the attack on the Paras and he took out General Alexander with the drone himself, just like the CIA taught him."

"What about the Christmas attack in England?"

"Swears he had nothing to do with it. He said he'd only hit military targets and, again, I actually believe him. He knows that Nawaz has multiple independent cells but doesn't know specifics. He was working his way up but he wasn't there yet. That's why he believed that Landry was running him for the CIA. It's actually quite genius."

"Yeah, but to what end? There is something we're missing. Why would Landry go rogue and run a former STU commando inside ISIS in Europe? He's not employed by the CIA anymore. What's his endgame?"

"I don't know, Freddy. Landry isn't bright enough to mastermind anything. He's not a thinker. Whatever he's doing, he's in it for the money or the rush."

"I'll pass all that to CIA and have them keep digging on Landry. Past associates, bank accounts, aliases. We'll catch a break eventually. Does Mo know where Nawaz is hiding?"

"He said he moves constantly but that he can lead us to him."

"Wait, he agreed? Just like that?" Freddy asked dubiously.

"Not exactly."

"What do you mean, Reece?"

"He'll lead us to Nawaz, but *only* if we give him a shot at Landry."

"A shot, like to kill him?"

"I'm sure he'd like to, but he wants answers."

"I would, too. Okay, let me talk to the bosses, but even if they agree, we are going to have to bring Mo in. We don't have a choice, Reece. He's a terrorist whether he was being run by a rogue CIA agent or not."

"I have another idea. Just hear me out on this. You ever hear of the Selous Scouts?"

"The Rhodesian guys with the FALs and the nut-hugger shorts? Yeah, I've heard of them. Did you spend too much time in Mozambique? What in the hell do they have to do with this?"

Reece detailed his plan, and Freddy gave it the critical review that his position demanded. In the end, Reece was able to counter each of his friend's well-directed arguments. Now it was a matter of selling it to the decision makers back at Langley.

CHAPTER 46

Burgas, Bulgaria
September

ANDRENOV HAD ARRANGED A French passport for Landry, which made sense given his heritage and reasonably good, though accented, command of the language. He couldn't pass for French in France, but he had no intention of going there. He didn't stay anywhere too long these days but he needed to be within reasonable proximity of his asset, so southern Bulgaria was ideal.

The Grand Hotel was nice, cheap, and right on the Black Sea coast. Landry spent most of his days working out in the hotel gym to maintain his bodybuilder's physique and to sweat out the sins of the previous evening. While most operators had adopted more functional fitness regimes over the past decade, Landry's vanity kept him focused on training individual muscle groups in isolation. Those workouts, and a healthy supply of anabolic steroids, kept him looking like a heavily tattooed version of a 1980s action movie hero. Too bad it was too cold to lie out by the pool. Landry loved the looks that the wives of the potbellied rich men gave him as he strolled the deck in nothing but a small swimsuit. He'd bedded more than a few when they went upstairs to "freshen up" while their husbands lazed drunkenly in their lawn chairs.

There were no such treats available this evening, as it was the slow season. There wasn't much to do here but work out and drink in the clubs, but lately, the booze hadn't been enough. The bartender had a source and soon Landry was adding cocaine to the mix. It took sleeping pills, Xanax, or opiates to come down from the blow in the early morning hours, sometimes all three, and marijuana to take the edge off when the new day came. Jules Landry had found himself in a cycle of stimulants, depressants, benzodiazepines, and sedatives, catalyzed by excessive testosterone levels and a level of alcohol consumption that would have been a problem all by itself. He may have looked like an inked Adonis to the women on the pool deck, but inside, he was a mess.

The post-dinner hour found Landry drinking in the hotel bar. He'd done a bump of coke after a shower and was three vodkas deep, which meant that he was at the peak of his chemically assisted relative normalcy. He'd done arms today and his biceps were pumped with blood; his black T-shirt clung tightly to them. He rolled his right wrist over and admired the vascularity of his forearm before doing the same on his left side. He looked good. He felt good. There was only one thing missing and he was certain the bartender could arrange it.

She arrived an hour later. She was cute; hot, actually. She had long, straight, jet-black hair that hung down to her midback, a decent face, and a body that looked to be flawless. She reminded him a little bit of a girl back home. Her long legs looked great in tight black leather pants and, when she removed her faux-fur coat, her glittery gold halter top rode up and exposed a six-pack of abdominal muscles. Her breasts were obviously enhanced, but she hadn't made the mistake of going too big with them. Yeah, she would do for sure.

She spoke no French and only a little English; they weren't going to do much talking anyway.

"I am Darina," she said, extending her hand.

"Jules," he responded, amused by the formality of the introduction.

The bartender brought her some type of vodka drink in a tall glass and Landry reached out his hand with two pills in the palm.

"What is?" she questioned.

"Ecstasy."

"What?"

"Ecstasy, you know, ecstasy," Landry said as he feigned dance moves with his fists up.

"Ahh, yes." She took a tablet from Landry's hand and popped it onto her tongue, washing it down with her drink. Landry swallowed the other pill. By the time the MDMA kicked in, both had downed two more drinks, and Landry motioned to her to follow him upstairs. She asked for the money as soon as they entered the large suite, and Landry handed her a stack of hundred-euro notes. Darina excused herself and disappeared into the bathroom to get herself ready. Jules made them each a drink from the bottle he'd brought from the bar and snorted a fat line of cocaine. He heard the toilet flush and then the click of the bathroom door opening. He pulled off his shirt and sat on the bed, holding his drink and waiting anxiously for what would come next.

Darina walked seductively into the room wearing only her black thong panties and high heels. Her body was even better than he thought it would be. He motioned to the nightstand, where her drink sat next to several more lines of cocaine; she skipped the drink and went for the powder. She climbed onto the bed and straddled the muscle-bound man who owned her for the next few hours. Minutes later they were both naked and he was doing another line of blow, this time off the small of her back. Landry was in heaven.

• • •

Landry's head pounded. The sun was beating through the windows. He'd forgotten to close the curtains in all of last night's excitement.

What time was it?

He rolled over and pulled a second pillow over his head, trying to go back to sleep. His foot slid to the right and he felt something solid on the other side of the sheet.

Is she still here?

He took the pillow from his head and rolled over far enough to see a nude female lying facedown, her head toward the footboard of the bed. Something about her didn't look right. Landry kicked her in the thigh in the hopes she would wake up, gather her things, and head out.

Nothing.

He kicked her again a little harder.

"Get . . . the . . . *fuck* . . . out," he said, kicking her a bit harder with each word.

Instead of responding, she slowly slid off the bed and slumped onto the floor.

Landry squeezed his eyes together in an attempt to quiet his pounding head. He reached down and touched her arm. Her pale body was unnaturally cool. He rolled her over and brushed her tangled mess of dark hair out of the way, exposing a large bruise on her cheek. Her eyes were wide open and lifeless. A path of dried blood led from her nose to her upper lip. He leaned in closer and saw that she had swollen purple marks on her fragile throat.

Instead of revulsion or horror, Landry looked at her in curiosity, trying to remember the events of the previous evening. He'd hit her, but it was just with an open hand. And he'd choked her, he recalled that. Her bulging eyes had filled with fear as he continued to fuck her. He liked that; being inside a prostitute as he took her life. Luckily, *shithole* countries the world over were filled with young girls for him to punish. He was upset with himself, though, not that he'd killed an innocent woman, but that he couldn't remember how he'd killed her. He'd cheated himself out of that pleasure.

Landry took a moment to admire what he could see of her breasts and abs before leaning over the nightstand to do the last line of cocaine. Then he grabbed her under the arms and positioned her on the bed for one last dance with the devil.

CHAPTER 47

CIA Station
Istanbul, Turkey
September

FREDDY AND REECE WENT over the pitch several times to ensure that they'd covered all the angles. Freddy knew the internal politics of the Agency well enough to realize that their concept had a better chance of gaining approval coming from him rather than Reece. To many back at Langley, Reece was a murderous loose cannon whose only use was his relationship with Mo. This needed to be about the operation.

Reece excused himself from the room when the time arrived for Freddy's video teleconference with his superiors back in Northern Virginia. Victor Rodriguez, a former Army Special Forces officer and current head of the Central Intelligence Agency's Special Operations Group, appeared on the screen, joined by the Agency's deputy director of the National Clandestine Service, Janice Motley. The tailored blue suits worn by both Rodriguez and Motley and the frosted-glass interior of the Langley SCIF were in sharp contrast to the shaggy-haired and polo-clad SEAL in the spartan conference room in Istanbul. At least he'd taken off his ball cap.

Despite climbing the ranks at the Agency, Rodriguez hadn't forgotten where he'd come from and could be counted on to watch the backs of his men in the field. Motley was an unknown quantity among the spies and trigger-pullers whom she oversaw in her new role. Her background as the lead staff attorney for the Senate Intelligence Committee didn't exactly fill the operatives with hope when it came to her view of paramilitary work.

"Mr. Strain, good to hear from you. Nice work in Morocco," Rodriguez began. "Let me introduce you to Deputy Director Janice Motley."

"Pleasure to meet you, ma'am. I appreciate both of you making time on such short notice. We have some extremely time-sensitive intel that needs attention," Freddy said, putting on his most charming smile as he transitioned from covert operator to salesman.

"Please go on, Mr. Strain." Motley clearly wasn't in the mood for pleasantries.

"Yes, ma'am. As you both know, we successfully recruited James Reece and brought him in to attempt to make contact with Mohammed Farooq, a former Iraqi special operations commander who worked with Commander Reece back during OIF."

"We are well aware of that, Mr. Strain, and you should know that decision was made over my objection," Motley added.

"Understood, ma'am. Earlier today, James Reece made contact with Farooq, who acknowledged his role in planning the attacks on the Colchester Garrison in England and the assassination of General Alexander in Brussels. He denied any role in the Christmas attack in Kingston but did say that Amin Nawaz operates multiple independent cells that do not have visibility of the others' missions for operational security purposes."

"Did Reece make any arrangements with him relative to Nawaz?" Rodriguez interjected.

"No, sir, there was an unforeseen twist in Mohammed's story. He claims to have been directed to carry out these attacks by a former Agency contractor named Jules Landry, who has been running Mohammed under the auspices of a legitimate CIA operation. Landry has been missing since 2013 and we have recently discovered that he may have entered the Agency's employ under fraudulent circumstances."

"Is Farooq's story credible?" Motley asked.

"We believe it is."

"So, you're saying that we have a green-badger who has gone rogue and is running terrorist networks under the guise of an official United States government paramilitary operation?"

"Yes, ma'am, that is our assessment."

"To what end?"

"We don't know at this point. As I said, we just became aware of this a few hours ago. My gut instinct is that Landry is running Mohammed at the behest of another entity, either a rogue state, terrorist organization, or what's termed a super-empowered individual or entity."

"I'm not interested in what your gut tells you, Mr. Strain, and I know the term."

"What I believe Mr. Strain is trying to say, Janice, is that there isn't evidence that Landry's defection was ideologically driven," Rodriguez interjected.

"So, what are you proposing we do with this information?" Motley continued without addressing Victor's comment.

Strain exhaled before responding, "Ma'am, are you familiar with the pseudoterrorist operations carried out by the Rhodesian Selous Scouts in the 1970s?"

Strain could see his boss's eyes widen at the mention of Rhodesia; Motley was African American and the racial implications of the Bush War made Rodriguez immediately uncomfortable.

Motley showed no reaction. "I am not, Mr. Strain."

"Well, they were arguably the most effective counterinsurgency unit in history. They used 'pseudoterrorists' who were either undercover Rhodesian soldiers or actual former insurgents to infiltrate enemy networks so that they could be targeted by conventional forces. We feel that we have a unique opportunity to utilize Mohammed Farooq in a similar role and not only take out Amin Nawaz but also infiltrate additional networks to include ISIS."

"You are proposing that, instead of incarcerating Mohammed Farooq for planning the murder of a U.S. general as well as killing and maiming numerous allied troops, we bring him in to work for us?"

"Yes, ma'am. As horrible as it is to have a rogue CIA agent running an asset against our allies, it also gives us a unique opportunity. As much as I hate to say it, we can take over from Landry and have a highly placed, and *legitimate*, asset in a leadership position of a major terrorist organization. Not unsimilar to how the DEA infiltrates the cartels."

After a pregnant pause, Motley continued: "How exactly would this happen, Mr. Strain?"

. . .

"What did they say?" Reece asked, his impatience evident.

"Well, they didn't shoot it down. They said they need to think about it. Vic seemed on board. I'm just not sure how to read Motley."

"So, what do we do now?"

"You had a long day of getting kidnapped, so I say we call it."

"And then?"

"Let's plan as if we're going to get the go-ahead."

By noon the following day, the two operatives had come up with a basic concept of operations that involved a direct-action mission to capture/kill Amin Nawaz, and the apprehension and rendition of Jules Landry. Either one of these tasks would be tricky to accomplish individually, let alone simultaneously.

With multiple unknowns this was a tough sell, and would be even harder to pull off once Murphy's law inevitably came into play; they didn't know the location of either Landry or Nawaz and wouldn't be sure of the latter until hours before the operation had to be executed. The entire plan revolved around their absolute trust in Mo, something that both of them hoped was not a naïve sentiment. They had plenty of leverage to motivate him but it was possible, perhaps even likely, he might disappear. Mo had been used by what he now knew to be a rogue CIA operative and had committed atrocities for reasons yet unknown. Reece and Freddy were counting on him wanting to find out why. A military chain of command would never greenlight such a harebrained operation, but the Agency wasn't the U.S. military.

By the following morning, Freddy received word from Vic Rodriguez that the plan was tentatively approved on several conditions: that the hit look like it was done by another Islamic entity, that the United States Department of Justice would formally charge Mo with terror-related crimes both to cover asses in Washington and to bolster his bona fides as an international terrorist, and, finally, that Landry would not enter U.S. custody at any point during the operation so that his civil rights would not be violated by any U.S. agency or asset, well, any agency other than the CIA. With those boundaries in place, Reece and Freddy dug into the details of their tactical planning. They were going back to war.

CHAPTER 48

Tirana, Albania
September

THE TINY APARTMENT HAD been abandoned by its occupants, who took little more than the clothes on their backs and what they could fit into a few plastic shopping bags. After years of waiting, their application for asylum in the United Kingdom had been mysteriously granted on the condition that they make the trip within twenty-four hours. As one of six hundred families packed into the squalid conditions of this communist-era housing project with no running water, they didn't have to be asked twice.

Institut was arguably the worst neighborhood in Tirana, which was saying something. It smelled of trash, human waste, and terrible food cooked in cramped and poorly ventilated one-room apartments. The un-paved streets were strewn with refuse and the drab concrete buildings' lone decorations came from the clothing that hung from nearly every window and balcony. The sights and smells reminded Reece of Sadr City and a hundred other places he'd fought in since 2001. The only things green were the weeds.

Nestled between the Republic of Macedonia to the east and the Adriatic Sea to the west, Albania was struggling with its national iden-tity. Now a market-based economy, member of NATO, and candidate for membership in the European Union, Albania continued to distance it-self from its communist past. Montenegro and Kosovo to the north and

Greece to the south allowed for ample trading of goods and services as the small Balkan nation worked to shed itself of its former status as North Korea's lone satellite state.

Albania's majority Muslim population was not traditionally radical or even particularly devout and, though the country was well known for exporting criminals, it wasn't a breeding ground for terrorism. That changed somewhat as a result of the killing and mass expulsion of Bosnian and Kosovar Muslims during the Balkans War in the 1990s. There is no better way to unite a people than to victimize them by identity; attempted genocide drew many Muslims in the region closer to their religion. As one of the Agency analysts put it during the pre-mission brief, "The Albanians became more radically Islamist during the 1990s the same way that the Irish became more radically Catholic during their conflict with the English in Northern Ireland."

Because some Albanians were sympathetic to his cause and because the government was improving but still dysfunctional, Amin Nawaz found the nation to be a perfect sanctuary on the European Union's periphery. In addition, the terrorist leader had a fondness for prepubescent boys, and one of the destitute families in Institut had offered their son in exchange for what, to them, was a vast sum of money. American troops had been shocked by the pedophilia that they witnessed first in Afghanistan and later in Iraq. Known as *bacha bazi*, or "boy play," in Pashto, this modern-day sex slavery was abhorrent to Westerners but accepted or at least tolerated by many in Central Asia and the Middle East. When drone strikes targeted the meetings of terrorist leaders, young "entertainment" boys were often found among the dead.

As a cell leader Mo wouldn't ordinarily have knowledge of Amin Nawaz's whereabouts. Sometimes even the inner circle wouldn't know travel plans until the last minute; this was a basic security protocol for a terrorist organization. However, Mo had known from the start that Landry's request for him to run a terrorist cell was outside of protocol, even for the CIA, and had recognized early in their relationship the need to create some leverage. While still in Syria, Mo had worked to infiltrate Nawaz's inner circle with his own asset, just as the CIA had taught him to do in Iraq. When Nawaz's operations chief was killed in an air strike by the Assad regime, an Iraqi with impeccable credentials stepped up, one of Mo's team leaders from the STU who had followed him to Syria. Mo was running his own small penetration operation to ensure he remained a valuable asset to who he thought was his CIA handler.

This Thursday evening, Nawaz would be visiting with a nine-year-old boy on this muddy street in Tirana's worst slum. Reece and Freddy had been inserted into the city in a baby blue minibus known locally as a *Furgon*. A local driver, who happened to be an Agency asset, parked the bus a block from the apartment building at 10:00 p.m. and walked inside to visit a girlfriend; any later and they may have aroused some suspicion by the local residents.

Reece and Freddy took turns napping intermittently under blankets on the van's floor until 3:00 a.m. They were both dressed in drab local clothing, over MultiCam combat uniforms worn by Albania's special operations battalion that had supported allied operations in both Afghanistan and Iraq. Freddy had worked alongside one of the Eagle companies on the Pakistani border and, as a gun and gear nut, knew their weapons and equipment firsthand. Fortunately, most of it was German-made and all of it was good. Reece carried a suppressed MP7, a weapon also conveniently used by the Albanians, inside his jacket. The helmet-mounted night-vision devices didn't match their disguises, so they kept them concealed until Mo's hand-drawn map led them to the second-story apartment without incident.

Once inside, the two men cleared the small one-room dwelling, confirming they were alone and that the place wasn't wired to blow. A set of jerry-rigged brackets on either side of the doorjamb held a two-by-four that Strain quietly slid in place to secure the door. They confirmed their line of sight to the target building and began constructing their urban hide site.

Freddy opened his pack and removed a 16.5-inch-barreled HK417 rifle that had been broken down into its lower and upper receivers. He snapped the two halves together and pushed the takedown pins into place to secure them. A SilencerCo Omega sound suppressor ratcheted onto the muzzle brake, and he loaded a twenty-round magazine of Black Hills 175-grain match ammunition into the weapon. To avoid the *clang* of slamming the bolt home, he slowly worked the charging handle and pushed the receiver's forward assist to ensure that the bolt was seated properly. A small AN/PAS-13G(v)1 L3-LWTS thermal optic was mounted to the rifle's top rail in line with the Schmidt Bender 3-12x50mm rifle-scope. The Albanians had better long-range sniper rifles in their inventory, but this would be a 250-yard shot at the most and the select-fire 7.62 would be plenty of gun to get it done. If the operation went south and turned into a firefight, a bolt-action sniper rifle would become a liability, whereas the HK would be an asset. An ATPIAL/PEQ-15 was attached to the rail. *Be prepared.* All the recent years of urban combat had taught the SEAL sniper community a great deal about life and death by the gun.

The apartment's former occupants had been fully debriefed on the interior of their residence, and the notes from that interview had been passed to the sniper pair. A handmade rug, the nicest item in the room, covered the concrete floor from corner to corner. A tattered couch sat against the side wall, facing a small television with a built-in VHS player. Two mattresses lay on the floor with their sheets neatly folded and a heavy wooden table with three chairs occupied the room's center. A gas burner rigged to some type of fuel tank alongside two empty buckets served as the kitchen. A bathroom was conspicuously missing.

A set of heavy blue curtains hung over a clothesline strung between the barred windows facing the street. Reece drew the curtains apart to allow a twelve-inch view between them and attached a dark, lightweight, see-through cloth to the curtain rod using metal binder clips. He unrolled it at an angle, securing it under the legs of the table. The forty-five-degree angle of the dark yet thin material allowed a sniper to observe a target area in an urban environment through what appeared to be just another empty window from the outside. The two snipers a clear view to their target building.

Freddy took a seat on the opposite side of the table from the window and unfolded the legs of the HK's Atlas bipod. Using the table as a bench rest to support the rifle, he adjusted his position in order to have a better view of the target area. Satisfied the site was ready, they removed their NOD-equipped helmets, stripped off their hot outer layers of civilian clothing, and settled in for a long day of waiting. Freddy took first watch on the rifle while Reece sat on one of the mattresses and took charge of their communications.

The Harris AN/PRC-163 Falcon III radio on Reece's vest was an incredibly capable piece of equipment, more of a computer, really, that did the work it would have taken two radios to do just a few years earlier. With it, he could talk to other units on the ground, satellites in orbit, and even UAVs loitering overhead. He plugged a ruggedized Android tablet into an L3 Technologies Rover 6 and powered it up. Within seconds, a satellite image of their location appeared on the seven-inch screen that looked like a higher-resolution version of Google Earth. Reece selected a menu that brought up a real-time ISR feed from an MQ-4C Triton drone operating high over the city. Confident all systems were working and were in the correct location, Reece sent an encrypted message to their operational commander on a vessel in the Adriatic Sea that was also received by higher headquarters back in Virginia.

Reece and Freddy had worked out a schedule in advance: each man spent an hour on the gun, observing the target area and working on a sketch that included ranges to potential enemy positions, while the other monitored the communications gear and slept. By Reece's second shift, the dark skies turned to gray and then pink as the new day began. He unclipped the thermal optic from the rail, visualizing possible shot scenarios. Nawaz wasn't expected until that evening, but his plans could change at any moment, and often did by design. Since most of the terrorist organization's communications were designed to avoid electronic intercept, and were therefore slow, it was unlikely that Mo would be aware of a change in time to adapt. They needed a bit of luck. Reece smiled, remembering an old commanding officer who preached that *luck was the residue of preparation*.

It was 184 meters to the front of the L-shaped building where the young boy lived and 213 to the side entrance. Both were well within the capabilities of a modern rifle and optic with a trained shooter behind the glass, but the target would likely be moving quickly and could be among a gaggle of other people, some of whom might be civilians. This was where experience and wisdom entered the picture. There was no such thing as an "easy shot" in the real world. Reece dialed 0.7 MILS of elevation into the scope, which would put the bullet's point of impact dead-on at 200 meters. At 175 meters the shot would be two inches high and at 225 it would be three inches low. Not knowing exactly where Nawaz would be clear for a shot, Reece would make the slight adjustment at game time. That was one of the differences between a marksman and a sniper.

By 7:00 a.m., most of Institut's residents were out and about. Old women with handkerchiefs tied over their heads carried water in five-gallon buckets or limped toward the city's markets. Elderly men stood in small groups and smoked while children in brightly colored jackets and backpacks walked toward what must have been their school. Like nearly all children around the world, these seemed oblivious to the poverty in which they lived; this was simply all they knew. As he watched them, Reece wondered whether the privileged children of the Western world would be able to compete in the twenty-first-century marketplace with kids like these, kids who would grow up with hunger, with grit. He fleetingly thought of what amazing assets these children could be to the world, if only they could escape the radicalization efforts of those like the man he hunted.

When it was Freddy's turn on the rifle, Reece did a quick check of the radio and tablet before closing his eyes. He smiled to himself, barely able to suppress his laughter as he thought about a strikingly similar urban sniper hide more than a decade earlier. He and his platoon had been tasked with training and advising an element of Iraqi snipers. His element had made their way into an apartment, similar to the one in which he now found himself, and began the painstaking process of setting up a proper urban hide. Reece was sitting behind the spotting scope, confirming that they had a good perspective on the street below, when an overwhelming odor filled the room. He turned and was shocked to find one of the Iraqi snipers squatting a few feet behind him, defecating on the floor. The Iraqi had no regard for the fact that they were expecting to spend the next twenty-four to thirty-six hours living and working in this small space; he had to go. A CIA reports officer summed it up with a saying that gained some traction in theater: "The *Haj* does what the *Haj* does." Maybe Iraq hadn't been as ready for Jeffersonian democracy as U.S. leaders may have hoped. One of Reece's enlisted SEALs took a digital photo of the offending turd on the floor and later displayed the print on the plywood wall of their makeshift bar back at base above a handwritten caption that read "Real World Shit."

Reece managed a few minutes of sleep and, at the top of the hour, he and Freddy traded places again. All communication was done using hand signals and facial expressions since the neighbors would expect the apartment to be empty and any noise from inside would arouse suspicion. The day dragged on, one rotation after another, observing the landscape of poverty like voyeuristic assassins from the first world. The room grew hot and stuffy and, by midday, they had stripped down to T-shirts and removed their low-vis body armor.

At dusk, they changed to a sniper/spotter arrangement with one operator on the HK rifle and one seated just behind and to the left so that he could spot using an additional L3-LWTS thermal. *Two is one, after all.* Because the optics used thermal rather than traditional night-vision technology, they worked in both daylight and darkness. Reece was on the rifle when an aging Mercedes microbus parked next to the target building's side entrance and six military-age males got out and took up security positions around the structure. One of them quickly disappeared into the apartment building. The locals gave them a wide berth. Everything about their behavior indicated that they were an advance security detail. No weapons were visible, but there was little doubt they were armed.

At 7:18 p.m., the ISR feed began tracking an Opel Monterey SUV, trailed by a small pickup truck, as they steered their way toward the area at a high rate of speed. The two-vehicle convoy fit the profile Mo had described and the timing was right.

The SEAL sniper team observed the area, sending photos back to

Langley via the Falcon radio. An hour after their arrival, Reece and Freddy noticed a perceptible shift in the advance team as they assumed a more aggressive posture. A man who appeared to be their leader reemerged from the side entrance along with another man in his thirties and a young boy. They both deduced the second man to be the boy's father; there was no sign of his mother, which was unsurprising in the Muslim world and likely also due to the nature of the transaction that was about to take place. The boy was dressed in a white cone-shaped *qeleshe* cap, *fustanella* dress-like shirt, and *xhamadan* vest, and wore an embroidered *brez* sash around his waist. His parents had clad their young son in traditional Albanian dress like he was some type of doll to make him a more hospitable sex toy for the visiting terrorist leader. The sight of it sickened both men and Freddy was happy to be the one who would be able to put a bullet into the pedophile before he could violate this innocent child. He suppressed the urge to put a second bullet into the boy's father.

Reece began whispering updates from the ISR feed as the SUV approached the target: "Five minutes out."

"Two minutes out."

"Thirty seconds out. He's passing our position."

Both men watched the silver SUV and pickup pass down the gravel roadway below and to the right of their position as they steered toward the target building's side entrance. It stopped next to the curb along with the truck, the back of which was filled with armed men.

The headache hit Reece with blinding speed and a pain worse than he'd yet experienced. An audible grunt and the thud of the handheld thermal hitting the floor took Freddy off the gun.

"Reece, you okay?"

Reece pushed as hard as he could on his temples as the pain continued to radiate and blind him.

"Reece?" Freddy whispered, looking back to the scene playing out in the streets below. "Reece, *shit!*"

Then it was gone.

"I'm okay, it's all right," Reece said, regaining his senses.

"Get back in the game, buddy; how far to the SUV?" his visibly concerned friend asked.

Reece picked up the thermal and consulted the range card they'd built in daylight: "Two ten to the SUV," he reported. Taking a breath, he studied the laundry hanging from the building's windows. "Wind is swirling, less than five. Hold dead-on."

A half-dozen men piled out of the truck's bed carrying a mix of Kalashnikov-style rifles that varied in barrel length and national origin. Some carried them slung over their backs and all of them had their stocks folded to make the weapons more compact. They surrounded the SUV, with four on the side near the building and two remaining on the street side of the vehicle. All four doors of the SUV opened and Reece heard the metallic sound of Strain moving the selector switch to FIRE.

An overweight man in his fifties stepped from the backseat of the Opel and was immediately flanked by the four security men. Though they saw him for only a brief moment, both Reece and Freddy were confident that he was their target. Amin Nawaz knelt by the vehicle, becoming totally obscured from view by his detail. He must have waved the boy over as he was prodded forward by his father and then walked sheepishly toward the stranger. The boy disappeared into the rugby scrum of terrorists until his head popped up. Nawaz had him seated on his shoulders like a father carrying his child at a carnival. *Shit. No shot.*

"What's the situation? Over," the radio headphone cackled in Reece's ear. *What asshole in Langley thinks this is a good time to be on the net?* He did not respond to the ridiculous query.

Freddy exhaled deeply as he struggled with what had effectively become a hostage situation and the ultimate sniper's dilemma. The gaggle of men began to move toward the door, the SEAL shooter tracking the position of Nawaz's head as it bobbed among the men of his security detail. Between the risk of hitting the boy and the low probability of a clean hit on the target among his security men, there was nothing the snipers could do but watch. Ten seconds after placing the boy on his shoulders, Nawaz and his detail were safely inside the building.

"Fuck!" Freddy whispered a bit too loudly, putting the weapon back on SAFE.

"You didn't have a shot, buddy. You did the right thing. Okay, two options: assault the building or wait to take him out when he exits."

"There's, what, twelve bad guys that we know of?"

"Yeah, I counted twelve. We wait him out."

"Damn it. I can't stand the thought of what's gonna happen to that kid while we wait. *Fucking* savages," Freddy hissed.

"I know, Freddy, me neither, but there isn't a damn thing we can do about that at the moment."

"Why in the hell wouldn't they authorize a drone strike on this vehicle on its way here in the first place?" Freddy said, even though he knew the answer.

"Politics with, in this case, a heavy dose of practicality. We need to protect Mo's cover to keep him a valuable asset to the U.S. government. A drone strike would look like exactly what it is, a U.S. assassination. We need this to look like an Albanian operation. We have to sit tight and take him on the way out."

CHAPTER 49

Edirne, Turkey
September

MO HAD SIGNALED TO Jules Landry that he needed to meet in person. The method was a simple one: a cryptic message left in the "draft" folder of the private messaging system on a Web forum dedicated to stamp collecting. Both men had a shared log-in and accessed the system on a regular basis to check for unsent messages left for each other. The same method was commonly used on webmail services, but the NSA was doing a better job of monitoring accounts with no incoming and outgoing emails, so the Swiss-based *philatélie* server provided an extra layer of protection for those who adapted in a tech-based world. General David Petraeus had used a similar technique with his mistress until a random series of events led to its discovery by the FBI.

Landry set up the meeting just outside the Greek-influenced city of Edirne, near Turkey's border with Bulgaria, so that he could use one of his EU passports to escape westward if something went wrong. He walked down the gray and white mosaic sidewalks of the city and climbed into his small rental Mercedes sedan. He'd spent the night locally and had scouted the route and the meeting site. Even in his chemically altered state, he remembered his tradecraft.

The road from town headed north, across a narrow stone bridge. Landry breathed easier once his car was past the choke point and over the wide-open swamp beyond. He turned right at the intersection and could see the ruins of the Ottoman Palace ahead. Pulling the car off the road, he parked on the grass, choosing to walk the last hundred meters of open farmland.

The twilight air was cool, and Landry was glad to be wearing a jacket. He had found that black leather made you all but invisible in this part of the world; his dark hair didn't hurt, either. He saw little sign of activity as he approached the ruins. It was primarily an agricultural area, not prone to crowds of tourists. Unlike most of Europe or anywhere in the United States, this historical site was open to the world with no fences, gates, or price of admission; it was simply part of the town.

He saw someone leaning against the opening of the Felicity Gate, a preserved doorway of what was left of a crumbled brick palace wall. Even at this distance, he could tell it was Mo. The man smiled as he approached. Mo jerked his head toward the larger labyrinth of ruins, Landry following a few steps behind. They passed under a columned archway and into one of the few standing rooms among the remains of the once-imposing structure. Mo lit a cigarette. That was the signal.

As Landry stepped inside, an electric stun baton emerged from the shadows and administered two and a half microcoulombs and thirty thousand volts just below his hip. He fell forward without the ability to raise his arms and crashed facedown onto the rocky ground. Mo and his paid accomplice worked quickly and had Landry flex-cuffed, with duct tape added for good measure, gagged, searched, drugged with a heavy dose of benzodiazepines, and rolled into a thick rug within minutes. They carried him into a delivery van filled with local carpets and hid him among the cargo. Mo powered off Landry's phone and zipped it into a bag designed to block all incoming and outgoing signals to prevent tracking and pocketed his car keys to dispose of along the route. Mo handed his accomplice an envelope of cash and bid him farewell before hoisting himself into the van and turning the key to begin the long trek toward the Ibrahim Khalil border crossing. Mo was headed home.

CHAPTER 50

Tirana, Albania
September

THE WAITING WAS BRUTAL. Not only were Reece and Freddy under the stress of the mission and the breakdown of the original plan, but they had to effectively stand by while an innocent child endured unspeakable abuse. The men's thoughts wandered to their own children, both living and deceased. Reece knew that Freddy would be thinking of his son Sam; you couldn't switch off being a father, no matter how hard you trained.

At 9:00 p.m., Reece took his place behind the rifle. Dusk had turned to darkness, but the clear visual through the thermal optic turned night almost to day. The security men outside the building glowed bright white through the scope, the warm concrete standing out against the cool ground beside it. Reece turned on the illuminated MIL-DOT "Police" reticle of the S&B rifle scope, the glowing red crosshairs giving him better contrast against the grayscale thermal image.

Despite a population of 3,500 residents, the grounds surrounding the apartment buildings were all but deserted: no children playing, no old men smoking, no women walking to or from the nearby shopping areas. The locals knew that something was going on. They didn't need to be told. This was home. They could sense it. The only signs of life came from televisions flickering in windows and the sounds of conversations echoing down the hallway outside their door. Thirty-five minutes into Reece's shift, the perimeter guards' behavior changed; the boss was coming out. Four men emerged from the building's side entrance and walked to the SUV, opening the doors. Now that darkness had fallen, the men were brandishing their weapons openly. *Six at the truck, six on the perimeter.*

Reece moved the rifle's selector back to FIRE and steadied the toe of the buttstock against the beanbag-like rear rest on the table. Two more armed men emerged from the building and stopped halfway to the vehicle, facing outward. Reece took a deep breath, exhaled slowly, and prepared himself for a precise shot. The security detail lead emerged next, with the shorter and heavier Nawaz trailing behind him. Reece took another breath and exhaled as he began to track the white-hot moving target with his crosshairs. The leader waved his hand toward the two men standing in front of them. They began to walk back in his direction. Reece had mere seconds before the target would be surrounded by security men.

He continued to track the target, holding the crosshairs on the front of Amin Nawaz's chest as he increased pressure on the trigger. Even suppressed, the shot was loud inside the confines of the room, especially after the men had worked in near silence for hours. The 175-grain Open-Tip Match bullet passed across the open courtyard in a quarter of a second before slamming into Nawaz's right arm. The bullet shattered the humerus on its way into his thoracic cavity, where it center-punched a rib, sending shards of bone into his lung like shrapnel. The bullet continued its slightly downward path as it shredded its way through both lungs and exited on the off side of his body, spraying blood, bone, and even bits of his ample body hair across the graveled ground.

His security men heard the sickening *thwock* of the bullet's impact an instant before the supersonic crack of the bullet's travel reached their ears. Nawaz lunged forward and down, crashing into his chief bodyguard. The security detail quickly became disoriented in the darkness, unsure how to react; they'd obviously spent their time intimidating civilians instead of rehearsing immediate action drills.

Amin Nawaz lay facedown, gasping unsuccessfully for breath as his lungs filled with blood. The two men closest to him finally reacted and began dragging his limp body toward the idling Opel. Reece and Freddy could hear the men yelling at one another as the rest of the team raced to surround their fallen leader.

"Hedgehog down. I say again, Hedgehog down, over," Freddy reported over the radio in a calm, even tone.

"Roger that, Hedgehog down," a distant command voice responded.

"SPARTAN, this is RENEGADE TWO-TWO, over," an animated voice joined in.

"I've got you, RENEGADE, preparing to move."

"Roger that, I'm ten mikes out."

"Good copy."

Within ten seconds of Freddy's radio call to Langley, the entire city of Tirana went dark. Agency hackers had breached a firewall for the Albanian power corporation known as KESH a week earlier and, with the target down, they signaled the servers to discontinue distribution of electricity to that sector of the nation's power grid. The hydroelectric plants continued to make power; the distribution points simply stopped relaying it. With Institut now thrown into absolute blackness, save for what came from the quarter moon, the terrorists' panic level increased exponentially.

As Reece and Freddy worked swiftly to ready their gear, they heard shots ring out. At first it was a few isolated bursts but the rest of the men caught on and soon full-auto gunfire was spraying in almost every direction. The suppressor had eliminated the rifle's muzzle flash and had muffled the report, so it was doubtful the men outside knew from which building the shot had originated. Their reaction was to wildly pump rounds into every structure in the vicinity in what professionals referred to as a "death blossom."

"RENEGADE TWO-TWO, this is SPARTAN. Hot extract. I say again, hot extract, over."

"Roger that, SPARTAN. Eight mikes out," a voice responded over the sound of a screaming diesel motor in the background.

Both operators had put on their helmets with the distinctive four-eyed NODs in place. Freddy had the magazines for the 7.62mm HK sniper rifle in his vest, so he carried the larger rifle. Reece checked the ATPIAL laser on his little MP7 submachine gun and nodded to his partner, who removed the two-by-four blocking the door and opened it, allowing Reece to creep into the deserted hallway. The sniper pair moved quickly but quietly toward the stairwell at the end of the hall, hearing animated voices from the apartments they passed. The residents of Institut were apparently unhappy with the power being shut off during their prime TV-watching time, not to mention the hail of bullets just outside their doors. They made it to the stairs and took the two flights down in seconds, pausing at the bottom to ensure that the hallway was clear. Halfway down the narrow ground-floor hallway, a beam of light washed out their night vision, and they heard a female scream. A surprised young woman dropped a flashlight and sprinted down the hall. The men raced to catch her, but she had too much of a head start.

"Polici! Polici!" she screamed as she burst through the metal doors and out into the open area between the buildings, pointing back the way she'd come.

Reece rounded the corner just in time to see a burst of tracers cut her down, the fire shifting to the doors. He dove back inside as the bullets impacted the concrete walls and metal doors, sending shards of dust and debris across the small entryway. Back on his feet, he and Freddy made their way swiftly toward the building's only other exit.

When they reached the side door, which was propped open with a rock the size of a soccer ball, they saw the headlights of a pickup truck racing toward their position. One of the terrorists riding in the bed of the truck had a belt-fed PKM machine gun resting over the cab and began firing toward the open doorway. Both men dropped to the ground and Freddy began firing methodically toward the PKM's muzzle flash while Reece put a long burst into the truck's windshield. The firing stopped, and the engine's whine slowed to an idle. The truck's momentum carried it forward as the pace slowed while both operators shifted their fire to the headlights.

The lull in the fire was temporary as the enemy began to zero in on the Americans' location. Within moments, more small-arms fire impacted around the doorway.

"I'll cover the other door," Reece yelled over the gunfire. "How far out is Ox?"

"RENEGADE TWO-TWO, what's your ETA, over?" Freddy called over the radio.

"Under five, I say again, under five."

Reece heard the transmission and flashed Freddy a thumbs-up as he jogged down the hallway. Rounds still passed through both of the building's openings, preventing either man from returning effective fire. Green tracers from a belt-fed weapon ricocheted as they impacted the walls of the hallway and 5.45mm AK rounds hit in a less frequent but equally deadly tempo. Reece slowly worked an angle on the doorway, firing short bursts as enemy muzzle flashes worked their way into his line of sight.

"I need a window," Reece heard his frustrated teammate call out. Seconds later, he heard the sound of a door being kicked in and the screams of the residents inside. The window gave Freddy a better position and after he dropped two terrorists with as many shots, the firing from that side of the building abated as the survivors took cover behind the bullet-laden pickup truck.

"Moving your way," Reece said into his radio.

Freddy fired repeated rounds into the truck to keep the enemies' heads down as Reece moved to exit the side door, scanning the area outside to ensure that he wasn't going to walk into a burst of machine-gun fire. Satisfied that it was as quiet as it was going to get, he sprinted through the door and ran around to the back side of the apartment building, where he took a knee to cover Freddy's exit. He didn't have to say a word; instead he fired short bursts from his MP7 under the pickup, his laser dancing across the open ground. Two of the rounds caught a shooter in the shin and he fell to his side, grasping his leg. The next burst hit his face. Freddy moved past Reece and took cover behind a small car, firing toward the enemy. They leapfrogged slowly, putting distance between themselves and the terrorist gunmen.

The scene was first world versus third, trained versus untrained, disciplined versus undisciplined. Reece and Freddy moved, fired, and changed magazines with practiced discipline while the terrorists sprayed rounds wildly on full automatic. The technological advantage of the NODs and IR laser–equipped former Frogmen was almost unfair: the terrorists fired at fleeting sounds and shadows while Reece and Freddy could clearly see not only the enemy, but each other's lasers. To the commanders and analysts stateside watching the scene from the black-and-white UAV feed, it was like watching a video game with the sound muted. IR strobes blinked on top of the helmets of the good guys while the bad guys' muzzle flashes identified them with nearly equal clarity.

Rick "Ox" Andrews had earned his nickname as a nineteen-year-old Ranger private first class by running across the runway of the Port Salines Airport in Grenada under fire, laden like an ox with a mortar tube across his shoulders and belts of linked M-60 ammunition crisscrossing his chest. He'd fought in nearly every armed conflict since that October day in 1983 and had served as a sergeant major in the Army's premier special operations unit before going to work for the CIA's Ground Branch in 2004. The special operations world was a small one, and he and Reece had crossed paths more than once in both Iraq and Afghanistan.

"Thirty seconds out," Ox called over the radio as he wove the green Land Rover Defender 90 toward the firefight around parked and slower-moving cars. He flipped his NODs down as he neared the target, his path illuminated by the vehicle's IR headlights. As soon as he did, he saw the beam from the powerful laser co-witnessed with the sights of the machine gun mounted on the Rover's roll bar. He hit the brakes, careful not to bounce his gunner around too badly, and turned sharply. The turn put them perpendicular to the pickup with the enemy totally exposed. Ox winced as the 12.7mm DShkM machine gun came alive above his head, its 855-grain armor-piercing incendiary bullets tearing the men, their weapons, and the truck behind them to shredded bits of flesh and metal.

Ox steered past the pickup and caught sight of the IR beams from Reece's and Freddy's ATPIALs two hundred meters ahead. He accelerated in their direction and saw one of their flashing IR strobes emerge from behind a compact car as he closed the distance. As he rolled to a stop, Reece opened the passenger-side door and climbed inside. He heard Freddy tumble into the truck's bed, and the massive gunner, whom they'd nicknamed Django after the movie character, slapped the truck's roof. Ox consulted the night vision–compatible LCD screen attached to the truck's dash as he accelerated away from the objective, confirming over his Peltor headset that their ride was inbound.

Reece changed magazines in the passenger seat and looked through the Rover's back window to see Strain covering the truck's rear with his rifle. *Full head count.* He let Ox handle the navigation as he ran through a mental checklist and subconsciously checked over his gear with his left hand. *Full mag in the gun and one more in the vest.* All Reece could see were buildings lining the darkened city streets as Ox wove his way toward the extraction point, his goggled head shifting between the road ahead and the screen to his right.

"Good to see you, buddy," Ox said as he drove. Reece could see his trademark grin below his NODs.

"*Damn* good to see you, Ox! We appreciate the ride."

"No worries, man, somebody's gotta keep you Navy guys out of trouble."

Ox steered the truck off the road and drove through a side yard between two houses at fifty mph. As they crossed the open field, a black shadow descended before them out of the heavens. The sound came next, the twin blades roaring through the night sky, the rotor wash forcing the high grass flat against the ground. Ox hit the brakes but was still moving at a faster pace than Reece had expected when he steered the Land Rover up the metal ramp of the MH-47G Chinook. It was a tight fit, too tight to open the truck's doors, but the Defender fit into the helicopter's cargo bay like it was made for it. Ox engaged the parking brake and shut off the engine, flashing a thumbs-up to the flight engineer. Seconds later, the pilot from the 160th Special Operations Aviation Regiment added power and lifted off.

. . .

As the helo gained altitude and turned west toward the Adriatic Sea, Amin Nawaz's dead body lay cooling in the backseat of the Opel, his frantic driver speeding to exit the city. Within an hour, cable news outlets were reporting that the terrorist leader had been killed in a raid by Albanian commandos and, an hour after that report, the actual commandos from Albania's Eagle 5 arrived on the scene of the firefight in their DShKM-armed, olive-green Land Rover Defender 90s. Thanks to a tip provided to the nation's State Intelligence Service, the Albanian SHISH recovered the terrorist leader's abandoned body in a discarded vehicle a few kilometers outside Tirana.

CHAPTER 51

Turkey-Iraq Border
September

IT TOOK THE TWO-VEHICLE convoy ten hours to reach the border. After passing through the town of Silopi, Turkey, Mo and his men crossed the Khabur River and approached the arched Frontier Gate at Ibrahim Khalil. The men manning the border were Kurdish Peshmerga, the most pro-U.S. troops in Iraq. Despite guarding an international border on behalf of their nation, they wore the sunburst flag of Kurdistan on their U.S.-made woodland BDUs rather than the flag of Iraq. Kurdistan was a nation within a nation, a place the CIA never really left after 1991.

The officer in charge of the checkpoint pointed toward a white Ford F-250 with a PKM machine gun mounted in the rear, operated by a balaclava-wearing Kurd dressed in desert tiger stripe.

CIA.

The skids had already been greased, and Mo passed through the checkpoint unhindered. Two Ford trucks with gunners manning the big guns in their beds fell in with Mo's van, one in front and one behind. Mo gave them a nod and a thumbs-up, following the lead vehicle in what was now a CIA convoy, returning to a country he had vowed never to set foot in again.

Mo briefly wondered if Landry would survive the journey; it was a long distance to travel wrapped up in a rug with feet, hands, and mouth secured with duct tape, and decided this was an appropriate time for an *Inshallah.*

The Agency operated with absolute autonomy in Kurdistan, even during the Saddam years. They had organized a coup there in 1995, one that was thwarted not by Hussein or his secret police, but by the national security advisor in the White House. The CIA and Iraqi dissidents had planned the coup early in 1995 but, at the last minute, the White House lost its nerve. Despite having two divisions and a brigade of the Iraqi Army ready to defect to the anti-Saddam forces, Agency personnel received a last-minute cable from Washington ordering them to stand down. Mo had no idea whether the plan for a coup would have succeeded, but having seen far too much bloodshed in the chaos that followed Saddam's removal in 2003, he believed the risk would have been worth it.

He briefly wondered what his life would be like had that coup succeeded, but quickly brushed the thought aside. He had work to do in the present, an assignment to break and question his treacherous cargo. The tables were turned, and soon Landry would answer for his sins.

CHAPTER 52

Aboard the USS Kearsarge *(LHD-3)*
Adriatic Sea
September

THE CHINOOK LANDED ON the deck of the amphibious assault ship under the cover of darkness, the only illumination on deck coming from a strip of green landing lights. Reece, Strain, Ox, and Django climbed out of the Defender through the top of its roll cage and down the helo's rear ramp while the aircraft and deck crews worked swiftly to move the MH-47 onto the elevator that would take it to a hangar belowdecks. A desert-cammie-clad Marine first lieutenant from the 26th Marine Expeditionary Unit led the men across the deck and inside through a steel hatch. All four commandos squinted as their eyes adjusted to the bright fluorescent lights of the ship's interior while their escort led them through the labyrinth of corridors. Members of the ship's crew stepped aside to let the visitors pass in the narrow space, eyeing the mysterious armed men with curiosity. The beards, nylon chest rigs, and salt-stained MultiCam combat clothing worn by the Agency men contrasted sharply with the blue and gray "Aquaflage" worn by the clean-cut sailors of the conventional Navy.

Wonder what admiral ever approved that uniform, Reece thought.

Reece hadn't been able to catch up with Ox much during the flight due to the noise. Now he was directly behind the Army legend as they moved through the bowels of what Reece often termed a "big gray ship" due to his mysterious inability to tell them apart.

"Aren't you getting too old for this, Ox? Happy seventieth birthday, by the way. Sorry I missed it."

"Easy, Reece, I'm not even sixty! Besides, the way my wife spends money, I can't afford to retire. I can still drive and shoot as long as I don't forget my glasses."

"Well, you must be the Dorian Gray of ███████."

"Who?" Ox asked.

"Never mind."

"Just don't ask him how to work the comms," the usually stoic Django deadpanned over his shoulder.

"Yeah, I need to start bringing one of my grandkids along to work the radios," Ox shot back at his partner. "Why do they make those things so complicated?"

Their Marine escort motioned to a closed hatch and the men shifted to a more professional demeanor as they entered the room for the mission debrief. The room was fairly large by ship standards and was one of the ready rooms for the LHD's helo pilots. A Marine helicopter squadron logo adorned the hatch as well as the podium at the front of the room, where two men and a woman, all dressed in civilian clothes, waited.

"Great job, boys, fantastic work. Mr. Strain, you and your friend here are going to make me take back all of the bad things I've ever said about SEALs. Mr. Reece, I'm Vic Rodriguez, very nice to meet you."

Reece was never a great judge of height, but he guessed Rodriguez at five feet six. He was a handsome man with short salt-and-pepper hair and olive skin that made his age hard to guess. Dressed in khaki pants, hiking boots, and a black polo shirt, he was fit and had an energetic air that made him immediately likable.

The two men shook hands, Rodriguez smiling warmly. He motioned toward the other individuals in the room and introduced them. Reece recognized Nicole Phan, the analyst from the videoconference in Istanbul; she looked even younger in person.

"Guys, this is Major Dave Harper. He's a liaison from █████," Rodriguez said, introducing the thin man with the high and tight haircut.

"Great job out there. I'm just here to coordinate the air, ground, and sea assets for this. Here to help however I can."

"Those helo pilots were nothing short of incredible," Reece said. "Please thank them for us."

"Will do," the Army major said with a nod.

The ship's galley had the room catered and the food, true to Navy form, was actually not bad, though Reece hadn't forgotten the differences between eating in the officers' mess and the enlisted one. *Night and day.* Reece and Freddy ate like they'd been shipwrecked for weeks before beginning the hotwash. He led them through each phase of the mission, answering questions from Rodriguez, Phan, and Harper as they went. The UAV images were displayed on the room's LCD screen, and the men gave play-by-play narratives from their perspective on the ground. Reece had been through hundreds of similar debriefs during his time in special operations, though none were as sensitive or as classified as this one. Following the three-hour meeting, Harper called for an escort to show the men to their assigned sleeping quarters.

Rodriguez shook Reece's hand on the way out and spoke in a muted voice. "Great work, Reece. Get some sleep. There's something I want to discuss with you in the morning."

Reece bid him good night, wondering what the morning's conversation would entail.

CHAPTER 53

REECE SLEPT WELL; THE ship's gentle roll a muted reminder of his time at sea aboard the Beneteau. That voyage seemed like years ago now. He dreamt of the ocean, how it offered him refuge, tested him, and delivered him, to what, he wasn't yet sure.

Voices passing outside the hatch of the small stateroom rousted him from a deep slumber. Reece stared silently into the pitch-black darkness and tried to remember where he was. After realizing that he hadn't failed BUD/S and been assigned to the fleet, he swung his feet onto the deck and felt for his Navy-supplied "shower shoes" with his toes.

The ship's company had left a package of new white T-shirts and a blue coverall jumpsuit for him on the bunk. He couldn't bring himself to put on the coveralls but he put on one of the fresh T-shirts and pulled on the Crye MultiCam pants that he'd worn on the Albania op. He brushed his hair back with his hands as best he could and put on a sweat-stained Padres cap he'd found under the bed. Heading out into the passageway and into the bustling heart of the ship during the morning watch, Reece asked directions to the wardroom and wandered in that direction. Navigating the internal passageways of a ship had never come easily to him.

Reece eventually found it with the help of a seaman apprentice who looked about twelve, and he wasn't surprised to see Ox already there when he arrived. He caught some strange looks from the khaki-uniform-wearing officers seated at one of the tables and begrudgingly took off his hat. He wasn't sure why he worried about it, the normal decorum of the officers' mess having already been shattered by the pasty-white former Army NCO clad in a tight T-shirt and a pair of black "Ranger panty" PT shorts, far too much of his anatomy on full display. The ship's officers apparently knew better than to say anything to the barrel-chested operator sitting by himself.

"Ox, you still wearing those Speedos in public? I think there's a regulation of some sort against that in the twenty-first-century military. You realize there are women on Navy ships now, right? You remind me of the old chiefs at Coronado who were still rockin' UDT shorts when I showed up as a new guy."

"Nothing more comfortable, brother. I'm not giving these things up. Get some coffee and come join me." Ox motioned to an urn full of the Navy's best jet fuel on a table nearby.

Reece filled his cup and doctored it carefully with sweetener and milk, a bit disappointed at the lack of honey.

"Good thing they *do* have women on ships now, Reece; otherwise you'd have to drink it black, like a man."

Reece gave his friend the one-finger salute over his shoulder, then took a seat at the round table, where his friend read a computer printout of a news story through a pair of half-glasses.

"What's happening in the world today, Ox?"

"Well, it says here that some Albanian commandos killed the most wanted terrorist in the world in a firefight last night."

"No kidding? Good for them."

"Yeah, pretty crazy. Says here in all that chaos somebody put a single round through his lungs."

"Wow! Kinda sounds like when Colombian forces killed Pablo Escobar," Reece said with a conspiratorial smile.

Ox looked at Reece over his glasses: "Very similar, my friend. Very similar."

"Are we the only ones up? What time is it?"

"Ha! It's 0930, Reece. Everyone has been up for hours. Freddy and Vic are off somewhere doing admin, and Django is in the gym, staying huge. He must have eaten a dozen eggs this morning. You need some chow?"

"No, I'm good with coffee for now."

Reece drank his java in silence, still trying to clear his mind from the fog of sleep while Ox droned on about something. Twenty minutes later, Vic Rodriguez walked into the wardroom dressed in pressed casual clothes: showered, shaved, and looking sharp.

"Good morning, Mr. Reece. Ox, glad to see that you haven't moved in two hours."

"Just catching up on the news, boss."

Rodriguez rolled his eyes.

"Reece, is this a good time for us to talk?"

"Good a time as any, I guess."

"Let's head topside. Top off your coffee if you'd like."

Reece nodded to Ox, who flashed him a grin as he refilled his coffee and followed the Agency man toward the upper deck. The irony was not lost on him that, as a career naval officer, he had to follow a former soldier to find his way through the ship. Vic led him through a hatch and onto the windswept flight deck. A crew member nodded to him and pointed toward the stern; this had obviously been arranged ahead of time. The two men stopped aft of the ship's superstructure, a few feet from the deck's edge, the chained railing the only thing between them and a long drop into the Adriatic Sea below. They were mostly out of the wind, but it was still present enough that no one standing more than ten feet away would be able to eavesdrop on their conversation, and no member of the ship's crew was within anything close to that distance. They had complete privacy. Rodriguez got right to the point.

"Reece, I want to thank you for what you've done; because of your efforts, the most wanted terrorist in the world is a corpse. Global markets are reacting to the news as we speak. We had a deal; as far as the U.S. government is concerned, you're a free man."

"I appreciate that, Vic. I get the feeling there's a 'but' here, though."

"You're right, Reece, there's a 'but.' You don't owe us a thing, *but* we sure could use you. I am offering you a job, no strings attached. You'd be a green-badger, a contract guy. You know what that means. It's not a bad deal. And you get to see this thing through."

Reece took a sip of coffee and stared out at the choppy green water on the horizon.

Rodriguez continued: "Okay, I guess you're going to make me sell it. You know what kind of evil is out there; you've been in these countries. Amin Nawaz was a big get for us, but someone is going to take his place tomorrow, smarter and even more determined. We need people we can count on to hunt these assholes down to the ends of the earth. And here's the other part: that plan that you came up with to flip Mo and use him as a 'pseudoterrorist'? It's brilliant, but I need you here to run it or else it'll get *fucked up*; you know that. Major Farooq, Mo as you call him, is on his way into Iraq with Landry right now. This isn't over by a long shot."

Reece nodded and took another sip of coffee, glad his friend was still alive and well.

"Listen, Reece, I don't know you personally, but I know your reputation. I've read all your EVALS, FITREPs, and medal citations, but more importantly, Freddy and Ox think the world of you. Come work for me. You do what you're good at, and I deal with the politics and the red tape."

Reece looked Rodriguez in the eye: "You really think they're going to let me go? They're just going to forget about all the people I killed?"

"Reece, all I know is that I can't protect you if you're not under my wing. Give me a few months on the job, focus on the mission, and I'll provide top cover. If you decide later that you want to walk, I won't try to stop you."

Reece was silent for a full minute as he weighed the different scenarios. He started to say no but stopped himself, looking out to sea, remembering the voyage from Fishers to Mozambique, his family, the tumor, and Katie. In the end, he made the decision for Mohammed, his friend with whom he had shared the bond of combat. This wasn't over. Mo had been played. He'd been played by a sociopath who had found his way into an intelligence agency that gave him the freedom to feed his sick fantasies. And somebody, possibly in the Agency itself, was running that sociopath. This wasn't over, and Reece couldn't walk until it was. He couldn't leave Mo halfway through the operation. To Reece, that was the same thing as leaving him behind on the battlefield. Vic was right, Reece needed to see it through.

"You forgot to mention something, Vic."

"Oh, what's that?"

"That you read my psych eval; that you knew I'd say yes."

Vic smiled. "Well, true, there is that."

Reece paused. "I'm saying yes to finishing this operation and then I'm out."

Vic Rodriguez smiled again and extended his hand.

"Welcome to the team, Reece. Surgery is planned either at Bethesda or at your clinic in La Jolla as soon as this is over. And by the way, you've got some money coming your way. We made it a condition of you coming on board that you got to keep the reward money for Nawaz. It was coming from the British government, so we worked it in as a term of your employment. It's a sizable chunk. Figured you could use it to get a fresh start."

"That might just about cover my old Land Cruiser, and I owe more than a few people beers. I do have one request to make, though."

"What's that?"

"I need you to track down a phone number for me."

. . .

After a pause and some clicks and beeps as the Iridium satellite phone connected, Reece heard it begin to ring. He was more nervous than he thought he would be. He hoped she'd answer the strange number.

C'mon, pick up.

He thought of all the times he'd called Lauren on the same type of phone, the same clicks and beeps followed by the strange satellite-transformed voice that made loved ones sound like aliens from another world. He'd always told her that everything was okay and not much was going on, even as he looked up at the night sky following a mission in which everything was *not* okay. No matter how tired he was, he always made time to call, feeling it was his responsibility to use the technical advantages afforded him that were not available to his late father in Vietnam or his grandfather in World War II.

"This is Katie."

Pause.

"Ah . . . Katie?"

"Yes?"

"Ah, it's um . . ."

"Hello, anyone there?"

Even through the Iridium satellite link he could detect her slight hint of an accent that most people wouldn't even notice.

"It's um . . ."

Shit! What am I, in junior high?

"Hello?" she said again.

Paralyzed, Recce remembered her on her knees with det cord twisted around her neck, with the thumb of a SEAL turned CIA operative turned mercenary on the detonator.

Reece, how did you know Ben didn't have that detonator connected? How did you know he wouldn't blow my head off?

"*Shit!*" Reece said out loud, hitting the END CALL button.

I didn't.

CHAPTER 54

Kurdistan, Iraq
September

LANDRY THOUGHT HE WAS going to die. As whatever drugs they'd given him wore off, panic began to set in. It didn't help that he was beginning to experience withdrawal symptoms from the cocktail of recreational and prescription drugs that had become his mainstay. His wrists and ankles were bound, there was tape over his mouth and eyes, and he was wrapped in something heavy. The heat was stifling, and the pillowcase over his head only exacerbated the claustrophobic conditions. The only sounds he could hear were those of tires on various combinations of asphalt, gravel, and dirt as the vehicle traveled for what seemed like days, his brain having no reference points to maintain his sense of equilibrium. He dry-heaved repeatedly from motion sickness, his clothing soaked in sweat and urine. His brain raced to process what had happened; he lived a paranoid existence as it was, expecting betrayal at nearly every moment. He struggled to make sense of what had gone wrong.

Betrayed by Mo, but to who and for what? Had Mo found out he wasn't really a CIA asset continuing his work for the United States government he'd started in Iraq?

This was more than misery. This was pushing Landry into the land of the insane. He squinted his eyes shut trying to make this nightmare end, only to open them to the darkness of the tape and hood, his muffled screams the only outlet for what had turned into an anxiety attack without end.

The van accelerated over gravel, made several sharp turns, and finally came to a stop, brakes squeaking. The driver was speaking to someone outside, and Landry heard the doors open. Whatever he was wrapped in was jerked from the vehicle. He landed on the ground with an unceremonious thud and rolled sideways as the rug unraveled. The effect was dizzying. Landry attempted to gasp for air, thwarted by the tape across his mouth.

It must be night, he thought, feeling the cool air against his skin. He could hear the distant hum of generators.

The scrape of a metal door penetrated the darkness and he was carried, facedown, by what felt like four men into a building of some kind. The footfalls of boots sounded as if they were walking on a concrete floor and he heard various doors open and shut in front of and behind them. No voices. The movement stopped and he was dropped onto the hard floor, his chin splitting on impact. He heard a strange sound that he couldn't identify until he realized it was a pair of EMT shears cutting the clothing from his body. The room was freezing cold, and he felt increasingly chilled as his skin was exposed to the air.

His boots were pulled from his feet and he was left totally naked on the cold, hard floor. The door slammed shut and, hands still bound with zip ties and duct tape, he curled up in a ball, shivering and convulsing, on the verge of madness.

CHAPTER 55

Over the Mediterranean Sea
September

THEIR FLIGHT TOOK CLOSE to three hours and nearly maxed out the V-22's fuel capacity. It was Reece's first time riding in the tilt-rotor aircraft and, though part of him thought it was an incredible feat of engineering, the almost-forty-something part of his brain couldn't help but remember how many times these aircraft had crashed during development. He and Freddy sat in the folding seats that lined the walls of the aircraft's cargo bay, which, to Reece's untrained eye, looked like a smaller version of the Chinook's interior. The inside of the fuselage was covered in an endless tangle of wires, metal lines, and hoses like something out of some steampunk artist's fantasy.

Reece thought of one of Ox's favorite sayings: "If you get in a helicopter and it's not leaking, get ready to crash because that means it's out of hydraulic fluid."

He looked up to see whether anything was dripping.

The Marine pilots steered them over the open Mediterranean before going "feet dry" over Turkey and finally passing into the airspace of northern Iraq. Their landing at Erbil International Airport was conventional by Iraqi standards, unlike the dive-bomber-like landings they'd all endured during approaches into Baghdad International Airport. *The surface-to-air threat must be pretty light here these days.* Their headsets allowed them to hear the chatter on the bird's intercom, which mainly consisted of the pilots conveying information to the crew chief riding with them in the cargo bay. It was all very routine.

Reece was curious whether the Osprey would land vertically or horizontally but, due to the generous runway, it touched down like a traditional fixed-wing aircraft. *Probably safer that way.*

After a short taxi, the twin turbine engines shut down and the rear ramp was lowered. Reece and Freddy went forward to thank the pilots and crew for the ride before unstacking their assorted gear strapped to a pallet on the aircraft's metal floor. The crew chief helped them carry the kit bags and Pelican cases to the tarmac, where a white F-250 had pulled up behind the Osprey. A small group of Peshmerga troops armed with SCAR-17s and dressed in surplus U.S. desert camo and black body armor stayed by the truck while a tall, blond-haired American wearing jeans and a tan polo shirt approached, looking like he'd just walked off the Norwegian ski team.

"Freddy, good to see you, buddy," the man said in recognition of Reece's partner.

"Hey, Erik! Appreciate the pickup. Meet James Donovan."

"Donovan, huh? *Okay.* Well, welcome to Kurdistan, James. Pleasure to meet you. I'm Erik Spuhr. I've heard good things."

Reece shook the man's extended hand. "Good to meet you as well."

"Let's get you boys loaded up and out of here. Your guest is waiting."

Spuhr waved to the Kurdish troops, who moved quickly to help retrieve the men's gear and load it into the truck. Reece and Freddy insisted on helping. They both noticed that Erik left the work to the Kurds.

They loaded into the crew-cab pickup, Spuhr behind the wheel, and drove east through the city.

"What's that?" Reece asked, turning in his seat to take in the huge fortress that occupied the high ground to his right.

"That's the famous Citadel of Erbil. They say it's been inhabited continuously since people first lived in this part of the world," Erik informed them.

"Good tactical position," Freddy observed. "Probably a good strategic one as well if it's been inhabited that long."

An hour east of Mosul, which had only recently been retaken from ISIS occupation, Erbil was the capital of Kurdistan, a relatively safe and quiet city of just under a million residents. It was an eclectic mix of modern and ancient structures and boasted beautiful green spaces, towering fountains, and winding, mosaic-tiled streets. Cars jammed the avenues, men sat and smoked outside coffee shops lining the sidewalks, families walked together in public, commerce was in full swing.

Leaving the historic city, they hit a main road that took them north. In contrast to much of Iraq, it appeared to Reece that the north was a virtual paradise. It reminded him of the Napa Valley wine country where he had been married.

"So, tell me about your crew," Freddy said, bringing them back to the present.

"All Yazidis," Spuhr began. "They're not Muslims and they've been heavily persecuted by Daesh—you know, ISIS. They hate the bad guys more than we do, so they're extremely loyal."

"Aren't all Peshmerga loyal to the U.S.?" Reece asked.

"Yeah, that's true for the most part. They have a chip on their shoulder, which is useful. They've been the ethnic and religious minority here forever; actually, they're a minority within a minority. I have them on loan from Qasem Shesho, the Old Tiger of Mount Sinjar. He's the commander of the Yazidi Pesh forces."

"What's the mission up here?" asked Freddy, his eyes scanning the road ahead.

"We're running a strike force against what's left of Daesh, ISIS, ISIL, whatever you want to call them this week. We have two commando squadrons of Yazidis trained up and we're doing a lot of direct-action work. We use their HUMINT networks along with all of our SIGINT assets and are hitting the enemy hard."

"Sounds like Baghdad 2006," Reece commented.

"Yeah, but this time we're not getting Americans killed. These people need to win back their own country."

Reece had seen plenty of Iraqi troops get killed or wounded fighting for their country, particularly from Mo's team, but he didn't press the point.

As they traveled farther from the city, the flat terrain transformed into rolling hills. Their journey led them into a wide valley where a modern compound had been built into the remote landscape. The exterior perimeter of sand-filled Hesco barriers, the modern-day equivalent of the lodgepole forts of the American frontier, screamed "U.S. outpost."

The force protection detail was a mix of local forces and Western security contractors. Inside the perimeter was a complex of concrete and steel structures at odds with the natural world outside its walls. The CIA had built its own fiefdom in this autonomous zone, a place where even the Iraqi Army was prohibited from entering by law.

"Freddy, does this remind you at all of *Apocalypse Now*?" Reece whispered, referencing the classic 1979 film by Francis Ford Coppola.

"Yes, and I expect we've already met our Kurtz."

. . .

Landry lay shivering on the floor, his body convulsing in its attempt to stay warm. With his hands bound behind his back, the best he could do was to draw his knees up to his chest. Without the stifling heat and claustrophobia of the rug, he'd begun to calm down and reenter the land of the sane. He'd tried scooting himself around the room to get his bearings and build up some body heat but the abrasive floors quickly rubbed his skin raw. He'd established that the room was roughly ten feet by ten feet and had a metal drain in the center of the floor. It was well built, almost clinical. The only ambient smell was that of the dried urine and feces that clung to his skin.

He was sure of one thing: his captors were state sponsored. Terrorist groups didn't run detainment facilities with massive air conditioners and clean concrete floors. He had to be within one thousand or so miles of where he'd been snatched. It wouldn't have made sense to take him deeper into Europe, which probably meant somewhere in the former Soviet Union, Syria, Iraq, or Iran. *Pakistan, maybe?* The Brits would want him desperately for the Christmas market attack in London, but, despite the effectiveness of their military, their government no longer had the stomach to operate in places like this; too many colonial memories.

Could the French have picked him up? They didn't play games when it came to terrorism. Instead of keeping their citizens from going to fight the infidel in foreign lands, France let them go. They let them go so that French special operations troops could hunt them down and kill them on foreign soil. But the French didn't have a footprint in this part of the world. That left the United States, the Russians, or maybe the Israelis.

Please don't let it be the Russians.

His thoughts were broken by a brief sound that was audible over the air conditioners, and seconds later his body was shocked by a blast of freezing-cold liquid. The water hit him like icy daggers, and he curled his body tighter into a more protective position. He tried worm-crawling away from the cold stream raining from above but it appeared as if the entire ceiling was equipped with shower nozzles; there was no escaping it. After an excruciating sixty seconds, the shower stopped as abruptly as it had started. A minute earlier, he hadn't thought he could be any closer to hypothermia, but that now seemed like a warm summer day by comparison. He knew this playbook. They were going to keep him on the verge of hypothermia coupled with sleep deprivation. For someone raised on the hot, steamy bayous of the Gulf Coast, this was torture, yet he knew what was coming and could play this game as well.

If it's the Americans, I still have a chance.

CHAPTER 56

Yazidi Strike Force Compound
Kurdistan
September

"WOULD YOU LIKE TO observe?" Erik asked Reece and Freddy with a tad too much enthusiasm, both men having stowed their gear in the dormitory-like rooms to which they'd been shown.

"No, thanks," Reece responded without hesitation, remembering his last experience with torture, extracting information from Saul Agnon in a Palm Springs hotel room for his role in the murders of Reece's wife and daughter.

"Me neither," Freddy chimed in. "I'd prefer to maintain some plausible deniability if this thing hits the news cycle. Remember what the last president did to the guys who interrogated Abu Zubaydah?"

Neither man had any moral objections to whatever interrogation techniques were being used on Landry; they simply weren't interested in watching. Landry was a traitor, a sellout who had become a terrorist due to a currently unknown motivation. His actions had taken innocent lives and he'd joined forces with his nation's number one enemy. On top of all that, he was a sadist who had tortured detainees under the guise of a CIA team leader. No, Jules Landry wasn't going to get any empathy from either of them.

"Suit yourselves. I'm going to go see how it's going," Spuhr said as he walked out.

They had been lounging in the Team Room, a combination club-house, living room, and meeting space used by small units around the globe. This one was nicer than most, but lacked the photos, captured enemy weapons, and other mementos that usually lined the walls and infused the space with the character of the occupying unit. With no such decorations, this room looked more like something you'd see in a nursing home or college dorm. It occurred to Reece that he hadn't watched television since he'd hastily departed the United States months ago, so he turned on the flat screen to see if he could catch the news. He found CNN International and, ironically, the segment was covering the killing of Nawaz by the now-famous Albanian Eagle commandos. He and Freddy exchanged eye rolls as a series of "counterterrorism experts" and retired military officers speculated wildly about how the mission had gone down. How these officers with high-level security clearances could spout off about ongoing military operations just days after they'd retired was beyond them both.

. . .

The freezing water soaked him at seemingly random intervals, leaving Landry constantly on edge in anticipation of the next icy blast, his body jerking uncontrollably. Then, just when his mind began to slip into delirium, the powerful air vents in the room started blowing warm air; the warmth was heavenly. As his body temperature began to rise, he was reminded of just how thirsty he was. He hadn't had anything to drink since before his capture and he was losing track of how long ago that had been. Every part of his body was soaking wet, save the inside of his mouth. Had his lips not been covered by tape, he would have licked the floor.

His head rose at the sound of the heavy metal door unlocking and quickly tucked it back against his chest, expecting a beating to begin at any moment. Footsteps sloshed across the wet floor. Whoever had entered the room smelled like cigarettes and was standing directly over him. The man pulled the wet cloth sack from his head, and the duct tape that had covered his mouth was torn swiftly away, the sharp pain only slightly diminished by the numbness of his face. His eyes were still taped over, so when something touched his lips he jerked away, causing water to spill on his chin. *Water!* His natural fear of physical pain was suppressed by his overwhelming thirst, and he extended his face toward the bottle. The cold liquid instantly brightened his mood as he gulped it down. The bottle was pulled away and something small was pressed into his mouth; it had a plastic taste to it. He tried to spit it out but the water returned and his thirst was too powerful; whatever it was, he'd just swallowed it. He pushed the thought aside and drank the water as fast as it was poured into his mouth by the plastic bottle.

The pleasure was short-lived. As quickly and abruptly as the water had come, the man left the room. Still, his body was shivering less as the room warmed, and he was no longer quite as dehydrated as he'd been just moments earlier. He'd learned during the various schools he'd attended in the Marine Corps to relish the brief moments of rest and relief when they came without thinking too much about what might happen next. He exhaled a deep breath and tried to put himself in a different place mentally, a "happy place." Just as he began to relax, his skin was blasted once again by the cold rain from above. It was like they were reading his mind.

· · ·

A sensor in the interrogation room's wall relayed the telemetry from the RFID device inside the detainee's body to the desktop monitor in the observation area. Roman Evdal, a Yazidi physician's assistant trained in the United States under an exchange program, watched the detainee's core temperature rise to 37 degrees Celsius and his heart rate slow to 65 BPM. "Rome," as he was called by the Americans at the facility, nodded to the man seated next to him, who touched his computer screen, activating the water pumps that fed the shower nozzles that covered the ceiling of the interrogation room. Rome couldn't hear the detainee scream through the thick Plexiglas with the speakers muted, but he could tell by the man's agonized facial expression that that was exactly what was happening. He looked over his shoulder toward the handsome Sunni whom he'd been instructed to address as "Major" and received an almost imperceptible nod in response. The "Major" didn't look like he was part of the Iraqi Army, and Rome suspected that he was part of the more powerful and secretive Interior Ministry. Not that it mattered; whoever he was and whoever he worked for, he was clearly in charge of this interrogation.

RFID-equipped body temperature monitors had been used for several years to monitor students' core body temperatures in the U.S. Navy's brutal Basic Underwater Demolition/SEAL training program. Breaking the will of would-be SEALs required keeping the men on the verge of hypothermia while going through Hell Week, the crucible of SEAL training that tied every generation of frogmen to the next. Men sometimes died as a result of this delicate dance, and the RFID monitors allowed instructors to instantly assess a trainee's body temperature by pointing a digital "reader" device at his torso.

Having experienced the debilitating effects of cold firsthand as a BUD/S student and later as an instructor, one of the Agency personnel involved in the construction of the interrogation facility had the bright idea of applying the technology in conjunction with "room temperature manipulations" as a method of breaking detainees without laying a hand on them. Not only could they keep them teetering on the edge of hypothermia, but they could prevent them from sleeping. Cold, exhaustion, and hunger are three of nature's most powerful forces, and they could use all three simultaneously with almost no risk of long-term physical harm. A healthy, fit male of Landry's age was unlikely to suffer a cardiac event under such stress, but a crash cart was available just in case. This was the first time this comprehensive system had been attempted on a real prisoner and, so far, it was working just as advertised.

CHAPTER 57

"HAS HE SEEN YOUR face yet, Mo?" Reece asked across the team room's dinner table.

The food here was exceptional, just like he remembered from his time attached to the Agency in Iraq. And they always had honey for his coffee.

"Not yet. I think we'll give it another day or so before I try to talk to him. The longer he goes without human interaction, the better. The cold and lack of sleep will break him. The isolation only helps exacerbate it."

"Mo, it always kills me that you have a better command of the English language than I do." Reece smiled. "And that British accent of yours makes you sound like an Oxford professor."

"You love to play the surfer boy, Reece, but I know better. I remember the stack of books in your room in Baghdad. No one has brought that much reading material to war since Churchill," Mo observed.

"Just trying to learn as much as I could about counterinsurgency and your country's history and culture. If you think I read a lot, you should see Freddy's book stack."

"I just look at the pictures," Freddy interjected.

Mo turned the conversation back to the issue at hand. "So, what do you want me to find out from Landry? He's almost ready to break."

"The big question is, who is he working for and why, but more *who* than *why*, if that makes sense," Freddy responded.

"And how many other agents and teams he's running," Reece chimed in. "We know he was handling at least two parallel teams: yours and the

STU from your old unit who hit us in North Africa. If he was also behind the Christmas market attack in London, that would bring us up to three at a minimum. There could very well be more we don't know about."

Mo scribbled some notes in a small spiral-bound book.

Reece leaned forward, his mind working the problem. "And we need to know how he knew to attack us in Morocco. No one outside of the Agency should have had that info. It's not like we got hit by some local militia group who found out there were some random Americans living down the road. That team was brought in specifically to target us. We've obviously got ourselves a leak and, Mo, your future depends on us finding out where that leak is."

CHAPTER 58

Fairfax County, Virginia
September

OLIVER GREY HATED DULLES airport. Its architecture was, to him, a glaring symbol of Cold War dominance, an obnoxious vision of America's arrogance during a period when so many in the world were rebuilding and suffering. He had a more practical reason to hate it as well: one never knew whether the Transportation Security Administration line would take five minutes or two hours. He found some ironic amusement in the fact that he used the Pre-Check lane, though; with the number of regular travelers in the D.C. area, it was barely faster than the normal security line.

The CIA analyst ordered a large Dunkin' coffee and picked up the latest Brad Thor novel while he waited impatiently for it to cool. *Spymaster*, he said silently to himself, already imagining himself in the lead role.

Surely, he'd be able to secure a good roast in St. Petersburg, but he assumed that there would be very few afternoons spent at his beloved sidewalk cafés in the immediate future due to the weather. It maddened Grey that he would have to transfer in Newark, in a middle seat no less, in order to make his connection to Europe, but it was a minor inconvenience on his way to his new life, a life of meaning. After this mission was complete, he would be the brains behind the rise of a new Russia. Andrenov appreciated his talents in a way the CIA never could.

The short flight was relatively painless but for the giant man and his filthy dog seated next to him. The figure was bearded and muscular, every inch of his arms covered in a web of tattoos. He had the military look so common these days, his "service" animal undoubtedly part of some silly veteran counseling program. Grey spent the flight leaning toward the old woman in the window seat who reminded him of his maternal grandmother with her knitting and constant jabbering.

Grey relaxed when he saw the Atlantic from the window seat of the United Airlines 757; there was no sadness even as he left the country of his birth for the last time. Thankfully, the middle seat next to him was empty, which allowed him to stretch out just a bit. He ordered a vodka soda from a middle-aged flight attendant who had the cheerful demeanor of someone working in a prison cafeteria. It wasn't very Russian of him to add the soda, or the ice for that matter, but at least he was making an effort. After two more drinks and a terrible movie, the cabin lights were extinguished. He put on his eyeshades and drifted off.

He slept surprisingly well for being in coach. The relief of finally slipping the bonds of his cover life had helped him relax. An announcement from the cockpit roused him, and he motioned to the annoyed-looking woman in the aisle seat that he needed to use the restroom. Forty minutes later, he was shuffling impatiently through the crowded aisle of passengers anxious to deplane after the overnight flight. The pale Portuguese customs officer eyed him with boredom and stamped his worn United States passport, a document he was using for the last time. The morning air was cold when he walked out onto the sidewalk in front of Humberto Delgado Airport but the sun was shining and the sky was pure blue. Grey had never felt so alive.

CHAPTER 59

Eastern Turkey
September

THEY WERE MORE LIKE artillery than small arms. The rifles weighed nearly thirty pounds each, even without the massive telescope-like optics. Both weapons had been waiting for them in the farmhouse, packed carefully in crates hidden under blankets. They didn't look like any rifles that Nizar had seen before. Tasho must have requested them. The stock looked almost skeletal, and the bipod mounted oddly above the long, thick barrel. The scope was as large as his forearm and would look right at home on the enormous rifle. Nizar spoke some English and was amused by the name of the scope, the "B.E.A.S.T."

After his assassination of President Hadad in Syria, Nizar had received his next assignment from General Yedid. That assignment had brought him to this remote land in eastern Turkey to prepare for a long-range shot, the longest Nizar had ever attempted.

The two men painstakingly mounted the U.S.-made optics, using machinist's levels to ensure that there was absolutely no cant to the reticle before torquing down the screws. The scope mount itself had a small bubble level attached so that the shooter didn't inadvertently cant the rifle while making a shot, something that could cause serious problems at extreme distances.

Packed with each rifle was a large amount of ammunition, hundreds of rounds, from the looks of it. Nizar removed one of the cartridges from its white cardboard box and examined it. He had never seen a rifle cartridge so large; it looked like something an antiaircraft gun would use.

Tasho appeared to be familiar with the equipment and worked quickly and efficiently. When he was done mounting his optic, he made sure that Nizar's was set up correctly as well. The scopes were secured using ERA-TAC adjustable mounts so that they didn't run out of vertical adjustment. Nizar didn't know who their target was, but from the looks of the sniper weapon systems, the shot was going to be a long one.

Nizar didn't care for the *Shishani*, as Tasho was nicknamed, despite his reputation. He was too cold, too solitary, too serious, but more than that, Tasho made him uneasy. He looked younger than Nizar had expected for someone with such a storied past. A pale face and red beard had become part of his calling card. When conventional forces in the Eastern world heard rumors of sightings of a sniper with red facial hair, they all prayed it was not the *Shishani*.

Nizar was not naïve enough to believe everything he had heard about the man with whom he now worked; not all of it could possibly be true. *But if a fraction of it was . . .* Still, he decided not to ask too many personal questions. Though he called him only by his first name, to Nizar he was still "the *Shishani*" as per his legend.

It was said that Tasho had begged his father to let him fight the Russians in the First Battle for Grozny. Though he was old enough to fight at age fifteen, his father would hear none of it, leaving him at home to care for his mother and two younger brothers. Tasho's father did not return that New Year's Day 1995, nor any day after. He was killed by the Russians early in the fighting, inadvertently causing exactly what he had attempted to prevent: Tasho now knew his life's calling, to kill Russians.

Choosing service in the Georgian army over life as a sheepherder, Tasho proved himself adept at shooting and stalking. Showing such promise as a tactical leader, he was recruited by the Georgian Special Reconnaissance Group, distinguishing himself in the Second Battle of Grozny in 1999. He killed fifty Russian soldiers in a single week. To Tasho, each was the Russian who had killed his father. The war also taught him his first practical lesson in asymmetrical warfare, guerrilla tactics being the order of the day: IEDs, suicide bombings, urban warfare, *a war of the rats.*

His youngest brother's death at the hands of the enemy in what became known as the Novye Aldi Massacre only sealed Tasho's resolve. When he buried his mother after the official end to hostilities, his last ties to his hometown of Shali were severed. Arrested for selling weapons to Chechen rebels, he served close to two years in prison. Identified as a prime target for recruitment and radicalization, he emerged as a full-fledged jihadi committed to the cause.

From 2004 to 2011 the cause was Iraq, where he plied his deadly skills against the infidels. He worked primarily in Ramadi, Fallujah, and Mosul, targeting coalition troops and civilians as the insurgency reached its deadly climax. As his reputation grew, so did his responsibilities in the organization known as al-Qaeda in Iraq, or AQI. One of Abu Musab al-Zarqawi's most respected fighters, he led cells of insurgents against the occupiers. With AQI's transformation into ISIS following the expulsion of U.S. forces, the *Shishani* turned his attention to Syria, where he fought Assad's forces under the new black flag. The battle for Aleppo in 2012 cemented his status as one of the most respected jihadist warriors in the Eastern world.

What his masters leading ISIS couldn't know was that Tasho's allegiance was to something other than Islam. Every time he pressed the trigger, regardless of the target, he was killing Russians.

Captured by Assad's special security forces in a raid in 2016, he was interrogated by the one man who had studied him enough to figure him out. He still remembered General Yedid's offer as he lay strapped to a metal mattress, car battery, cables, and water at the ready.

"How would you like to work for me?" the general had asked politely. "Come work for me, and I'll give you a chance to kill Russians."

.   .   .

Nizar couldn't care less about politics or revenge; to him this was just a job. He had joined the Syrian Army to appease his father and found success in the ranks. He was recruited by the Interior Ministry thanks to his intellect and physical stamina, and had been trained as a sniper.

As the political uprisings in his country escalated into all-out civil war, Nizar played a key role in suppressing the insurgents by actively targeting their leadership. He preferred head shots, as they had a devastating effect on the enemy's morale; there's nothing quite like having your commander's brains splattered on your face to suppress your will to fight. He felt neither joy nor sadness in taking the lives of his targets, only the satisfaction of a successful hit.

As established media outlets fled the war-torn nation, freelance journalists from the "new media" tried to document the fighting using their own video cameras and smartphones. They became his targets of choice. He racked up an impressive record of one-shot kills at increasingly greater ranges. Syrian arms and training were relatively crude compared to first-world armies, but what he lacked in technical training and equipment he made up for in real-world experience and predatory instinct.

Nizar's skills caught the attention of General Yedid as he built his network of mercenaries to operate outside Syria. With the money that he would receive from this off-the-books job, Nizar could walk away from Syria before his luck ran out and make his way into Europe, where opportunity awaited.

That Nizar and Tasho had fought on opposite sides of the Syrian Civil War didn't seem to bother either of them. They were snipers and they had a job to do.

. . .

Nizar had painted the steel target with orange spray paint and driven back to the farmhouse in the small pickup truck. These trips were getting longer as he moved the heavy steel plate increasingly farther across the open field. They had begun at five hundred meters, which Nizar had protested was too easy a shot, and had steadily increased the range as they'd learned to release their rounds simultaneously. He climbed onto the flat roof of the house and found Tasho lying prone, already staring through his scope toward the target.

"Did you have me in your sights?"

The other man grinned in a rare signal of emotion. "Never miss an opportunity to train, Nizar," the elder sniper offered. "I read that on social media in a post from one of the infidel military social media *influencers*."

Nizar looked quizzically at the legendary sniper with whom he now trained. Though they were both part of General Yedid's network, Tasho was the lead. What he didn't know was that General Yedid had entrusted Nizar with a follow-on mission known only to the two of them.

"Never mind, Nizar. On my mark, at two thousand."

Nizar climbed behind his own rifle, identical to Tasho's, and moved the towel that he'd used to cover his ammunition. At first, they'd blown primers as they fired, which was an indication of excessive chamber pressure. They'd discovered that keeping the loaded rounds in the sunlight during the heat of the day was getting the cartridges too hot and raising the pressure. Tasho was no fun to be around but he was a competent professional and had passed along the towel trick, which had eliminated the problem.

Nizar found the tiny target in the scope as Tasho entered the range and environmental data into his handheld computer. The software accounted for everything from bullet drop to temperature, barometric pressure, wind, Coriolis effect, and even the spindrift caused by the barrel's right-hand rifling. The rifles were zeroed precisely at one thousand meters, which was only halfway to their current target.

"Come up thirteen MILS."

"Thirteen MILS up," Nizar repeated as he made the elevation correction using the dial on top of the optic.

"Hold three MILS right."

"Three MILS right." Nizar placed the appropriate hash mark on the scope's reticle at the target's center to account for the wind call.

"Ready."

"Ready." Nizar began to exhale.

"On my count: three . . . two . . . one."

Both rifles spoke in unison, sending a combined seven hundred grains of copper across the plowed field. Even with the long tubular sound suppressors attached, the rifles' reports were still quite loud. It took the bullets nearly three seconds to reach the target and an additional six seconds for the sound of their impact to echo back to the shooters' position. Two hits. A few more days' training and they would be ready.

CHAPTER 60

Yazidi Strike Force Compound
Kurdistan
September

LANDRY'S NERVES WERE COMPLETELY shot. He wasn't sure which was worse, the exhaustion or the cold. The hunger was bad, but it didn't compare to the lack of sleep and constant state of near hypothermia. He hadn't eaten in days, and his metallic breath indicated that his body was in a state of ketosis, burning his fat stores to stay alive. As his body transitioned to fat as a fuel source, a blinding headache was added to his list of agonies.

Keeping track of time had become impossible, but Landry estimated that it had been close to a week since his captivity began. He knew that the bitter cold and the sleep deprivation were part of a well-scripted interrogation regimen. He also knew that it was working; he simply didn't have much will to resist at this point. Whatever it is they wanted to know, they would soon find out. Besides, he was in this for the money, not some *ideology*. His best plan would be to cut some kind of deal. At least they'd traded his wrist and ankle restraints for hand and leg cuffs that provided some level of circulation to his extremities; he'd been afraid that he would lose his hands and feet due to the lack of blood flow.

The door opened and Landry heard the familiar sound of boots on the wet floor. They'd entered the room more than once a day to give him water and, as best he could tell, he was due again. The water was the only thing that he had to look forward to in this hellish cycle of cold and heat, and his dry lips pursed to accept his drink. To his surprise, instead of the liquid refreshment he'd been craving, he was jerked aloft by strong hands on both sides and found himself seated on the cold steel of a chair that had been carried into the room. Each leg was secured to the chair with restraints and the same was done with his hands. That he didn't hear the multiple sets of boots enter the room was yet another sign that he was losing his grip on reality.

The door slammed but Landry could tell that he was not alone. He could smell the food, some type of fresh meat with onions coupled with nicotine clinging to his captor's clothing. The smell caused him to salivate. He sat in silence for what seemed like minutes before the tape that had covered his eyes since his capture was torn from his face. His skin was as soft as tissue paper from the constant cold water soaking and he was sure that he'd lost some skin as well as his eyebrows when the tape was removed. Strangely, it didn't hurt. The room's bright lights were blinding to his senses and he squeezed his eyes shut, bowing his head to avoid the shocking LEDs that ringed the room like crown molding.

"Look at me," he heard the man say. He knew the voice instantly.

Landry blinked his eyes and tried to focus on the floor, his naked body brutally exposed by the room's illumination. Slowly, he turned his squinting gaze upward and took in the slim figure of Major Mohammed Farooq, formerly of the Iraqi Interior Ministry's Special Tactics Unit. Farooq was dressed in winter clothes, toasty warm in a room that felt like a walk-in freezer. Landry had worked for years to trick Mo into working for his employer under the ruse of helping the American government, and now the shoe was on the other foot; Mo had Jules Landry by the balls. Landry had seen the calm, sophisticated Iraqi officer display serious brutality toward his enemies and knew that he would show no quarter. Now was the time to make a deal and preserve what was left of his physical self before Mo decided to cross the line from "enhanced interrogation" to downright torture.

"Tell me about the girl that you raped, Jules."

"What? What girl? I didn't rape any girl!" *Why does he want to know about some stupid girl?*

"The girl in Louisiana, Jules. Before you joined the Marines to stay out of jail."

How in the hell . . . ? "Oh, that. That was a long time ago, Mo . . . I . . ."

Mohammed Farooq rose from his chair without saying a word and as the steel door slammed shut behind him, the room went totally dark. A second later, the cold shower was activated. All Landry could do was scream.

CHAPTER 61

Lisbon, Portugal
September

GREY WAS FLUENT IN Spanish, having spent many years working in Central and South America. The bad news was that, as he'd discovered in Brazil many years ago, Portuguese was not as close to Spanish as many would have you believe. He struggled to communicate with locals who did not speak Spanish or English, relying mainly on common words and gestures in order to get by. His train would leave that evening, so he had an entire day to kill in Europe's second-oldest capital city. He took a taxi to the Hotel Jerónimos, where he checked his bags and washed his face in the lobby's restroom.

Lisbon was physically attractive with its gray, black, and white stone mosaic streets, bright buildings with red-tiled roofs, classic streetcars, and waterfront views. The city's mood was, to Grey, relatively bleak. Citizens shuffled the streets with little joy and many of the buildings appeared dingy and neglected. Lisbon had the feel of a city whose best days were behind it.

Joy radiated from the faces of the numerous immigrants he saw, undoubtedly former residents of Portugal's many former colonies, places like Mozambique, Angola, and Equatorial Guinea. A once-mighty empire that had mastered deepwater navigation, commanded the seas, and spanned the globe was now one of the smallest economies in Europe, only its language left as a mark on its former territories, a faded tattoo as a reminder of what once was.

After a café breakfast, Grey wandered to the waterfront to see the fourteenth-century Belém Tower, the small Gothic castle that guarded the narrow waters leading to the city. He took some photos with the old green Leica in his shoulder bag before making his way toward the train station for a rail ticket. Purchasing the ticket online was out of the question, since this was the point where Grey would abandon his old identity and assume a new one. As he strolled along the walkway that led from the tower to the shoreline, he tossed his iPhone into the choppy waters of the Tagus River. No part of him felt like turning back.

The olive felt fedora on his head and Wayfarer sunglasses on his face would help hide him from the prying eyes of the security cameras and their facial recognition algorithms. His beard, though patchy, was starting to come in. After a frustrating conversation in bad Spanish and even worse English, he was told that he could buy his rail pass only online or at the station from which his train would depart. The ticket agent pointed animatedly at a pamphlet for the Estação de Lisboa-Oriente, a station east of the airport and well beyond walking distance. He triple-checked the departure time as 9:34 p.m. local and decided that he would buy his ticket at the station that evening rather than make two trips across the city and back.

Grey impatiently explored the city as he passed the hours until his departure, his body adjusting slowly to the time difference. Walking had always helped him fight jet lag, and he logged many miles afoot as he saw the sights, cataloging them with his camera as he went. He bought two bottles of Capitulo, a local red wine, along with some fresh bread and butter for the train ride. After retrieving his larger bag from the hotel, he waited for the afternoon traffic to subside before hailing a taxi to the station.

The Oriente Station was a modern marvel of white metal arches, illuminated by artificial lighting as the sun set on the opposite side of the city. Grey paid extra for a private compartment on the Renfe train and bought the ticket from a wad of euro notes he'd accumulated over many years of travel in the employ of the United States government. When asked for his passport, he proudly produced a red-jacketed book identified in Cyrillic and ISO Latin letters as belonging to the Russian Federation. Thanks to the Colonel's contacts, the passport was entirely authentic but for the name, Adrian Volkov, a man who until this moment had never existed.

He ate a small dinner in the station as he waited for the train to arrive, having traded his sunglasses for a pair of prescription eyeglasses. Glancing at the steel Rolex on his wrist, he thought for a moment about the man who had previously worn it, a man who had almost stopped all this from happening before it had even begun. A man he had bested, not with brawn, but with intellect.

Boarding his train, he found his way to his small but clean first-class compartment, locked the door, and poured himself a paper cup of red wine, savoring the flavor and the civilized nature of rail travel. The city lights dimmed in their wake as the train made its way into the quiet countryside, small cities and tiny villages visible along their path. Drinking through all of the first bottle and most of the second, he then pulled down both the bunk and the window shade. The train rocked rhythmically along the rails beneath him, and he quickly fell asleep.

CHAPTER 62

Yazidi Strike Force Compound
Kurdistan
September

"HER NAME WAS AMY, Amy Bertrand!"

When the water stopped, Landry began speaking to the empty room, confident that it was wired for sound and that they could hear him. The thick Louisiana accent that he'd worked for years to suppress had returned.

"She had long beautiful black hair and green eyes. Stunning. She always wore dresses. She never paid me no mind; rich girls like that don't even notice white trash like me. 'Rich Bitch' is what we called her type. Everybody in school was gettin' into college. Kept hearin' her talk about Tulane and how she was gonna join her momma's sorority. Tulane . . . I had a better chance of endin' up in Angola like my dad. He was doin' hard time. Girl like Amy Bertrand don't know nothin' about no hard times."

Landry paused; his eyes fell to the floor and his voice dropped to a whisper. "She was workin' in the nursery at the church, holdin' babies and changin' diapers. It was after Mass on Holy Thursday, the day before Good Friday. Everybody's Catholic where I come from 'cept for the black folks. I snuck in the room behind her where she was in there cleanin' up after all the parents had picked up their young'uns. I locked the door real quiet and she looked up and seen me when she heard the door click. She smiled and called me by my name, I didn't even know she knew my name.

Soon as she saw me walk toward her, she stopped smilin'. I was a pretty good linebacker. 'Fore she knew it I tore that pretty little dress right up the back. Had my hands over her mouth so she couldn't scream. I told her I'd kill her and her baby sister if she told anybody, especially the cops. She was down on her knees cryin' when I left. Guess I shoulda felt bad for what I done to her but I didn't, I just ain't that way. Never did see her again after that night."

The room was bathed in light as the white LEDs were switched back on, once again shocking Landry's darkness-adapted vision. The muscular and tattooed man who was ordinarily physically intimidating now looked like a shell of his former self. He sat with his shoulders hanging forward, his chin resting on his ink-covered chest.

The steel door opened, and Mo closed it behind him as he entered, taking a seat across from Landry in silence. Landry kept his eyes on the floor.

"What happened then, Landry?" Mo asked calmly.

"My uncle worked for the sheriff's office and Amy's parents had reported it. Her 'Miss Perfect' reputation would have been shattered in a small southern town like that. No more sorority, no more rich boys linin' up to marry her. My uncle and the sheriff made a deal with her old man; I join the Marines and never come back to town and they don't press charges. I signed the delayed-entry papers the next day and two months later, the Monday after graduation, I'm on my way to Parris Island.

"Who do you work for now?"

"Now hold on, Mo. You know I need some assurance that I'm not goin' to prison if I sing."

"Want me to turn the water back on?"

"Just listen, Mo, just listen. I'm low-hangin' fruit. If you want the main enchilada you know I need somethin'."

Mo took a breath and produced a paper from his coat pocket. Landry's eyes lit up like it was the golden ticket. *A way out.*

"Verbal acknowledgment is enough. This is the best deal you are going to get. It's not immunity, Landry, but it puts you in a minimum-security U.S. prison and gives you the possibility of parole in twenty years. It's a country club. But it's got to be everything. If you leave out one detail you are going to the deepest, darkest prison we can find. It won't be a U.S. prison. It'll be an Iraqi one. You might even know a few of the prisoners. They'll treat you like you treated Amy Bertrand for the rest of your miserable life. When you're not getting gang raped, you'll be in solitary confinement until your ass heals enough for another round."

Landry's eyes scanned the document. It looked official, and he wasn't in a position to push his luck.

"I accept," he said, nodding at the corners of the room, where he assumed there were cameras. "I accept."

"Talk."

"I was workin' embassy duty after a couple of Afghanistan deployments, down in Buenos Aires. I got to know one of the Agency guys there; he wasn't a field spook, just an analyst. I ran into some trouble with a local girl. We was on a date, and she come back to my hotel room knowin' what was gonna happen. Anyway, this little CIA guy offered to fix it, to make that problem go away. After that he helped get me the CIA job. He smoothed over my trouble back home and in Argentina where nobody could see the paperwork, and he taught me how to beat the poly. I was makin' good money workin' as an Agency contractor and he was getting me cash on the side in a Swiss account. He had me start recruitin' you once Reece left the unit."

"Who was the Agency man, Landry? What was his name."

"He had me just call him Bond. Ha! Pudgy paper-pusher fancies he's 007."

"So he never told you his name?"

"He didn't, but I figured it out. I'm not as dumb as people think. We both worked for the CIA after all."

"Name, Jules. What's his name?"

"Grey. Oliver Grey."

Mo looked up at the camera and nodded.

"Does Grey still work for the Agency?"

"Sure does, he's workin' at Langley."

"Was he running this entire operation or was he working for another intelligence service?"

"Not for another country, Mo. He worked for a person. Some Russian, but he don't live in Russia. He's Swiss now. They call him the Colonel."

"Do you have a name?"

"No, Grey just called him the Colonel."

Mo didn't pursue it, moving from topic to topic to keep Landry on his toes. "Who is your contact in the Interior Ministry now?"

"Major Saeed, from your old unit. I just pass along the messages from Grey. We set it all up before I left Iraq."

"Who gave you the target in Morocco?"

"Grey did. He gave photos with the layout of the compound and arranged the transport. All I was supposed to do was get Saeed to put his crew in motion and make sure they knew to kill everybody on target. Whoever was at that place musta known they was coming 'cause them boys never came back."

"Where is your other team? The ones you used in London?"

"I only dealt with one guy: a Syrian. There's cells all over the West now; their handlers put 'em to work cheap. They get to get their jihad on, so they're all happy."

"What Syrian? We were both there after Iraq. Do I know him?"

"General Yedid. General Qusim Yedid."

Mo's face betrayed no recognition, but he knew the man, if only by reputation. Formerly one of Assad's inner circle. It was rumored he had left Syria to act as a private broker of mercenaries to places and causes that benefited Assad's regime.

"Where does General Yedid live now?"

"I don't know, I swear I don't know," Landry groaned as he thrashed against his restraints. He was a broken man and he was beginning to lose it.

"How many teams do you have left out there?"

"None, I got nobody out there but you, Mo. I swear it. Yedid, he's got teams all over Europe, maybe even some in the U.S. All I was supposed to do was those attacks to scare the shit outta everyone. Grey had some other stuff goin' for sure but I wasn't part of it. He told me to lay low and just keep runnin' you like I was doin'."

"Who set up the Christmas market attack in London?"

"I told you, the Syrian. I was just the go-between."

"Landry, I am going to be very clear here," Mo stated. "And I'm going to speak slowly so that even you will understand. Your deal depends on your telling us everything you know. If we find out later that you left anything out, the deal is off and you become a *bitch* for life. Imagine how they'll treat an American CIA officer in an Iraqi prison. I almost feel sorry for you. So, scan your brain; is there anything else you want us to know?"

"No, I've told you everything. *Wait!* A few months ago Grey decided he wanted to go direct to Yedid and take me out as the go-between. I'm not sure why; it just exposed him to more risk."

"Why do you think that is, Landry?"

"I dunno, I got the impression that he needed a lot of guys for whatever he was planning. Something major, maybe even 9/11 major."

"Tell me more."

CHAPTER 63

THE TWO SEALS WATCHED the video in the team room, Reece taking notes while Freddy paced the room anxiously. They had watched it in real time but now reviewed it segment by segment with Mo.

Mo pressed the pause button when Landry mentioned General Qusim Yedid. "I know this man; know of him, I should say. He was in charge of finding members of the various resistance factions in Assad's army. His tactics were brutal. If he even suspected someone of being a traitor, he would order the family rounded up and torture the wife and daughters. If the man didn't have a wife, he'd find the mother or even the grandmother. I'm probably not as squeamish about such things as you Americans are, but even I am disgusted by this man. It was also rumored he was a primary advocate of using chemical weapons against villages with questionable loyalties."

"Why would Grey take the risk of going straight to this Syrian? Why not continue to use Landry as a cutout?"

"Trust?" Freddy guessed. "He was losing confidence in Landry?"

"Maybe, or maybe because whatever they're planning is big enough to blow Grey's cover," Reece speculated.

"Maybe it's both? Grey is a highly placed agent in the CIA. That would have to be one big mission. That's not typical for a long-term plant."

"Remember, we are not talking about a Foreign Intelligence Service here," Reece reminded his friend. "Now we know that we are dealing with an individual. A super-empowered individual. This is bigger and more complex than we've suspected so far. See what else you can find out, Mo.

Landry has to have more in that head of his that can help us. This is po-tentially actionable intel on a major attack. We need details."

"Gladly." Mo put down the remote and left the room.

"What do we do about Grey?" Reece asked.

"I'll call Vic. He'll get the counterintel guys on him and start working things from his end."

Five minutes later, Freddy was talking to Rodriguez from the facil-ity's secure conference room.

. . .

"Grey is a senior analyst at the Russian desk," confirmed Rodriguez. "He's had overseas postings in Central and South America. He's currently on leave in Portugal. We just checked with the hotel on his approved leave papers and he never checked in. No one has heard from him. He's disap-peared."

Hanging up the phone, Freddy relayed the new information to Reece.

"I don't like this, Freddy; it smells like something moving into a final phase. Grey left before he knew we had Landry, so he wasn't spooked. This was deliberate. Whatever it is will happen soon."

"I agree. Vic is going to do some more digging on Grey. In the mean-time, he suggested that we talk to a guy named Andy Danreb. I don't know him, but Vic says that if anyone is going to know anything about some Russian they call 'the Colonel,' it's Andy."

"Let's call him."

"That's where it gets prickly; Andy is old-school. He's an analog guy. If we want him to help us, we've got to go to him. He's at Langley."

"They're really going to let me, the guy that blew up the WARCOM commander and shot the SECDEF, into CIA headquarters?"

"Yep."

"Guess I better find those nice clothes they bought me in Istanbul."

CHAPTER 64

Madrid, Spain
September

THE PLAZA MAYOR WAS busy, even well after the summer tourist season. Grey had been here a handful of times over the years but had never seen this much of an armed security presence. Municipal and national police officers, soldiers, and even a pair of the nation's Guardia Civil, mounted on horseback, patrolled the large public square and its surrounding streets wearing their distinctive tricorne hats. The security forces were out in a show of force to deter would-be terrorists. As he sipped his *café con leche*, he took in the sights and sounds of Spanish life and was reminded of his days in Buenos Aires. He ordered in lisping Castilian Spanish and, despite a slight Argentine accent, could pass as something close to a local.

All the trains for Paris departed in the morning and, after overnighting on the Lisbon-to-Madrid route, Grey needed a day to stretch his legs. His room at the nearby Hotel Carlos V would not be ready for a few hours, which gave him a chance to stroll the sidewalks of one of his favorite cities. He spent the day window-shopping and practicing his Spanish. He dined at Sobrino de Botín, a favorite of Hemingway's and reportedly the oldest restaurant in Europe, and devoured the roast suckling pig along with a nice bottle of reserve Rioja. His train would leave early in the morning, so, after just a couple of glasses of house red at a café on the plaza, he retired to his room. The hotel was nothing special, but their security cameras looked old and they didn't ask too many questions.

The morning train to Paris left at seven and Grey spent his day staring at the countryside as it rolled by. He overnighted in La Ville-Lumière before traveling, again by rail, to Strasbourg, where he boarded one last train for the final leg of his long journey. Flying would have been faster and more direct, but this method was far more secure and allowed him to spend time with his new identity. He was shaking with excitement as he walked through the doors of Basel's SBB station in search of his contact.

It didn't take long to spot him, a severe-looking man with a shaved head dressed in all black. The man's dead eyes were locked on him from across the room and, when Grey finally met his gaze, the man nodded without smiling. He didn't offer to take Grey's bag, but led him to a black Mercedes AMG G63 idling in front of the station. The driver, who looked about as friendly as his partner, stepped out of the SUV and loaded the bags into the rear cargo area. Grey climbed into the backseat and shut the door. After the long journey on public transportation and among so many strangers, the feel and smell of the soft leather interior was another indication that he had almost arrived.

CHAPTER 65

THE ROYAL JORDANIAN AIRLINES flight left Erbil at 4:00 a.m., which meant that both Reece and Freddy hadn't slept a wink all night.

Shouldn't a possibly imminent terrorist attack qualify them for a Gulf-stream? Reece wondered.

Their diplomatic passports got them through the check-in process quickly, neither had checked a bag. The guns all stayed behind, making Reece feel naked, even in jeans and a dress shirt with suit coat. The business-class seats on the Airbus 319 were comfortable, but Reece's sleep was soon interrupted by their approach in Amman, where they would have three hours to kill until their Frankfurt flight.

They drank coffee and put a serious dent in the Royal Jordanian Lounge's breakfast spread before boarding the late-morning flight to Frankfurt. Located in Germany's fifth largest city, Frankfurt Airport was Europe's hub to the Middle East, and had certainly seen its share of American trigger-pullers and spooks pass through over the years. Reece got a few more hours of sleep on the next flight and was starting to feel almost human again when they touched down in London.

Another four-hour layover, another airport lounge, another pot of coffee. At least this airport had an international bookstore with some interesting titles. Reece always enjoyed perusing international bookstores, as he often found interesting military nonfiction written by Brits, Aussies, Kiwis, and South Africans. In this particular bookstore he found a copy of *Three Sips of Gin*, by Tim Bax, about the Selous Scouts and pseudoterrorist operations in Rhodesia.

Catchy title, Reece thought.

They boarded the United 777 at 4:30 p.m. local and found their seats for the nine-hour flight to Dulles. Reece read his new book, dozed off a few times, and switched back and forth among the cable news channels available on the in-flight monitor, hoping subconsciously that he might catch a glimpse of his favorite journalist.

The sky stayed in a perpetual state of sundown as they flew west across the time zones, nighttime teasing but never quite falling. The big Boeing touched down right on schedule at 8:05 p.m., startling Reece out of his slumber. He was more than ready to get off the plane after nearly two days of constant travel. Fortunately, their business-class seats put them near the exit.

Reece was expecting to ride on one of Dulles's Chrysler-built "mobile lounges," the obsolete aircraft boarding buses that looked like something devised on a 1950s-era drawing board as "the future of passenger comfort." Instead they docked at a jet bridge at C Concourse that dumped the passengers directly into a Federal Inspection Station, where bored but alert U.S. Customs and Border Protection officers were waiting in their dark blue uniforms. A man with a clean-shaven head and an ID lanyard hanging outside his light gray suit was standing off to one side as the bleary-eyed returning tourists and stoic business travelers shuffled off the aircraft. Freddy spotted him and gave him a quick wave, showing the man both of their credentials. The slightly portly man motioned for them to follow and he swiped his ID card and punched a four-digit code into a nondescript doorway that led to an elevator.

If this was some type of trick to get Reece back to the United States so that he could be arrested, this was where it would go down. Their path allowed them to bypass Passport Control and Customs as their escort showed them to an uncrowded stop on the airport's AeroTrain. Moments later they were walking through Dulles's unique concrete-and-glass wing-shaped terminal, another relic of Draperesque 1950s design.

I guess I really am a free man.

It was late enough that the legendary D.C. area traffic was light, especially heading toward the city. Their CIA driver didn't say a word as he negotiated the route. Reece was amazed by all the new tech- and defense-related office buildings that lined the Dulles Toll Road; this area had been built up significantly since his last visit.

It was strange being back home; Reece felt like he was getting away with something. He'd pocketed a pack of gum from a 7-Eleven as a kid, the only time he'd ever stolen anything in his life; this feeling was oddly similar.

The Tysons Corner Hilton was their destination for the night and both Reece and Freddy, whose bodies were operating on the assumption that it was long past midnight, opted to skip dinner and head to bed. Thanks to the time difference, Reece was wide awake at just after 4:00 a.m. and couldn't make himself go back to sleep. He hadn't packed workout clothes or athletic shoes, so he made do in his room wearing the T-shirt and boxer briefs he'd slept in. After a few minutes of stretching, he knocked out a hundred burpees, leaving him soaked in sweat. It felt good to move. Fitness is perishable.

He watched cable news with the volume low, all the channels obsessed with a tropical wave off the coast of Africa that they expected to become a hurricane. Meteorologists clad in raincoats bearing the logo of their respective networks had been pre-positioned all over the Caribbean, waiting to report on the storm's violence that was still days away. Outside of terror attacks, bad weather seemed to be the only thing that tore people away from television's many streaming services and back to watching the news. The networks responded by hyping up every storm as if it were "the next big one." Reece turned off the giant LCD screen and hit the shower.

He and Freddy were both downstairs and waiting when the hotel's restaurant opened for breakfast at 6:00 a.m., the normally scraggly operators looking almost dapper in their business suits. Neither man said much, as what occupied their minds wasn't something that they could discuss in public. They did make sure to get the U.S. government's money's worth from the twenty-six-dollar breakfast buffet.

Their ride pulled up just before 8:00 a.m., and the traffic was at its peak as they made the short drive through McLean to their destination.

They were cleared through the security gate, the black Tahoe stopping in front of the six-story George Bush Center for Intelligence. Reece wasn't impressed by much, but he was wide-eyed as they approached the entrance to the "old" building, which was completed in 1961. As they made their way past the doors and through the electronic security turnstiles, Reece spotted something in the lobby and asked Freddy to stop for a moment.

On a wall of white Alabama marble were 129 stars, flanked by the flags of the nation and the Agency. Each star carved into the wall stood in silent testimony of a CIA officer or contractor killed in action.

Reece read the inscription:

IN HONOR OF THOSE MEMBERS
OF THE CENTRAL INTELLIGENCE AGENCY
WHO GAVE THEIR LIVES
IN THE SERVICE OF THEIR COUNTRY

A black goatskin book sat in a glass case below the stars, listing the names of ninety-one of the slain officers: the remaining names still classified. His eyes took in locations and dates from Vietnam, Bosnia, Somalia, El Salvador, Ethiopia, Iraq, and Afghanistan. Two had even been killed when a Pakistani national opened fire at the line of cars waiting to enter headquarters in 1993. He saw the names of Glen Doherty and Ty Woods, men he'd known in the SEAL Teams who had died defending the U.S. consulate in Benghazi, and of ██████████████████████████ ████████████████████████. He searched for his friend ████, killed by an EFP doing Agency work ██████████████████ just after Reece had left the unit, but didn't see it. Along with thirty-seven others ████'s star still kept its secret.

Reece looked at all the names of those killed in 2003. The one he was searching for had only a simple star followed by a blank space where the name should have been. He took a moment to reflect, to remember. Then, exhaling deeply, he turned to Freddy, who gave him an understanding nod before leading him to the elevators.

CHAPTER 66

CIA Headquarters
Langley, Virginia
October

ANDY DANREB WAS A big man, taller than Reece, with broad shoulders and large Slavic hands. He wore his graying hair short and carried himself in a way that suggested he'd once served in uniform. Though his oxford blue dress shirt was neatly pressed and his pants were clean, he wore the exhausted expression of a man who'd been beaten down by the government's bureaucracy for his entire career. He greeted his visitors with little enthusiasm. His small office was cramped thanks to the stacks of books, papers, and files that sat upon every surface, including the floor. Without apology, he cleared stacks of books from the two chairs opposite his desk and motioned for Reece and Freddy to sit. He was one of the Agency's foremost Russian experts, a relic of the Cold War kept on ice for occasions such as these. *Break glass in case of war.*

"We came a long way to see you, Andy." Freddy spoke first.

"Probably a giant waste of your time but we'll see. What can I do for you?"

There was a slight Chicago accent there that Danreb hadn't shaken.

"We need your help on something. Have you ever heard of a Russian expat living in Switzerland who people in intel circles call 'the Colonel'?"

"*Кукольный мастер*, 'the Puppet Master' . . . his name is Vasili Andrenov."

Danreb switched between Russian and English effortlessly.

"Who is he?"

"He was a colonel in the GRU, Soviet military intelligence. If there was a tin-pot insurgency or coup during the latter half of the Cold War, he was there stirring the pot and handing out weapons. He specialized in spreading chaos and misery around the world."

"So, the KGB didn't run those operations?" asked Reece.

"No, military-specific operations were always GRU. KGB was busy fucking off in the capital with all the embassy intrigue BS, regardless of what all the eighties spy movies would have you believe. GRU was out doing most of the wet work in the field."

Danreb spun his chair and dug into a stack of files cluttering the top of his inkjet printer. Within seconds he turned back around and opened the folder to an eight-by-ten black-and-white photo of a young Andrenov standing among some soldiers holding Soviet weapons in what looked like Africa. A shock of sandy hair hung below the brim of the dress cap worn pushed back on his head, the distinctive striped undershirt of the Soviet airborne and Spetsnaz forces visible inside the open collar of his camouflage jacket.

"This is him in Mozambique, I think, no, maybe it was Angola . . . no, Mozambique. He almost single-handedly provided the weapons for all the African insurgencies in the seventies and eighties."

"Would he have been the one who supplied the MANPADS that shot down the two Rhodesian airliners, one in '78 and the other in '79?" Reece asked.

"I'd bet on it."

Reece's eyes narrowed, thinking of Rich Hastings's sister who had perished in the second attack.

"How did this guy get to be such a player?" asked Freddy.

"The same way everyone does in a communist system. His father got him the job. Oh, he was a real monster, that one; one of the orchestrators of Stalin's purges. He coordinated the Katyn Massacre in Poland during the war."

"I'm not familiar with it," Freddy admitted.

"I'm not surprised to hear that. What's twenty thousand dead among sixty million? Basically, the Russians had a long-term plan to take over Poland after the war. They didn't want to leave anyone who was going to make trouble, so they did what they always did: killed everyone with a brain. They rounded up officers, lawyers, professors, anyone who could organize. They marched them one by one into a soundproof room and shot them in the back of the head. They had a door on the other side of the building where they'd sling the bodies into the back of a truck. The bodies were dumped in the Katyn Forest, hence the name of the massacre. That's what happens when you don't have a Bill of Rights. The German army actually discovered the bodies when they invaded. The Russians tried to blame it on them. The Nazis documented it in typical German fashion, and the Russians finally fessed up to it at the end of the Cold War." He paused. "I'm rambling. Anyway, Andrenov the elder came out of that as a big shot, and his son's path was set early. No muddy plows or greasy factory work for young Vasili."

"What a legacy. Is Andrenov still working for the Russians?" Reece asked.

"No, not for the government at least. Russian president Zubarev is a moderate, at least by their standards. Andrenov is a hard-core Russian nationalist trying to stoke the fires of the empire's last gasp."

"What does that mean?"

"Russia is a dying nation, literally. Their life expectancy is so bad that the average Russian never makes it to retirement age. Booze, drugs, HIV, heroin, TB, overall bad health—they are in rough shape as a people. On top of that, their birth rate has been in the shitter for generations. Don't you guys read Zeihan?"

"Who?"

"Forget it. Anyway, ethnic Russians are dying off in droves and there's no one to replace them. The only group that's growing in Russia is the Muslim population and to folks like Andrenov, they aren't real Russians. The nationalists want the Russians to push their boundaries out to places like Ukraine and Poland to grab both their people and resources. If they can *annex* those people, Mother Russia will live on."

"A land grab to save a dying empire," Reece stated.

"That's it," Danreb confirmed. "Look at human history. It's what nations do. Stalin forcibly relocated people in an attempt to grow the empire. I actually think they're going to push south as well, into places like Azerbaijan and maybe even Turkey."

"What about NATO?" Freddy asked.

"It's already begun in Crimea. What did NATO do about that? Don't get me wrong, they've got Europe nervous. Sweden has reinstated their draft, which has everything to do with this, but without U.S. leadership, no one except perhaps the Germans are in a place to oppose Russian expansion. Remember, they shot down an airliner full of Europeans over Ukraine, and the world shrugged its shoulders."

"But the current Russian administration didn't invade Crimea. That was the last guy," Freddy said.

"Exactly, he was one of Andrenov's people and, with him out of power, the Colonel is out of favor with the current administration. Andrenov would love nothing more than to see Putin, or someone like him, back at the helm."

"Would Andrenov be bold enough to attempt a coup?" Reece wondered aloud.

"He's spent his entire career doing just that around the world, so I wouldn't doubt it for a minute."

"Sounds like someone could scoop up Andrenov and charge him with war crimes or something to get him out of the picture," Reece offered.

"Yeah, good luck with that; between his bullshit charity and all of the K Street suits he has on retainer, he's untouchable. I've been sounding the alarm on him for years, but it all falls on deaf ears. This asshole should be behind bars but instead he's throwing galas that are attended by half of the U.S. Senate."

"What do you mean?" Reece asked.

"Andrenov runs a foundation focused on 'helping the downtrodden across the globe,' or some such nonsense. It's really a front for influence peddling around the world. You want to drill for oil in Nigeria or mine for lithium in the 'Stans, you give the foundation eight figures and their people on the ground open those doors. The funds are cleaned up and distributed to politicians through Stewart McGovern's lobbying firm. Money makes a lot of friends in D.C., especially in an election year."

"Sounds like someone we should talk with," Reece observed. "Any idea who he might use as hired help if he were going to make a move?"

"Impossible to say. Between his GRU days and his foundation, he has endless contacts around the world."

"We have some single-source intel that he may be using an ex–Syrian general to hire mercenaries," Freddy added.

"I'll buy that. I think his fingerprints are on both sides of the Syrian Civil War, but that's not my area. If I were in your shoes and had that information, I'd be waterboarding Syrian generals until I could link Andrenov to something concrete." He paused. "But that's probably why they don't let me leave this building."

Reece was starting to like this guy.

"We'll do our best. On another topic, do you know Oliver Grey?" Reece asked.

"What about him?" Andy replied, his demeanor stiffening.

"What are your thoughts on him? One hundred percent off the record."

"I've never trusted that little weasel. I brought up some questionable behavior of his a few years back and was told to *stay in my lane*. You wouldn't believe the PC bullshit in this place."

"Any chance that he's somehow associated with Andrenov?"

"It wouldn't shock me in the least. I'd honestly be surprised if Andrenov *didn't* have a minion somewhere in this building."

"Appreciate your candor."

"What are they going to do to me? Put me out to pasture in a tiny office somewhere and bury me in paperwork?" Danreb waved his hand around at his surroundings.

The two frogmen exchanged looks.

"We seriously appreciate your help," Freddy said.

"Don't let your guard down with Andrenov," Danreb warned. "He's evil, but more importantly, he's a *capable* son of a bitch."

"We won't. Thanks again for your time," Freddy said.

"Hope it was worth the trip. Call me if you need anything." Danreb handed each man a business card.

"So, we could have called you instead of flying halfway across the world to meet with you?" Reece couldn't resist.

"That was before I liked you guys." He rose and extended his hand. "Welcome home, Mr. Reece."

CHAPTER 67

Basel, Switzerland
October

COLONEL ANDRENOV WELCOMED GREY into his opulent home like a returning son, something that meant a great deal to someone who had grown up without a father. Grey wasn't naïve, but he wanted to think that he was more than a mere asset to Andrenov. Nonetheless, he was relieved and excited to have finally arrived. He had never felt more important, more *needed*.

A lavish lunch had been prepared for them by Andrenov's staff, and Grey's appetite met the challenge, putting down roast beef, lobster, and a variety of desserts. Andrenov was unapologetically Russian but his world travels had expanded his taste in cuisine far beyond the steppe.

Chilled vodka, Russian, of course, was served with the meal and Grey's head swam as he followed his mentor into the library. The room was nearly three stories high, with an elaborately carved and paneled bookcase rising to the ceiling. A black and gilded wrought-iron staircase allowed access to the upper levels of the collection, where leather-bound editions of Russian literary classics and treasured manuscripts pilfered from third-world libraries and museums lined the shelves.

Andrenov's desk sat opposite the books in front of a large granite fireplace, where flames danced around the logs as if trying to escape. Above the mantel hung a masterfully done copy of his favorite painting, *Reply of the Zaporozhian Cossacks*. The 1891 oil depicts a crowd of laughing men composing a profane and insulting reply to Sultan Mehmed IV of the Ottoman Empire's demand as the *"Son of Mohammed; brother of the sun and moon; grandson and viceroy of God..."* that they *"voluntarily and without any resistance"* submit to Turkish rule. The Cossacks' irreverent response read, in part, *"O sultan, Turkish devil and damned devil's kith and kin, secretary to Lucifer himself. What the devil kind of knight are thou, that canst not slay a hedgehog with your naked arse? The devil shits, and your army eats. Thou shalt not, thou son of a whore, make subjects of Christian sons; we have no fear of your army, by land and by sea we will battle with thee, fuck thy mother."*

Ilya Repin's original painting hung in the State Russian Museum in St. Petersburg but it would soon find its way into Andrenov's home if his plans came to fruition. The painting, as well as the Cossacks' letter to the sultan, epitomized Andrenov's disdain for his enemies. It was an ever-present reminder that the struggle between East and West was an enduring one.

Grey admired the painting as well as its surroundings; it was a grand and masculine room. It had been three years since he had seen the cold warrior. He had aged visibly but wore his years well for a man who had seen and done so much. Grey guessed Andrenov's age at seventy but couldn't be sure and would never dare ask. He wore a brown custom suit of what looked like fine cashmere with a starched white shirt underneath, open at the collar. The Edward Green country boots on his feet were highly polished, and he looked every bit the wealthy European gentleman. A paisley pocket square completed the ensemble. His hair was salt-and-pepper and his neatly trimmed beard matched, framing an unremarkable face. His eyes, though, were anything but unremarkable, a hypnotic gray, nearly silver in their luminescence. They could calm or strike fear, seduce or amuse. Grey wondered what mood Andrenov's eyes would betray next.

"Let us drink to your journey, Oliver," the Russian offered.

The men raised their glasses and toasted to victory.

"You have come so far and are at my side, where you belong, at long last."

"You will soon lead Russia back from the brink," affirmed Grey.

"This is your home, at least for now. You are safe here. You have worked hard for me, Oliver, for Russia. You have brought us the keys to our country's future."

"You believed in me when my own country didn't."

"That's because that was not your country, Oliver, just an unfortunate place of birth. Their oceans and their wealth make the Americans arrogant. They are like the rich man's son who thinks he's earned his wealth. They would never see in you what I see. You recruited one of our very best assets, Oliver, and the mission that you planned in London was executed beyond our expectations. I am proud of you."

"Thank you, Colonel. What can I do now? How can I help?"

"You must be my eyes. You must travel where I cannot. We are close, Oliver, so close, but only you can get us there. I say this without exaggeration, Russia's future depends on you. Islam is destroying us from within. The Muslim population continues to grow, while our ethnic population is in a steady decline. President Zubarev is too weak to stand up to them, too weak to do what must be done. We need justification, Oliver, justification to liberate the ethnic Russian people of Ukraine and push all the way to Azerbaijan in the south and Poland to the west."

"Are the snipers ready?" Grey asked.

"They are. And they are en route to the site as we speak."

Grey nodded. He was finally part of the varsity team and it was almost time for the championship game.

"Oliver, I fear that a simple assassination will not be enough to achieve our goal. It is not 1914 anymore. Assassinating Archduke Ferdinand was enough to plunge the world into the Great War back then. Today it will take something more."

"I see."

"Today the assassination of a world leader would be met by days of mourning and sanctions. The Chechen, Tasho, will help give us the justification we need but that will not be enough. We require something that cannot be ignored."

"What is that?" Grey asked, though he already knew the answer.

"The West calls it a CBRN attack, for chemical, biological, radiological, and nuclear. We are going to focus on the chemical."

CHAPTER 68

REECE WAS GLAD TO have Freddy for a guide as they made their way from the den of analysts where the Agency had stashed Andy Danreb to the executive level where Vic Rodriguez's office was located. Unlike Danreb's broom closet, Rodriguez's space was large and uncrowded, with natural light pouring in from windows that lined an entire side of the room. Photos, plaques, and memorabilia from Vic's days as a Special Forces and Paramilitary Operations officer lined the walls and adorned the bookshelves.

"Gentlemen, welcome to Langley. Reece, do you believe me now that this wasn't an ambush?"

"I'm beginning to." Reece smiled, looking around the office, a faded black-and-white photograph on the wall catching his eye.

The image was of a group of proud-looking young men wearing World War II duck hunter camouflage uniforms and carrying a variety of U.S.-made weapons, including a 1941 Johnson semiautomatic rifle.

"Is this what I think it is?" Reece inquired, walking toward the framed photo for a closer look.

"Brigade 2506 in '61. That is my father's squad just before leaving for *Bahía de Cochinos*, the 'Bay of Pigs.' He was the only one in that photo to survive," Vic explained.

"Brave men" was the only thing that Reece could think to say.

"That they were, Reece. Just like the operatives we have in the field today. We need all the good people we can get," he continued, directing his comments at Reece. "Let's take this into the conference room."

Vic motioned for the men to follow. Reece and Freddy removed their phones, storing them in the designated small safes that looked like tiny post office boxes outside the door to the secure room.

"Can I get you guys anything? Coffee, water?"

"I'm good, Vic; you want anything, Reece?"

Reece shook his head in response, not wanting to slow things down to doctor up his coffee.

Everyone took a seat and the men gave Rodriguez an update from Jules Landry's interrogation and Andy Danreb's thoughts on Vasili Andrenov.

Vic took it all in and looked at the ceiling for a moment before responding.

"Andrenov sure makes a compelling conspirator. We need to figure this out, but I want it done quietly. I don't want Andrenov's friends on Capitol Hill sticking their noses into this and tipping our hand. I also have some disturbing news on Oliver Grey. The counterintelligence team is putting a picture together that isn't going to boost any careers at the Office of Security. It's clear that he's been turned. What isn't clear is how much damage he's done. This breach could be on the Aldrich Ames level. As you may know, he passed multiple polygraph examinations while spying for the Soviet Union and Russia. We're keeping it compartmentalized for now while we figure out how to play it. We need to know when he was turned and to whom he's been passing intelligence. Any ideas on how we pursue this Syrian general lead in Greece?"

Reece responded first. "Assuming we can find General Yedid, the second that we or the Greeks snatch him up, the network will go to ground and the trail will go cold, so things are going to have to happen fast. If this is big enough for Andrenov to burn a CIA asset, then it's 9/11 big," he continued. "We need to get the Geographic Combatant Commanders to recall their deployed SOCOM components, particularly their CIF companies, CRF, or whatever we're calling them now, and have them on standby. Spin up ▮▮▮▮ back here and get the standby squadrons ready to roll. In the meantime, we will keep pushing Landry for information while you get your analysts and assets turning over every stone for a location of General Qusim Yedid. We also need you to start working for approvals to wrap him up, so whatever channels you need to manipulate or favors you need to call in, do it. We need SECDEF or POTUS approval to capture him regardless of where he is, and it needs to be us. We'll have a short window to extract information and act on it, so it can't be a partner or allied force. This has to be unilateral. And while all that is going down, we need to ensure Mo doesn't get burned as working for U.S. intelligence. Am I forgetting anything, Freddy?"

"That's some good officer stuff, Reece. Very impressive." Freddy smiled.

"Well, I used to get paid for that sort of thing." Reece grinned back.

"You still do, Reece," Rodriguez interjected. "I'll get the ball rolling on my end. The approvals are going to be a pain in the ass. They always are. And having seen my share of high-level missions over the years, I can tell you this one might take a while."

"Well, do what you can, Vic," Reece said. "We'll be standing by to stage for a mission to capture Yedid as soon as you give us the approval. From there we'll flex based off his intel."

"I can do that, but we have a problem," Rodriguez said.

"What's that?" Reece asked.

"While you guys were in the air, Mo disappeared."

CHAPTER 69

Kurdistan, Iraq
October

LANDRY'S BLINDFOLD WAS REMOVED to reveal his worst nightmare. He had been dragged out of the sterile interrogation room and was in some type of storage building. It was hot, and he was beginning to sweat out what little moisture his body had left. He was naked, standing on an uneven, rickety wooden stool with his hands cuffed behind his back. A piano wire had been tied to the rafter above and looped around his genitals in a way that ensured it would tighten like a noose if more downward force were applied. He had to stand on his toes to prevent the wire from tightening painfully, which was exhausting after days without food, little water, and constant cold. One slip from the stool and he would be instantly separated from his testicles and penis.

He was familiar with the technique because it was one of his favorites. He had used it against more than a few Iraqis and Syrians, both militants and civilians, over the past decade. One night, after more than a little gin, Landry had used it on a suspected insurgent as the man's wife was forced to watch. When the man refused to admit to any wrongdoing, Landry shoved him off the stool and forced his wife to watch him bleed out. It was later determined that he'd been snatched from the wrong house. Landry had murdered an innocent man, radicalizing his wife in the process and ensuring their children would become the next generation of determined jihadis.

"It's just you and me, Landry. No soft Western interrogation room. No water and temperature fluctuations. No Americans. No supervisors. No doctors. No CIA. *No rules.*"

Landry's eyes darted around the room as he struggled for balance.

"I don't have to tell you how this could end, Landry. I need you to tell me everything there is to know about General Qusim Yedid: where he lives, how you contact him, security, everything, or I'm going to turn you into a woman."

"Mo, please don't do this. I'll draw you a map. I'll take you there myself. I'll do anything. I've got money, Mo, lots of money that the Russian gave me. We can go to Switzerland. I'll give you all of it. It's enough money to disappear on, Mo, and it will all be yours. Yedid lives in Athens but spends a lot of time on a boat in the Med. He's still brokering jobs."

"Why didn't you tell us any of this back in the official interrogation cell?"

Landry stayed silent, focusing on his balance. Apparently he was more afraid of Yedid than he was of years of incessant gang rape in prison.

"What kind of jobs?" Mo continued after he'd given Landry enough time to think.

"Whatever someone needs: kidnapping, hits, car bombs, you name it."

"Like sending my old unit to Morocco to attack a CIA compound?"

Landry's mouth went dry. "Yeah."

"Tell me more."

"There are Syrian refugees in every city in Europe, former fighters, and General Yedid has connections to all of them."

"What's the next target?"

"I honestly don't know, Mo, I swear to God. Grey asked to be put in touch with him, and I told him where to find him."

"Why would Grey want to do that, Landry?"

"I don't know. I figured it was none of my business," Landry squeaked as he caught his balance.

"Take an educated guess for me."

"It's got to have something to do with the Russian."

"The one in Switzerland?"

"Yeah, that's him. He and Grey have got to be behind all of this. I'm just a small part. I'm a nobody."

"Oh, I know that, Landry. What was the last thing Grey asked of you before he took over comms with Yedid?"

"He asked me to have General Yedid track down a sniper."

Sweat poured from the former CIA man as he did everything he could to steady his quivering legs on the shaky stool.

"A sniper?"

"Yeah, the best in Syria."

"Who is that?"

"I don't know, exactly. They call him the *Shishani*. It means like 'day-shooter' or 'day-Chechen' or something. Red beard. That's all I know. I *swear* to you, Mo. I'd tell you if I knew anything else. *Please cut me down!*"

Mo took notes as Landry continued to talk, wobbling on the decrepit stool, almost losing his balance and begging for Mo to cut the wire that encircled his manhood. He explained details of the operation, providing descriptions of those involved along with dead-drop locations and security practices. Landry was becoming increasingly helpful the longer he balanced.

Mo left the room, walking outside to make a phone call, leaving Landry trembling on the stool.

"I'll be back. Don't go anywhere."

"Mo! Mo! Don't leave me here!"

Mo dialed Reece's number and conveyed the new information from Landry. Minutes later, the analysts at the CIA were adding Landry's information to the growing target package they were putting together on one General Qusim Yedid.

Mo ended the call and walked back into the room where Landry's muscular and tattooed physique was perched on the tiny stool like a circus elephant.

"Please, please," Landry pleaded, looking into the deep, dark, unforgiving eyes of his former asset. "I've told you everything I know."

"I believe you," Mo stated, before quickly kicking the stool across the room and sending Jules Landry straight to the ground.

All two hundred and fifteen pounds of him hit the gravel-strewn concrete floor with a brutal thud, less a few ounces of tissue that hung for a moment on the wrong side of the piano wire until landing beside his body. An animalistic scream followed. With his hands secured behind his back, Landry could do nothing to stop the massive bleeding from what was left of his groin. As the bright red arterial blood pulsed out in spurts, the volume of his screams decreased, eventually becoming a mere groan. He lost consciousness within a minute and was clinically dead before Mo had his truck in drive.

PART THREE

REDEMPTION

CHAPTER 70

Washington, D.C.
October

WHAT BEGAN AS A calculated late-night leak to select reporters was confirmed as true by the Office of the Director of National Intelligence the following day. The cable news channels devoted all their coverage to the story and even the networks preempted their daytime broadcasts. Terrorism, it seemed, trumped both soap operas and *Judge Judy*. U.S. and European intelligence agencies had identified a former Iraqi major from the Ministry of Interior, Mohammed Farooq, as the mastermind behind the recent terrorist attacks across Europe. Farooq had served as a cell leader for Amin Nawaz, using his skills as a trained special operations commander against both civilian and military targets. Farooq had slipped through the net that had led to Nawaz's death by Albanian commandos and was believed to be on the run somewhere in Turkey. A dated, pixelated image of Farooq was broadcast to an international audience, giving terror a face. The United States would supply allied intelligence and law enforcement agencies with both assets, including classified biometric information that would aid in his capture.

What allied intelligence services did not know was that the human and signals intelligence provided by the United States would be intentionally misleading and that the biometric data—facial recognition, fingerprint and voice recognition—did not match Farooq's.

Within hours, Mo was the most wanted man in the world. He had instant "cover for status" with any Islamic terrorist organization on the globe.

CHAPTER 71

Odessa, Ukraine
October

ONE OF ANDRENOV'S SECURITY detail could certainly have completed the task, but Grey insisted upon doing it himself. He'd been kept mostly behind a desk for his entire career and would suffer that fate no longer; he would be out in the field where the action was. He would prove himself to his Russian master.

Andrenov's contact had arranged the safe house, which was a simple but clean apartment on Hretska Street. Its location put him near the Philharmonic Society and the Museum of Art in addition to numerous bars and restaurants. Nearly everyone here spoke Russian, in addition to the national language, which gave him ample opportunity to improve his latent skills.

It didn't take much cash to get him access to the docks, euros being the local preference. Andrenov had provided him with enough currency to bribe half of Ukraine, which made the tiny favor of parking a certain ship at a specific berth quite simple. He was shown where the ship would be tied, and he walked down to the exact site to inspect it himself.

It took a few minutes for the GPS unit to locate a sufficient number of satellites to obtain the accuracy that this mission required. This was not a consumer handheld GPS, but a large dual-frequency OmniSTAR-capable commercial unit designed for mapping and surveying. While a consumer GPS was accurate to within a few meters, this system provided both horizontal and elevation information within five to ten centimeters. So long as the ship was moored as directed and the container placed in the proper position, the assassins would be within range of their target.

That evening Grey carefully recorded the distance and elevation information onto a spreadsheet and printed it along with digital photographs that he'd taken from various vantage points at both the firing and target positions. Everything was checked and triple-checked before he sealed the documents into a DHL Express envelope. He was not going to let this operation be compromised by electronic communications. The information would be in Turkey in two days, and his contact there would deliver it personally to the farmhouse. Grey was about to change the world.

CHAPTER 72

Washington, D.C.
October

ALL REECE AND FREDDY could do now was wait—wait for the CIA analysts to build a target package on General Qusim Yedid and wait for Rodriguez to get approvals to detain him.

Freddy rented a car and made the eight-hour drive to Beaufort, South Carolina, to spend a day with his family. It was Sam's birthday and he had missed too many of them already.

Reece had turned on the TV as he got ready for a workout when he heard a familiar voice. Turning his attention to the screen, he saw Pulitzer Prize–winning journalist Katie Buranek on *Fox News Sunday* talking about unwarranted surveillance. *She is right down the street!*

After his last disastrous attempt, he'd decided that now was not the time to surprise her with the news that he was alive over the phone. But, knowing she was just a few miles down the road at Fox's D.C. bureau, he was having second thoughts. He grabbed his phone from the nightstand and stared at the display.

Should I try this again?

What do I even say? Hi, Katie, it's Reece. I'm not dead and I knew that detonator wasn't going to blow your head off last time I saw you. Want to meet up for dinner?

Shit!

He tossed the phone on the bed, trying to focus on what she was saying in the interview.

Should I surprise her at the station? He could be there in minutes.

Reece looked at his RESCO watch.

Yes, that's it. In person would be way better than a phone call.

He quickly changed back into his best clothes and headed for the lobby.

. . .

Reece had his taxi drop him off at a Starbucks catty-corner to the Fox News D.C. bureau, located just north of the Capitol and surrounded by America's traditional institutions of power. Reece had always liked D.C., even though he wasn't a city guy by any means. D.C. was different. There was an energy in the air. There was a sense that no matter how bad things were, this was still the United States. This constitutional republic had weathered storms that would have destroyed most nations, and had prevailed. As Reece ordered a Venti Blonde Roast and asked that the barista leave room for honey and cream, he couldn't help but think that not long ago, all these instruments of federal power had been focused on finding and killing him.

He exited onto E Street NW and found his way to North Capitol NW. Reece strolled toward the parking lot across the street from the cable news giant, pretending to look at his phone while he observed the front of the building.

Fox News Sunday should be finishing up any minute. Wonder how long she stays after taping?

What are you doing, Reece? You are going to scare the living daylights out of her if you surprise her. What if she doesn't want to see you? What if she leaves by a different door? Is this going to creep her out?

You are overthinking this, Reece.

His thoughts were broken by the sight of Katie's blonde ponytail swinging behind her as she exited the building and walked toward the parking lot where Reece waited. There was no mistaking her, even at two hundred yards.

As he stepped toward her, he felt his phone vibrate. Not many people had this number, so he resisted the urge not to answer it. A number with the local 703 area code was displayed on the LCD screen and he swiped the icon to answer the call.

"Yeah."

"Reece, it's Vic. Where are you now?"

"Uh, I'm in D.C. Getting a cup of coffee."

"The hotel coffee not good enough?"

"Well, they didn't have honey," Reece said, frozen in his tracks, watching Katie take a left on Capitol and walk north away from the parking lot.

"Okay, well, I need you on a plane ASAP. We have actionable intel, we have approvals, and we are moving resources to respond. Can you be at Dulles in thirty minutes?"

"I'll be there," Reece said without hesitation.

"Better yet, I'll have an Agency car pick you up at the hotel. Get back there, grab your stuff, and meet the car out front."

Reece ended the call. *Shit.* He took one last look at Katie as she walked away before jogging toward the street to flag down a ride.

CHAPTER 73

Virginia Beach, Virginia
October

THE PAGERS HAD GONE off at 11:42 a.m. on Sunday, catching what appeared to be ordinary families in the middle of the most mundane of Sunday morning tasks: church services, mowing the lawn, playing with kids. Many of those without wives and children, and a few with, were nursing hangovers from a late night out in a series of Virginia Beach bars. To the untrained eye this group could be mistaken for a rugby team. Upon closer examination, a few dead giveaways betrayed them as anything but normal, least of which were the odd-looking cigarette-pack-sized pagers that were never more than an arm's length away. Though most people had turned in their pagers for mobile phones in the mid-1990s, a few elite special operations units still used them as a secure way to connect via satellite with a very select group of lethal men, always on standby for an emergency just such as this.

Forty-five minutes later they had assembled in the team room of the most exclusive club on earth. There would be no more contact with families, friends, or loved ones; the sole focus was now the mission. The families whose lives had once again been interrupted by the now-familiar buzz of the Iridium pagers were acutely aware that this might be the last time they saw their husbands and fathers off to work. They shared them with a larger and oftentimes more demanding family, that of the Naval Special Warfare Development Group.

"Team leaders, do we have everyone?" called out Master Chief Pete Millman in a commanding tone to silence the small talk.

"One's up."

"Two's up."

"Three's up."

"Four's up."

"Roger. Okay, guys," Pete continued, looking around the huge table, flanked on either side by individual desks adorned with computers connected to a net even more secretive and secure than the SIPR computers usually found in military briefing rooms.

Pete was all business and he suppressed an urge to smile looking out at the assaulters and Team leaders ███████████████████████. This was likely to be one of his last times briefing the guys as their troop chief. He'd been around for a long time, graduating the ███████████████ in the first post-9/11 class, and he'd been deploying ever since. His body had taken more abuse than an NFL lineman over the years, and though he hated the thought, he had a GS position in the operations shop that would start up next year. His first marriage had ended in disaster, before kids had entered the picture. His second marriage was to the Command, and he couldn't quite bring himself to separate from her even after twenty-three years in the Navy.

"Quick turnaround on this one, gentlemen. The NSC just green-lighted the ███ package to capture a Syrian general . . . one Qusim Yedid, on a yacht in the Med between Libya and Malta. He's not someone on our HVI or war-criminal top ten, but he just moved up to the number one spot. The Agency has him pegged as a key player in a plan that's already in motion and a direct threat to the United States. This is time sensitive and has visibility at the highest levels. Yeah, Smitty," Pete said, acknowledging his newest Team Leader.

"Direct threat? As in we need to exploit him for additional information?"

"That's right. This is a capture/kill mission, *not* a kill/capture. It was stressed to me in no uncertain terms that we need to take Yedid alive. The intel folks are putting the final touches on the target package, which will include a list of questions to which we need specific answers. Everyone will have a photo of the target and the list of questions."

"How rough can we get with this guy, Master Chief?"

"Don't get excited, Smitty, we are also jumping in an interrogator from Langley, Dr. Rob Belanger, who will take care of that part. He's flying down from D.C. now. If something happens to him, then we take over. BIT guys," Pete said, using the acronym for Battlefield Interrogation Team, "you'll have it from there. Just be aware that this is not some hovel in Afghanistan. This will have a lot more eyeballs on it, so act accordingly."

"I think it's called TQ now." Smitty smiled. "That's tactical questioning, for you older guys."

"Ah, yes. I keep forgetting. Much more PC."

"What's the general's background?" asked a SEAL who looked more like an endurance athlete than one of America's top frogmen.

"Interesting cat," Pete continued. "He was a general in Assad's regime. Earned his stripes carrying out chemical weapon attacks against the populace not supportive of Assad's policies. Somewhere along the line he was connected to Al-Furat, Syria's main oil producer. At least it looks like that's where his money comes from. He's listed as one of their security consultants, but that's just to muddy the waters. The CIA has him as essentially a broker of talent."

"What the *hell* does that mean?" Smitty asked.

"Well, Syrian forces have received training from Russian advisors, and they've gotten a lot of experience exercising that training in putting down rebellions. Remember, Syria is one of the only countries to escape the Arab Spring."

"Yeah, and look how well that worked out for everyone."

"As far as we've been able to tell, he has a line on military talent and parlays it out to governments, rogue regimes, terrorist organizations, as long as their interests are in line with those of Syria, and, you guessed it, Mother Russia. Need an explosives expert, a sniper, an assault team, a chemical weapons specialist? General Yedid will set you up."

"I thought Russia had a moderate in power right now."

"They do, Smitty, but some of the policies from the old president are still in place, as are leaders of powerful institutions, both private and the government agency type, that don't agree with their current president's more progressive stance."

"Like the FSB and SVR?"

"Exactly like that. Russia's reincarnation of the KGB and GRU."

"What's security on the yacht look like, Pete?" another Team leader asked.

"It's a 135-foot superyacht called the *Shore Thing*. I know, I know, it's an awful name. It looks like a damn spaceship and rents for $175,000 a week. Specs are for eight crew and ten guests. CIA estimates there are four to six Syrian bodyguards on board with the general and probably a couple of guests. Apparently the general doesn't like to party alone. CIA doesn't have eyes on board, so this is all a best guess. He's rented it before. Sometimes he brings friends. It's the usual fare: girls, vodka, and your drug of choice. Agency managed to get a prostitute in the mix last year, which is why they have a good idea of his PSD and profile."

"Are the hookers included in that $175,000?" Smitty asked. "Seems a bit high."

Pete rolled his eyes. "I think they're extra. Let's finish this up and get to the bird. It's waiting on us at Oceana. So, let's review: bad-guy general contracts out Syrian military specialists to those willing to pay and those that advance Assad's agenda. We need information about one of those specialists. In this case, we need information on a sniper."

• • •

Fifty-two minutes later they were wheels-up over Virginia in two C-17s on standby for just such a contingency. It had been ninety-seven minutes since the first pagers started beeping.

CHAPTER 74

Somewhere over the Atlantic Ocean
October

SMITTY WATCHED HIS TROOP chief huddled in conference with their squadron commander. The squadron commander was new to ■■■■ but he seemed like a good enough guy. Smitty could tell that his troop chief was mentoring the cake-eater into his new role. Officers just rented lockers at this command; enlisted assaulters ran the show.

As leader of one of the four assault teams split between two aircraft and four boats that would jump in to take control of the motor vessel *Shore Thing* to capture/kill Syrian general Qusim Yedid, Smitty took a breath and thought through the contingencies for the next phases of the operation. He had done more than a few ship-boarding operations in the Northern Arabian Gulf to enforce the UN embargo on Iraq just prior to the U.S. invasion in 2003, but this was the first time he would do it as part of his current command. *What if a boat burned in?* Aside from being a multimillion-dollar loss, it would not be the end of the mission. They could lose two boats and still accomplish their task. *What if, God forbid, an operator burned in?* Two boats would stay to recover the body with minimal assaulters while the other two moved to the target vessel. They would still get it done. They would owe that to their fallen brother. His troops carried an assortment of HK 416s and MP7s. The breachers had torches and saws but those heavier tools would stay on the assault craft;

intel suggested that Benelli shotguns set up to breach should be able to get them through any doors on the expensive yacht.

Underway Maritime Interdiction Operations were a prime mission set for this elite unit. If there was an opposed boarding that needed to be done to protect the national security of the United States, Naval Special Warfare Development Group got the call. The warriors in its esteemed ranks were the most highly trained in the U.S. arsenal, and though most of their missions since the towers fell had been against land-based targets, they kept their ship-boarding skills sharp.

. . .

It had been years since Dr. Rob Belanger had fired a weapon and he didn't have so much as a handgun on him tonight. He didn't know much about boats, nor had he ever jumped out of a plane, certainly not at night into the ocean. Tipping the scales at 140 pounds with a thick mane of graying unkempt hair and a smile that kept those around him wondering what he was thinking, he had established himself as one of the CIA's best interrogators. The U.S. Air Force had paid for his medical school along with follow-on training in neuroscience. Rob had started working his way up the military medical corps chain when the world changed forever on a sunny Tuesday morning.

With the country's appetite for retribution at a peak after the brazen attack on the homeland, administration lawyers issued a classified memo giving the CIA authority to research, test, and evaluate interrogation techniques that went beyond those labeled "enhanced." Those techniques would be the subject of scrutiny in Op-Eds, debated on panels, and argued on the political and legal fronts for years to come. At the recommendation of the head of neurosurgery for the Air Force, Rob found himself detailed to a covert CIA research facility buried four stories underground in the arid mountains outside Monterrey, Mexico. While pundits, politicians, activists, and talking heads were focused on sleep deprivation and stress positions of detainees held at the detention facility in Guantanamo Bay, Cuba, Rob and his team of doctors were experimenting, studying, refining, and documenting the most effective and efficient ways to extract information from the most senior and hardened al-Qaeda prisoners.

Whatever mixed emotions Dr. Belanger had felt about the coupling of politics and ethics beneath the Mexican soil were guided by his devotion to country. He didn't want to cause these prisoners any undue pain, the key word being *undue*. To Dr. Belanger it was like the challenge of a complex puzzle: how could he extract the necessary information from a religious fanatic, causing him the least amount of pain possible while ensuring that the intelligence gleaned was accurate and reliable? He couldn't pick up a weapon and charge into battle in defense of his country, but he could help the war effort in a different way, and the doctor intended to do just that.

With the change in administration and the nation feeling the fatigue of what some had termed "the Long War," Dr. Belanger was reassigned to the medical staff of the CIA in Northern Virginia. The interrogation files from the team's experiments in Mexico existed only in hard copy in the depths of a vault deep in the bowels of an off-site medical clinic with no discernable clientele. It existed in name only as a shell corporation for a company that didn't exist.

As one of only a few doctors in the United States with the knowledge and experience to extract information from a noncompliant subject, Dr. Belanger was a valuable commodity. On very rare occasions, he would pack a Pelican hard case with the tools of his vocation and be flown to a foreign country to ply his trade. This was the first time he would be jumping out of a perfectly good airplane. He knew he could not be in better hands than those of the SEAL senior chief seated next to him, but he was still nervous. Who wouldn't be? He wasn't even a very good swimmer.

The doctor's black hard case would be jumped in by another SEAL. He would be reunited with it once the assaulters had secured what he heard them refer to as the VOI, or Vessel of Interest. Then it would be his turn to work.

Dr. Belanger watched as the SEALs went into what looked to him like the well-rehearsed movements of a Team that knew their business. Chutes were donned, weapons and gear secured, then double- and triple-checked by teammates to ensure multiple sets of eyes were inspecting every detail of the lifesaving equipment that would guide them safely into the waters of the Mediterranean Sea.

The doctor stood and turned around as his harness was clipped to the tandem rig of the large SEAL next to him. His life was now in the hands of the blond-bearded Viking he'd met only hours earlier. There was nothing he could do now but consign himself to fate.

The roar was deafening even through his foam ear protection, as the ramp of the C-17 opened to the unforgiving elements. With the adrenaline, Dr. Belanger felt something that he hadn't experienced since the early days of the war when the first al-Qaeda prisoner was delivered by a team of CIA operatives: *purpose.*

A gray pilot chute shot from the palletized assault boat, violently pulling it from the cargo hold and out into the night. No sooner had the first boat been pulled from view than the second followed closely after. Dr. Belanger knew a second C-17 would be going through the same sequence right behind them just like he'd been told in a quick brief in the hangar before they launched. As his jumper moved with him closer to the open door, he barely noticed the steady stream of assaulters and boat drivers piling out the back of the aircraft in quick succession, following their sleek high-speed assault crafts falling from the sky.

The edge of the ramp was suddenly before him and they stepped off into the abyss.

CHAPTER 75

Mediterranean Sea
October

GENERAL QUSIM YEDID'S FIRST indication that something was wrong was when the door to his stateroom flew open and smashed into the bulkhead. His second was when his security detail lead burst in waving his Makarov 9x18mm pistol, frantically yelling at him to get out of the bed he was occupying with a tall Ukrainian redhead who had a penchant for cocaine.

Yedid sat up just in time to watch his head of security cut down as he took a burst of bullets to his upper back, dropping to the floor just shy of the bed.

The general had the lights dimmed to enhance the mood but still illuminate the lithe body of the beautiful young Ukrainian who had her head between his legs until the first two apparitions from another world shattered the sanctity of his domain. He knew instantly they were Americans. The four-eyed night-vision devices attached to their helmets were a telltale sign that his life had just irrevocably changed. Popularized by the military-inspired television shows and movies in the wake of the Osama bin Laden raid that made them famous, these technological wonders were tilted slightly up so the predators could use the light of the room as they searched for more targets.

Yedid had never been on the receiving end of an assault. He'd ordered plenty but always left the deed to others. He was more of a planner. He felt a paralyzing fear unlike any he'd ever known. Even if he had a pistol nearby, he would not have reached for it.

He was unceremoniously thrown to the floor by the larger of the two intruders and flex-cuffed with an efficiency he had seen only from the Russian advisors to the Mukhabarat, the military intelligence unit controlled by Assad.

His female friend was cuffed as well but was given a bedsheet to preserve some of her dignity and was gently led from the room, her initial screams having subsided. Even though the patch was subdued gray and black on the shoulders of the invaders, she recognized the Stars and Stripes of the United States and knew her night was not going to end at the bottom of the Mediterranean Sea. She wasn't quite as certain about the general.

Still facedown on the deck, Yedid was roughly turned on his side as someone grabbed his chin, twisting it to get a better view of his face and comparing it to what Yedid correctly guessed was his most current photo. A flashlight blinded him as another commando approached, comparing it to another photo on his wrist coach. Nodding to his Teammate, he pressed a button on his chest and said a word that Yedid knew did not bode well for his future: "Jackpot."

CHAPTER 76

Over the Atlantic Ocean

THE GULFSTREAM WAS IN the air less than an hour after Reece had received Rodriguez's call. At least he'd finally made his way onto a private jet. The G550 landed briefly to pick up Freddy at Marine Corps Air Station Beaufort before heading eastward over the Atlantic. Reece could tell by the look on his partner's face that it was crushing him to fly out in the middle of his son's birthday party. Things like that never got easier, especially with a special needs child like Sam.

As the standby squadron from Dam Neck hit the target, Reece and Freddy would be airborne and able to flex as necessary based off exploited intelligence. Their weapons were being stored at the Agency base in Kurdistan, so a basic weapons package from the Ground Branch armory had been loaded onto the plane for their use. Strain opened a black Pelican case and inspected the HK416D assault rifle inside.

"Just one?" Reece asked.

"Looks that way," Strain responded. "Maybe they don't trust you yet."

"Terrific."

"Hey, with what I've experienced in my short time at Langley, we're lucky to even have that. Here," Strain said, "you take the two pistols. I'll take the rifle."

"Wonderful, no extra magazines?" Reece commented, inspecting the 9mm SIG P320 X-Carry and P365. "What kind of operation are you guys running over there?"

"At least they included two nice holsters," Freddy countered, tossing Reece an ankle rig for the 365 and a BlackPoint Tactical Mini WING for the larger handgun.

"I like these Elcans," Freddy remarked, referring to the expensive optic mounted on his HK as he broke the weapon down into its upper and lower receiver and placed it in a low-vis backpack.

"No armor?" Reece asked.

"Doesn't look like it. Guess we better not plan on getting shot."

While they were loading magazines the jet's onboard satellite phone system chirped. The conversation was mostly one-sided and Freddy jotted down some notes before hanging up.

"▆▆▆ just hit Yedid on his yacht. He survived. We have an Agency interrogator working on him now. They said the general was scared shitless when the boys interrupted his party. We should know more soon."

"Any theories, Freddy?"

"It's quite a cast of characters. We've got a former Russian GRU colonel clearly at odds with the current regime and very connected in D.C., a turned CIA Russia analyst on the run, a Syrian general tied to Assad and essentially brokering mercenaries out of Syria and Iraq and God only knows where else, all connected to a rogue CIA Ground Branch sadist running a former friend of yours who thought he was working for the U.S. government. They certainly aren't doing it because they have nothing better to do."

The two former frogmen turned intelligence operatives began discussing various scenarios when another call came in.

"This is Strain."

"Mr. Strain, this is Andy Danreb at the Russian desk. I've come across something that I think you need to know about."

"Hey, Andy! What time is it there?"

"I'm not sure, it's late. This idea hit me, so I came back to the office. My wife was thrilled."

"I bet. I'm putting you on speaker with Reece. What do you have?"

"After our conversation, I started thinking more and more about Oliver Grey. We know he's dirty. What I couldn't figure out, though, was, *why now?* Why, after what must have been years of working for Andrenov, did he do something he knew would blow his cover?"

"We've been asking ourselves the same question, Andy," Reece chimed in.

"Well, I think I've found the answer. I started looking through some of the raw intelligence coming across his desk; he was looking at a ton of signals intercepts, which is really well below his pay grade. I've been searching all weekend, but I didn't find anything that made any sense. It hit me tonight that he would have hidden whatever it was, that he would have removed it from the system, so I couldn't pull it up. He couldn't hide the raw feed, though, so I went back and found an intercept that wasn't in message traffic."

"What was it?"

"It's the Russian president's itinerary. NSA intercepted some communication between the Russian FSO, the Federal Protective Service, and the president's Executive Office. The FSO is their version of the Secret Service. We have a thirty-day snapshot of where President Zubarev will be, hour by hour. It's this month, Strain; we are halfway through the calendar that we have."

"Where is the Russian president now?"

"He's scheduled to give a speech in Odessa tomorrow at noon. Then he flies to Moscow early the following morning."

"Grey didn't randomly choose this month to disappear. That schedule is the key. We'll need some analytical assets at our disposal, Andy. You think you can help?"

"I thought you'd never ask; what can I do?" Danreb felt like he'd been liberated from prison.

"I need your best team, people you can trust, in a secure conference room. I need you to be our eyes, ears, and brain as this info comes through."

"I'll get on the phone and start waking people up."

"I need you to be absolutely sure that none of these people are tied to Grey."

"That's not a problem. Let's just say that he and I don't run in the same circles around here."

"Do you know Nicole Phan at CTC?"

"I've heard the name, but I don't know her."

"She's been helping us on this; you might want to bring her in if you can."

"Will do. I better run if I'm going to get this thing up and running."

"Thanks, Andy. Great work." Freddy ended the call and turned to his friend. "Reece, I almost forgot."

"What?"

Strain pulled a duffel from a compartment behind his seat. "I saw what you gave to Richard Hastings in Africa and thought you might need a new one," he said as he pulled a Winkler tomahawk from his bag and handed it to his friend.

Reece stared at the masterpiece of wood and steel, slowly pulling the small bungee cords that secured the Kydex sheath to its deadly head and examining its razor-sharp blade.

"I can't accept this, brother. It's your Squadron ax," Reece said, honored and humbled.

"I've never carried it. As you know, I prefer my guns," Freddy said smiling, clearly enjoying the moment. "Keep it. Think of it as a thank-you for nailing that *haji* that was climbing the building to take me out in ▮▮▮▮▮▮▮. Plus, I know how much you love those things."

"Thank you, Freddy. I'll hold on to it for you; how about that?"

"Sounds good, Reece."

CHAPTER 77

Somewhere over the Mediterranean Sea
October

THE TOUGHEST PART WAS going to be getting word to the Russians. Ordinarily, the State Department would have been the appropriate channel, but in this case, more urgency was required. Strain had relayed what information he knew to Vic Rodriguez, who was working the phones on his way into the office. After speaking with Janice Motley, it was decided that the best course of action was to have the Moscow station chief reach out to the Federal Protective Service, responsible for President Zubarev's security. Sources and methods had to be protected, so the communication was simple: the United States government had reason to believe that individuals, possibly Syrian nationals, were targeting the Russian president during an upcoming trip to Odessa, Ukraine. The head of the FSO was polite and appreciative but offered no information in return.

Their apprehension about sharing and their skepticism about a threat were not unfounded. Single-source intelligence, hunches, and assumptions were how one got into trouble. Of course, that ran contrary to the sixth sense that had kept warriors alive in battle since the beginning of time; sometimes you just needed to trust your gut.

The CIA jet was within thirty minutes of landing at Odessa International Airport when the phone rang again. This time it was the Agency doctor who had accompanied the SEALs on the takedown of Yedid's yacht calling with an update.

"This is Strain."

"Freddy, this is Dr. Rob Belanger. I've got an update for you."

"Give me good news, Doc."

"Well, as you know I don't make the good or bad determination. It's information and I would rate it reliable."

"Understood. What do you have for us?"

"CIA analyst Oliver Grey went through General Qusim Yedid to hire a sniper team. Their last known location was two weeks ago along the Turkey-Georgia-Armenia border near a town called Göle. General Yedid identified the sniper team as Tasho al-Shishani, a Georgian, and a Syrian named Nizar Kattan. Langley is doing a workup on them now. They'll send you photos if they have any, along with anything else they can dig up."

"And the target?"

"He said he didn't know. Grey wanted to run the operation himself."

"How confident are you in what Yedid told you?"

"Mr. Strain, I didn't even need to open my case, which is always the best way. He isn't a radical, ready to die for Allah. Those are my specialty. He is a businessman and has no interest in dying for the cause. I am not at liberty to discuss his deal, but rest assured the Agency will put him to good use as an asset."

"Understood. Anything else?"

"Yes. General Yedid had a female companion with him when he was detained."

"You mean a prostitute?"

"Yes. She told us that there was an American on the yacht a few days ago. Yedid confirmed it was Grey. They dropped him off when they picked her up."

"Where was that, Doc?"

"Odessa."

. . .

Freddy pulled an iPad from his pack and selected the icon for LeadNav Systems, a sophisticated imagery program used by special operations forces. He pulled up the area surrounding Göle and turned the screen so Reece could see it.

"That was Dr. Ron Belanger. He's a CIA interrogator that ████ jumped in on the Yedid takedown. He says that Grey hired General Yedid to find him a sniper team and he got him one. And get this, their last known location was just across the Black Sea, right here," Freddy said, moving the cursor to a place on the screen. "Notice anything?"

"Looks pretty rural," Reece offered. "Good place to shoot a rifle without attracting too much attention."

"I agree. They're training for something. Look at how close it is to the coast. Let's say these snipers board a ship somewhere here," Freddy said, pointing to the screen, "then cross the Black Sea. They're in Odessa."

Freddy zoomed the image out to show the entire Black Sea and its coastline, with the snipers' last known location directly opposite the landlocked body of water from the Russian president's destination.

"Can you pull up port information on that thing?" Reece asked.

"Nothing too specific. We'll need Andy's team for that. It looks like the closest port of any size would be Batumi, just across the border in Georgia."

The engines had powered back and the jet was descending rapidly over the Ukrainian countryside. The pilot came over the cabin's speakers and indicated that they would be on the ground in ten minutes. Both men put on their seat belts and took a few moments to think through the newest information. The puzzle was coming together, but Reece still felt like they were missing a big piece.

CHAPTER 78

Odessa, Ukraine
October

UPON THEIR ARRIVAL IN Ukraine, Reece and Freddy were met by a case officer assigned to the embassy in Kiev, who was not happy to have made the six-hour drive to retrieve some bearded commando types from the Odessa airport. Steve Douglass was polite but not overly friendly as he greeted them outside the terminal. The men stowed their backpacks in the back of the small black Lada four-by-four SUV and climbed inside.

"So, I'm assuming that you guys are here for the president's visit?"

"Something like that," Reece responded.

"I guess the Secret Service needed some extra bodies? Not sure why they couldn't pick you up."

"We aren't super close with the FSO," Freddy added.

"What do you mean, the FSO? I'm talking about the Secret Service."

"The United States Secret Service?" Reece asked.

"Of course. POTUS is here."

"The president of the United States is here, in Odessa?"

"He will be in a couple of hours. You're telling me that's not why *you're* here?"

. . .

Freddy immediately called Rodriguez on the sat phone and gave him the rundown. The interagency wheels, however inefficient, began to turn in

Washington as the Agency made contact with the Secret Service. Much like presidents' recent visits to war zones in Iraq and Afghanistan, this visit was being kept a secret until the last moment. The White House pool reporters would not even be aware of their destination until Air Force One landed in Odessa, and as can be the case in a bureaucracy as big as the United States intelligence and federal law enforcement apparatus, the right hand often did not know what the left hand was doing.

In the meantime, Steve Douglass made a phone call and determined which hotel the advance team was using as a base of operations. By the time the local agents were informed that a pair of CIA officers were on the ground with specific threat intel, Douglass was parking outside their temporary command center in Hotel Otrada.

As the trio entered the hotel lobby, a petite female agent with a lapel pin on her blue pantsuit approached them. Freddy fished his green agency identification badge out of the inside pocket of his jacket. All Reece had was his black U.S. passport, which he handed over. She scrutinized both, returning Freddy's badge before handing over Reece's passport.

"You look just like a guy I saw on a wanted poster, Mr. Donovan," the agent said, staring at Reece with bright, unflinching eyes.

"I get that a lot."

She slowly broke into a smile and shook their hands. "I'm Kim Scheer. Follow me."

It looked as though the Secret Service had occupied the entire hotel; uniformed and plainclothes agents were moving around the lobby as they readied for the arrival of their principal, the president of the United States. Agent Scheer led the way to a suite on the hotel's highest floor. The room was packed with tables filled with computers and communications gear as well as at least fifteen agents and technicians. A tall man in his early fifties stood in the center of the room, clearly in charge. He wore a dark blue three-button business suit and his head was closely shaved, having given up the battle with his receding hairline a decade earlier. He turned to greet Reece and Strain like a man with a great deal on his plate.

"What can I do for you two gentlemen?"

His accent was from Minnesota or perhaps the eastern Dakotas.

"We're from the Agency, Ground Branch. I'm Freddy Strain, and this is James Donovan. We have reason to believe that there is a specific threat against the president of Russia and/or the president of the United States here in Odessa."

They had his undivided attention.

"What kind of threat?"

"A sniper. A sniper team, to be precise. A Georgian national they call the *Shishani* and a Syrian named Nizar Kattan. Last known location was across the Black Sea in Turkey. The president needs to cancel whatever public appearance he has planned."

"How credible is this?"

"It's credible," Freddy responded.

"I hate to break it to you guys, but a lot of people want to kill the president and we can't shut down his schedule every time some nutcase makes a threat. I'm going to need specifics, gentlemen."

"Look, we have a Syrian general brokering mercenaries at the behest of a former GRU colonel named Vasili Andrenov set on a transfer of power in Russia who's put a sniper team within a stone's throw of Odessa at the same time the presidents of Russia and the United States just happen to be here. One or both of them are the targets." Reece was starting to lose his temper.

The man put up a hand. "I'm sorry, guys, I didn't mean it that way. I'm up to my eyeballs here and now I've got two scraggly-looking Agency guys telling me about some plot to kill the president. Let's start over. I'm Lee Christiansen."

The taller man shook both their hands and his demeanor changed appreciably.

"Lee, the president needs to cancel this speech or move it inside," Freddy said.

"If it were up to me, we'd never let him leave the White House, but that's not how a republic functions. We can't cancel his itinerary every time there's a threat."

"This isn't some whacko posting threats on Twitter from his mom's basement. This is a trained sniper team," Freddy stressed.

Christiansen sighed. "Here's what I'll do. I'm going to pair you guys up with one of my agents so you'll have full access to our resources. Agent Scheer, you're going to be our point person on this. Whatever these guys need, you make sure they get it and call me directly if someone gets in your way. I'll talk with the White House and fill them in. Will that work for a first step?"

"That works for us," Freddy answered.

Agent Scheer led them down the hallway into a smaller room that had been set up with a conference table. A whiteboard stood in the corner on a tripod stand. All three took seats with Scheer at the head of the rectangular table.

"So, what do we have, guys?"

Reece spoke up first. "We're going to tell you some things that you're probably not cleared for, so hopefully your memory isn't the greatest."

"I drink a lot."

"Perfect. Here's what we know: a former Russian intelligence officer, with a history of planning coups and assassinations, is living in Switzerland. He is on the outs with the current Russian administration led by President Zubarev and would love to have his hard-liners in power. Through an intermediary, he contracts with a Syrian general to hire a sniper team whose last known location was in rural Turkey near the Georgian and Armenian borders."

Freddy passed his iPad to Scheer and pointed to the spot.

"Looks like a good place to train," she observed.

"Our thoughts exactly."

"May I?" Scheer asked rhetorically as she zoomed out of the image so that the entire region was visible. "I don't like it that they're so close to the Black Sea, and the presidents are going to speak on the coastline near a major port."

"Where's the speech?"

"Here." Scheer scrolled the map to center on Odessa and zoomed in on a site near the coastline. "It's called the Boffo Colonnade. It's located on the grounds of the Vorontsov Palace. It's a tourist attraction and major landmark."

The curved narrow structure was lined with ten massive columns on each side and sat like a raised amphitheater in front of a cobblestone pedestrian area that led to a wide set of stone steps, framed on either side by elevated statues of full-maned African lions.

"What's the sniper risk at the site?" Freddy asked.

"We evaluated it as moderate. To the front there are buildings that block the line of sight to the lectern and we have them secured and covered with our own countersniper teams. It's all low ground behind the colonnade all the way to the sea. There are some structures on the port with exposure, but we'll have everything there secure out to two thousand meters. The entire harbor will be shut down during the speech and we'll have eyes out that direction."

"Is that the president's only public appearance in Odessa?"

"Other than the airport tarmac and the route to the speech, that's it."

"Tell us about the route."

"Nothing ideal for a sniper, especially not in the Beast," Scheer said, referring to the president's heavily armored Cadillac limousine.

"Anything else peculiar about this site?"

"Yes, there are catacombs underneath used during World War Two, but they existed well before that. The partisans used them to fight the Nazis. The plaza was a restaurant in the 1800s. The owner would supposedly drag drunk customers down into the tunnel system, bring them straight down to the docks, and sell them to the slave ships waiting in the harbor."

"Really? Rough way to wake up. I'm assuming you've secured the tunnels?" Freddy asked.

"Correct, but they have three levels and they've never been fully mapped. We've secured all known entry points, but people are discovering new ones all the time. There's an entire industry built around exploring them, discovering new passages, new artifacts."

"Terrific." Freddy checked his phone and saw an email from Andy Danreb.

"Looks like the analyst team is up and running. Let's see if they have anything for us." He dialed into a secure conference number and put his phone on the center of the table with the speakerphone engaged.

"Danreb here."

"Andy, it's Freddy and James. We're in Odessa with Agent Kim Scheer from the Secret Service."

"Agent Scheer, I'm Andy Danreb here at Langley with Nicole Phan and Fabian Brooks, our computer whiz."

"Appreciate you all pulling this together on short notice. Anything new?" Reece inquired.

Nicole spoke up. "We are exploring anything and anyone with a connection to Vasili Andrenov, Jules Landry, and General Yedid. Andrenov's political connections and charitable giving have muddied the waters since there are so many paper trails to follow, but we are working it through. It looks like Landry's network was pretty slim. Yedid is connected to just about every radical Islamist refugee in the Middle East and southern Europe."

"In other words, we don't have shit," Danreb chimed in.

"Keep on it, Andy, we have . . . how long, Kim?" asked Reece.

"Three hours and thirty-two minutes until Umbrella lands. Four hours until he goes onstage."

Every protectee, or "principal," had a Secret Service code name: "Umbrella" was a reference to the 187th Infantry Regiment of the 101st Airborne Division, nicknamed by the Japanese as *Rakkasan*s, which meant "falling-down umbrella men." The president had commanded the Rakkasans during Operation Iraqi Freedom in 2003 before being selected as vice president by the previous administration.

"We have less than four hours, so do what you can. I know you'll come up with something. Out here."

Freddy ended the call and turned to their Secret Service liaison. "Can you take us to the site?"

"Let's go. I'll drive. And let me get you two some lapel pins."

CHAPTER 79

Odessa, Ukraine
October

REECE AND FREDDY RETRIEVED their gear bags and weapons from the back of the Agency SUV and thanked Douglass for the ride. Agent Scheer led them to a white Hyundai minivan that was obviously from a local rental agency's fleet.

"No Suburban?" Reece teased.

"*Please!* The advance team gets the shaft. All the cool guys on the PPD, ah, that's the president's detail, get their vehicles flown in on C-17s for game day and we get whatever Avis can't rent out that week."

Kim pulled out of the hotel and navigated the local streets like a native. She'd obviously spent some time in the area as part of the advance team.

"What's your background, Kim? Did you come straight to the Secret Service?" Freddy asked.

"No, I went to Annapolis. Then the Marine Corps. Got out as a captain, tried to go to work in the family insurance business, but that made me want to blow my brains out. Applied for this job five years ago and have been here ever since. I love it."

"What did you do in the Corps?" Reece asked.

"Intel, mainly. Supported some high-speed units but didn't leave the FOB much."

"MARSOC?"

"They call them 'Raiders' now but, yeah, I was attached as an intel officer."

"That's right, 'the artists formerly known as MARSOC.' Hard to keep up with all of the name changes. I was attached to DET ONE in 2004 for a couple of months," Reece responded. "That was a solid group. I really learned a lot from them, especially Major K. He used to run their mountain warfare training center. Great guy!"

"He was squared away," Kim remembered.

"Was Gunny Gutierrez still around when you were there?" Reece asked.

"He sure was. Small world."

"It is, indeed."

After showing her credentials to local police and making her way through the roadblocks, Agent Scheer parked the minivan on Prymorskyi Boulevard and led the men toward the site of the speech. They walked along the gray cobblestone driveway past an impressive nineteenth-century columned building that had, at some point, been the residence of someone important. The gated perimeter had already been set up and the temporary fences funneled pedestrians into a tent with several airport-style magnetometers and package scanners. The uniformed personnel recognized the Secret Service agent and waved her through. As they cleared the checkpoint and rounded the building, the colonnade they'd viewed on the iPad imagery was directly in front of them.

The area was smaller than Reece had expected it to be. The site had obviously been chosen for television viewing rather than its ability to accommodate a large physical audience. A stage had been built in front, with two lecterns a few yards apart from each other. Last-minute preparations were being made by a variety of workers while security personnel from the United States, Russia, and Ukraine moved busily about.

They walked up onto the stage and looked around. The site of the speech sat on a high bluff, with the ground falling off sharply toward the sea below. From the land side of the colonnade, the site left very few options for a sniper. Tall trees and buildings surrounded the structure, leaving no discernible line-of-sight shooting lanes that wouldn't be locked

down by the Secret Service. A long and modern pedestrian bridge connected the area from stage right to a more built-up area of the city, but
only the rooftops and high windows of those buildings offered a shot toward the stage, and all would be occupied by authorities. Each member
of the team spent several minutes taking in the scene, looking for something that had been overlooked by the other dozen sets of eyes that had
studied it as part of the overall security assessment.

Reece broke the silence first. "I'll be honest, Kim, this is a good spot."

"I agree," Freddy added. "The only thing that bothers me is the port,
but you're saying it's been locked down?"

"Yep. Everything within two thousand meters has been searched
and secured. We have drones up looking for IR signatures and dog teams
have been working it all night and morning. The port is secure."

"What are we missing?" Reece asked himself as much as the others.

Far out on the horizon, past the closest set of docks and through
a forest of dock cranes, sat a massive green and red tanker-style vessel
with a handful of colorful shipping containers stacked on the deck. Strain
pulled a laser rangefinder unit from his pack and aimed it toward the
ship, bracing it against one of the columns for stability.

"Twenty-one hundred meters. Technically, you could make a shot
from that far pier but it would be a long one."

"Sure would, especially in this wind. You think that's a legitimate
threat, Freddy? What's the world-record shot these days anyway?"

"These records are changing every year or two but the longest confirmed real-world shot was taken in Iraq by a Canadian sniper in 2017,
went 3,871 yards. He used a McMillan TAC-50 like the ones we used to
use. The shot took ten seconds to reach the target."

"That's crazy," Reece said, shaking his head.

"It's damn fine shooting, buddy."

"No, I meant that you can remember all that stuff." Reece smiled.
"How about on a controlled range?"

"To the best of my knowledge, a shooter out of Texas hit a three-
mile shot with a .408 Chey Tac in 2018. Before that, one of our old sniper
instructors had it at 2.8 miles with the same round. Keep in mind those

are not under combat conditions and were done with the best rifle-scope combinations available, shot by the most highly trained and capable snipers on earth."

"So, from those cranes and that ship," Reece said, gesturing to the distance, "it's a low-percentage shot but not out of the realm of possibility. With the guns and optics that are out there now, it could be done. Could you have some people take a look at that far pier, Kim?"

"It's outside of the perimeter but, sure, I'll have someone check it out."

Agent Scheer walked off a few steps and made a phone call. Gesturing with her hand as she spoke, she tried to describe the exact location of the tanker, before hanging up and rejoining the group.

"That's the oil terminal, so it's not open to the public. It's gated, and local police are manning it. They're sending some of our people over there to look around and will do a sweep with the UAVs as well."

"Okay, good, let's keep looking. I still feel like something is off."

"The Secret Service does extensive research into the threats to POTUS," Kim explained, "at every location on every itinerary. Ever since President Kennedy we have been extremely sensitive to sniper threats against the president, for obvious reasons. No one wants to relive the nightmare that was Dallas, so ever since 1963 we've kept data of every military and law enforcement sniper, and with the advent of social media we've kept tabs, using open-source information, on civilians going to shooting schools run by former military snipers. Anytime POTUS makes a stop, we've cross-referenced everyone in a given area, including incoming travelers whose names we get from TSA, to those former MIL/LE and civilian-trained long-range shooters. They each get checked out, and any in the vicinity of a POTUS stop are flagged. Facial recognition technology helps a lot."

"That's thorough," Reece remarked, "but here you don't have that information on foreign-trained snipers."

"The database is fairly robust thanks to the folks at the NSA, but you're right, nothing's a hundred percent. We have good intel on U.S., Canadian, and European-trained snipers, who are the ones that coincidentally have the best shot at taking out the president. According to our assessment, other countries just don't have the training or equipment required to make a shot past two thousand yards. That's stretching it even for us."

Reece nodded and looked out to sea. "The *Shishani* is here, Kim. I know it. He's in place. He's waiting. That sniper is here."

. . .

Oliver Grey recognized James Reece from the media coverage following his attacks on various civilian and military individuals across the United States the previous year.

He looks a lot like his father did.

Reece and his two colleagues had taken no interest in him as they walked past in front of the Bootlegger, a gangster-themed pub that sat on the ground floor of a taller building near the colonnade. Grey was sitting at a table on the sidewalk, reading the local Russian-language newspaper and drinking coffee like just another local going about his day. Since the pub sat well below the high ground where the presidents would speak, the street where it was located would remain open until just before the event began.

The fact that Reece was walking with another Westerner and what looked to be a female Secret Service agent meant that he had worked his way back into the good graces of the U.S. government. This explained why Jules Landry had fallen off the radar, which meant that this operation had been compromised. Still, it was too late to call it off now. They would never get another opportunity like it. Grey had long since passed the point of no return, and the operation had reached a similar point. There was no going back.

CHAPTER 80

"TELL ME ABOUT YOUR countersniper setup," Reece said.

The three Americans were standing on the roof of a large apartment building in the midst of renovation that overlooked the colonnade. A Secret Service sharpshooter, dressed from head to toe in black BDUs, was setting up what looked like an AR-10 on the roof parapet. A giant pair of well-worn 1980s-vintage Steiner binoculars sat nearby. Next to the American was another black-clad sniper wearing a matching beret with a colorful badge. His rifle, a black chassis-style bolt-action with a Nightforce scope, was cradled in a tripod mount alongside a separate tripod that held both a Leica spotting scope and a pair of rangefinding binoculars. It wasn't lost on Reece or Strain that the Russians seemed to have superior equipment to the Americans', at least when it came to optics.

"Well, it depends on where we are but, in this case, we have our guys paired up with Russian counterparts from the FSO, one U.S. shooter and one Russian," Kim explained. "In some countries, our folks aren't permitted to carry weapons, but they always at least shadow the local shooters so they can coordinate with the PPD."

"Don't your people usually work in pairs?" asked Freddy.

"Generally, yes, but not on this trip. This arrangement was a negotiated deal between the Russians and the Ukrainians. Besides, budget cuts hit us hard. We're low on agents as it is. This allows us to spread our people over a wider radius."

"Sounds like a recipe for disaster," Freddy commented.

"Let's hope not."

"What rifle is that, Freddy?" asked Reece.

"I think it's called a *Tochnost*. It's Russia's new sniper rifle. Supposedly a great gun, but I don't have any experience with it."

"What about assaulters? What assets do we have on the ground?" Reece asked, beginning to pace.

"CAT, that's our Counter-Assault Team, will be near the stage. Their job is to cover the PPD while they get Umbrella to safety. The Russians have their own team with a similar role. Neither is going to divert away from their principal. If there's a threat somewhere that we need to move on, the Ukrainian Alphas will be the ones to do it."

"Forgive me for bringing up the elephant in the room, Kim, but don't the Russians and Ukrainians hate each other? Russia is occupying Crimea, for Christ's sake," Freddy pointed out.

"Our threat assessment teams analyze all that. Us agents, we leave the politics to the politicians."

"That reminds me to check in with Andy." Freddy stepped away from the countersnipers and made a call. Reece and Kim followed and leaned in to hear the conversation.

"This is Andy."

"It's Strain, anything new?"

"I was actually about to call you. I just heard from a contact at State. During his speech today, President Zubarev is going to announce that they're giving back Crimea. In exchange, the United States will drop its sanctions against Moscow, and the EU will buy a bunch of Russian natural gas. Our president praises Russia, and everyone shakes hands and sings 'Kumbaya.'"

"That doesn't sound like it's in line with Andrenov's vision," Reece chimed in.

"Not at all. This is the kind of move that would make him want to take out a president. And if I know Andrenov, he'll find a way to spin it to his advantage."

"How so?"

"If President Zubarev goes down, the new president will have the support he needs to retaliate. That means he's going to blame it either on the Ukrainians, Azerbaijanis, or someone within their own borders that they want to take out, probably Muslims in the Caucasus. When Russian tanks start rolling farther into Ukraine or Turkey on another land grab, they'll be able to wave around a photo of their dead president as justification. Like I told you when you were here, this is the last gasp of a dying empire. Desperate people do desperate things. *Hell,* if our president was hit as well, we might even support them! And I'm just giving you my best guess as to what's going on. We're not perfect; we thought Iraq had WMDs, remember?"

"That rings a bell," Reece said. "Keep working it. I'm going to see if Agent Scheer can get you a list of the local security forces. Maybe we're overlooking someone there."

"I'll have PID send them a full list," she confirmed.

"Okay, thanks all, out here." Freddy ended the call.

"I think we just checked the motive block," Reece observed.

Agent Scheer looked at her watch. "I'll pass all this along but we're going to need more. Umbrella lands in less than an hour."

CHAPTER 81

"UMBRELLA IS EN ROUTE, five miles out. He'll be here in ten minutes."

Strain had kitted up with a low-vis mag carrier. His carbine was slung to his left side. Reece had both 9mm pistols courtesy of his new employer. They were on their own radios, which were not compatible with the ones used by the Secret Service. That meant that Reece stayed close to Agent Scheer so she could relay any relevant information from her feed. It was the best that they could muster on such short notice.

The former SEALs had placed themselves on opposing ends of the Tioschin pedestrian bridge, an elevated structure that gave them a good vantage point and reasonable mobility. Reece and Scheer were closest to the colonnade where the presidents would be speaking while Freddy was positioned on the west end. He had given Reece the sat phone since he was in a better position to coordinate assets and intelligence should that become necessary.

The streets had been closed, and the route had been cleared. A crowd of several hundred people, all having been frisked physically and electronically by uniformed Secret Service agents, filled the space in front of the colonnade. No backpacks, satchels, or briefcases were allowed inside the perimeter. A brass band was set up at stage left, facing the direction of the pedestrian bridge. Television cameras were ready to film the event with the agreement that the live feed would be sequestered until the respective leaders were on-site.

A team of Ukrainian police had searched the pier that had concerned the Americans and found nothing out of the ordinary. Reece peered into every probable hide site that he could find using his binoculars. The tough part was that this area had virtually no middle ground; the shooter was either very close or extremely distant.

I know you're here. Where are you hiding?

"Umbrella is five minutes out."

"You see anything, Freddy?"

"Negative, Reece," his friend responded over the radio.

• • •

The shipping container sat at the top of the large stack of identical boxes riding on the deck of the freighter, giving them a commanding view of the harbor. They had no communications devices in the container, so everything depended on the clock. Cell phones, satellite phones, and radios all gave off electronic signatures that could be detected remotely and would give away their location. If there was anything the Americans were good at, it was locating and targeting communications equipment, specifically cell phones. *Lessons learned the hard way.*

The ventilation system had been shut off twelve hours earlier to prevent heat signatures from escaping, and though the oxygen tanks that had been fitted inside allowed them to breathe through medical masks, the heavily insulated container had become incredibly hot, humid, and stagnant. Nizar closed his eyes and tried to remain calm. Finally, after what seemed like days, Tasho nodded to Nizar that it was time to open the doors. Both men donned dark sunglasses.

They each turned a crank that raised a metal panel inward, much the same way that residential windows functioned. A red cloth mesh that matched the outside paint of the container remained in place, allowing them to see out while limiting their exposure to all but the closest visual inspection. The air that rushed into the space felt like heaven but, even darkened by their sunglasses and the cloth screen, the light was blinding. The rifles were already positioned behind the openings, resting on their bipods and beanbag-like sandbags at the rear. Tasho and Nizar easily found the distinctive architecture of the colonnade in their scopes and made adjustments to their bodies and to the rifles until they found what was called a natural point of aim. Heat and moisture emanating from Nizar's breath and sweat-soaked forehead quickly fogged the rear lens of his scope. He wiped it hastily to clear the image.

They had already dialed for elevation, the exact distance from their hide site to the target had been calculated and sent to them before they'd entered the container. They knew the precise width of the ship and its position against the pier. The wind was another story. It was blowing from the southwest, which made it almost full value. At this extreme distance, knowing the wind at the muzzle wasn't enough, as it could change multiple times between rifle and target. Fortunately, coastal winds such as these were fairly consistent and there were few terrain features in their path to cause disturbances in the air.

Tasho studied the visual mirage, the movement of the water below, the sway of the tall trees near the target, and even the flags mounted atop the pier's numerous cranes through his Swarovski spotting scope. As he studied each indicator, he began to build a picture of the wind call that would determine the success or failure of their mission.

. . .

"I've got something here, Andy."

It was Fabian, the computer expert who was supporting their frantic search for some shred of evidence that could assist the team on the ground in Odessa.

"What is it?"

"I've been searching known associates of Andrenov and bumping them against every database that we have. Yuri Vatutin is Andrenov's head of security and, like most of them, he's a former FSB commando. One of the men under his command in Chechnya was Grigoriy Isaev. There's a very similar name, Gregory Isay, on the Russian Federal Protective Service roster the Secret Service just emailed us. Isaev means 'son of Isay' in Russian. I think it might be the same person. The computer didn't match the names because it wasn't an exact match. We run into this problem constantly with Muslim names, so it's something I think about. I've just never had to do it with Russians."

Danreb snatched the list from the analyst's hands. *"Get Strain on the phone! Now!"*

CHAPTER 82

"UMBRELLA IS ONE MINUTE out."

"One minute, Freddy, it's game time."

"Roger that."

The Agency sat phone vibrated just as the band fired up, playing whatever the Russian equivalent was to "Hail to the Chief" as President Zubarev took to the stage. Reece held his hand over the radio earpiece on his left ear and put the phone up to his right. "Donovan."

"It's Andy. We think one of the FSO agents served with Andrenov's head of security. His name is Gregory Isay."

"Say it again, Andy, it's really loud here."

"FSO agent Gregory Isay may be your shooter!"

Fuck!

Reece communicated the name to Scheer, who made a radio call of her own. He then hit the transmit button on his radio.

"Freddy, FSO Agent Gregory Isay could be our shooter. Scheer is finding out where he is."

Reece and Freddy began frantically searching the rooftops as they waited for information from Scheer. On nearly every high building they saw a pair of figures staring through either binoculars or spotting scopes, scanning their assigned areas for threats.

On the nearby roof of a pink and white corner building, Strain saw a Russian sniper with no sign of an American counterpart. He looked around for a path to the building from his high perch on the pedestrian bridge. The street below was too far to drop. He would break both his legs if he were lucky. Running farther to the west, Freddy found what he was looking for and swung his slung HK416 behind his back and out of the way. He climbed over the bridge's six-foot chain-link railing. *I'm too old for this.* He took a deep breath and dropped onto the tiled roof of a two-story apartment building below. He half-slid, half-ran down the roof before dropping another floor down to the flat roof next door, twisting his ankle as he landed. Limping across the flat roof, he swung his legs over the side, finding the stone wall with the toe of his boot, and dropped six feet onto the roof of a Volvo sedan parked on the sidewalk. Hobbling across the intersection as fast as his tender ankle allowed him with his weapon trained on the roofline, Freddy moved toward his new objective.

Out of breath from the exertion, he keyed the mic button attached to his armor: "Reece, I'm headed to a building northwest of your position. I think that's where the shooter is."

"Roger that! I'm having Scheer send people there now to support."

Freddy took the three doorway steps as fast as he could with his injured ankle and jerked on the wood-framed glass door. Locked. Without hesitation, he smashed through the glass with the suppressor and raked away the standing panes before stepping inside. The ground floor of the three-story building was a clothing boutique that was dark except for the sunlight filtering through the canopied windows. Using the light mounted on his weapon's rail, he located the unlocked back door and made entry. An old wooden stairway began at the end of the narrow hallway behind the door and he moved as quickly as he could while searching the area above for potential threats. *Don't rush to your death.*

Freddy had made his way up four flights of stairs and was turning the corner to approach the third floor. It was dead quiet inside the building but for the creaks of the stairs below his feet. It actually startled him when the radio came alive in his ear.

"Freddy, the countersniper at your location is not answering his radio call. Alpha Group is moving toward your location, but I doubt they're going to get there in time to help."

Freddy keyed his mic twice in understanding.

CHAPTER 83

THE LONE FIGURE STANDING on the rooftop was the sign that President Zubarev had taken the stage. The snipers couldn't distinguish facial features at such a distance, so everything depended on time, place, and the signal from inside the perimeter. It was time to take their shots. Tasho moved from the spotting scope to his rifle. He took a final look at the wind and decided to bracket the shot. Calling wind was as much an art as a science, especially at this distance. He would make one wind hold himself and give Nizar a slightly different hold, statistically increasing the chances that one of their shots would find its mark. Winds were tricky.

"Confirm twelve-point-nine MILS of elevation."

Nizar looked at the dial on top of the optic. "Twelve-point-nine MILS confirmed."

"Hold two-point-nine MILS right."

"Two-point-nine MILS right," Nizar repeated.

"Ready."

"Ready."

"Three . . . two . . . one."

Boom! The sound inside the container was deafening, the overpressure event of their shots reverberating through the enclosed space. The propellant gases from the muzzle blew the cloth screens off the openings before the bullets left the barrels, the copper projectiles exiting the muzzles at just under three thousand feet per second. The bullets' arc took them high above the physical obstacles that lay beneath the container and the colonnade during their 3.171-second flight. Their total drop was over 970 inches from the muzzle to the target, accounted for by the 1,000-yard zero and elevation adjustments made in the scope. The 13-mph west wind pushed the bullets 221 inches laterally as they flew.

Tasho had called the wind perfectly for his own shot, which meant that Nizar's 350-grain bullet smashed into one of the colonnade's pillars, showering the area with a puff of white dust that many onlookers mistook for an explosion.

The *Shishani*'s bullet created a different, grislier shower as it passed through President Zubarev's abdomen, sending blood, bone, bowel tissue, and digested matter across the stage. The bullet severed the Russian president's vertebrae, and gravity sent his body crashing downward before anyone knew what had happened.

Even had the band's noise not drowned out the rifle's report or the bullet's sonic crack, he would have been on the ground before anyone heard it. Tasho and Nizar had completed their mission. *Inshallah*, it was time for the other shooter to complete his.

Reece saw the formation of agents moving toward the stage react instantly. Umbrella was shoved down and away from the stage by the agents closest to him. The crowd's confused cries transformed into panicked screams as the band members dropped their instruments and dove for cover. A team of black-clad Counter-Assault Team agents wearing Kevlar body armor and helmets, armed with KAC SR-16 carbines, emerged from around the Vorontsov Palace and moved to dominate the terrain as Umbrella was rushed to safety by his detail.

With POTUS out of the line of fire, Reece turned his attention back to the Russian sniper that Freddy had seen standing alone on the roof. Unable to see him from his current vantage point, Reece moved to higher ground.

· · ·

Freddy reached the roof level of the stairway and, not surprisingly, the door had been blocked. With no breaching equipment in his kit, Strain moved the selector switch on his carbine to full auto and emptied a magazine into the door, blasting the dead bolt and doorjamb into splinters of wood and metal. He ejected the empty magazine, inserted a fresh one from his chest rig, and slapped the bolt stop before kicking the door open and taking the corner onto the roof. He moved quickly since the element of surprise had been spoiled by the thirty brown-tip rounds that he'd sent through the door. He stepped laterally and saw a pool of blood expanding across the flat metal roof. As he continued, he saw the source of the blood ten yards away, the supine figure of the Secret Service agent assigned to the rooftop countersniper position. He wasn't moving. Freddy took another step to his right and saw the long barrel of a Russian sniper rifle turning to face him, the sniper rising from his knees as he turned.

· · ·

Freddy found the sniper in his scope and squeezed a half-dozen rapid-fire rounds into his torso, shooting him into the ground as he fell sideways onto the roof, his heavy rifle hitting the deck next to him. The SEAL fired two additional security rounds into the Russian's head and dashed forward to assess the wounds of the American agent.

"Reece, we've got a man down up here. The threat is down, too. I say again, the threat is down. Over."

The Secret Service countersniper had been shot in the throat, undoubtedly by the suppressed Yarygin handgun lying on the roof beside the Russian sniper. Strain applied pressure to the American's wound. He could feel a faint pulse as he pressed on the source of the bleeding, bright red blood flowing between his fingers as he knelt beside the gravely wounded agent.

"Reece, we need a medic on this roof ASAP. I've got a critical patient here, over."

"I'm working on it, Freddy. Over."

· · ·

Nizar worked the bolt instinctively and loaded another round from the rifle's magazine. Per his orders, he transitioned his scope to the three-story building to the right of the stage and corrected his elevation for the closer shot. He had already done the math on the wind and used the reticle to hold for the drift. His target was kneeling instead of in the prone position that Nizar expected, which made for an even easier target. He exhaled and began to take the slack out of the trigger.

. . .

Reece had lost sight of Freddy kneeling behind the roof's parapet wall but, from his elevated position, he had a view of the SUVs containing the Ukrainian Alpha Group assaulters headed to support.

"Freddy, be advised the Alpha Team is on your street. They'll have a medic with them, so just hold tight. Over."

"Roger that, Reece, is Umbrella safe?"

"Check, he's secure, Freddy, but President Zubarev is down. No idea where the shot came from, so stay down."

A chirping on the satellite phone alerted Reece to an incoming call.

"Freddy, we have a call coming in on the secure line. Stand by."

His right hand squeezing the wounded agent's neck, Freddy reached his left hand up to activate his radio.

Reece would never get a response.

. . .

Nizar felt the recoil and muzzle blast. *Russian down. Two Russians down.*

He turned to face Tasho.

"We did it, Tasho," a smiling Nizar said.

"That we did, Nizar."

The older sniper put his head back to his scope for one last look at the chaos they had created and almost simultaneously felt a strange slap to the right side of his head. His face felt warm and wet as he turned back toward Nizar, wondering why he was having trouble seeing.

Nizar fired two more rounds from the suppressed Stechkin pistol into his sniper partner's head, just as he had been instructed by General Yedid. A Chechen needed to be blamed for this. Nizar understood that he was an expendable asset, like the legend he had just killed. Today he was thankful that he wasn't Chechen. He wiped Tasho's blood from his eyes and saw his lifeless body slumped forward over his rifle in a pool of crimson. *The student bests the master.* His ears rang both from the suppressed rifle shots and from the even louder blast of the 9x18mm in the close confines of the container; the darkened steel box stank of sweat, blood, and burnt gunpowder. It was time to disappear.

. . .

"Hello," Reece said into the phone.

"Mr. Strain?" the voice asked over the encrypted satellite link.

"No, it's Ree . . . uh, Donovan," Reece answered.

"Ah, Mr. Donovan, this is Dr. Belanger. May I speak to Mr. Strain. It's an urgent matter."

"You'll have to settle for me, Doc. Things just got crazy here."

"Very well. Something didn't sit right with me on General Yedid's interrogation, so I spent some additional time with him. I'll spare you the details but after some additional persuasion, I have something for you."

"Tell me, but make it quick."

"The snipers are not your only threat."

"What?"

"Have you heard of the nerve agent Novichok?"

"I have. Isn't it what killed that Russian spy in London recently?"

"That is correct. The assassination in Great Britain was of a GRU agent named Sergei Skripal. The Russian government always denied any involvement. It would not be a stretch to think that it was a test of Novichok on an adversary of Andrenov. They would have known each other in the GRU. And remember, that was just a minute portion. Novichok is a binary compound that . . ."

"Binary? What does that mean? You need to mix it?"

"Yes. It was made to be stored in two parts in an attempt to bypass the Chemical Weapons Convention. Combined, they are more toxic than VX or sarin. Seven to ten times as lethal, to be precise. It was developed in Uzbekistan but that facility was dismantled by international inspectors led by the United States in 1999. It was always suspected that those binary compounds were sent to Russia and Syria."

"What are you telling me, Doc? That Yedid has a chemical weapons attack planned here?"

"That's exactly what I'm saying."

"*Shit!* Is there an antidote?" Reece asked urgently.

"Atropine can counter the chemical, but the doses required are in and of themselves lethal."

"How would they disperse it?"

"Airborne would be the most effective."

"Airspace is shut down. It's something else."

"Stand by, Mr. Donovan. I'll ask our new source—General Yedid."

Reece waited an excruciating few minutes while filling in Agent Scheer on the latest development.

"With everything you've told me, this makes sense," she said. "The president is on his way back to the airfield. He'll be airborne in minutes."

"*Mr. Donovan. Mr. Donovan!*" the satellite phone barked back to life.

"Yeah. Go."

"It's the catacombs. It's not coming down from the air. It's coming up from the catacombs beneath the square!"

Shit!

"*Kim!* Where was that entrance to the catacombs? The one that led to the bar that's sealed up!"

"Follow me!" she shouted as she sprinted for the door.

"Freddy?" Reece keyed his radio. "*Freddy!*" *Damn radios.*

There had not been an attempt on the president's life since Reagan in 1981, and no matter how well trained, disciplined, and prepared the Secret Service was, an attempt on their principal with shots fired and another head of state down still resulted in chaos.

Reece knew chaos well. He'd lived with it as a constant companion in combat, learned to expect it and thrive in it. In chaos there was opportunity. In this case, it had led to opportunity for the enemy. Reece recognized that fact as clearly as if he'd planned it himself. If the Secret Service was converging on the president, as was their primary responsibility, that left local law enforcement liaisons covering down on the areas that had formerly been secured by the most effective protection force on the planet. It left those locations vulnerable.

Reece and Agent Scheer hit the street at a full sprint. As a member of the advance team, part of Kim's job was to know all the routes of ingress and egress. She didn't even pause to get her bearings. She knew exactly where to go.

"This is Scheer!" The Secret Service agent yelled into her lapel mic as she wove through the street that was now clogged with people moving away from the confusion and congestion of the promenade. Police whistles blared, punctuating an already confusing scene.

Reece wished he had a long gun but also knew that might put him in the crosshairs of a local police officer just trying to do his job. Both Americans kept their sidearms in their holsters as they rushed toward the water.

"Where are we going?" Reece yelled above the crowd.

"Stay close! We had an agent and local PD at all known entrances to the catacombs in the area. The closest is just at the base of these cliffs," she said, motioning ahead. "From what we could tell, none of them led directly under the colonnade."

They slowed their sprint as they approached the nearest cross street that hadn't been shut down for the presidents' speeches. Kim flashed her Secret Service badge at a police officer, who looked confused as to what to do in all the commotion as they darted through a chorus of blaring horns to the walkway that overlooked the Black Sea.

"There," Agent Scheer said, starting to move down the makeshift trail and pointing to the rocky beach about a hundred yards down from their position. "Let's go."

"Hold on," Reece said, catching back up with her, scanning the beach and the surrounding area. "Where's your agent?"

"He should be moving to a link-up point and then converging on the president's position," Scheer confirmed.

"Okay, looks clear," Reece said, "but I don't see the local PD anywhere."

His eyes instinctively took in all the probable hide sites a sniper would use to cover the entrance to the catacombs below.

Take a breath, look around, make a call.

"There should be a uniformed officer down there, but you never really know with the host nation fo—"

Agent Scheer never finished her sentence. Reece was already throwing her to the ground as fully automatic rifle fire raked across their position. Kim was in the lead and took two rounds on her way to the dirt, Reece grabbing the back of her shirt and dragging her as he crawled to cover behind a huge boulder.

Three hundred yards down, halfway down the embankment.

It wasn't the best position for the shooter. The fully automatic fire told Reece it wasn't a sniper. Most likely it was the least experienced of the group whose responsibility was to guard the entrance, and he was doing just that.

"Where are you hit?" Reece yelled, his hands searching for entrance and exit wounds, quite aware that they were in a bad position if there was a flanking element ready to maneuver.

"I, I . . ."

"Where?" Reece demanded.

"Leg . . ." Kim said breathlessly.

Reece finished his assessment, his head on a swivel, going between Kim and the avenues of approach to their location. In the intensity that was combat it was easy to treat the first wound you found, while another, less obvious one drained the life from your injured comrade.

"Pressure, here!" Reece ordered, placing Kim's hand on her thigh. Blood had begun to seep through her pant leg. It didn't look like an arterial bleed or a broken femur but now was the time to do the basics. He knew he should win the fight first but something in his DNA wouldn't let him leave her in a growing pool of blood. He needed to work quickly.

"Do you have a tourniquet?"

"Yes, ankle."

Reece reached down and pulled up her left pant leg. *Nothing.* Then the right. Wrapped around her leg, just above the ankle, was a combat tourniquet. Reece recognized the North American Rescue tourniquet as the same type he'd taken downrange on many a deployment, and he knew just how to use it. Sliding it over her leg just above what looked like at least two bullet wounds, he cinched it down, twisted the spindle, and secured it under a plastic catch.

"Give me your radio," Reece said, snatching it off her waist and yanking the wire out that led to her earpiece.

"This is James Donovan," he said into the radio. "I'm with Agent Scheer at just across . . . Kim, where are we?"

"Across, across Chornomorsoka Street. Southwest of the colonnade," she panted, pain obvious in her eyes.

Reece pressed transmit again. "On the sea side of Chornomorsoka Street. Agent Scheer has been shot in the leg. We need agents and medical personnel on scene. Be aware, we have one enemy combatant approximately three hundred yards south of our position halfway down the hill. At least one shooter with a rifle. We have a chemical weapon threat to the area. Clear the colonnade. It's Novichok and it's in the catacombs now. Delivery mechanism unknown."

Reece didn't wait for a reply. Instead he shoved the radio into Kim's hand, ripped off his long-sleeve shirt, and started shoving it into her wound cavity.

"Fuck! That hurts!" Kim gritted through clenched teeth.

"You are going to be fine. Keep monitoring the radio and guide them in. How many rounds do you have in that *pistola*?" Reece asked.

"Twelve. One extra mag."

"Okay. Good," Reece said, recognizing the SIG P229 in .357 SIG that Kim drew from her holster.

"You have a flashlight?" Reece asked.

"Yes."

"Give it to me," Reece said, stuffing it into his pocket.

"I want you to start putting rounds into our bad guy or at least in his general vicinity. He's about three hundred yards in front of us and about halfway down the embankment. There's a lone tree just above him. Find that tree and start shooting about twenty yards down from it. Can you do that?"

"Yes. What are you going to do?"

"I'm going to flank him. You ready?" Reece asked.

Kim looked up at the man who had transformed before her eyes into an instrument of war.

"*Kim!*" Reece shouted. "Are you ready?"

Kim nodded and pushed her back against the rock that had provided them sanctuary.

Reece moved to a knee, drawing the larger pistol the CIA had issued him for the trip, and handed it to the wounded Secret Service agent.

"I want you to start sending rounds as soon as I break cover. Action is faster than reaction, so I'll be fine, but I need you to keep his head down. Shoot both your mags. You hold on to mine. That's a backup in case they have anyone in the area we haven't accounted for. That's your last resort."

"What about you?" Kim asked in astonishment. "Don't you need a weapon?"

"I've got an extra," Reece said.

Kim gazed into his brown eyes and shivered.

"Ready?" he asked again. "*Go!*"

Reece broke from cover as Kim rolled around the opposite side of the rock. She searched frantically for the tree, finding it and looking below it just as muzzle flashes began to erupt, sending rounds in Reece's direction. Kim started shooting.

. . .

Reece charged up the embankment to the road and out of the line of fire, sprinting along the path at the top of the ridge. He felt strong. Traffic was at a standstill to his right, and pedestrians whose curiosity had drawn them to the sound of gunfire stopped to watch the strange man with the black backpack running at breakneck speed along the coast. He could hear the sound of Agent Scheer's .357 SIG behind him. The fully automatic fire stopped, its owner either behind cover or trying to find the source of the incoming rounds.

Always improve your fighting position.

Reece swung the backpack off his shoulders and reached inside, still moving at full speed. His hand found the wooden shaft of Freddy's tomahawk. Leaving the backpack in his wake, Reece flipped the Kydex sheath off the ancient weapon and let it fall to the ground. He needed intel on the opposing force and the hawk would give him options that his pistol couldn't. His legs pumped, his eyes evaluating the terrain while searching for threats.

Reece spotted his landmark. The lone tree on the slope. It was a hundred yards away, and he was closing fast. He had attempted to track Kim's shots, knowing that she had only twenty-four rounds, but wasn't sure of the exact count. It didn't matter. He was committed.

Reece broke from the trail and cut down the steep embankment. Their assailant had found Kim's position and was back on target. His fully auto approach was his mistake and it was going to cost him. Reece watched the earth move ahead of him as he charged down the incline. His target was concealed under a brown blanket and had rolled to his side to change mags when Reece pounced from above and just behind his left flank.

Reece drove the tomahawk down and deep just to the right of the shooter's spine. With no body armor to contend with, the sharp blade made short work of the bone and muscle protecting the terrorist's vital organs. Reece's momentum and the intense spasms of the shooter's body in reaction to the violent intrusion sent them tumbling fifty yards to the base of the hill.

They hit hard but not hard enough to do any real damage. Reece scrambled to his feet as his target struggled to untangle himself from his sling.

Reece was on him in a heartbeat, forcing him onto his back. The human body can take a lot of abuse and Reece's initial strike was not enough to kill. As much as the primal side of him wanted to end it, he needed information. The former SEAL trapped the AK-type rifle with his left knee, crushing the windpipe with his left arm, tomahawk at the ready in his right.

"English?" Reece hissed, glaring into the eyes of the man beneath him.

The eyes betrayed recognition and revulsion, but nothing more. Reece had seen eyes like that before. Eyes that revealed such burning hatred that the threat of death had no effect; death only delivered them to salvation.

With a possible chemical weapon attack on a civilian population imminent, Reece wasn't about to wait for direction. *Take charge and lead.*

"How many men are in the tunnel?"

This guy wasn't going to say a word.

Knowing that he had been an active participant in a WMD attack made Reece's next decision an easy one. He didn't have time to take this guy apart piece by piece in the hopes he'd paint a clearer picture of the opposition awaiting him in the catacombs. A city of innocent men, women, and children needed him to finish this, and it didn't matter how many enemy combatants were in the tunnels, Reece was going in. He pulled away from the man who had moments before had him pinned down with bursts of AK fire and swung the spike on the hilt of Freddy's tomahawk down at an angle, through his temple into his brain. The body shuddered as Reece removed the hawk, spun it in his hand, and drove it blade-first through the skull to finish the job.

Reece removed and inspected the AK from the dead man. *No magazine.* He checked the chamber. *Empty.* He removed the last magazine from the shooter's chest rig, pushed down on the top round with his thumb to ensure it was fully loaded, inserted it into the mag well, and racked the charging handle before moving back up the shoreline to a cement bunker with a rusted metal door: the entrance to the catacombs.

CHAPTER 84

THOUGH AKRAM COULDN'T BE sure, he thought he heard gunfire outside. If true, that meant that local police had made a move toward the beach and Ziad had killed them with his AK. Well, maybe not all of them. Ziad was the youngest of the group, and he was nothing if not enthusiastic. In all likelihood, reinforcements were being called in, and soon Ziad would be dead. *Martyred for the cause.* He would hold them off and buy the team time to complete their mission. It was too late to stop them at this point. As the most senior member of the team, and with his years of experience in the Syrian Army and then the military side of the Mukhabarat, Akram was the only one who knew how to mix the binary compounds to create the Novichok nerve toxin.

His most recent posting had been to the Syrian Scientific Studies and Research Center in Masyaf. Located on the eastern side of the Jabal Ansariyah mountains in northwestern Syria, it had somehow managed to escape targeting by the latest round of attacks from the West; air strikes launched by the British, the French, and, of course, their American masters. It was not lost on Akram that it was in Masyaf that the Islamic sect known as *assassins* were formed in the eleventh century. General Yedid had paid him well, looked over him, and ensured his upward trajectory in the Mukhabarat. Now, just like the famous *fida'i* from centuries past, Akram was being passed the torch. The four other men and one woman who made up the team were there to get him to this point; they were there to protect him.

General Yedid did not give Akram the exact target but had said enough for him to believe it was someone important, perhaps even a leader from one of the countries responsible for the cowardly attacks on his country. He was to be the personal scepter of President Bashar al-Assad and strike back against the West. They had targeted his homeland with sanctions and the might of their military.

Unfortunately for them, they've missed the chemical research center built into the mountain that had been the birthplace of the assassins, he thought. *Today they will reap what they'd sown.*

Launched from hundreds of miles away, missiles could miss their targets. The white powder he had just mixed by combining the two Novichok binary compounds would not miss. This weapon did not need to be as precise as a rifle's bullet or a smart bomb dropped from above—this was a weapon of terror. Unseen and unavoidable, it would not discriminate.

They had successfully tested it in a minute portion in the rebel town of Douma and seen its effectiveness firsthand. One touch of the toxin on the skin was enough to cause violent convulsions, followed by paralysis and then respiratory and cardiac arrest. Western intelligence agencies had misinterpreted it as a chlorine gas attack when it had in fact been a test of the Novichok that had been moved to Syria from Nukus, Uzbekistan, after the fall of the Soviet Union in advance of UN chemical weapons inspections. There, it had been studied and improved upon. Now it was ready. Safe in its binary components, the mixture of the two substances created the deadliest nerve toxin known to man. Most people had heard of sarin gas and had a healthy fear and understanding of its devastating power, but until recently Novichok had remained a mystery. While it was a similar class of toxin, Novichok was over a thousand times as potent as sarin, rendering any antidotes completely ineffective. A microgram of exposure was lethal and would, in the amount ready to be unleashed onto the streets of Odessa, render the entire area uninhabitable for generations. The perfect substance for terror's lasting legacy. It would be the most severe blow to the West since the attacks of 9/11 and would be the revenge that President Assad had publicly promised his people. General Yedid had even passed along blessings from the president himself.

I will not fail.

It had taken some effort to carry the equipment into the tunnels, but they were able to do it, moving to their set point ahead of schedule. Faya and Tawfiq had taken care of the two men guarding the entrance without much trouble. That was the benefit of having a female on the team. It gave them the ability to close with an unsuspecting male target. It was rumored that President Assad had mandated the creation of the all-female commando battalions himself. These Lionesses of National Defense now made up a battalion of the elite Republican Guard. After five years as a Lioness, Faya had been recruited into the Mukhabarat following her performance on the front lines subduing insurgent forces in Damascus in 2015, and General Yedid had been paying her a retainer ever since. That she was also attractive didn't hurt. In this case it allowed her to hold hands with Tawfiq as they walked the beach, stopping to ask the two local police officers guarding the catacombs what all the commotion was about in the streets above. Lovers looking to spend some time alone by the sea, oblivious to the world around them.

Their stab wounds were savage and lethal as the counterfeit lovers went right for the throats of the unsuspecting police officers just as they had been trained to do in service to their country. A whistle brought Akram and Hassan down from the trail above; Akram carrying the fan in a large backpack while Hassan carried the two small canisters that would forever change the world. Ziad was set up with his AK on the hillside with a clear view of the entrance to the tunnels.

Now, deep in the tunnel system, it was time. Condensation had built up inside the protective clothing and soaked Akram in a layer of sweat. He knew the others were in a similar condition, the thin plastic suits designed as airtight barriers against the evil they were unleashing. They had secured the cylindrical tube leading off the fan directly to the side shaft with a combination of tape and rubber cement, forming an airtight seal leading to the street above. Originally constructed and connected to the catacombs as drainage to allow water trapped in the colonnade to find its way to the ocean, it was now a conduit of death.

Each member of the team worked for the military side of Syria's famed Mukhabarat, and each also worked for General Yedid. He had chosen to activate them for this mission because they all had extensive training in unconventional chemical munition delivery systems. The thin plastic suits would serve their purpose. All they needed to do was carefully pour the mixed compound into the yellow tube, then attach the fan and turn it on. So simple. So effective. There was no stopping them now.

CHAPTER 85

DARKNESS.

No NODs. No suppressor. No team.

Reece slipped inside and began to work his way down the tunnel. That he wasn't killed right away told him whoever was ahead had been counting on the rear security he had just eliminated to cover their six. That, or they had someone barricaded deeper in the tunnel.

He had what was probably twenty-eight or thirty rounds in the AK, his SIG P365 in the ankle holster, a SureFire flashlight from Agent Scheer, and the tomahawk.

What lay ahead in the blackness? One man? Two? A squad of heavily armed terrorists? Had they already mixed the binary components of the Novichok? Were thousands of Ukrainians already dead and dying from the deadly compound? Reece pressed on.

Reece remembered stories of the tunnel rats in Vietnam from his father's unit, descending into the subterranean labyrinths carrying nothing but a flashlight and a 1911 handgun. And, he remembered his friends and teammates going into tunnel complexes in the mountains of Afghanistan at the start of the war.

He refrained from using the flashlight as he didn't want to telegraph his arrival, though it was in his left hand pressed against the stock of the AK. He was one man against an entrenched enemy force, with an unknown number of weapons, in possession of a deadly nerve toxin, hidden somewhere ahead in complete darkness, beneath the streets of an ancient city in what amounted to an unmapped labyrinth of caves and tunnels three levels deep.

The passage began to narrow, the air cold and heavy. Reece used his left shoulder to guide him forward along the corridor, the cold damp limestone walls bearing witness to yet another battle in a new war.

Reece heard them first. Coming to a stop, he listened.

Did they have night vision and IR lights? Reece was about to find out.

Like he had done as a bow hunter making the final approach on his prey, Reece removed his shoes to quiet his movement as he inched forward.

A light began to illuminate the tunnel and Reece worked his way toward it. As much as he wanted to sprint into the breach, he knew he wouldn't do anyone any good if even one of those he pursued lived to launch the toxin.

A new sound made Reece freeze in his tracks. *What was that?* It sounded like a vacuum. Then it went silent. Reece moved forward more quickly, the light ahead getting brighter.

He was close and could hear a strange, almost computerized whispering in Arabic. Taking a knee, Reece leaned to his right, away from the wall, to get a better angle on his target.

Twenty yards down the tunnel was a puzzling sight that turned to horror as Reece's brain processed the scene. A lantern illuminated a man standing guard with an AK similar to the one Reece now carried. His attention wasn't on security, though he did look in Reece's direction every few seconds. His focus was on his companions.

Three people wearing white chemical suits with respirators were working to attach what looked like an industrial fan to a bright yellow tube, the type used to ventilate sewer systems through manholes or construction tunnels that could be maneuvered in and around corners like an oversized vacuum. It was fixed to the wall of the cavern. It took a moment for Reece to process what was happening, but then it all came together. Designed to ventilate small spaces, the fan and its attached tube had been turned into a weapon of terror. The high-powered fan was on the floor of the tunnel, plugged into a mobile battery pack. Strewn around it were two discarded plastic containers with Cyrillic writing. They were in the final stages of setting up their system designed to blow the lethal Novichok down a side tunnel and into the colonnade above. It was ready to go. Just as Dr. Belanger had briefed, the toxin was inside the mazelike catacombs, and the fan was set to blow it into the crowded streets of Odessa.

"Ziad?" Reece heard the digitized voice-altering challenge through the respirator from the guard with the AK, who now peered attentively in Reece's direction.

The fan started to turn.

Shit!

Reece answered with five rounds from the AK, but without illumination to line up his sights in the dark his shots went wide. The guard immediately began firing on full auto in Reece's direction, forcing him back and out of the cone of fire. The rifle fire was deafening inside the confines of the cave, and the muzzle flashes were blinding.

Fortune favors the bold.

Reece depressed the button on his flashlight and dropped it to the ground, at the same time moving to the opposite side of the tunnel.

With his enemy's attention on the bright light, Reece stitched him up with another ten rounds from the rifle and charged forward toward the fan.

. . .

As their accomplice dropped dead on the floor of the catacombs, one of the conspirators reached for an AK as two others retreated into the darkness, disappearing down the tunnel complex. Rounds from Reece's AK found their mark in the upper chest of the chemical-suit-clad terrorist, and two more exploded through the respirator's face mask, dropping him in a bloody heap. Reece resisted the urge to pursue and instead stopped in front of the large fan, the high-pitched whine of the electric motor pushing the chemical agent toward daylight. Within seconds, the deadly vapor would reach ground level, killing hundreds if not thousands of civilians, transforming the entire area into a toxic wasteland.

Reece's finger began to take the slack out of the heavy trigger as he aimed at the fan's motor. Then he stopped and released the pressure.

Think, Reece. Adapt.

Fuck it!

Reece couldn't read whatever language was on the dial, but it was as intuitive as could be. Reaching down he cranked the dial to the left and felt the fan switch directions, pulling the Novichok back into the ventilation tube, returning it to the catacombs.

Turning to run, Reece stopped and directed the fan deeper into the tunnel system toward those who had unleashed it. As it sucked the deadly nerve toxin into the underworld he sprinted back the way he had come.

CHAPTER 86

BY THE TIME REECE emerged from the depths of the catacombs, the beach was teeming with local police, Ukrainian military, and a few Secret Service agents left behind to coordinate with the host nation.

Reece spotted CIA case officer Douglass and briefed him on what he'd seen in the tunnels, stressing that two terrorists in white chemical suits were contaminated with a nerve toxin and needed to be shot on sight if they made it to an exit. Dr. Belanger had sounded the alarm after his call to Reece, which set off a chain reaction and triggered the Ukrainian Ministry of Emergency Situations WMD response protocol, which was on its highest level of alert, due to the high-profile event in Odessa. HAZMAT teams were already sealing off the catacombs, while the military coordinated an evacuation of the immediate and surrounding areas.

"How's Scheer?" Reece asked as soon as he was able.

"She's going to make it, Reece. But I do have some bad news. It's about your friend."

. . .

By the time Reece made his way back to Freddy's last position, Alpha Group had secured the scene. The wounded Secret Service sniper had been transported to a local hospital where U.S. medical personnel were fighting to save his life. There were black tarps over two bodies on the roof. Reece knelt at his friend's side and pulled back the dark plastic. Tears welled up in his eyes as he cradled the head of the devoted husband

and father of three who had given an entire career in service of his nation and now his own life to protect its president. After the shock of losing his entire troop in Afghanistan and his pregnant wife and child in his own home, Reece didn't think he could feel any more grief. He was wrong.

Reece's world went into slow motion as activity swirled around him. The Ukrainian reaction force efficiently maintained security while doing their best to protect what was now more than a crime scene. This had been an act of war. All Reece could manage was to stare into the lifeless face of one of the best men he'd ever known.

CHAPTER 87

Ramstein Air Base, Germany
October

FREDDY'S BODY HAD BEEN bagged and was surrounded by ice to keep it as cool as possible. Reece accompanied his friend's remains on the C-17 that also carried the Secret Service's vehicles from the president's motorcade. The Air Force loadmasters had carefully and respectfully secured Freddy's body bag to the aircraft's metal cargo floor. Reece sat next to it.

When they'd landed in Germany to refuel and link up with the president and the rest of the Presidential Protection Detail, an agent approached Reece with an offer to ride in Air Force One at the president's invitation. Reece politely declined; he wasn't leaving his teammate's side. The NCIS investigation in Afghanistan had robbed him of his duty to accompany the fallen members of his troop home, and he wasn't about to let that happen again.

Reece had spoken to Vic Rodriguez on the sat phone and helped him coordinate the notification of Freddy's family. When Joanie Strain's bedroom light turned on in Beaufort, South Carolina, at 6:13 a.m. the following morning, Rodriguez knocked quietly on the front door.

The knock sent her heart racing as she realized that the dreaded moment that every military wife fears had come, a nightmare from which she would never awake.

Joanie didn't know Vic, so she didn't recognize him when she cracked the door in a light robe, but she knew the master chief in dress blues from

Freddy's last military command who accompanied him. Her eyes moved from his ribbons to the Trident to his sad eyes; her knees buckled and she collapsed to the floor.

. . .

At Landstuhl Regional Medical Center, Freddy was transferred to an aluminum metal casket and repacked with ice. Reece couldn't help but think that the casket, with its metal handles and locking clasps, looked a lot like a large rifle case; Freddy would like that. To his credit, President Grimes had waited in Germany for the SEAL's remains to be prepared, making an impromptu visit to the air base and hospital to boost morale and thank the men and women recovering from wounds sustained in combat before their transfer back to the United States. Six uniformed airmen loaded the flag-draped box back onto the C-17, the Secret Service agents forming an honor guard between the military cargo van and the aircraft's ramp. Nearly all of them had served in the military, and many had lost friends and teammates in the process.

Reece felt the dread building in his body as the massive jet approached the homeland. He knew he would have to face Joanie and he wasn't sure he could. *What can I say to her? The only reason he's dead is because they sent him to find me. If I'd turned down their offer, Freddy would still be alive.* His own grief over the loss of his friend was overshadowed by overwhelming guilt. He had to be strong for her, though, as Freddy would have been for Lauren if their roles had been reversed. But Lauren was gone; *everyone was gone.*

As the aircraft landed at Andrews Air Force Base in Maryland, Reece could see the crowd of people and vehicles arranged near one of the hangars: a hearse, a limousine, a crisp formation of men dressed in black. The C-17 taxied toward the hangar, and the pilot shut down the powerful Pratt & Whitney turbofan engines.

The aircrew quietly removed the straps securing the metal casket to the floor and stood aside. As the ramp lowered, Reece could see two lines of Freddy's highly decorated former teammates, many of them with thick beards but still dressed immaculately in their blues, forming a cordon between the aircraft and the waiting hearse.

Joanie stood on the tarmac, her hands on Sam's shoulders, their two other children at her side, her face a mask of stoic grief. Vic Rodriguez had escorted her throughout her tragic journey and was an arm's length away. A couple who must have been her parents stood beside her along with an older couple whom Reece recognized as Freddy's parents. *Every-one looks so old.*

Reece stood at attention at the head of the casket as a SEAL detail approached. Reece knew the master chief leading the grim progression and caught an almost imperceptible nod of recognition as the two men made eye contact. They had to be wondering what in the hell Reece was doing there; they'd sent a team to kill him at the Pentagon's orders just months prior and had followed the ensuing fallout closely. The smart money had been on him being dead.

The press had been kept away at the family's request and because every face in this crowd was from a unit that the Pentagon doesn't pub-licly acknowledge. Freddy's fight was over, but these men were still very much a part of it at the tip of the U.S. military's powerful spear. Reece watched as the flag-draped casket was carried toward his family and, as the wind blew across the open tarmac, noticed that one of the SEALs carrying him wore a prosthetic lower leg. *Where do we find guys like this?*

After the casket was loaded and the honor guard dismissed, Reece approached Joanie, who was speaking to one of the senior enlisted SEALs. When she caught sight of Reece she moved to him and hugged him so tightly that it stunned him, her big blue eyes red and swollen from endless crying.

"I'm so sorry about Lauren and Lucy, Reece."

Her husband came home in a box and she still offers me condolences for my family.

"I . . . I'm sorry about Freddy. He died like he lived, a hero."

"Vic told me that you were with him, Reece. It means so much to me that you were there, that he didn't die alone. I didn't even know where he was."

"I'm sorry I couldn't save him, Joanie. It was instant; he wasn't in any pain."

"I know. Vic told me." Reece felt the almost imperceptible nod of her head against his chest through the tears.

"When he left the Teams, I was so relieved. He said this job would be safer, and that I wouldn't have to worry."

"It should have been, Joanie. I'm so sorry. It's my fault, Joanie. It should have been me."

Joanie's head snapped back. "Don't you ever think that, James Reece. Not ever. Do you understand me?"

"Pardon the interruption, ma'am, but the president wishes to see you," said a Navy O-5 standing nearby.

Joanie Strain stood up straight and took a deep breath. She wiped her tears with a tissue and looked her husband's friend directly in the eye. "Thank you for bringing him home to me, Reece."

"I'll find who did this, Joanie. I'll find everyone responsible. I promise."

"I know," she said, then nodded and turned away.

CHAPTER 88

CIA Headquarters
Langley, Virginia
October

REECE SAT IN VIC'S office while the CIA man read from a stack of papers on his desk.

"The FBI is assisting the Secret Service. It will be a while until we have the final report, but we have some initial findings. They found a shipping container that had been rigged up as a sniper's hide: it was insulated to conceal any thermal signature. The shooters had spent at least a few days living in it waiting for the presidents' arrival."

"So it was definitely a sniper team, just like General Yedid told Dr. Belanger," Reece said.

"That's what it looks like. Two simultaneous shots targeted the Russian president, one connected. The other hit the column next to him. They found two U.S.-made CheyTac rifles with Nightforce scopes, a ballistic computer, spotting scopes, the works."

"Two shooters. Two wind calls," Reece said.

"Exactly. Then one of the shooters turns the gun toward the sniper that Freddy took out so that he couldn't talk. At that range, they wouldn't have been able to tell who was who. He was just shooting at a shape."

"So the close-in sniper was supposed to take out POTUS?"

"That's the theory, but there's no one to interrogate. We confirmed that he was Gregory Isay, a sniper on President Zubarev's FSO protection detail. His grandparents were Ukrainians who were forcibly relocated to Russia decades ago. Andrenov's PR machine is spinning Isay as a nationalist with an ax to grind, but we're not buying it. He's a known associate of Andrenov's head of security, Yuri Vatutin. Of the long-range team, one of them was found dead in the container. Looks like his partner, whom General Yedid identified as Nizar Kattan in his interrogation, took him out with a nine-by-eighteen before vanishing. The dead sniper has been positively ID'd as Tasho al-Shishani."

"So, one sniper shoots the close-in shooter on President Zubarev's overwatch who was supposed to take out POTUS, only it turned out to be Freddy. Then Nizar kills Tasho before getting away?"

"That's how it looks, Reece."

"How did they even know President Grimes would be there? That was close-hold information. We didn't even know until we got there."

"We are digging into that now. The NSA is pouring their considerable resources into mining all electronic data that even comes close to touching Andrenov. Danreb isn't one hundred percent convinced that he doesn't have sources in the U.S. government but admits that it's highly probable that President Grimes's itinerary came from the Russian side late in the game. Andrenov still has an intelligence network loyal to him in Moscow, just waiting for him to take the reins and promote them into what they see as their rightful positions of power. Danreb's analysis is that the primary target was President Zubarev and that when Andrenov found out that President Grimes would be there, they activated Isay. President Grimes was a bonus, and his assassination by a Ukrainian nationalist would have ensured the U.S. wouldn't oppose a Russian move into Ukraine."

"And to think we got here from simply trying to flip Mo to give us Nawaz," Reece said, shaking his head. "Where did the sniper weapons come from?"

"ATF is looking into that, along with State since a lot of their gear was ITAR-restricted. Somebody pulled a string with SOCOM and had the rifles shipped to Turkey. That's not easy to do. We're not sure who did it yet, but we'll find out. It will be a short list."

"And the Novichok? How did that come into the picture?" Reece asked.

"Yedid connected Andrenov with the head of Assad's chemical weapons program, who, for an ungodly fee, provided the compounds to a cell whose job was to release the toxin into the colonnade in Odessa. Five hundred grams would have killed everyone there and untold thousands in the vicinity. That's a softball-sized portion, Reece. Exposure of that magnitude is eighty to ninety percent fatal, and if you were to survive, the neurological damage would be so severe that you would wish you were dead. It's not water-soluble, which means you can't decontaminate an exposed site. The entire area wouldn't have been habitable for the next twenty years, which is what we are looking at for the catacombs now. All known entrances and exits have been hermetically sealed up by hazmat teams. Thanks to your actions, the only Novichok casualties are the four terrorists you entombed down there."

"But that doesn't make sense. They were already planning to kill the president. Why plan a chemical attack as well?"

"Andrenov knows our security protocols almost better than we do. He's also a geopolitical strategist. I talked with our chem-bio guys. They estimated that the amount of toxin Andrenov's team had ready to disperse would have killed two hundred thousand people. The president's limo is equipped with an overpressure system designed to keep the outside air out and seal it off from a chemical or biological attack. The idea is, if the Secret Service got the president to his vehicle he would be protected. The president of Russia had a similar countermeasure in his vehicle. The snipers were for the presidents, and the Novichok was for the crowd and the worldwide response to a CBRN attack. It qualifies as a weapon of mass destruction, and you know what that means."

Reece did know what that meant. An attack by a country or entity with WMD meant all bets were off. The attacked country had carte blanche to respond en masse. From what Reece knew of Andrenov, it would have meant a consolidation of hard-liners in power and tanks rolling into Ukraine.

"So, Andy was right," Reece stated. "This whole operation was about political positioning. Taking Zubarev out opens the door for Andrenov to step up. A Russian nationalist ready to lead his country back to prominence as a dominant superpower. If a Ukrainian killed President Grimes it would all but ensure the U.S. wouldn't put up more than rhetorical resistance to a Russian invasion of Ukraine. And a Chechen responsible for the death of President Zubarev would allow the Russians to possibly maneuver right up to the borders of Turkey and Iran. That's quite a land grab."

"And the Novichok nerve agent would seal the deal. The UN probably wouldn't even pass sanctions if Andrenov moved forces south in response to counter a WMD threat at their border. Andrenov needed both," Vic continued. "He needed President Zubarev out of the picture and he needed world opinion and support for an invasion of Ukraine. With Andrenov convinced that Islam poses an existential threat to the long-term survival of ethnic Russians, Danreb thinks a hard-line party led by Andrenov would result in large-scale Muslim eradication efforts on a scale not seen since Stalin's Great Purge."

"Well, he's nothing if not thorough."

"There's something else, Reece. Novichok is different. Like I said, it's extremely stable in that it doesn't wash off. If the president brushed up against his vehicle or against a contaminated Secret Service agent when they transferred him to Air Force One, even with a decontamination station, he wouldn't have made it."

"Well, he can thank Dr. Belanger for going back in to question General Yedid."

"He did. He also wants to thank you, Reece."

Reece's eyes narrowed.

"This assassination attempt and the chemical scare really shook him up. He's expedited the presidential pardons for you, for your friend Katie and"—Vic looked down at a file on his desk—"for Marco del Toro, Clint Harris, Elizabeth Riley, and Raife Hastings."

Reece nodded, remembering all that his friends had done to help him avenge his family and his Team. There had been an emptiness to those killings. Born of pure rage, their purpose had been death unto itself. What he'd done since Freddy tracked him down in Mozambique had been different. The purpose of the killing he'd done on this new mission had been *life*.

"The president also wanted me to express his sincere condolences on Freddy's death and, uh, and on the deaths of your family."

Reece nodded again.

"He wants you to get that tumor of yours checked out ASAP. Any string he can pull, any favor he can ask, you just say the word. He wants you to get your surgery and then he wants you to come back in."

"Back in?"

"Like we talked about on the *Kearsarge*, Reece. He wants you to come work for me. We briefed him up on what we know about the past few months; Andrenov, snipers, Amin Nawaz, Mohammed, Landry, a CIA mole, nerve toxins. It all gave him pause. He wants you to keep doing what you did to keep the country safe."

Reece took a deep breath, seeing the smiling faces of his beautiful wife, Lauren, and little daughter, Lucy, waving good-bye on that last deployment, eternally frozen in time. They'd never grow old, feel hurt, pain, disappointment, joy, or love. They would remain forever young, an indelible fixture in his memory.

"Tell him I'll think about it," Reece said, remembering Freddy and the sniper still out there who put him down.

"I figured you'd say that. There's also this," Vic said, handing Reece a series of still photos taken from news footage of the event in Odessa. Reece stared down at them, unsure of what he was looking at.

"Who's this?"

"That's Oliver Grey, Andrenov's mole. Facial recognition has him in the colonnade just prior to the hit. We don't know where he is now."

Reece looked closely at the photos, suddenly interested in what was on Grey's wrist, a vintage Rolex Submariner.

Coincidence? Reece wondered. *A lot of people wear Rolexes.*

"When we find him, I'd like to know about it. When do we hit Andrenov?" Reece asked.

"We can't, Reece, at least not yet. That foundation of his has bought him a lot of friends, including plenty in Congress."

"He killed the president of Russia and attempted to kill the president of the United States. My partner's three little kids are about to bury their father, and you're telling me that he threw one too many fund-raisers?"

"He'll go down, Reece. It's just going to take some doing. We know he's behind all of this, but we've got to sell it to the right people, and we have to do this *legally*. We need tangible evidence and, trust me, we will find it. We're tearing apart his electronic life right now."

"Where is he?" Reece asked quietly.

"Reece, this agency has congressional oversight. We just can't kill whoever we want and keep it a secret, as much as we might want to."

"Where is he?" Reece asked again, his voice cold.

"Working on that now, Reece."

"Well, while you work on it, I'm going to take some leave. While I'm gone, could you have someone put together a timeline of Grey's movements, both duty stations, and leave dates and locations for me, with a special emphasis on all travel between 2001 and 2004?"

"Of course, why?" Vic asked, a bit puzzled.

"Just curious. Probably nothing. And could you get what you have on Andrenov during that same time frame? I'd appreciate it."

Vic nodded. "I can do that for you, Reece. Does that mean you are coming onboard?"

"It means I'm considering it."

"I'll let you know when we coordinate the ceremony for Freddy's star on the wall. I know the president will want to be here, too."

"I'll be there." He stood, shook Vic's hand, and walked out of the office.

"Ah, Mr. Reece?" Rodriguez's assistant said, stopping him on the way out and handing him a folder.

"What's this?" he asked.

"You never set up your direct deposit, so those are your paychecks and some other documents from Human Resources."

"Oh, uh, okay. Thanks."

Reece shoved the stack into his small pack and walked toward the elevators. On his way out of the building, Reece stopped at the Memorial

Wall and placed the palm of his hand on the spot where Freddy Strain's star would be carved. *I'll handle this, Freddy. Rest easy, brother.*

. . .

In his hotel room that afternoon, Reece pulled out the paperwork and glanced at each page. There was a welcome packet from Perryman Inc., a Rosslyn, Virginia–based company that he'd never heard of that, apparently, was his current employer. There were a handful of paychecks, some information about setting up a direct-deposit service, and a letter-sized envelope with a crest and "HM Treasury of Westminster, London" printed as a return address.

Intrigued, he opened the envelope, tossed it into the small trash can below the desk, and opened a letter printed on heavy embossed stationery. It was signed by the Chancellor of the Exchequer and the Permanent Secretary of the Treasury. He skimmed the letter and quickly retrieved the envelope from the trash. Inside was another slip of paper: a check in the amount of $4,171,830.00. It was the 3 million British pound reward for the killing of Amin Nawaz, courtesy of Her Majesty's Treasury.

God Save the Queen.

CHAPTER 89

Reston, Virginia
October

REECE TURNED ON THE television in his hotel room as he packed a small bag for his trip south for Freddy's funeral.

The late President Zubarev wasn't even in the ground when the talking heads in Washington began suggesting that he be replaced with "proven leader and global philanthropist Vasili Andrenov."

Senator Phillip Stanton, another protégé of super-lobbyist Stewart McGovern, was one of the leading voices supporting Andrenov's return to Russia. Stanton, who always insisted that "Combat Wounded Ranger Veteran" accompany his formal title, had become a staple on the cable news channels since his election to the U.S. Senate.

Stanton had won the Wisconsin Republican primary and breezed through the general election thanks, in no small part, to his status as a veteran of the Iraq War. Though he did serve as an Army officer in Iraq, his position as a signal officer meant that he rarely left the safety of the Forward Operating Base to which he was assigned. On one of his few forays outside the wire, his unit's convoy was struck by an IED. The nineteen-year-old private first class driving his vehicle slammed on the brakes, causing then-lieutenant Stanton to suffer a laceration on his forehead when his head hit the dashboard of the up-armored HMMWV. He put himself in for a Purple Heart after receiving two stitches on his forehead, the same award that went to the young men who were killed in the lead vehicle that took the full force of the explosion. He spent the rest of his deployment writing a book about his overseas exploits and had reserved the Web domain www.phillipstantonforpresident.com years before. He now had three books published, all ghostwritten, leading some of his former soldiers to joke that he had completed more books than deployments.

Stanton wore a dark gray suit with a miniature Ranger tab and Purple Heart ribbon on the lapel and had grown a beard to complete the special operator "look" that had become popular on social media.

Reece shook his head as the senator espoused his expertise on global strategic policy thanks to his single overseas assignment as a junior officer. Calling himself a "Ranger" was intentionally misleading; he attended the Army's grueling eight-week Ranger School after completing the Signal Basic Officer Leaders Course, but never served in the famed 75th Ranger Regiment. Technically, he was "Ranger-qualified" or "Ranger-tabbed" but was not "Ranger-Scrolled." Having worked with Rangers on numerous deployments, Reece had nothing but respect for their capabilities, professionalism, and bravery. By calling himself a "Ranger," Stanton was intentionally misleading the public to believe that he had been a member of the elite special operations unit rather than a graduate of the school. *There was no dishonor in being a Ranger-qualified signal officer; why did guys like this have to make a good story better? Not really stolen valor. Borrowed valor, perhaps?*

"Once again," Senator Stanton stated in a tone that made Reece think he'd practiced his delivery more than a few times, "we have seen Islamic extremism rear its ugly head in its desire to build a worldwide caliphate. The murder of President Zubarev was yet another battle in the broader conflict. Russia needs a proven leader in the struggle against these terrorists. If the U.S. doesn't act, our democracy could be next. To think that a fellow combat leader like President Grimes was nearly killed by these terrorists sickens me. We need a leader in Russia who will stamp out this aggression before it spreads. Vasili Andrenov has devoted his life to providing aid to the most impoverished countries in the world and he understands the geopolitical struggles of our time. The United States and the broader international community should support immediate elections in Russia. Andrenov would be a key U.S. partner in Moscow and, together, the United States and Russia can defeat Islamic extremism wherever it appears."

The host of *Morning Edition* turned to Senator Bolls, who sat flanking her Senate colleague at the news desk with her hands folded in front of her.

"This is a rare issue on which the senator from Wisconsin and I can agree," she began. "Though I don't share his characterization of the many peace-loving Muslims in places like Chechnya and Syria, I do believe that Vasili Andrenov would be a natural choice to lead Russia in this time of crisis. The achievements of Mr. Andrenov's foundation speak for themselves, and he would be a steady hand to stabilize the unrest that is seizing his country. His leadership would help stop the spread of toxic nationalism in Ukraine and help bridge the divide between Russia and the United States as well as the European Union."

"Well," the host responded, "when two leaders of our highly partisan Congress can agree on something like this, the world should take note."

As pictures of a presidential-looking Vasili Andrenov filled the screen, Reece press-checked his SIG and deliberately placed it into the holster on his belt.

· · ·

Stewart McGovern smiled as he watched the monitor backstage in the greenroom; both senators had delivered their talking points perfectly, and Stanton was even sounding presidential on foreign affairs. If he could actually get Andrenov elected president of Russia, he would turn his greatest client into his most lucrative financial asset. Every U.S. company wishing to build a business relationship with Russia, and its vast natural resources, would have to hire his law firm to make the deal. He would be the de facto trade minister of Russia. Maybe he would buy that house in Aspen that his wife had suggested they add to their growing list of properties?

CHAPTER 90

Beaufort National Cemetery
Port Royal Island, South Carolina
October

THE SERVICE HAD BEEN solemn but at times humorous as the pastor honored the life of Senior Chief Petty Officer Fredrick Alfred Strain (Ret.). It was obvious that the man knew him well despite Freddy having moved to Beaufort just a few months earlier. Reece figured this must have been Joanie's congregation growing up. The church was crowded with family and friends as well as former and active SEALs. The media stayed away; none of them had yet made the connection between the attempt on the U.S. president and a local veteran's funeral. Reece rode in the limousine at Joanie's request as the procession made the short trip to the nearby veterans' cemetery. It was a beautiful spot in South Carolina's low country: live oaks dripping in moss shaded the graves of soldiers who had fought on both sides of the nation's bloody Civil War and every conflict since. Freddy would rest surrounded by fellow warriors.

Reece helped Joanie out of the limo and gazed upon the line of cars parked along the cemetery's asphalt driveway. A supercharged Range Rover with a custom flat-black paint scheme and green Vermont plates caught his eye. The door opened and a tall, fit man wearing a dark suit emerged. His eyes found Reece within seconds and, even at a hundred yards, Reece recognized Raife Hastings.

At the graveside ceremony, before military honors were rendered, the pastor read a passage from Isaiah 6:8. To some in attendance it had a special significance.

"Then I heard the voice of the Lord saying, 'Whom shall I send? And who will go for us?' And I said, 'Here am I. Send me!'"

Vic Rodriguez presented Joanie with the folded American flag and the SEALs in attendance lined up to press their golden Tridents into the mahogany veneer of their brother's casket. Reece joined the line of frogmen, reaching into his pocket to run his thumb over the insignia that represented the brotherhood. Superimposed over an anchor signifying the naval service were a trident spear, an eagle with its head down searching for prey, and a musket that was cocked and ready for war. Those symbols represented the three mediums in which SEALs operate: sea, air, and land.

For a moment Freddy's casket was replaced with that of Reece's wife and daughter, his teammates lining up to render similar honors. Reece closed his eyes, then opened them and looked at Joanie, her arms around two of her three children, a daughter just shy of her teen years and seven-year-old Fred Jr., providing them comfort and support. Sam could not attend due to his genetic condition and was at home with a caretaker provided by the church. Reece removed the protective backings from his Trident and placed it on the coffin. He looked back to Joanie, then at the casket that held his friend before slamming his fist down onto the Navy SEAL Trident and cementing it into the mahogany, his dark sunglasses concealing his pain. As Reece passed the grieving widow, little Fred Jr. pushed himself off his chair and stood before the coffin. Then, standing at attention, he slowly lifted his hand in salute. He remained standing until the last Trident was embedded in its final resting place. There was not a dry eye in attendance.

At the conclusion of the ceremony, the assembled parties gathered into groups of friends and loved ones. Soon the Team guys would find an Irish pub and give Freddy a proper send-off. The local sheriff's office was informed of the commando's death and had offered to drive any of the SEALs where they needed to go, no questions asked.

Reece offered condolences to Strain's parents, whom he'd met years before, and stood uncomfortably between the groups, not feeling particularly at home among any of them. He was all too aware of the toxic environment created by some of the senior officers. The late Admiral Pilsner still had some friends in high places, and Reece didn't want to put any of the active-duty SEALs in a bad position with rumors of them being too chummy with the man who had blown the admiral into tiny bits in his own office.

Reece felt a hand on his shoulder and turned to see Vic Rodriguez.

"Thanks for being there for Joanie and the kids, Vic."

"Freddy was one of my guys. I brought him in. You're one of mine, too, Reece."

"We can talk about that later. I owe you a thank-you, though. I got the queen's check. Didn't think you guys would actually follow through with that."

"I told you it was part of the deal. Regardless of what you may think, Reece, even in the intelligence business, our word is our bond."

Reece nodded.

"I'm still working on the travel records for Grey and Andrenov. I should have it soon."

"Thanks, Vic," he said, turning to leave.

"There's one more thing, Reece. After you left my office the other day, I asked myself, 'What would my father do?'"

"What do you mean?" Reece asked, remembering the Bay of Pigs photo on Vic's office wall.

Rodriguez pulled a manila envelope from his jacket pocket, handed it to Reece, nodded, and walked away.

Reece peered into the envelope and saw part of an aerial photo. *What the?* He took a few steps away from the other mourners and looked at the contents of the envelope: maps, photos, surveillance logs, and a flash drive. It was a target package.

Distracted by the package, he almost didn't see Raife approach. Unlike the suit that Reece had bought at a local men's store the day before, Raife's was finely tailored and likely cost ten times as much. His skin was tanned to a deep copper, making the scar on his face all the more noticeable. His sandy blond hair looked sun-bleached from living in the elements. It was the eyes, though, that set Raife apart, those glowing green eyes. If he hadn't opted to spend his life as a frogman, rancher, and businessman, he could have gone to Hollywood.

Reece shoved the envelope into his jacket pocket and extended his hand to his friend.

"Sad day, Reece."

"It is, brother."

"Were you with him?"

"I was," Reece confirmed, "but I didn't see it; sniper got him. We were in Odessa. He saved the president's life."

"Figured that was it. Timing was too close."

Reece hesitated. "Thank you for what you did for me."

"I owed you one."

"Well, not anymore. I thought a lot about that on the boat, and about what's important."

"I have too, Reece. I don't blame you for anything that went down in Iraq. I want you to know that I was angry at the system, and truth be told, angry with myself."

Reece looked at his friend and knew it was best not to push.

"I spoke to Uncle Rich," Raife said, changing subjects. "He sends his best. He says that you saved Solomon's life and that's what blew your cover. You're a good oak, Reece; you always were."

Raife broke into a rare smile as the men shook hands.

"Freddy told me what your family did for Sam. *Incredible*."

Raife nodded. "It was the least I could do."

Reece thought for a moment. "I have a question for you: do you miss it?"

Raife thought for a moment before responding. "Not the action. The mission. I miss the mission."

"How would you like to avenge the deaths of both Freddy and your aunt?" Reece asked, bringing up the airline shoot-down he'd learned about in Mozambique. "Two birds with one stone?"

"How do you know about that? Ah, the PHs. They talk too much."

"That Strela-2 that brought down her airplane. The guy that supplied that missile is the mastermind behind President Zubarev's assassination and Freddy's death."

Raife turned his green eyes toward the gravestones and then back to Reece. "When do we leave?"

CHAPTER 91

Buenos Aires, Argentina
November

OLIVER GREY LOVED BUENOS AIRES. It was so *alive*. It reminded him of Madrid with its rich history and Old World architecture but there was a spark here that Europe lacked. Spain's best days were behind her, but this nation had a bright future. San Telmo was not his favorite part of the city but, thanks to its Russian population, it was the safest place for him until things settled down. He would have loved to have explored his old neighborhood of Juncal but the chances of being spotted there by someone from the U.S. embassy were too great.

This working-class neighborhood was home to a group of Russian expatriates to which, of course, Andrenov's network was connected. Grey was to go to ground until the next phase of the operation unfolded. Once the inevitable elections were held, Grey would take his place at Andrenov's side in Russia. He got a taste of his future home each day when he looked to the bright indigo domes of the Cathedral of the Most Holy Trinity, shrine to the Russian Orthodox religion that Andrenov loved so deeply. Perhaps Grey himself would attend services there as part of his transformation.

He took a bite of the Milanesa and washed it down with half a glass of the house Malbec, his third. The hearty meal made him crave a smoke and he thought of the fresh supply of local flue-cured leaf that he'd bought for his pipe that morning. The operation had been a success, despite the escape of the U.S. president and the thwarted chemical attack. The lynch-pin of the entire plan was the assassination of President Zubarev and the subsequent blame game. Zubarev was lying in state in Moscow and the international media was whipped up into a frenzy over the apparent alliance between Chechen, Syrian, and Ukrainian conspirators. It was a perfect storm, calculated and set in motion by a genius. Grey liked to think that he had picked the right mentor, conveniently forgetting that it was Andrenov who had selected him.

The sights, sounds, and smells of Buenos Aires brought him back to his first real field operation for Colonel Andrenov, one that took place on these very streets more than a decade before. After he'd discovered the identities of the U.S. MACV-SOG recon team members operating in Laos in 1971 in the Agency's files, Andrenov had asked for his help in locating the team leader. Grey's research was thorough. So much time had passed that no alarm bells went off at CIA headquarters when an analyst requested files on CIA operations in Vietnam. It was ancient history. Grey discovered that the same SEAL chief petty officer who had led RT Ozark on the raid that had killed a senior Soviet officer had become part of the Agency's Clandestine Service after leaving the Navy. The man had been one of the famed Cold War operators who had dedicated his life to countering the Soviet threat. Grey could still remember his excitement at having successfully completed his first mission and could see the man's name clear as day at the top of the dossier: Thomas Reece. *Oh, how the world is small.*

Though Tom Reece had retired from the Agency, he was one of those hard-core spooks who'd never really left and he had agreed to help with an operation in South America after 9/11. Grey had already recruited that sociopath Landry from the local embassy and this had been his first true test of loyalty. The old spy had been wise, but age had slowed his reflexes, and the four *sicariatos*, assassins from the Los Monos drug gang in Rosario whom Landry had hired to complete the task, had the drop on him. He bled out quickly in a dark corner of the German section of the Cementerio de la Chacarita, the city's historic cemetery. Grey glanced at the stainless-steel Rolex that Landry had brought him back as a trophy, its colors faded and edges worn smooth by decades of hard use. The death had been ruled a homicide and attributed to a robbery gone wrong, thanks in part to the theft of the very wristwatch Grey had worn ever since. He wished he'd had the courage to have done the deed himself, but he knew his limits. His weapon was his mind; it was up to Neanderthals like Landry to do the dirty work.

It was only after that operation that Grey had dug deeper into the Agency files and had come to appreciate its importance. The Russian officer had been Andrenov's father, and the death of Thomas Reece, the man who'd killed him in the steaming Laotian jungle, was revenge decades in the making. That Grey had brought such closure for Andrenov cemented their relationship. By avenging the death of Andrenov's father, Grey had found a father figure of his own. A father who was poised to become Russia's next leader, a president who would lead Grey's ancestral homeland back to greatness. All it would take now was patience, a virtue that was easy to embrace in the land of silver.

CHAPTER 92

Basel, Switzerland
November

YURI VATUTIN ALWAYS FELT exposed on Sundays. He had warned Colonel Andrenov more than once that his monthly church visits made him a predictable target but the old spymaster was stubborn about the church. They could vary the three-mile route over one of four bridges that crossed the Rhine without venturing across the borders of either France or Germany, but when leaving the compound and arriving at the church, they were completely exposed. He subconsciously tapped his left side, feeling the spare rifle magazine concealed beneath his suit jacket the way a civilian would confirm that he was carrying his wallet. Once he'd received word from his men that the route appeared clear, he nodded to his man at the door.

The front door opened and Andrenov walked toward the idling Mercedes with an extra spring in his step. They had been successful in putting the weak Zubarev in the ground, which had been their primary objective. Killing the president of the United States had always been a long shot. "Icing on the cake," as the Americans were fond of saying. Even though he had lived, the world believed that Zubarev was assassinated by lunatic jihadis out of the Caucasus. Even NATO would have to support a Russian military response. Andrenov's people in the Russian government were already setting the stage for the former GRU officer's return. It was only a matter of time before he would lead Russia back to greatness.

Yuri noticed that Andrenov was wearing a gold "double-headed eagle" coat of arms on his lapel. The pin was more than one hundred years old and had belonged to one of the czar's ministers. Russia needed a leader and Colonel Andrenov was already dressing the part.

After a final radio check, the gates opened and the three-vehicle convoy began to move. Once they made their way out of the tight confines of the residential neighborhood, their route would take them through the city and across the river on the A2, a modern highway that left few spots for likely ambushes. Yuri looked over his shoulder as they approached the on-ramp. Andrenov was reading a Russian-language news site on his iPad. The chase vehicle was right where it should be.

Their path took them past the rail depot and below a concrete scramble of highway overpasses as they exited the A2. Yuri clutched the grip of his AK-9 as they took a sharp left turn, crossed a small two-lane bridge, and steered through a roundabout on Riehenring. Their right turn took them into the narrower neighborhood streets near St. Nicolas and into a more vulnerable position.

Two more turns.

. . .

"One minute out, coming south on Hammerstrasse," Raife said into his radio.

Reece nodded to Mo and turned to the north, his position on the six-story apartment rooftop gave him a clear view above the trees that lined the narrow road. Thirty seconds later, he saw the three black vehicles emerge. The S600 sedan was flanked fore and aft by matching black AMG sport utility vehicles.

As the lead car slowed to make the right-hand turn onto Amerbachstrasse, it did so directly beneath Reece's position. The vertical range to the target exceeded the horizontal distance; the shot was basically straight down. He pulled the black cocking lever downward and trained the sight on the roof of the sedan below. As the sedan made the turn, he pressed his gloved thumb on the red trigger button. The solid rocket motor ignited in milliseconds, sending the fin-stabilized PG-32V 105mm anti-armor HEAT round hurtling toward the target at 140 meters per second. To Reece's eye, it was as if the car exploded the instant he pressed the trigger.

The rocket's shaped charge detonated upon impact with the lightly armored roof of the S600, sending a stream of liquefied metal into the passenger compartment. The overpressure from the explosion blew the roof off the Mercedes and sent fragments of window glass in every direction, along with what was left of Colonel Vasili Andrenov, his head of security, and their driver.

The remainder of the detail performed admirably, despite the traumatic brain injuries that each of them sustained in the blast. They emerged quickly from their SUVs, the windows of which had all been shattered, and set up a hasty perimeter around the mangled and burning sedan. Some of them scanned the nearby rooftops, the muzzles of their suppressed carbines trained upward.

With car alarms blaring and the sirens of emergency vehicles sounding in the distance, Mo made a show of rappelling down the face of a building at 192 Hammerstrasse, in full view of multiple surveillance cameras and onlookers filming the scene with their smartphones. In all the confusion, no one noticed the tall bearded Caucasian male climbing into the white Audi rental car driven by American citizen and Zimbabwean expat Raife Hastings a block away. As Swiss, German, and French security forces scrambled to find the Middle Eastern abseiler, the two old friends began a leisurely if circuitous drive toward the French border.

• • •

That evening, they boarded a Global Express jet at Nice–Côte d'Azur Airport with a final destination of Billings, Montana. There would be a brief stop at Ronald Reagan Washington National Airport for fuel, and to allow one passenger to deplane. As much as he'd love to get off the grid and decompress at Raife's ranch, Reece had a reporter to see. As the aircraft reached its cruising altitude and passed above the Bay of Biscay, Reece pulled a bottle of Basil Hayden's bourbon, Freddy Strain's favorite, from the bar and poured two triple shots over rocks. Handing one to Raife,

Reece raised his glass in tribute to their fallen brother, repeating the words immortalized by legendary SEAL Brad Cavner:

"To those before us, to those amongst us, to those we'll see on the other side. Lord let me not prove unworthy of my brothers."

"Until Valhalla, Freddy."

CHAPTER 93

Naples, Florida
6:00 a.m., Christmas Eve

CHRISTMAS WAS ALWAYS AN extravagant affair for the McGovern family, and their new winter home had enough bedrooms to house three generations comfortably. Despite Andrenov's untimely demise, Stewart McGovern still had a powerful client list and much to celebrate. The previous night's bar tab had been a hefty one at the Country Club of Naples, so only the youngest grandchildren were awake when the battering ram shattered the paneled cypress front door of the multimillion-dollar home.

McGovern was awakened from his scotch-induced slumber by the screams of his wife as the black-clad helmeted agents entered their expansive bedroom with M4s at the ready; the home was cleared within minutes. Shocked and bleary-eyed family members were gathered in the living room as one of the members of the joint BATFE/FBI Task Force read the search warrant aloud. The elaborately decorated fourteen-foot Douglas fir surrounded by wrapped presents made for a tragic backdrop as adults, teenagers, and small children knelt on a Persian rug with their hands on top of their heads. All eyes were on the family's patriarch, still clad in his silk pajamas, as he was led past his children and grandchildren in handcuffs. The reactions of the family members ranged from horror to disbelief and, in the case of Mrs. McGovern, righteous indignation.

Though there were no reporters at the residence to film McGovern's uncharacteristically disheveled appearance during his "perp walk," plenty of camera crews were present outside his D.C. office, where agents in lettered windbreakers carried box after box of documents and hard drives into waiting cargo vans. The ninety-six-page indictment included a range of charges and, thanks to the sworn statements of two U.S. senators who had flipped on him in order to escape prison time, the Department of Justice's case was a solid one. Senator Lisa Ann Bolls was extremely helpful in providing information on her former friend, admitting she had directed her staff to facilitate the transfer of sniper rifles in violation of ITAR restrictions, one of which had fired the bullet that had killed the Russian president. Though the congressional ethics committee already had her in their sights, she was more than willing to cooperate with the U.S. attorney's office to avoid federal prison.

The investigation into McGovern resulted in collateral damage for Wisconsin senator Phillip Stanton when it was discovered that the veterans' charity he spent so much of his time promoting and fund-raising for was a slush fund used to support his family vacations and multiple not-so-successful business ventures. Investigators determined that he had diverted funds from the foundation to pay the ghostwriters of his books that exaggerated his wartime exploits to advance his political career. In addition, foundation dollars had been used to buy large quantities of his books in order to game the system and ensure they were purchased in a way that guaranteed they made the *New York Times* bestseller list. Added to that indignity, email traffic exposed his affair with the highly compensated executive director of the foundation, a fact that didn't align with his "family values" conservative façade. He quickly turned against McGovern and, like Bolls, would stay out of jail but was forced to resign his Senate seat due to the outcry from his constituents and media back home.

The results of the search warrants executed on McGovern's home and office would no doubt add to the list of charges, but law enforcement officials felt it necessary to move ahead with his immediate arrest for national security reasons. His bank accounts were frozen and most of his assets were seized, a move that would make his costly legal defense a challenge. The timing of the Christmas Eve arrest was, according to law enforcement officials, a mere coincidence.

Deputies of the Collier County sheriff's office had formed a cordon to seal off the cul-de-sac where McGovern's home was located. Among the contingent of federal and local law enforcement officers was a man with dark features and short hair. He was given a courtesy call earlier the day before and had made the drive down from Tampa along with agents from that FBI field office. He walked with a limp.

Sergeant Major Jeff Otaktay's eyes didn't betray a thing as one of Washington's most powerful lobbyists was ushered into the backseat of a black Chevy Tahoe by armed federal agents. It was the first time he'd circumvented the chain of command, going around his boss in the SOCOM Acquisition Office. With results like this he might have to do it more often.

CHAPTER 94

Beaufort, South Carolina
10:00 p.m., Christmas Day

JOANIE STRAIN WAS SEATED at the kitchen counter surrounded by vestiges of the holiday; stray wrapping paper was scattered among small stacks of presents and the dishes that didn't make the first washer load were stacked in the sink. She was spoonfeeding Sam plain oatmeal, one of the few foods he could eat, as she watched cable news coverage of the shocking arrest of political lobbyist and former senator Stewart Mc-Govern. Sam couldn't share in the Christmas dinner earlier with the rest of the family; he required one-on-one care and needed every bit of her attention. Her two other children had gone to bed an hour ago, and her parents had long since left after an exhausting day that required them all to wear forced smiles for the sake of the kids.

Like most moms, Joanie was an expert multitasker, feeding Sam with one hand while she went through a stack of mail with the other, anything to postpone the depressing task of cleaning up what was left of Christmas dinner by herself. It wasn't like they had never spent Christmas alone. Freddy had been deployed for many a holiday, leaving Joanie to push the dangers of his chosen profession to the back of her mind. That's how women like Joanie survived. They focused on the kids. They focused on running the household. They focused on living. Every now and then the fear they worked so hard to lock away would find its way

out, roused from the recesses of the mind by a news broadcast announc-
ing the deaths of U.S. servicemen in a HMMWV, a helicopter, or on a raid.
In those moments, Joanie had always glanced toward the door, wondering if Freddy was among the dead and if at any moment she would hear
the dreaded knock. That knock had come for Joanie and her children.
Freddy would never again bound through the door to scoop his kids into
his arms or sweep Joanie off her feet. She shook her head and fought back
the urge to cry. She had to be strong for her kids. She had to be strong
for little Sam and she attempted to persuade him to eat just a bit more
oatmeal before glancing back at the TV.

A young female reporter was making a connection between the Mc-
Govern fiasco and a recent car bombing in Switzerland that had left a
former Russian intelligence official turned global philanthropist named
Vasili Andrenov dead. According to the broadcast, Andrenov had long
utilized McGovern's services for access to the Washington, D.C., power
establishment and may have coordinated transfer of the ITAR-restricted
weapons used in the Russian president's assassination. A terrorist and former Iraqi commando named Mohammed Farooq was wanted in connection with Andrenov's death but had thus far evaded capture. The weapon
used in the attack was suspected to be a Russian-designed RPG-32 that
had been supplied by Russian intelligence assets to pro-Assad forces in
Syria. A launch tube had been recovered from a rooftop above the scene.
Joanie smiled to herself as she imagined her late husband giving her five
minutes on technical details on the RPG-32, had he been sitting there.

Joanie hadn't brought herself to open the condolence cards in the
ever-growing stack of mail. She would get to them eventually, after the
holidays when the kids were back in school. As she sifted through the letters, sorting the personal ones from the bills, she saw an envelope from a
local law firm she didn't recognize.

Wonder what this is?

Joanie tore the end of the envelope open with her teeth and fished
the letter out with her left hand. As she began to read, she dropped the
spoon.

Dear Mrs. Strain:

This letter will serve as confirmation of establishment of the Samuel Strain Special Needs Trust which was established by our firm on behalf of an anonymous donor. The balance of the trust is $4,171,830.00. Please call our office at your earliest convenience and we can discuss the details of this account. We are at your service.

Sincerely,
T. Sullivan, IV Esq.

Joanie looked back at her son and began to cry.

EPILOGUE

Athens, Greece
Kolonaki District
January

GENERAL QUSIM YEDID ADMIRED the young lithe body of his Russian "escort" for the evening, maybe more than a few evenings, if she was as good as he'd been promised. He'd requested a redhead and instead this blond Russian had been delivered. No matter, there were plenty of young Russian girls to keep him busy, and his future looked brighter than it had in quite some time. If this girl didn't work out, he could order another tomorrow. He'd be sure to confirm they understood he wanted a redhead.

Just northeast of the Acropolis, the Kolonaki district was *the* place to shop for those with means in Athens. Bars, restaurants, and art galleries were spaced between high-end boutiques where jewelry, clothes, and shoes cost a small fortune. General Yedid noticed he wasn't the only older gentleman with arm candy looking young enough to be the daughter or, in some cases, the granddaughter of those they accompanied.

The shopkeepers didn't seem to mind the tight black dress she wore that made her look more or less like what she actually was. If they did, the serious-looking man in sunglasses who followed the couple at a respectful distance kept them on their best behavior.

Yedid was able to afford the exorbitant prices for the clothes she admired, but he'd rather let her just look, to warm her up for what was to come. Some lingerie and shoes from Kalogirou should do the trick. He had already reserved a table at Cinderella nightclub, one of the trendiest clubs in the city, where patrons could dance to music from the seventies and eighties into the early hours of the morning. It was just down the street from their next stop in the ancient city heralded as the birthplace of democracy. He'd decided on seafood tonight and steered his companion toward the world-renowned Papadakis restaurant. He favored the *kakavia* soup to start, while finishing his vodka before switching to a nice bottle of *Marquis de la Guiche–Le Montrachet* to go with his main course, probably a grouper with truffles. Too bad the exquisite wine would be entirely lost on the young girl by his side.

It didn't quite compare to the meals prepared by his private chef on the *Shore Thing*, but it would have to do for now. The yacht he usually rented was still impounded, but his American benefactors should have him back on the high seas soon enough; appearances had to be kept up, after all. In exchange for information, the CIA was allowing him to continue working in his past profession and even keep the money he earned from brokering teams of Syrian mercenaries around the globe to those willing to pay. In exchange, he was expected to feed the Agency information on all transactions. The Americans were even compensating him, albeit a small pittance, for his troubles. If the time came when he could pass them information that helped thwart a 9/11-style attack on their homeland that resulted in a blown cover, then they had a nice property waiting on him in horse country outside Washington, D.C., for his "retirement." He wondered, how hard would it be to find Russian hookers in Northern Virginia?

All in all, his was not a bad deal for someone who had hired the team that had successfully assassinated the Russian president and almost killed the American one. This was a high-stakes game, and Yedid knew that if he was discovered to be working for the Americans, he could expect to be skinned alive before his beheading as a warning to others who might be tempted to side with what the Iranians called the Great Satan. He felt fortunate he hadn't ended up like his associate Vasili Andrenov, blown to bits by perpetrators yet unknown. He knew he was lucky to escape with his life after the American commandos had stormed his boat, and even luckier to have made a deal with that CIA doctor. He shuddered at the thought of the small academic-looking man with the Pelican cases, and he was smart enough to know not to press his luck.

The Agency had set up surveillance on Yedid for a month to establish his pattern of life, run countersurveillance and ensure that his tradecraft was polished enough to communicate with his case officer working out of the American embassy. Once they felt comfortable, they had backed off to allow him to continue to build his business while gathering intelligence for his new masters.

. . .

Mohammed Farooq waited patiently outside and just down the street from the Syrian general's flat, the 1988 Mercedes G230 wagon blending in perfectly with the night's light traffic going two and from the more popular night spots in Athens. The general had retired earlier than usual, just shy of 2 a.m. and had even opened the gate for his companion; this one looked to be about twenty. The large bodyguard followed, scanned the street, eyes coming to rest on Mo's vehicle, before closing the gate, ensuring it was securely locked and walking up the steps to the front door.

Twenty minutes later the G-wagon's passenger side door opened and a tall westerner in dark clothes slid inside.

"I thought we might be doing this another night, my friend," Mo said, turning to face the American.

"Nope. It happens tonight," James Reece replied. "Do you have what I asked for?"

Mo reached into the backseat and handed Reece a leather satchel and a pair of black gloves.

"It's in there. The pistol's a bit on the antique side. If investigated, it will be traced back to a deceased *Bratva* enforcer," Mo said, referencing the Russian mafia. "It certainly won't be linked to anyone who will lead them to either of us."

After putting on the gloves, Reece reached inside and pulled out a small black pistol. Inspecting it, he looked at Mohammed with a questioning eye. "Will it work?"

"It will work for your purposes."

Reece ejected the magazine from the Beretta M1934 pistol and pressed down on the top round with his thumb to ensure it was fully loaded, then inserted it into the weapon and racked the slide before engaging the safety. Chambered in the small 9mm Corto, known to Americans as .380 ACP, it wouldn't have been Reece's first choice, but he was pleased that the old pistol was fitted with a suppressor. Stealth was an important component of tonight's operation.

Reaching back into the bag, Reece extracted a small box and carefully cracked the hinge to find a bottle wrapped in an old rag.

"I wasn't sure you'd be able to get this. How'd you do it?"

"Reece, I am now one of the world's most notorious terrorists, thanks to you and the CIA. My Nawaz-affiliated networks are still in place. I say the word, and it gets done. You'd be surprised at how deep these cells are embedded into both the Western and Eastern worlds, my friend."

Reece nodded.

"I know this is non-sanctioned, so I won't ask too many questions," Mo continued. "There are easier ways for the CIA to liquidate their own asset than by sending you to Greece. Were it not for you, I'd still be working for Landry—*may God curse him for eternity*—so whatever you need, I shall provide."

"Thanks, buddy. Is your man inside?"

"He is. With Yedid's protective detail either dead or in a black-site prison, he needed someone with the right credentials—a Syrian, who just happens to work for me," Mo said with a sly smile. "The CIA will get their money's worth out of me, I assure you. Pity the same cannot be said for our Syrian general."

"I know they will. And, I'm going to do what I can to get you out of this deal. I'll need some time, but I'll make it happen."

"Gratitude, my friend. Eventual freedom from *indentured servitude,* I believe you call it?"

"Something like that. After tonight there are two more people I need to put in the ground: the men directly responsible for Freddy's death. As far as I can tell, the CIA doesn't know where they are yet. As soon as I use all assets at the Agency's disposal to find them, I'm out."

"So, we shall work together once again at the behest of American intelligence, just like the old days in Iraq."

"Looks that way," Reece affirmed.

"Inshallah, one day we shall both be free."

"Inshallah," Reece responded.

Reece looked at his watch. "Let him know I'm coming."

Mo texted a single word via his cell phone and nodded to Reece. "He knows. I'll be here if you need me. *Allah yusallmak."*

Reece exited the vehicle, pulled the satchel over his shoulder, and moved up the street, toward his target.

. . .

What was taking her so long?

She'd enjoyed dinner and downed her share of wine followed by champagne at the club; he hoped she hadn't passed out on his bathroom floor. He liked watching her dance, turning down the advances of men much younger than he, returning to him when he'd beckoned. Back at his flat, she hadn't been interested in the drugs, instead having a final drink before going to the washroom to change into the lingerie he'd purchased for her earlier in the evening. She seemed genuinely attracted to him, a result of the unnecessary but pleasant wining and dining. The sex was always better with these young ones if they thought it was more than just a business transaction. They still had hope.

A sharp rap at the door startled him.

"Maada turiid?" He shouted angrily from his bed.

The door opened, and a man who was not his bodyguard entered the room, a black suppressed pistol in his outstretched hand.

"Where is she?" the man asked in a tone that conjured images of death itself.

Yedid looked to the nightstand drawer, knowing he could never make it to his Makarov pistol in time, then nodded toward the bathroom.

Reece moved across the room, his eyes and pistol still trained on the overweight general in white boxers propped up against the throw pillows, and opened the door.

"Get your things," he said to the small blond girl whose eyes betrayed a mixture of fright and dismay, as he ushered her to the bedroom door and into the waiting hands of Yedid's bodyguard, who would escort her away.

"Fucking traitor," Yedid spat.

"Do you know who I am?" Reece asked, his voice devoid of emotion.

The general took a deep breath and eyed the intruder suspiciously in the dim yellow glow coming from a single lamp next to the bed.

"Well, you are American. That I can tell. You can't be Agency, as they have other means to contact me. Ah, but this might be a test. The Central Intelligence Agency is famous for testing their sources to assess loyalty."

"I'm not Agency, and this is not a test. I'm here for information. Whether you live or end up like your buddy Andrenov depends on the quality of that information. Do you understand?"

Yedid nodded slowly, digesting everything he'd just heard. He had not been a frontline soldier. He'd chosen an even more dangerous career path. He'd been a politician in uniform under Bashar al-Assad and his father, Hafez al-Assad, before him. He was more adept at political maneuvering in a game during which one small error or lapse of judgment meant torture and death. He'd played the game well.

"I understand. What can I do for you?"

"The sniper, Nizar Kattan, and Oliver Grey. I need to find them."

Yedid studied the bearded American, weighing his options.

"I've told my handler everything I know, that's part of my deal," Yedid said, gesturing to the room. "I don't believe you are not Agency. They are the only ones, how do you say it, privy to those names?"

The small-caliber bullet entered General Yedid's right knee just above the kneecap, breaking bone and tearing cartilage and ligaments along its path before terminating its flight halfway through the thick mattress. The general's eyes opened wide in horror as he inhaled sharply at the pain, grabbing his leg, too shocked to even scream as his mind raced to catch up with what had just happened.

Reece covered the five steps to the bed in less than a second, whipping the pistol down and across the Syrian general's face, careful not to impact the jaw or temple, instead shattering the cheekbone and leaving a nasty gash in its wake.

"Look at me," Reece hissed down at the terrorist he knew was part of the conspiracy that left his friend's wife and children without a father and had helped almost unleash a nerve toxin on a civilian population, all for money.

Yedid looked up in a mixed state of shock and confusion. *Who was this man?*

"I told you, I'm not Agency, but I do want answers."

Reece stepped back and aimed the suppressed pistol directly at Yedid's head.

"It's too late for the leg. You'll lose it above the knee. If you want to keep the other one, and your life, I better believe what you have to say."

"Yes, yes," the general panted, frantically trying to stem the flow of blood soaking his sheets.

"Nizar and Grey. I need to know what you didn't tell the Agency. I need to know where they are now."

"I don't know! I swear to the Prophet, I don't," Yedid pleaded.

"The only prophet you worship is the god of money," Reece said, nodding toward an armoire set up as a bar with an assortment of drugs at the ready.

"Then what do you want?"

"I want you to guess. And it better be a good one. I know Andrenov hired you to put the team together. And I know that Grey wanted to run this himself, which puts you at a severe disadvantage tonight. I need your best educated guess as to where they might go and who they might contact."

His leg in tatters and his face dripping blood, the American the very incarnation of death standing over him, General Yedid weighed his options. He thought once again about his pistol in the drawer a mere few feet away but decided that discretion was the better part of valor in this particular situation. He could talk his way out of this.

"It's so painful. I need something for the pain. Please."

Reece walked to the armoire and eyed the selection of drugs and alcohol, giving General Yedid a moment to contemplate his pain and his future.

"Vodka?" Reece asked.

"Please. Yes, vodka," Yedid responded through gritted teeth.

"Think carefully, Yedid. You don't want this drink to be your last."

Reece kept an eye on Yedid in the mirror as he set his Beretta on the armoire and administered a healthy pour, taking a moment to empty the contents of a small bottle from his satchel into the liquid with his gloved hand. He picked up his pistol, turned back around, and approached the bloodied overweight man breathing heavily and still gripping his leg above what used to be his knee.

The general looked up and reached for the drink.

"Not yet, Yedid. First tell me where you think Grey and Nizar would go to ground."

"Okay, okay," the Syrian said in defeat. "As I told the CIA in my debrief, I don't know. What I *can* tell you is that Andrenov is connected, both in D.C. and in Russia. Grey certainly can't go back to the United States, and neither can Nizar, for obvious reasons, but they can go to Russia."

"Russia? But they assassinated the Russian president. Why would they go to Russia?"

"I see, you do not understand Russia. You are too young. My guess from the looks of you is that you spent your time in Iraq and Afghanistan."

"Continue," Reece commanded, holding the drink a bit closer to the Syrian.

"Russia is a puzzle even more complex than the Middle East," Yedid continued, still gripping his leg. "Andrenov, although excommunicated from the echelons of power, still had supporters in the government who had hedged their bets in anticipation of his eventual return. But, more important, he had deep connections to Russian organized crime, the mafia. If I were to guess, I would speculate that the plan for this contingency was a fallback involving the Bratva, somewhere in Russia, or in a Russian mafia–controlled city."

"Who would they contact, exactly?" Reece pressed.

"I don't know." Yedid prayed. "How could I? That is Andrenov's territory."

"Who?" Reece ordered again, moving the pistol to the general's one good knee.

"I don't know! I swear to it. I don't know!"

Reece contemplated the man before him—shot, beaten, crushed—and lowered the gun.

"I believe you," Reece said, handing the general his drink.

Yedid reached for it with both bloodied hands and brought it to his lips, taking two huge gulps of the strong liquor, closing his eyes in momentary relief from the torture this man had wrought.

Something was wrong.

Instead of the expected respite, he felt an intense burning in his mouth, followed quickly by a pain, sharper than anything he'd ever experienced, attacking his lungs and stomach. His eyes moved questioningly to the man standing over him but were quickly torn away as they rolled back in his head, his back arching, the drink falling onto his chest, convulsions racking his body as the dose of Novichok liquid soluble precursor seized control of his musculoskeletal system and threw him into an exorcistic seizure. As fluid began to flow into Yedid's lungs, his mouth filled with a white froth that leaked down his chin and out of his nose, his body deteriorating into a writhing mass of agony. His last vision, before his respiratory system shut down and his heart seized, was of the American tossing his pistol onto the bed, looking down at him without a hint of remorse.

. . .

Reece exited the building and made his way through the early morning darkness to the waiting Mercedes. He'd carefully removed his gloves and left them at the scene. One of Mo's people would leave an anonymous message in Russian for Greek authorities that warned them of the contamination so that appropriate HAZMAT crews could respond; the flat would be uninhabitable for years to come.

Traffic was extremely light and none of the drivers paid much attention to the tall figure climbing into the passenger side of the older-model German vehicle.

He didn't dwell on what he'd just done. The Syrian general had been at it long enough to know that eventually the reaper comes to call. Reece had gotten the information he needed. His sights were now set on Russia. It was time to hunt.

GLOSSARY

160th Special Operations Aviation Regiment: The Army's premier helicopter unit that provides aviation support to special forces. Known as the "Night Stalkers," they are widely regarded as the best helicopter pilots and crews in the world.

.260: .260 Remington; .264"/6.5mm rifle cartridge that is essentially a .308 Winchester necked down to accept a smaller-diameter bullet. The .260 provides superior external ballistics to the .308 with less felt recoil and can often be fired from the same magazines.

.300 Norma: .300 Norma Magnum; a cartridge designed for long-range precision shooting that has been adopted by USSOCOM for sniper use.

.375 CheyTac: Long-range cartridge, adapted from the .408 CheyTac, that can fire a 350-grain bullet at 2,970 feet per second. A favorite of extreme long-range match competitors who use it on targets beyond 3,000 yards.

.375 H&H Magnum: An extremely common and versatile big-game rifle cartridge, found throughout Africa. The cartridge was developed by Holland & Holland in 1912 and traditionally fires a 300-grain bullet.

.404 Jeffery: A rifle cartridge, designed for large game animals, developed by W. J. Jeffery & Company in 1905.

.408 CheyTac: Long-range cartridge adapted from the .505 Gibbs capable of firing a 419-grain bullet at 2,850 feet per second.

.500 Nitro: A .510-caliber cartridge designed for use against heavy dangerous game, often chambered in double rifles. The cartridge fires a 570-grain bullet at 2,150 feet per second.

75th Ranger Regiment: A large-scale Army special operations unit that conducts direct-action missions including raids and airfield seizures. These elite troops often work in conjunction with other special operations units.

. . .

AC-130 Spectre: A ground-support aircraft used by the U.S. military, based on the ubiquitous C-130 cargo plane. AC-130s are armed with a 105mm howitzer, 40mm cannons, and 7.62mm miniguns, and are considered the premier close-air-support weapon of the U.S. arsenal.

Accuracy International: A British company producing high-quality precision rifles, often used for military sniper applications.

ACOG: Advanced Combat Optical Gunsight. A magnified optical sight designed for use on rifles and carbines made by Trijicon. The ACOG is popular among U.S. forces as it provides both magnification and an illuminated reticle that provides aiming points for various target ranges.

AFIS: Automated Fingerprint Identification System; electronic fingerprint database maintained by the FBI.

Aimpoint Micro: Aimpoint Micro T-2; high-quality unmagnified red-dot combat optic produced in Sweden that can be used on a variety of weapons platforms. This durable sight weighs only three ounces and has a five-year battery life.

AISI: The latest name for Italy's domestic intelligence agency. Their motto, "scientia rerum reipublicae salus," means "knowledge of issues is the salvation of the Republic."

AK-9: Russian 9x39mm assault rifle favored by Spetsnaz (special purpose) forces.

Al-Jaleel: Iraqi-made 82mm mortar that is a clone of the Yugoslavian-made M69A. This indirect-fire weapon has a maximum range of 6,000 meters.

Alpha Group: An elite Russian counterterrorist unit that is part of the Federal Security Service (FSB). Alpha Group units also exist in numerous nations of the former Soviet Union, including Ukraine.

AN/PAS-13G(v)L3/LWTS: Weapon-mounted thermal optic that can be used to identify warm-blooded targets day or night. Can be mounted in front of and used in conjunction with a traditional "day" scope mounted on a sniper weapons system.

AN/PRC-163: Falcon III communications system made by Harris Corporation that integrates voice, text, and video capabilities.

AQ: al-Qaeda. Meaning "the Base" in Arabic. A radical Islamic terrorist organization once led by the late Osama bin Laden.

AQI: al-Qaeda in Iraq. An al-Qaeda–affiliated Sunni insurgent group that was active against U.S. forces. Elements of AQI eventually evolved into ISIS.

AR-10: 7.62x51mm brainchild of Eugene Stoner that was later adapted to create the M16/M4/AR-15.

Asherman Chest Seal: A specialized emergency medical device used to treat open chest wounds. If you're wearing one, you are having a bad day.

AT-4: Tube-launched 84mm anti-armor rocket produced in Sweden and used by U.S. forces since the 1980s. The AT-4 is a throwaway weapon: after it is fired, the tube is discarded.

ATF/BATFE: Bureau of Alcohol, Tobacco, Firearms and Explosives. A federal law enforcement agency formally part of the U.S. Department of the Treasury, which doesn't seem overly concerned with alcohol or tobacco.

ATPIAL/PEQ-15: Advanced Target Pointer/Illuminator Aiming Laser. A weapon-mounted device that emits both visible and infrared target designators for use with or without night observation devices. Essentially, an advanced military-grade version of the "laser sights" seen in popular culture.

Azores: Atlantic archipelago consisting of nine major islands that is an independent autonomous region of the European nation of Portugal.

Barrett 250 Lightweight: A lightweight variant of the M240 7.62mm light machine gun, developed by Barrett Firearms.

Barrett M107: .50 BMG caliber semiautomatic rifle designed by Ronnie Barrett in the early 1980s. This thirty-pound rifle can be carried by a single individual and can be used to engage human or vehicular targets at extreme ranges.

BATS: Biometrics Automated Toolset System; a fingerprint database often used to identify insurgent forces.

Bay of Pigs: Site of a failed invasion of Cuba by paramilitary exiles trained and equipped by the CIA.

BDU: Battle-dress uniform; an oxymoron if there ever was one.

Beneteau Oceanis: A forty-eight-foot cruising sailboat, designed and built in France. An ideal craft for eluding international manhunts.

Black Hills Ammunition: High-quality ammunition made for military and civilian use by a family-owned and South Dakota–based company. Their MK 262 MOD 1 5.56mm load saw significant operational use in the GWOT.

Browning Hi-Power: A single-action 9mm semiautomatic handgun that feeds from a thirteen-round box magazine. Also known as the P-35, this Belgian-designed handgun was the most widely issued military sidearm in the world for much of the twentieth century and was used by both Axis and Allied forces during World War II.

BUD/S: Basic Underwater Demolition/SEAL training. The six-month selection and training course required for entry into the SEAL Teams, held in Coronado, California. Widely considered one of the most brutal military selection courses in the world, with an average 80 percent attrition rate.

C-17: Large military cargo aircraft used to transport troops and supplies. Also used by the Secret Service to transport the president's motorcade vehicles.

C-4: Composition 4. A plastic-explosive compound known for its stability and malleability.

CAT: Counter-Assault Team; heavily armed ground element of the Secret Service trained to respond to threats such as ambushes.

███

███.

Cessna 208 Caravan: Single-engine turboprop aircraft that can ferry passengers and cargo, often to remote locations. These workhorses are staples in remote wilderness areas throughout the world.

CIA: Central Intelligence Agency

CIF/CRF: Commanders In-Extremis Force/Crisis Response Force; a United States Army Special Forces team specifically tasked with conducting direct-action missions. These are the guys who should have been sent to Benghazi.

CJSOTF: Combined Joint Special Operations Task Force. A regional command that controls special operations forces from various services and friendly nations.

CMC: Command Master Chief, a senior enlisted rating in the United States Navy.

CQC: Close-quarter combat

CrossFit: A fitness-centric worldwide cult that provides a steady stream of cases to orthopedic surgery clinics. No need to identify their members; they will tell you who they are.

CRRC: Combat Rubber Raiding Craft. Inflatable Zodiac-style boats used by SEALs and other maritime troops.

CTC: Counterterrorism Center; CIA office tasked with disrupting terrorist groups and attacks.

CZ-75: 9mm handgun designed in 1975 and produced in the Czech Republic.

DA: District attorney; local prosecutor in many jurisdictions.

Dam Neck: An annex to Naval Air Station Oceana near Virginia Beach, Virginia, where nothing interesting whatsoever happens.

DCIS: Defense Criminal Investigation Service

DEA: Drug Enforcement Administration

Democratic Federation of Northern Syria: Aka Rojava, an autonomous, polyethnic, and secular region of northern Syria.

Det Cord: Flexible detonation cord used to initiate charges of high explosive. The cord's interior is filled with PETN explosive; you don't want it wrapped around your neck.

DOD: Department of Defense

DOJ: Department of Justice

DShkM: Russian-made 12.7x108mm heavy machine gun that has been used in virtually every armed conflict since and including World War II.

DST: General Directorate for Territorial Surveillance. Morocco's domestic intelligence and security agency. Probably not afraid to use "enhanced interrogation techniques." **DST was originally redacted by government censors for the hardback edition of *True Believer*. After a five-month appeal process that decision was withdrawn.**

EFP: Explosively Formed Penetrator/Projectile. A shaped explosive charge that forms a molten projectile used to penetrate armor. Such munitions were widely used by insurgents against coalition forces in Iraq.

Eland: Africa's largest antelope. A mature male can weigh more than a ton.

EMS: Emergency medical services. Fire, paramedic, and other emergency personnel.

EOD: Explosive Ordnance Disposal. The military's explosives experts who are trained to, among other things, disarm or destroy improvised explosive devices or other munitions.

EOTECH: An unmagnified holographic gunsight for use on rifles and carbines, including the M4. The sight is designed for rapid target acquisition, which makes it an excellent choice for close-quarters battle. Can be fitted with a detachable 3x magnifier for use at extended ranges.

FAL: Fusil Automatique Léger: gas-operated, select-fire 7.62 x51mm battle rifle developed by FN in the late 1940s and used by the militaries of more than ninety nations. Sometimes referred to as "the right arm of the free world" due to its use against communist forces in various Cold War–era insurgencies.

FBI: Federal Bureau of Investigation; a federal law enforcement agency that is not known for its sense of humor.

FDA: Food and Drug Administration

FLIR: Forward-Looking InfraRed; an observation device that uses thermographic radiation, that is, heat, to develop an image.

Floppies: Derogatory term used to describe communist insurgents during the Rhodesian Bush War.

FOB: Forward Operating Base. A secured forward military position used to support tactical operations. Can vary from small and remote outposts to sprawling complexes.

Fobbit: A service member serving in a noncombat role who rarely, if ever, leaves the safety of the Forward Operating Base.

FSB: Russia's federal security service; like the FBI but without all the charm.

FSO: Federal Protective Service; Russia's version of the Secret Service.

G550: A business jet manufactured by Gulfstream Aerospace. Prices for a new example start above $40 million but, as they say, it's better to rent.

Game Scout: A wildlife enforcement officer in Africa. These individuals are often paired with hunting outfitters to ensure that regulations are adhered to.

Glock: An Austrian-designed, polymer-framed handgun popular with police forces, militaries, and civilians throughout the world. Glocks are made in various sizes and chambered in several different cartridges.

GPNVG-18: Ground Panoramic Night Vision Goggles; $43,000 NODs used by the most highly funded special operations units due to their superior image quality and peripheral vision. See *Rich Kid Shit.*

GPS: Global Positioning System. Satellite-based navigation systems that provide a precise location anywhere on earth.

Great Patriotic War: The Soviets' name for World War II; communists love propaganda.

Green-badger: Central Intelligence Agency contractor

Ground Branch: Land-focused element of the CIA's Special Activities Division, according to Wikipedia.

GRS: Global Response Staff. Protective agents employed by the Central Intelligence Agency to provide security to overseas personnel. *See 13 Hours.* **GRS was originally redacted by government censors for the hardback edition of *True Believer*. After a five-month appeal process that decision was withdrawn.**

GRU: Russia's Main Intelligence Directorate. The foreign military intelligence agency of the Russian armed forces. The guys who do all the real work while the KGB gets all the credit, or so I'm told.

GS: General Schedule; federal jobs that provide good benefits and lots of free time.

Gukurahundi Massacres: A series of killings carried out against Ndebele tribe members in Matabeleland, Zimbabwe, by the Mugabe government during the 1980s. As many as twenty thousand civilians were killed by the North Korean–trained Fifth Brigade of the Zimbabwean army.

GWOT: Global War on Terror; the seemingly endless pursuit of bad guys, kicked off by the 9/11 attacks.

Gym Jones: Utah-based fitness company founded by alpine climbing legend Mark Twight. Famous for turning soft Hollywood actors into hard bodies, Gym Jones once enjoyed a close relationship with a certain SEAL Team.

Hell Week: The crucible of BUD/S training. Five days of constant physical and mental stress with little or no sleep.

Hilux: Pickup truck manufactured by Toyota that is a staple in third-world nations due to its reliability.

HK416: M4 clone engineered by the German firm of Heckler & Koch to operate using a short-stroke gas pistol system instead of the M4's direct-impingement gas system. Used by select special operations units in the U.S. and abroad. May or may not have been the weapon used to kill ████████████.

HK417: Select-fire 7.62x51mm rifle built by Heckler & Koch as a big brother to the HK416. Often used as Designated Marksman Rifle with a magnified optic.

HUMINT: Human intelligence. Information gleaned through traditional human-to-human methods.

HVI/HVT: High-Value Individual/High-Value Target. An individual who is important to the enemy's capabilities and is therefore specifically sought out by a military force.

IED: Improvised Explosive Device. Homemade bombs, whether crude or complex, often used by insurgent forces overseas.

IR: Infrared. The part of the electromagnetic spectrum with a longer wavelength than light but a shorter wavelength than radio waves. Invisible to the naked eye but visible with night observation devices. Example: an IR laser aiming device.

Iron Curtain: The physical and ideological border that separated the opposing sides of the Cold War.

ISIS: Islamic State of Iraq and the Levant. Radical Sunni terrorist group based in parts of Iraq and Afghanistan. Also referred to as ISIL. The bad guys.

ISR: Intelligence, Surveillance, and Reconnaissance

ITAR: International Traffic in Arms Regulations; export control regulations designed to restrict the export of certain items, including weapons and optics. These regulations offer ample opportunity to inadvertently violate federal law.

JAG: Judge Advocate General. Decent television series and the military's legal department.

JSOC: Joint Special Operations Command. A component command of SOCOM, ██ ███████.

Katyn Massacre: Soviet purge of Polish citizens that took place in 1940 subsequent to the Soviet invasion. Twenty-two thousand Poles were killed by members of the NKVD during this event; many of the bodies were discovered in mass graves in the Katyn Forest. Russia denied responsibility for the massacre until 1990.

Kudu: A spiral-horned antelope, roughly the size and build of an elk, that inhabits much of sub-Saharan Africa.

Langley: The Northern Virginia location where the Central Intelligence Agency is headquartered. Often used as shorthand for CIA.

LaRue OBR: Optimized Battle Rifle; precision variant of the AR-15/AR-10 designed for use as a Designated Marksman or Sniper Rifle. Available in both 5.56x45mm and 7.62x51mm.

Law of Armed Conflict: A segment of public international law that regulates the conduct of armed hostilities.

LAW Rocket: M-72 Light Anti-armor Weapon. A disposable, tube-launched 66mm unguided rocket in use with U.S. forces since before the Vietnam War.

Leica M4: Classic 35mm rangefinder camera produced from 1966 to 1975.

Long-Range Desert Group: A specialized British military unit that operated in the North African and Mediterranean theaters during World War II. The unit was made up of soldiers from Great Britain, New Zealand, and Southern Rhodesia.

M1911/1911A1: .45-caliber pistol used by U.S. forces since before World War I.

M3: World War II submachine gun chambered in .45 ACP. This simple but reliable weapon became a favorite of the frogmen of that time.

M4: The standard assault rifle of the majority of U.S. military forces, including the U.S. Navy SEALs. The M4 is a shortened carbine variant of the M16 rifle that fires a 5.56x45mm cartridge. The M4 is a modular design that can be adapted to numerous configurations, including different barrel lengths.

MACV-SOG: Military Assistance Command, Vietnam—Studies and Observations Group. Deceiving name for a group of brave warriors who conducted highly classified special operations missions during the Vietnam War. These operations were often conducted behind enemy lines in Laos, Cambodia, and North Vietnam.

Mahdi Militia: An insurgent Shia militia loyal to cleric Muqtada al-Sadr that opposed U.S. forces in Iraq during the height of that conflict.

MANPADS: MAn-Portable Air-Defense System; small antiaircraft surface-to-air guided rockets such as the U.S. Stinger and the Russian SA-7.

Marine Raiders: U.S. Marine Corps special operations unit; formerly known as MARSOC.

Mazrah Tora: A prison in Cairo, Egypt, that you do not want to find yourself in.

MBITR: AN/PRC-148 Multiband Inter/Intra Team Radio. A handheld multiband, tactical software–defined radio, commonly used by special operations forces to communicate during operations.

McMillan TAC-50: Bolt-action sniper rifle chambered in .50 BMG used for long-range sniping operations used by U.S. special operations forces as well as the Canadian army.

MDMA: A psychoactive drug whose clinical name is too long to place here. Known on the street as "ecstasy." Glow sticks not included.

MH-47: Special operations variant of the Army's Chinook helicopter, usually flown by members of the 160th SOAR. This twin-rotor aircraft is used frequently in Afghanistan due to its high service ceiling and large troop- and cargo-carrying capacity. Rumor has it that, if you're careful, you can squeeze a Land Rover Defender 90 inside one.

MH-60: Special operations variant of the Army's Black Hawk helicopter, usually flown by members of the 160th SOAR.

MI5: Military Intelligence, Section 5; Britain's domestic counterintelligence and security agency. Like the FBI but with nicer suits and better accents.

MIL DOT: A reticle-based system used for range estimation and long-range shooting, based on the milliradian unit of measurement.

MIL(s): One-thousandth of a radian; an angular measurement used in rifle scopes. 0.1 MIL equals 1 centimeter at 100 meters or 0.36" at 100 yards. If you find that confusing, don't become a sniper.

MIT: Turkey's national intelligence organization and a school in Boston for smart kids.

Mk 46 MOD 1: Belt-fed 5.56x45mm light machine gun built by FN Herstal. Often used by special operations forces due to its light weight, the Mk 46 is a scaled-down version of the Mk 48 MOD 1.

Mk 48 MOD 1: Belt-fed 7.62x51mm light machine gun designed for use by special operations forces. Weighing eighteen pounds unloaded, the Mk48 can fire 730 rounds per minute to an effective range of 800 meters and beyond.

MP7: Compact select-fire personal defense weapon built by Heckler & Koch and used by various special operations forces. Its 4.6x30mm cartridge is available in a subsonic load, making the weapon extremely quiet when suppressed. What the MP7 lacks in lethality it makes up for in coolness.

MQ-4C: An advanced unmanned surveillance drone developed by Northrop Grumman for use by the United States Navy.

MultiCam: A proprietary camouflage pattern developed by Crye Precision. Formerly reserved for special operators and airsofters, MultiCam is now standard issue to much of the U.S. and allied militaries.

NATO: North Atlantic Treaty Organization; an alliance created in 1949 to counter the Soviet threat to the Western Hemisphere. Headquartered in Brussels, Belgium, the alliance is commanded by a four-star U.S. military officer known as the Supreme Allied Commander Europe (SACEUR).

Naval Special Warfare Development Group (DEVGRU): A command that appears on the biographies of numerous admirals on the Navy's website. Vice President Joe Biden publicly referred to it by a different name.

NCIS: Naval Criminal Investigative Service. A federal law enforcement agency whose jurisdiction includes the U.S. Navy and Marine Corps. Also a popular television program with at least two spin-offs.

Niassa Game Reserve: Sixteen thousand square miles of relatively untouched wilderness in northern Mozambique. The reserve is home to a wide variety of wildlife as well as a fair number of poachers looking to commoditize them.

NODs: Night observation devices. Commonly referred to as "night-vision goggles," these devices amplify ambient light, allowing the user to see in low-light environments. Special operations forces often operate at night to take full advantage of such technology.

NSA: National Security Agency; U.S. intelligence agency tasked with gathering and analyzing signals intercepts and other communications data. These are the people who can listen to your phone calls.

NSC: National Security Council; this body advises and assists the president of the United States on matters of national security.

NSW: Naval Special Warfare. The Navy's special operations force; includes SEAL Teams.

Officer Candidate School (OCS): Twelve-week course where civilians and enlisted sailors are taught to properly fold underwear. Upon completion, they are miraculously qualified to command men and women in combat.

OmniSTAR: Satellite-based augmentation system service provider. A really fancy GPS service that provides very precise location information.

Ops-Core ballistic helmet: Lightweight high-cut helmet used by special operations forces worldwide.

P226: 9mm handgun made by SIG Sauer, the standard-issue sidearm for SEALs.

P229: A compact handgun made by SIG Sauer, often used by federal law enforcement officers, chambered in 9mm as well as other cartridges.

P320: Striker-fired modular 9mm handgun that has recently been adopted by the U.S. armed forces as the M17/M18.

P365: Subcompact handgun made by SIG Sauer, designed for concealed carry. Despite its size, the P365 holds up to thirteen rounds of 9mm.

Pakistani Taliban: An Islamic terrorist group composed of various Sunni Islamist militant groups based in the northwestern Federally Administered Tribal Areas along the Afghan border in Pakistan.

Pamwe Chete: "All Together"; the motto of the Rhodesian Selous Scouts.

Panga: A machete-like utility blade common in Africa.

Peshmerga: Military forces of Kurdistan. Meaning "the one who faces death," they are regarded by Allied troops as some of the best fighters in the region.

PETN: Pentaerythritol TetraNitrate. An explosive compound used in blasting caps to initiate larger explosive charges.

PG-32V: High-explosive antitank rocket that can be fired from the Russian-designed RPG-32 rocket-propelled grenade. Its tandem charge is effective against various types of armor, including reactive armor.

PID: Protective Intelligence and Threat Assessment Division; the division of the Secret Service that monitors potential threats to its protectees.

PKM: Soviet-designed, Russian-made light machine gun chambered in 7.62x54R that can be found in conflicts throughout the globe. This weapon feeds from a non-disintegrating belt and has a rate of fire of 650 rounds per minute. You don't want one shooting at you.

PLF: Parachute Landing Fall. A technique taught to military parachutists to prevent injury when making contact with the earth. Round canopy parachutes used by airborne forces fall at faster velocities than other parachutes, and require a specific landing sequence. More often than not ends up as feet-ass-head.

POTUS: President of the United States; leader of the free world.

PPD: Presidential Protection Detail; the element of the Secret Service tasked with protecting POTUS.

President's Hundred: A badge awarded by the Civilian Marksmanship Program to the one hundred top-scoring military and civilian shooters in the President's Pistol and President's Rifle matches. Enlisted members of the U.S. military are authorized to wear the tab on their uniform.

Professional Hunter: A licensed hunting guide in Africa, often referred to as a "PH." Zimbabwe-licensed PHs are widely considered the most qualified and highly trained in Africa and make up the majority of the PH community operating in Mozambique.

Protocols of the Elders of Zion: An anti-Semitic conspiracy manifesto first published in the late 1800s by Russian sources. Though quickly established as a fraudulent text, *Protocols* has been widely circulated in numerous languages.

PSO-1: A Russian-made 4x24mm illuminated rifle optic developed for use on the SVD rifle.

PTSD: Post-traumatic stress disorder. A mental condition that develops in association with shocking or traumatic events. Commonly associated with combat veterans.

PVS-15: Binocular-style NODs used by U.S. and allied special operations forces.

QRF: Quick Reaction Force, a contingency ground force on standby to assist operations in progress.

Ranger Panties: Polyester PT shorts favored by members of the 75th Ranger Regiment that leave very little to the imagination, sometimes referred to as "silkies."

RFID: Radio Frequency Identification; technology commonly used to tag objects that can be scanned electronically.

RHIB/RIB: Rigid Hull Inflatable Boat/Rigid Inflatable Boat. A lightweight but high-performance boat constructed with a solid fiberglass or composite hull and flexible tubes at the gunwale (sides).

Rhodesia: A former British colony that declared its independence in 1965. After a long and brutal civil war, the nation became Zimbabwe in 1979.

Rhodesian Bush War: An insurgency battle between the Rhodesian Security Forces and Soviet-, East German-, Cuban-, and Chinese-backed guerrillas that lasted from 1964 to 1979. The war ended when the December 1979 Lancaster House Agreement put an end to white minority rule.

Rhodesian SAS: A special operations unit, formed as part of the famed British Special Air Service in 1951. When Rhodesia sought independence, the unit ceased to exist as part of the British military but fought as part of the Rhodesian Security Forces until 1980. Many members of the Selous Scouts were recruited from the SAS.

Rich Kid Shit: Expensive equipment items reserved for use by the most highly funded special operations units, usually part of ███████.

RLI: Rhodesian Light Infantry; an airborne and airmobile unit used to conduct "fireforce" operations during the Bush War. These missions were often launched in response to intelligence provided by Selous Scouts on the ground.

Robert Mugabe: Chairman of ZANU who led the nation of Zimbabwe from 1980 to 2017 as both prime minister and president. Considered responsible for retaliatory attacks against his rival Ndebele tribe as well as a disastrous land redistribution scheme that was ruled illegal by Zimbabwe's High Court.

ROE: Rules of engagement. Rules or directives that determine what level of force can be applied against an enemy in a particular situation or area.

RPG-32: 105mm rocket-propelled grenade launcher that is made in both Russia and, under license, in Jordan.

SAP: Special Access Program. Security protocols that provide highly classified information with safeguards and access restrictions that exceed those for regular classified information. Really secret stuff.

SCAR-17: 7.62x51mm battle rifle produced by FN. Its gas mechanism can be traced to that of the FAL.

Schmidt & Bender: Privately held German optics manufacturer known for its precision rifle scopes.

SCI: Special Compartmentalized Information. Classified information concerning or derived from sensitive intelligence sources, methods, or analytical processes. Often found on private basement servers in upstate New York or bathroom closet servers in Denver.

SCIF: Sensitive Compartmented Information Facility; a secure and restricted room or structure where classified information is discussed or viewed.

SEAL: Acronym of SEa, Air, and Land. The three mediums in which SEALs operate. The U.S. Navy's special operations force.

Secret Service: The federal law enforcement agency responsible for protecting the POTUS.

Selous Scouts: An elite, if scantily clad, mixed-race unit of the Rhodesian army responsible for counterinsurgency operations. These "pseudoterrorists" led some of the most successful special operations missions in modern history.

SERE: Survival, Evasion, Resistance, Escape. A military training program that includes realistic role-playing as a prisoner of war. SERE students are subjected to highly stressful procedures, sometimes including waterboarding, as part of the course curriculum. More commonly referred to as "camp slappy."

Shishani: Arabic term for Chechen fighters in Syria, probably due to "Shishani" being a common Chechen surname.

SIGINT: Signals intelligence. Intelligence derived from electronic signals and systems used by foreign targets, such as communications systems, radars, and weapons systems.

SIPR: Secret Internet Protocol Router network; a secure version of the Internet used by DOD and the State Department to transmit classified information.

SISDE: Italy's Intelligence and Democratic Security Service. Their suits are probably even nicer than MI5's.

SOCOM: United States Special Operations Command. The Unified Combatant Command charged with overseeing the various Special Operations Component Commands of the Army, Marine Corps, Navy, and Air Force of the United States Armed Forces. Headquartered at MacDill Air Force Base in Tampa, Florida.

Special Boat Team-12: The West Coast unit that provides maritime mobility to SEALs using a variety of vessels. Fast boats with machine guns.

Special Reconnaissance (SR) Team: NSW Teams that conduct special activities, ISR, and provide intelligence support to the SEAL Teams.

SR-16: An AR-15 variant developed and manufactured by Knight Armament Corporation.

StrongFirst: Kettle-bell-focused fitness program founded by Russian fitness guru Pavel Tsatsouline that is popular with special operations forces.

S-Vest: Suicide vest; an explosives-laden garment favored by suicide bombers. Traditionally worn only once.

SVR: Russia's foreign intelligence service, formerly known as the KGB.

Taliban: An Islamic fundamentalist political movement and terrorist group in Afghanistan. U.S. and coalition forces have been at war with members of the Taliban since late 2001.

TDFD: Time-delay firing device. An explosive initiator that allows for detonation at a determined period of time. A fancy version of a really long fuse.

TIC: Troops in contact. A firefight involving U.S. or friendly forces.

TOC: Tactical Operations Center. A command post for military operations. A TOC usually includes a small group of personnel who guide members of an active tactical element during a mission from the safety of a secured area.

TOR Network: A computer network designed to conceal a user's identity and location. TOR allows for anonymous communication.

TQ: Politically correct term for the timely questioning of individuals on-site once a target is secure. May involve the raising of voices.

Troop Chief: Senior enlisted SEAL on a forty-man troop, usually a master chief petty officer. The guy who makes shit happen.

TS: Top Secret. Information, the unauthorized disclosure of which reasonably could be expected to cause exceptionally grave damage to national security, that the original classification authority is able to identify or describe. Can also describe an individual's level of security clearance.

TST: Time-sensitive target. A target requiring immediate response because it is highly lucrative, is a fleeting target of opportunity, or poses (or will soon pose) a danger to friendly forces.

UAV: Unmanned aerial vehicle; a drone.

UCMJ: Uniform Code of Military Justice. Disciplinary and criminal code that applies to members of the U.S. military.

UDI: Unilateral Declaration of Independence; the 1965 document that established Rhodesia as an independent sovereign state. The UDI resulted in an international embargo and made Rhodesia a pariah.

V-22: Tilt-rotor aircraft that can fly like a plane and take off/land like a helicopter.

Numerous examples were crashed during its extremely expensive development.

VBIED: Vehicle-Borne Improvised Explosive Device; a rolling car bomb driven by a suicidal terrorist.

VC: National Liberation Front of South Vietnam, better known as the Viet Cong. A communist insurgent group that fought against the government of South Vietnam and its allies during the Vietnam War. In the movies, these are the guys wearing the black pajamas carrying AKs.

VPN: Virtual Private Network. A private network that enables users to send and receive data across shared or public networks as if their computing devices were directly connected to the private network. Considered more secure than a traditional Internet network.

VSK-94: Russian-made Sniper/Designated Marksman rifle chambered in the subsonic 9x39mm cartridge. This suppressed weapon is popular with Russian special operations and law enforcement units due to its minimal sound signature and muzzle flash.

War Vets: Loosely organized groups of Zimbabweans who carried out many of the land seizures during the 1990s. Often armed, these individuals used threats and intimidation to remove white farmers from their homes. Despite the name, most of these individuals were too young to have participated in the Bush War. Not to be confused with ZNLWVA, a group that represents ZANU-affiliated veterans of the Bush War.

WARCOM/NAVSPECWARCOM: United States Naval Special Warfare Command. The Navy's special operations force and the maritime component of United States Special Operations Command. Headquartered in Coronado, California, WARCOM is the administrative command for subordinate NSW Groups composed of eight SEAL Teams, one SEAL Delivery Vehicle (SDV) Team, three Special Boat Teams, and two Special Reconnaissance Teams.

Westley Richards Droplock: A rifle or shotgun built by the famed Birmingham, England, gunmakers that allows the user to remove the locking mechanisms for repair or replacement in the field. Widely considered one of the finest and most iconic actions of all time.

Whiskey Tango: Military speak for "white trash."

Yazidis: An insular Kurdish-speaking ethnic and religious group that primarily resides in Iraq. Effectively a subminority among the Kurds, Yazidis were heavily persecuted by ISIS.

YPG: Kurdish militia forces operating in the Democratic Federation of Northern Syria. The Turks are not fans.

ZANLA: Zimbabwe African National Liberation Army. The armed wing of the Mao-
ist Zimbabwe African National Union and one of the major combatants of
the Rhodesian Bush War. ZANLA forces often staged out of training camps
located in Mozambique and were led by Robert Mugabe.

Zimbabwe: Sub-Saharan African nation that formerly existed as Southern Rhodesia and later Rhodesia. Led for three decades by Robert Mugabe, Zimbabwe
ranks as one of the world's most corrupt nations on Transparency International's Corruption Perceptions Index.

ZIRPA: Zimbabwe People's Revolutionary Army. The Soviet-equipped armed wing
of ZAPU and one of the two major insurgency forces that fought in the Rhodesian Bush War. ZIRPA forces fell under the leadership of Josh Nkomo, who
spent much of the war in Zambia. ZIRPA members were responsible for shooting down two civilian airliners using Soviet SA-7 surface-to-air missiles in the
late 1970s.

Zodiac Mk 2 GR: 4.2-meter inflatable rubber boat capable of carrying up to six
individuals. These craft are often used as dinghies for larger vessels.

ACKNOWLEDGMENTS

"There are only two plots in all literature: a person goes on a journey, a stranger comes to town." Though its original source is debated, this quote is often attributed to **Fyodor Dostoyevsky**, **Leo Tolstoy**, or American novelist and professor **John C. Gardner**. Throughout my life I naturally gravitated to books and movies that echoed those two narratives. In no small way was I influenced by **Joseph Campbell's** *The Hero with a Thousand Faces*, which details the similarities in the hero's journey across cultures. During my high school years, I became enthralled with Campbell's work after watching his series of interviews with **Bill Moyers** which aired on PBS in 1988, called *The Power of Myth*. What many consider to be Campbell's seminal work still occupies an honored place on my shelf. As a lifelong reader and student, I've always been captivated by the hero's journey: *The Epic of Gilgamesh*, *Beowulf*, the *Iliad*, the *Odyssey*, and *The Aeneid*. The reluctant hero, his journey, and resulting transformation resonated with me. Just as they have since time immemorial, those myths and their modern incarnations inspired me to undergo my own formative journey in the military. Did I emerge transformed? Perhaps. Wiser? One can hope.

I trace my life through the novels I was reading at various stages along the path. It may have all started in a hammock under the pines of the Sierra Nevada mountains. With a mother who was, and is to this day, a librarian, I grew up surrounded by books, imagining a day when I would enter the real world I was visiting on the written page. That literature would lead me into a twenty-year odyssey in special operations and eventually catapult me into the world of publishing.

I distinctly remember my parents reading **Frederick Forsyth**, **Ken Follett**, **Robert Ludlum**, **John le Carré**, **Ian Fleming**, and former British Royal Marine Commando **John Edmund Gardner** when he picked up the torch. I longed for the day when I could pull those books from the shelves of our old cabin and, truth be told, I've been training to write thrillers since I tipped that first spy novel from its perch.

As we entered the 1980s, I began my early education in storytelling. My professors in those formative years were **David Morrell**, **Nelson DeMille**, **J. C. Pollock**, **Tom Clancy**, **Louis L'Amour**, **Marc Olden** and **A. J. Quinnell**. I'd spend all day immersed in the pages of *Centrifuge*, *Man on Fire*, *Oni*, *The Charm School*, *Last of the Breed*, *The Hunt for Red October*, and what is now called the *Abelard Sanction* series. In fact, it was David Morrell's classic espionage thriller *The Brotherhood of the Rose* that confirmed I wanted to serve my country as a SEAL and then follow his footsteps into the writer's fray. That early reading, two decades in the SEAL Teams, time in combat, and an academic study of war, terrorism, and insurgencies now provide ample fodder for the pages of my political thrillers.

I started reading Tom Clancy in the sixth grade, and since his first appearance in *The Cardinal of the Kremlin*, I have been a John Clark fan. *Without Remorse* would hit shelves while I was in college, and, already having my sights set on the SEAL Teams, I was there to purchase it on publication day. That novel remains an old friend.

Just prior to enlisting in the Navy, I discovered the great **Stephen Hunter,** whose work continues to influence me today. In the days following 9/11, I rushed to print calling cards inspired by *Point of Impact*, pirating **Steve McQueen's** famous line from *The Magnificent Seven*: "*We deal in lead, friend.*" I had long been fascinated by the sniper, but it was Stephen Hunter's personification of "Bob the Nailer" that cemented it as my future specialty in the profession of arms. The idea of the lone man with a rifle appealed to me: alone, outnumbered, behind enemy lines, only wits and skill with the great equalizer keeping him alive. The ultimate test. *The Most Dangerous Game*. For his magnificent work, for his inspiration and friendship, and for giving the world Bob Lee Swagger, I thank you.

My experience with the CIA in the pre-9/11 days was primarily informed by popular culture to include the three remarkable **Daniel Silva** novels I had read before my August 2001 CIA phone interview (I have since read them all and eagerly await the next installment in the evolution of Gabriel Allon). The world would change just a few weeks later, and after serving and fighting alongside the quiet professionals of CIA's Ground Branch, they extended an invitation, though this time I decided to stay in the fight as a frogman. This very novel was inspired by events in Iraq in 2006 when I was attached to a CIA covert action program which ended up being one of the highlights of my time in uniform. The mission behind that inspiration will remain known only to the team that was there and those who read the classified cables. That experience, coupled with **Peter Zeihan's** *The Accidental Superpower*, provided the basis for *True Believer*.

The events of September 11, 2001, ushered us into a new age of prolonged warfare, and as a young SEAL, I was in the thick of it. I wouldn't emerge from a combat-focused posture for more than a decade, during which time I devoted myself to the study of war and of our enemy. I devoured books, articles, and interviews by and with counterinsurgency specialists **Dr. David Killcullen, Dr. Kalev Sepp, Dr. John Arquilla, Dr. Hy S. Rothstein, Dr. Heather S. Gregg, Dr. Anna Simons, Ahmed Rashid, John A. Nagl, Thomas X. Hammes, Antonio Giustozzi, Eliot A. Cohen, Martin Van Creveld, H. R. McMaster**, and the classics from **David Galula, Robert Taber, T. E. Lawrence, Vo Nguyen Giap, Roger Trinquier, Mao Zedong, George K. Tanham, Che Guevara, Napolean D. Valeriano, Alistair Horne, Charles T. R. Bohannan, Bernard B. Fall, B. H. Liddell Hart**, and **Walter Laqueur**. It was my responsibility to immerse myself in the word of asymmetrical warfare in order to make the best decisions possible under fire.

I pulled my head from the study of conflict to discover the late legendary **Vince Flynn** and read *Term Limits* on a plane to Afghanistan in 2003. Upon my return home I immediately caught up and read *Transfer of Power, The Third Option,* and *Separation of Power.* I haven't missed one since, including the newest in the series, *Red War,* by **Kyle Mills,** who is doing an outstanding job keeping Vince's legacy alive.

I snuck in my first **Brad Thor** novel on the way to Ramadi, Iraq, in 2005. I read *The Lions of Lucerne* on the flight into what was arguably the most dangerous city in the world at the time. The entire Task Unit had read it by the end of deployment, and we've all been Scot Harvath fans ever since. Little did I know then what a profound impact Brad would have on my life. Brad, thank you for breaching the door for me. Without you, none of this would be possible. I am forever in your debt.

More recently in my post-military life, I was introduced to **Mark Greaney**. If you have not read his Gray Man series, add it to the top of your list.

These incredible authors have created the iconic characters of Mitch Rapp, Scot Harvath, Gabriel Allon, Bob Lee Swagger, Jack Ryan, John Clark, and Court Gentry. Thank you for sharing your gifts with the world.

I remain a student of war, and that study continues to inform my writing, hopefully tempered by wisdom and the benefit of time and distance from the battlefield. I borrowed much of Reece's Islamic studies teacher in Morocco from the real-life **Maajid Nawaz** and his fascinating book, *Radical*. The Grand Mosque seizure really did happen in Mecca in 1979. Unofficial estimates put the death toll at more than four thousand, not counting the sixty-plus rebels publicly beheaded in eight cities around the country in its aftermath. What would have happened between the West and Islam, had the House of Saud not taken a road toward increased authoritarianism while allowing religious conservatism to flourish in the wake of the siege? Would fifteen of the 9/11 hijackers have been sons of Saudi Arabia? Would The Kingdom still be the most significant source of financial support to terrorist groups around the world? We will never know.

Aside from the legendary authors who have led the way, I owe a debt of gratitude to a number of people who made this novel a reality. Their levels of knowledge and expertise certainly eclipse mine. Any errors on these pages rest with me alone.

On the Africa front, to the professional hunters and anti-poaching units I worked with in Mozambique and South Africa as both research for this book and to repurpose some of my old skills for a new cause, thank you for what you do day in and day out on the front lines to protect African wildlife. To **Jumbo Moore**, **Jacques Hartzenberg**, **Ryan Cliffe**, **Louis Pansegrouw**, **Paul Wellock**, and **Darren Ellerman**, you might recognize your contributions to the novel. To **John Burrell** and everyone at **High Adventure Company** for setting everything up and for always doing an exemplary job. To my friend **Billy Birdzell** for spearheading our trip to train an anti-poaching unit in the Kalahari focused on saving some of the last rhino on earth. To **Tony Makris** for always pointing me in the right direction. To **Gus van Dyk** for sharing your deep knowledge of conservation efforts in Africa and to former South African police officer **Nic de Kock** for answering all my questions on poaching syndicates and the black market trade in illicit wildlife. To "**Hubert**" for an incredible life story, one that will make it into fictionalized form in my next novel. To **Shane Mahoney** for all you do to defend the wild others. And, to **Jeff Crane, Phil Hoon** and **PJ Carleton** at the **Congressional Sportsman's Foundation** for fighting the legislative battles.

To those who live by the gun: **Larry Vickers, Ken Hackathorn, Pat McNamara, "Goat," Eric Frohardt, Jeff Houston, Mickey Schuch, Sean Haberberger, Keith Walawender, D'Arcy Echols, Tim Fallon, Dave Knesek, Doug Prichard, Chip Beaman, Cory Zillig, Eddie Penny, Kyle Lamb, Mike Pannone, Tim Clemit, Bill Rogers, Joe Collins, Bill Rapier, Johnny Primo, Caylen Wojcik, Travis Haley, Mario Garcia, Clay Hergert**, and everyone who puts in the time to responsibly train in defense of themselves and their loved ones.

To **Clint and Heidi Smith** of **Thunder Ranch,** thank you for inviting us in all those years ago, and for all you do for law enforcement, our military, and my family.

To "**Biss**"—great things on the horizon.

To **James Yeager** for everything you did to make *The Terminal List* such a success.

To **Susan Hastings** for the generous year-long loan of her collection of Rhodesian history books. I promise to return them soon.

To **Shahram Moosavi** for all the life lessons in the ring and on the mat. Training with you made BUD/S seem like a walk in the park.

To **Dom Raso** of **Dynamis Alliance**, thank you for everything you've done for me and my family. Keep crushing!

To **Daniel Winkler** and **Karen Shook** of **Winkler Knives**, thank you for doing more than most will ever know for those who operate on the edge. It is appreciated more than any of us can express.

To Chief Special Warfare Operator (SEAL) **Brad Cavner**, killed in a training accident on June 23, 2014. He left an indelible impact on the SEAL Teams and everyone who was fortunate enough to meet him. Thank you to the **Cavner Family** for allowing me to honor his memory by incorporating his toast into the novel.

To **Andrew Arrabito** and **Kelsie Bieser** of **Half Face Blades** for always saying an enthusiastic *yes* to my blade ideas and for always diving in to help.

To neurological spine surgeon **Dr. Robert Bray** for your service and sacrifice, what you continue to do for veterans, and for always patching me up after the scrapes that come with the territory. Your kindness and generosity are never far from my thoughts. Thank you to you and **Tracey** for making our post-military life possible. We couldn't do it without you.

To **Chris Cox**, **David Lehman**, and **Graham Hill** for always being there.

To **Rick and Esther Rosenfield** for your love and support.

To **Nick** and **Tina Cousoulis** for your inspiration.

To all our friends who have been there every step of the way: **Garry and Victoria Peters, Jim and Nancy Demetriades, Josh and Audrey Waldron, Larry and Rhonda Sheakley, Martin and Kelly Katz, Razor and Sylvia Dobbs, Mike Atkinson, Mac Minard, Mike Port, Jonny Sanchez, Alec Wolf, George Kollitides, Bob Warden, Wally McLallen, Nick Seifert,** and **Jeff Kimball**.

To **Jimmy Spithill** and **Jerome Sammarcelli** for your assistance on the sailing portion of the story. One would think I would know a bit more about boats after twenty years in the Navy.

To **Tuck Beckstoffer,** your wine was a constant companion well into my late writing nights.

To **Jeff Rotherham** for once again guiding me through the world of IEDs and homemade explosives. I hope no one ever pisses you off.

To **Jon Dubin** for your time at the FBI, for **Pineapple Brothers**, for our past adventures and those to come.

To **Trig and Annette French** for your friendship and early enthusiastic support of *The Terminal List*.

To **Andrew Kline, Frank Lecrone, Kevin O'Malley**, and **Jimmy Klein**: *Pals*.

To **Darren LaSorte** for a lifetime of friendship and for everything you've done to support the cause.

To **Scott Naz** for answering all my fishing questions.

To **Frank Argenbright** for the opportunities.

To **Shane Reilly** for moving my family while I was deployed. I may have planned it that way.

To **Hoby Darling, Erik Snyder, Mike Augustine, Brian Sudler, Jesse Mease, Jason Bertrand, Tom Brace** and **Paul Swedenborg** for keeping me humble in our morning workouts.

To **Scott Grimes** and **Jason Salata**, let's get back on a river soon.

To **Craig Flynn** for always dropping everything to come to the rescue. Someday it will pay off.

To **Lacey Biles** for all you do in defense of freedom.

To **Michael Davidson, Adnan Kifayat** and **Ben Bosanac** for your *very* early support.

To **Damien and Jennifer Patton**, you are poised to change the world.

To **James Jarrett**, soldier, horseman, professor, writer, gunman, and patriot. A graduate of the jungles and tall grass of Southeast Asia, his short story, "Death in the Ashau," is required reading. A brilliantly written piece that highlights the underlying disconnect between the operator in the mud and the starched-uniformed brass in the Pentagon, it's a less-than-subtle critique of the McNamara-era numbers and data-driven war through a fixed ten-power scope and the business end of a .308-caliber 168-grain International Match Boat Tail Hollow Point. You can hunt it down in *De Oppresso Liber: A Poetry & Prose Anthology by Special Forces Soldiers* published by Old Mountain Press.

To those who continue their work in the shadows and cannot be named, thank you for living at the tip of the spear.

To **Jeff and Kristi Hoffman** at **Black Hills Ammunition** for your support, technical expertise, and for making rounds that have put more than a few of our nation's enemies in the dirt.

To the legendary **Ross Seyfried** for an education in African rifles and cartridges.

To **Andy B.** for your expertise in all things Russian intelligence.

To **Jocko Willink** and **Jeff Johnston** for lending a hand with the jiujitsu and combatives.

To **Elias Kfoury** for help on the tactical medicine front and for keeping our friends alive downrange in some of the worst situations imaginable.

To **Dylan Murphy** for all your help with the blade work—you are the reason I carry a gun.

Thank you to **Brock Bosson and the team at Cahill Gordon & Reindell** for being the equivalent of Tier One operators on the legal front.

Thank you to **Mitch Langberg at Brownstein Hyatt Farber Schreck** for your advice, counsel, and for always having my back. Don't know what I'd do without you.

Thank you to the politicians, committees, attorneys, lobbyists, journalists and influencers who helped usher this novel through the "30-day" Department of Defense Office of Prepublication and Security Review process. It truly was a team effort . . . all seven months of it.

To **Ironclad Media** for a next-level video trailer for *The Terminal List*. You certainly raised the bar.

To **Dan Gelston** for your time in uniform and for all your support. If things at L3 Technologies don't work out, you have a bright future in copy editing. Thank you for all your help.

To **Teddy Novin, Olivia Gallivan, Jason Wright, Hana Bilodeau,** and "**Mato**" at SIG Sauer for treating me like one of the family. A SIG P226 was at my side on every deployment and remains my go-to pistol to this day.

To all those who took a chance by inviting me on your podcasts, radio shows, and TV programs, and to everyone who promoted the novel at the grassroots level—you made *The Terminal List* a success. I'll never forget, nor take for granted what you did for me. Among many others, thank you to **Andy Stumpf, John Dudley, Evan Hafer, Jarred Taylor, Marcus Torgerson, Mat Best, Porter Berry, John Barklow, Jonathan Hart, Max Thieriot, AJ Buckley, Neil Brown Jr., Justin Melnick, Hank Garner, Adam Janke, Amy Robbins, Tom Davin, Mike Ritland, Ryan Michler, Trevor Thompson, John Devine, Jason Swarr, Ben Tirpak, Mark Bollman, Maddie Taylor, Rick Stewart,** and **Rob Olive—** author of *Essential Liberty*.

To **Katie Pavlich** for being there once again. This is starting to become a habit.

To **Gavy Friedson** for the future novel ideas. I'm looking forward to a research trip to Israel.

To **Ryan Steck**, aka **The Real Book Spy**, for all you do for the thriller genre and for all you've done for me. It is sincerely appreciated.

To **Desiree Holt**—you make me blush. Thank you for energy and enthusiasm.

To all the bookstores and booksellers, thank you for all you do and for always making me feel at home.

To **Barbara Peters** of **Poisoned Pen**, thank you for your guidance and for all you do for authors and readers.

To everyone at **Dolly's Bookstore** in Park City, thank you for always making me feel right at home.

To **Lucky Ones Coffee**, thank you for employing and empowering people of all abilities and disabilities, and for keeping me fueled up throughout the writing process.

To **K. J. Howe**, thank you for making **Thrillerfest** a not-to-be-missed event and for putting together such an incredible assembly of authors. I'm looking forward to doing some additional damage to New York's Guinness supply with **Eric Bishop**, **A. J. Tata**, and **Brad Taylor**. Eric, good luck with *The Body Man*. I can't wait to read it.

To **Lee Child** and **Steve Berry** for your support of those of us new to the ranks and for welcoming us into the club of scribes.

To the staff at **Bouchercon**, thank you for bringing together authors and readers in such a special event. Being able to talk, exchange stories and build friendships among those with a collective love of books is invaluable. I am an author, reader, and fan, so getting to spend time with my friends and fellow authors **Mark Greaney**, **Christine Carbo**, **Simon Gervais**, and **Josh Hood** is almost too much fun.

To fellow author and Marine **Matthew Betley** for leading the way.

To **Ray Porter**, narrator of the audio version of *The Terminal List* and *True Believer*, thank you for knocking it out of the park.

To **Mystery Mike**, thank you for sharing your passion and knowledge, and for tracking down my new collection of first editions.

To **Carolyn Reidy**, president and CEO of **Simon & Schuster**. Thank you for taking a risk on an unknown and for always making time for me. I am all in!

To **Jon Karp**, president and publisher of **Simon & Schuster**. Thank you for being such a champion!

To **Libby McGuire**, senior vice president and publisher of **Atria Books**, thank you for all your support.

To **Suzanne Donahue** of **Atria Books**, your excitement is infectious, especially surrounding your favorite chapter in *The Terminal List*.

Thank you to the best publisher and editor in the business, the incredible **Emily Bestler** of **Emily Bestler Books**. Your leadership, insight, experience, and friendship mean more to me than you will ever know. Without you, James Reece would still be imprisoned on my hard drive. Thank you for everything!

To **David Brown**, publicist extraordinaire. Nobody does it better. Thank you for your expertise, energy, and direction and for keeping the Atria Mystery Bus charging full steam ahead. I owe you more than a few drinks. Much appreciated, my friend.

To **Lara Jones** for staying on top of everything and for keeping us all in line. Thank you for all your efforts!

To **Al Madocs**, the most understanding production editor on the planet. Thank you for your patience, expertise, and for making this all come together.

To **Jen Long** at **Pocket Books** for a fantastic paperback edition of *The Terminal List*. I absolutely love it!

To my agent, **Alexandra Machinist**, for your honesty and expertise. Maybe someday I'll even get you to the range.

To **Garrett Bray,** your creativity and skill in the digital marketing domain are second to none. I can't thank you enough.

To my parents for instilling in me a lifelong love of reading.

To **Chris Pratt**, thank you. And to **Jared Shaw** for connecting the dots. Who would have thought that a conversation all those years ago in my office in the SEAL Teams would have led us where it has. I'm fired up for what's ahead!

Thank you to the readers who have enjoyed these first two James Reece adventures. There are more to come!

Above all else, I want to thank my beautiful wife, **Faith**, for putting up with this crazy enterprise: late nights, research, copious amounts of **Black Rifle Coffee**, glass after glass of my favorite **Mockingbird Blue**, more than a few whiskeys, days spent locked in the library, trips to Africa to immerse myself in the illicit world of poaching, and revisiting memories from the battlefield best left in the dust. Thank you, my love. And, to our three children who put up with Dad going into lockdown for the final phases of editing, you are always in my thoughts.

And finally, to those who continue to hold the line and run to the sound of the guns, I am eternally grateful.